DOOR TO DOOR
QUILTS

Second Novel in the
Door County Quilts Series

ANN HAZELWOOD

PUBLISHING

Publisher: Amy Barrett-Daffin

Creative Director: Gailen Runge

Acquisitions Editor: Roxane Cerda

Managing Editor: Liz Aneloski

Executive Book Editor: Elaine H. Brelsford

Proofreader: Managed Editing

Cover Designer: Michael Buckingham

Book Designer: April Mostek

Production Coordinator: Zinnia Heinzmann

Production Editors: Jennifer Warren and Alice Mace Nakanishi

Front cover photography owned by Gately Williams; back cover photography owned
by twenty20photos / elements.envato.com

Portrait photography owned by Michael Schlueter

Published by C&T Publishing, Inc., P.O. Box 1456, Lafayette, CA 94549

Library of Congress Control Number: 2021935672

Printed in the USA

10 9 8 7 6 5 4 3 2 1

Dedication and Thanks

A writer is only as good as her editor, and my history has shown this to be true. Prior to writing for AQS Publishing, I wrote Missouri travel books for Virginia Publishing and Reedy Press in St. Louis, Missouri. That was where I learned all that an editor does to make an author look good.

Writing nonfiction requires researching a subject and then writing about what's been learned. Fact checking is necessarily a priority. That was true both with the travel books and also with the 100 Series I wrote for AQS Publishing.

When I started writing fiction for AQS, there seemed to be a series of editors that came and went. Each one was different, but I was always pleased that they remained respectful of my story line and concentrated on grammatical corrections instead. Each had their own style of editing, but as a new fiction author, I was always grateful for their advice.

Andi Reynolds was my first editor at AQS. She and Meredith Schroeder lobbied successfully that quilt fiction needed to be a part of their offerings. They warned me that I was their guinea pig in this new venture, but my first series enjoyed immediate success. Thank you both!

Elaine Brelsford has been my editor for the last few series, and I can only say that she's a gem. She knows my writing style, has good taste, and shares my success. Thank you, Elaine!

I don't think editors get enough credit for all they do. I'm not saying that just because I have a son who is one, but because I know how an editor can make or break the outcome of a published piece. To all my past and present editors, I dedicate this book to you! Thank you!

Thanks also to the Coulson's of The White Gull Inn for letting us show their beautiful facility on the cover of this book.

—*Ann Hazelwood*

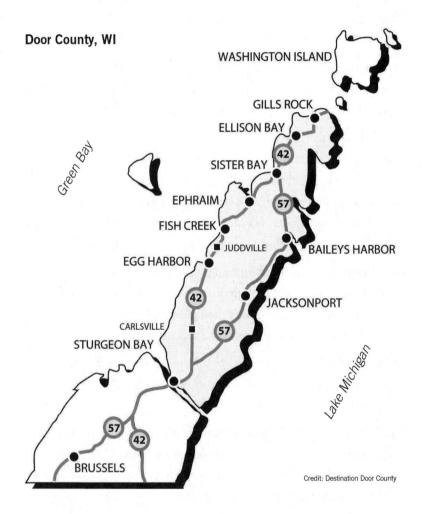

Door County, WI

WASHINGTON ISLAND

GILLS ROCK
ELLISON BAY
Green Bay
SISTER BAY
42
57
EPHRAIM
FISH CREEK
JUDDVILLE
EGG HARBOR
BAILEYS HARBOR
42
JACKSONPORT
CARLSVILLE
57
STURGEON BAY
Lake Michigan
57
42
BRUSSELS

WHO ARE THE QUILTERS OF THE DOOR?

GRETA GREENSBURG is Swedish, in her sixties, and is one of the charter members of the club. As she leads the group, she holds firm in keeping to the tradition of only nine members who are diverse in their quilting styles. Greta makes quick and easy quilts and is one of the few members in the club who machine quilts.

MARTA BACHMAN is German. She's 57 and lives in Baileys Harbor. Her family owns a large orchard and dairy farm. Marta makes traditional quilts by hand. She typically has a large quilt frame set up in her home.

AVA MARIE CHANDLER is 54 and loves any kind of music. She served in the Army where she sang for anyone who would listen to her. She's blonde, vivacious, and likes to make quilts that tell a story. She loves her alcohol, so no one knows when her flamboyant behavior will erupt. She lives in a Victorian house in Egg Harbor.

FRANCES McCRAKEN is the eldest member of the group at 78 years old. She regularly spends time in the local cemetery where her husband is buried. She lives in the historic Corner House in Sturgeon Bay and has a pristine antique quilt collection that she inherited. The quilts she makes use old blocks to make new designs.

LEE SUE CHAN is Filipina and is married to a cardiologist. They live in an ornate home in Ephraim. She is 48 years old and belongs to the Moravian Church, also in Ephraim. Lee is an art quilter who loves flowers and landscapes. She is an award-winning quilter who is known for her fine hand appliqué.

OLIVIA WILLIAMS is Black and lives in an apartment over the Novel Bay Booksellers in Sturgeon Bay. She is 40, single, and likes to tout the styles of the Gee's Bend quilts as well as quilts from the South. She is quiet in nature, but the quilts she makes are scrappy, bright, and bold.

RACHAEL McCARTHY and her husband, Charlie, live on a farm between Egg Harbor and Fish Creek. She is 50 years old and has a part-time job bartending at the Bayside Tavern in Fish Creek. They have a successful barn quilt business and sell Christmas trees in season. Rachael makes their business unique by giving each customer a small wall quilt to match their purchased barn quilt.

GINGER GREENSBURG is a 39-year-old redhead who is Greta's niece. She and her husband own a shop in Sister Bay where they sell vintage and antique items. They reside upstairs and have two children. While she works in the shop, Ginger likes to make quilted crafts to sell and takes old quilt tops and repurposes them.

CLAIRE STEWART, 55, is single and is the main character of the series. She is the newest member of the quilting club because her friend Cher moved back to Missouri to take care of her mother. Claire was eager to leave Missouri and moved into Cher's cabin in Fish Creek. Greta and the club made a rare exception to let Claire replace Cher until Cher moved back to Door County. Claire, a blonde who is showing some gray streaks, is a quilter and watercolor artist who sells her art-work in galleries and on her website. Claire has a brother in Missouri who is a journalist and author, and her mother also lives in Missouri.

Chapter 1

"Austen! What are you doing here?" I gasped in disbelief.

"Aren't you going to ask me in?"

In shock, I opened the door. He strode confidently into the living room and glanced at the glass of wine sitting on the table.

"Would you like some company?" he asked, gesturing toward the glass.

"You haven't answered my question," I said tersely, still standing at the door. "Why are you here, and how did you find me?"

He grinned, but it was not a grin that conveyed friendliness. "Claire, in a small town, word gets around. You know that. I have to admit, I didn't think you had the guts to do what you did."

I took a deep breath to tamp down the anger that seethed inside me. "I came to the conclusion that I was doing you a favor."

Austen then went into the kitchen, spied the bottle of wine, and proceeded to search for and retrieve a glass out of the cabinet. He remained silent as he filled it. Still facing the cabinet, he took a sip and then walked slowly back into the room. "Pretty good wine," he said thoughtfully as he looked around. "I find it interesting that you left such a beautiful home for this ... cabin ... in the woods," he said slowly, again taking in the surroundings.

"If you came here to insult me, please leave."

He chuckled.

"Why come here now?" I asked, frustrated.

"Well, it's obvious that you're not happy to see me after all this time."

"Why would I be? You didn't even bother to call to find out why I left or where I was," I said, making every effort to choose my words carefully.

"I knew where you went," he said dismissively. "I'll admit I was pretty angry at first. You should be glad I didn't contact you then!" He took another sip and paused before saying quietly, "I thought I provided a pretty good life for you."

"A lot of men provide their mistresses with a nice lifestyle."

With that, his expression turned angry. "Claire, you were never a mistress and you know it!" he said, coming toward me. "I'll admit that my work had to be difficult to contend with at times, but you never complained."

"Exactly! What kind of person would I be to complain to a doctor about his spending too much time with his patients? I got that part, but I was lonely. I had to decide if I planned to be lonely for the rest of my life," I explained.

"So, are you happy now?"

"Actually, I am. I love it here," I said as I began to calm down. "I feel that it was meant to be. It's incredibly beautiful here. I've met new friends, and my artwork is taking off."

"I beg to differ regarding its beauty! I couldn't have picked a worse time to come. It's bitterly cold, snow is everywhere you look, and it seems like most of the businesses are closed! I drove around a bit yesterday and wasn't impressed," he blurted out.

"Your impression doesn't surprise me," I said, shaking my head. "This happens to be the locals' favorite time of the year."

"That's interesting," he said. "When you refer to the locals, does that include you?"

"I'm very happy and content," I replied.

"Aah, so does that contentment indicate that you have a new sweetheart?"

I paused and gave him a disapproving look.

"Am I wrong?"

"It's none of your business what my life is like, nor do I care about yours," I said icily.

He sat down in a nearby chair and heaved a big sigh. "Okay, Claire, now that we've both had an opportunity to vent, let's try to remember what we had and how much in love we were."

I looked at him in disbelief, and I'm sure my eyes were wide in surprise. "Honestly, Austen, I can truthfully say that I don't spend a lot of my time reminiscing about the time we spent together."

"Please stop, Claire. You know we had a lot going on between us," he said, leaning forward and looking at me pleadingly. "You're the only one who can make me laugh at myself. You're the only one I can really talk to. You're the only one who ever made me think about getting married."

"Getting married? You've got to be kidding! You avoided that topic at all costs. Yes, we didn't want to have children, but that didn't mean I didn't want some kind of commitment."

"I see. It was the commitment and marriage thing that made you leave."

"No, it was everything, Austen," I began, suddenly needing him to understand my feelings. "My body and soul were just done. I simply ran out of reasons to convince myself to stay with you. I was lonely. I felt alone—not at first, but certainly as more time went on."

"Why didn't you express any of that sooner? I love you—and love you still—or I wouldn't be here. Look at me. I know what I lost—trust me."

When I looked into his eyes, I felt a tinge of what had connected us in the first place those many years ago. I used to love those gorgeous eyes of his. "Well, if it makes you feel any better, I have no regrets. There was a lot about you to adore. Your patients adore you still, and I loved seeing you interact with the children. We had some good times and some fun trips, but I always felt like they offered only fleeting moments of happiness."

"So, you felt your clock ticking and wanted more security, right?"

"Perhaps. I guess I just wanted a return on my investment of five years. I felt like I was being taken for granted. There were times when I didn't even think you saw me at all. Being in a relationship with you made me feel invisible," I admitted, my voice quieter.

"You can't possibly mean that," he said, lowering his voice as well. "You know we had more than what you say. I miss you. Is that what you want me to say? If it's marriage you want, I'm willing to do that," he offered.

I stared at him, wondering how far he'd go. "No, a wedding ring is the last thing I want now. By the way, how in the world did you manage to take the time off to come here?"

"You haven't been listening to me. I couldn't let you go without seeing you again. I want you to give us another try." He rose from the chair and approached me, coming closer than I wanted.

"It's all too late, Austen. I have a new life of my own now. I'm not beholden to anyone. I don't have to try to impress your friends just so they'll buy my artwork. I can't go back when I'm moving forward."

"If you think I'm leaving town without trying to change your mind, you have another thing coming. I'm staying at the Eagle Harbor Inn in Ephraim. Let's have a nice dinner tomorrow night and talk about things," he suggested.

"You're welcome to stay in Door County as long as you like, but I'm not available. You may like it so much that you'll want to move here."

"Is that an invitation?"

"No, it's not!" I stated firmly. "I think you need to leave now."

"Okay, but please think about everything I've said. You know where to find me." He turned away and left, but I caught the look of sadness on his face as he departed.

Chapter 2

I shut the door, retrieved my drink, and went upstairs. My mind was reeling from the surprise visit. It had been nearly a year since I'd seen Austen. I took a good-sized swallow of wine and got ready for bed. I was in shock over the things he'd said, and he knew me well enough to know that I'd go over those things in my mind again and again. Unlike most of our conversations, this one hadn't included an interruption of any kind. As a pediatrician, he was always on the run, returning home from work just to turn around and rescue a sick or needy child. Even on trips, he was often sidetracked by an emergency. He was either on his phone or checking messages. For him to drive all this way to see me was impressive. He said he knew where I was all this time, but he didn't try to contact me because of his pride. I suspected that he was lying about some of the things he'd said. In his mind, he probably didn't think he'd have to do much to persuade me to return to the relationship.

Once I was in bed, the hours passed but sleep didn't come. Mentally, I played back painful memories of when I'd left Austen behind while he was at a medical convention. Austen Page enjoyed a reputation as a marvelous pediatrician. He was extremely beloved by the families he served. I lived with Austen for five years but gradually became lonelier and lonelier. For me to leave him and have a clean break, it had to be when he was gone so he couldn't try to make me change my mind. It was hard to give up a beautiful home with a lovely and spacious art studio, but after a while, those things became less and less important.

When Cher, my best friend, suggested that I move to Door County, it seemed like the perfect place to get away. She had returned to Perryville from Door County to help her ailing mother. My staying in Cher's cabin would allow her to keep her place while she returned to our hometown. I took Cher up on her offer and moved into her little log cabin in Fish Creek. Within a short time, I simply fell in love with it.

Door County offered me a beautiful environment and an opportunity for a whole new life as an art quilter. The Wisconsin peninsula was known for its artists and magnificent galleries, so it didn't take me long to find a spot where I fit in with my quilting art. My label was "The Quilted Palette by Claire" because I frequently painted on my quilts. In the short time I'd been here, I'd already secured a gallery that would take my work on consignment. I'd also been commissioned to paint a piece for a customer who noticed my work in that gallery.

The bed covers were a mess as I continued to toss and turn. Why did Austen have to come and spoil the peace I'd felt since moving here? I absolutely wouldn't entertain the possibility of getting back together with him. At four, I turned on the light and checked the clock. I also looked at my phone to see if there were any messages or texts.

Puff, the cat I'd inherited from Cher, lifted her head as if to wonder if it was time to get up.

Morning would be here soon, and my sleeplessness left me opportunity to think about Rachael and Charlie. Rachael, my dearest friend since I'd moved here, had lost her husband recently, and I intended to be there for her. I'd gotten to know Charlie and Rachael when I'd agreed to help them out at their barn quilt business during the Christmas season. Rachael was also a member of the prestigious quilt club that I was privileged to join after Cher moved back to Missouri. The club had reluctantly agreed that I could fill her spot until she returned.

Rachael had sent a group text stating the details of the funeral. It'd be held at Stella Maris Catholic Parish in Egg Harbor. It was so hard to think of Charlie's passing. Charlie and Rachael had been experiencing financial difficulties. Now, Rachael would have to face those challenges without him. Just like at home in Missouri, there were deaths and disappointments here in Door County as well.

I turned out the light and longed for just five or ten minutes of sleep, but Austen's image wouldn't go away. He was spending the night in the small town of Ephraim, just down the road. Was he awake as well? My hope was that he'd take my message seriously and head back to Missouri.

Chapter 3

I woke up late after a stressful night, forced myself out of bed, and went downstairs to feed Puff. I decided to call Cher and tell her about Austen's surprise visit. I sat down at the kitchen table, hoping she was already awake as the phone began to ring.

"What's this early call all about?" Cher asked, as if she'd read my mind.

"Guess who showed up at my door last night?"

"It's too early, and I'm in no mood to play games, Claire Bear. The movers changed my date again, and it's made a mess out of everything."

"That's upsetting. Can I do anything on this end?"

"No, sorry. It's especially hard for the folks who are waiting to move into this house. My things are all packed up, but the movers are really making me frustrated."

"Well, here's something to get your mind on something else. Are you sitting down?"

"No, I'm actually reclined. Is that okay? Did I mention that you called awfully early?"

I smiled to myself. "Late last night, I heard a knock at the door. When I answered it, my visitor was Austen."

"Are you kidding me?"

"I wish. He just walked right on in! He saw my glass of wine on the table and helped himself to a glass as if he lived here."

"Unbelievable! How did he find you?"

I told her the entire conversation. When I got to the part about him claiming that he missed me and telling me how sorry he was, I could hear Cher heave a sigh of disgust. When I told her that he said he'd go as far as marriage, I thought she was going to lose it.

"Did you laugh or cry? Where is he now? How did you get him to leave?"

"He's staying at the Eagle Harbor Inn. I'm sure he'll return. You know how sure of himself he always is. I know how I feel, but what should I do?"

"All I can say is that you really need to think about this. I give him credit for making the trip. If you have any feelings or doubts about moving to Door County, you need to take advantage of this because you may never get another chance."

"It kept me up all night. I can't go back. I just can't."

"Does Grayson have anything to do with your answer?"

I paused before I answered. "Perhaps. We're getting off to such a nice start, plus I love Door County. Even if I still had feelings for Austen, returning with him would mean going back to the same situation. I won't do that."

"It sounds as if you have your answer, but I'm not sure he'll accept it. You'd better be firm in your response, or you'll never get rid of him. Do you hear me, Claire Bear?"

Cher and I had called one another Cher Bear and Claire Bear since elementary school years. "You're right as always,

Cher Bear," I replied, grateful for her listening ear. "I wish you were already back here."

"I do, too. I need some normalcy in my life again. I don't regret moving back home to take care of my mother, but I feel like my life has been on hold for so long. You know how we artists are! Door County was perfect for me. There's nothing in this town, just like we said in high school! I hope I find a gallery connection like you did with Carl when I return to Wisconsin. I have a great bay window in my new condo. I hope to set up an area there where I can paint."

"I remember your mentioning that when we went to look at it. You talked about the lighting, just like I have here on your porch."

"I'm glad that living in the cabin is working out for you." Cher paused and then said thoughtfully, "I hope you'll be strong with Austen. I'm sure it can't be easy."

"I'll get through it somehow. Have you talked to my mother lately?"

"I have plans to call her today to tell her about the delay in my move."

"Please don't tell her about Austen coming here. It'll only cause her to worry. When I know he's on his way back to Missouri, I may tell her. Goodness knows what she'd advise me to do."

"She's so great, and she's pretty savvy as well. She wants what's best for you, as do I. Keep me informed, okay?"

"I will! Love you, Cher Bear."

Chapter 4

As always, it was a relief to share my feelings with Cher. In grade school, we'd huddle by ourselves at recess and share all sorts of things. Throughout middle and high school, we wrote notes and passed them to each other between classes. We were hardly ever separated. After we attended art school together as young adults, Cher moved to Green Bay, Wisconsin, married, and then quickly separated. She talked with me every single day through the whole divorce. She didn't want to come back to a small town, so she found Door County and settled there. The rustic log cabin in Fish Creek suited her as an independent artist until she returned home to take care of her ailing mother. I'll never forget the day she suggested that I move here to get away from Austen. I made the decision and never looked back. It was the change that I needed. I went upstairs to dress for the day and got a call from Olivia, a quilt club member.

"Good morning, Claire. I got the notice about Charlie's funeral taking place tomorrow. Do you think all the club members should attend?"

"Well, I hope they can if they're able. After all, Rachael has been in the club for a long time. Are you going?"

"I'd like to, but Frances isn't sure that she's going. I want to go with someone."

"I'll save you a seat. Why wouldn't Frances come? She's all about this kind of thing."

"Claire, she gets carried away sometimes about things. Knowing her, she'll visit his grave instead."

"Well, whatever. Rachael will be thrilled to see us all, so I hope all of the group members who can attend will come."

"I'll be there. I feel better now. I may not stay for the luncheon, but I want to pay my respects."

"I understand. I may not go to the lunch either." With that, we chatted for a few more minutes and ended our conversation. I was glad that Olivia felt close enough to call me. I suspected that there were times when she felt uncomfortable being the only African American in the group. She had a reserved personality, but when I'd suggested a raffle quilt, she jumped in and the project received her full support. She went to the quilt shop down the street from her apartment and purchased the supplies. As the group members worked together to create the quilt, we even won over Greta, our stoic leader. She came through in the end and offered to machine quilt it for us! It was the first time the club had ever done such a thing, which was hard for me to believe. Quilt guilds in Missouri made quilts and raffled them off to raise funds for all sorts of things!

This quilt club baffled me from the day they'd accepted my membership. I still haven't figured out what all the fuss is about with this club. Its strict membership seems to instill mystery and envy among local quilters who aren't members. The group did something they had never done before when they accepted me in Cher's place. I had a certain feeling that Greta would never view me as a legitimate member.

I went about my business while trying not to think about Austen being in town. I ordered flowers for the funeral and then got settled on the porch to resume working on my painting. It was about three in the afternoon when I stopped working. The phone rang, and it was Austen. I almost didn't answer, but curiosity got the best of me. Maybe he was calling to say goodbye.

"I hope you're having a good day," he began. His voice sounded cheerful. "Listen—I found a wonderful restaurant called The English Inn. I made reservations for us to have dinner there tonight."

I took a deep breath to give myself time to gather my thoughts. I replied, "That's nice. It's a very good place to eat. I hope you enjoy it."

"Don't play hard to get, Claire," he said, keeping his tone lighthearted.

"Austen, unless you want to travel around the area as a tourist for a few days, I suggest that you go home. We have nothing else to say to each other."

"I came all this way to see you. There's no need to be rude."

His voice was even and controlled. That was how Austen worked when he wanted to get his way. Typically, it was just easier to go along with whatever he wanted. I took the time to draw in another deep breath before saying slowly, "Some folks just don't make good choices. Enjoy your dinner."

I hung up before he could register any protests and realized that my hands were shaking. I couldn't believe I'd found the nerve to stand my ground! It was just like him to assume that I'd go to dinner with him. Just the sound of his voice brought back unpleasant feelings that I had not experienced since leaving him. If I'd accepted this dinner invitation, it'd have been too easy for me to fall back into my pattern of just giving in to whatever Austen wanted rather than thinking about what I needed. I knew myself that well.

Chapter 5

Despite how the phone call from Austen had stirred me up, I managed to get a good night's sleep and woke up the next morning feeling refreshed. Poor Rachael would bury her husband today. It was hard to imagine how painful that would be for her. I put on my robe and went down for that first swallow of coffee for the day. Puff had something different on her mind and let me know by standing at her dish and meowing. While I was feeding her, Cher called.

"I couldn't sleep. What's the latest? Is he still there?"

"I don't know. Yesterday, he called to tell me that he'd made reservations at The English Inn. I refused to go."

"You did? Good for you!"

"I have to get dressed for Charlie's funeral in a bit."

"Oh, I know. I wish I could be with all of you. I did send flowers. Please give Rachael a hug for me."

"I will," I said, realizing that I was about to cry.

"Oh, Claire Bear, I know that this is a rotten time for you. Austen will be gone soon, and you have so much going for you. Rachael will have to make some big decisions. I'm so glad the two of you became such good friends. You'll be able to help her through this really challenging time."

"Thanks, Cher Bear. I love you." With that, we hung up and I went upstairs to assess what I had in my wardrobe that would be appropriate to wear to the funeral. I selected black pants and a sweater and put them on. I was glad the sun was shining, but the weather app on my phone said it was only twenty-two degrees outside.

Once in my car, I headed toward Egg Harbor. This particular stretch was one of my favorite sections of Highway 42. I had to admit that I was curious about seeing the inside of the magnificent church. From the looks of the crowded parking lot, the service was going to be well attended. Everyone loved Charlie. I got out of my car and saw Nettie and Fred, who were great friends of Rachael's from the Bayside Tavern. They would be thoughtful enough to brave the cold for this event. Since I wasn't Catholic, I knew I'd be unsure about the mass and how to participate, so I took a seat in the back of the church. Minutes later, I was pleased to see Olivia walk in with Frances, Ginger, and Ava. I caught Olivia's eye, and the group of them squeezed into the pew with me.

"Marta will be coming with her husband. I didn't hear from Greta or Lee," Olivia whispered.

"Good to see all of you," I whispered, smiling.

As I glanced around the room, I recognized many familiar faces from the large Christmas Eve party Rachael and Charlie had hosted. The service began, and everyone stood as they rolled the casket down the aisle. It was followed by Rachael and the family members. It was a dreadful sight. Rachael looked dazed. I felt sure that she was exhausted. As I blinked away tears, I glanced down the pew and saw that my quilting friends had tears in their eyes as well.

Harry stood to give the eulogy. That made sense since he was Charlie's best friend. He, too, looked weak and had to clear his throat many times before beginning to speak. It was quiet as we waited to hear his first words.

"Charlie was my brother and buddy. There are no words to describe our grief today," he began. His message was brief but lengthened by his need to stop every now and then to clear his throat. He was eloquent and brave. It was hard for everyone to listen to his tribute without choking back tears. At one point, he made us laugh, something Charlie would have appreciated. After he finished, he left the podium and walked straight to Rachael and gave her a big hug. It was another one of those moments when I had to concentrate hard to keep from breaking into sobs. At one point in the eulogy, Olivia reached over and took my hand. I don't know whether she did it to comfort me or herself, but I appreciated the warm gesture of friendship.

After the service, the family was first to file out of the sanctuary. Out of the corner of her eye, Rachael spied our pew and her eyes welled up with fresh tears. It was gratifying to know that she felt our support. The group of us agreed not to go to the grave site or the luncheon. As we walked out of the church, we were able to acknowledge Marta, her husband, and Lee, who came with someone we didn't know. There was no sign of Greta. I said a simple goodbye to everyone and headed home. I was emotionally drained and wanted to have some time to myself.

When I got home, I collapsed on the couch. I thought of Rachael trying to visit with family at the meal while feeling the loss of her husband. How could I be a friend and help her through this experience? The situation perplexed me, and I didn't come to any firm conclusions. Exhausted, I dozed off.

Chapter 6

A tickle of cat fur came across my face. Of course, it was Puff. I quickly sat up, realizing I'd slept most of the afternoon. I felt hungry so I opened a can of soup, ate it slowly, and then walked around the kitchen in a daze until I heard my phone ring. It was Austen. I couldn't believe he was still here—or was he? I let it go to voicemail. A few minutes later, I listened to the message. "I love you, sweetheart," was all he said before hanging up. I didn't know what to make of it. Hearing sweet talk from Austen was awkward. I wasn't falling for it. It didn't even sound sincere.

I changed clothes and made a fire. There was something soothing about making and enjoying a fire. I remained concerned that Austen could knock on my door at any moment. The phone rang again. I assumed it'd be Austen, but it was Grayson instead.

"I thought about you today while you were at Charlie's funeral," he said kindly. "I just couldn't get away."

"Thank you, Grayson. It was difficult. There were so many people there! I couldn't believe it."

"They're well known, so I'm not surprised. Are you okay? You sound drowsy."

"I came home and took a nap."

"Well, I have some good news. Final plans for the Honors Dinner have been made. It'll be held at Alexander's, which will be really nice. I put in a word about auctioning off the quilt and they said there shouldn't be any problem."

"Thanks so much. I haven't shared all of this with Rachael yet."

"I was wondering if you'd like to be my date for the banquet."

I smiled. "As in a third date with Grayson Wills?" I asked teasingly.

"Well, by then the number may be higher," he replied with a smile in his voice. "By the way, there are signs of an early spring with all the ice breaking away at some of the piers. My offer still stands to take you out to see the lighthouse in Sturgeon Bay. It would be very cold, however."

"I think I'd like to wait on that for a bit. I'm painting the background now, and I want to see it against a clear sky."

"You're the artist! How about coffee in the morning at the Blue Horse? We can make it later in the morning if my usual visit there is too early."

"How about eight?"

"Great. See you there."

I hung up feeling like I'd scored for the day. I was wide awake now. I even picked up Puff and gave her a hug. I got comfy by the fire and picked up one of my Quilted Snow quilts. I'd always remember my first winter here in Door County. There had been so much snow! I'd made a quilt to reflect a winter scene and consigned it at the gallery. After it sold quickly, I was asked to make another to consign. Would I love this piece as much done in spring and summer themes? Maybe I needed to consider all seasons! My mind began racing with ideas. I could do Quilted Blooms in the spring, Quilted Sun in the summer, and Quilted Leaves in the fall. Perhaps someone would want them all! I could offer them as a set. Door County was such an inspiration. I settled into bed that night with thoughts racing about my new idea.

Chapter 7

I felt butterflies in my stomach on my way to meet Grayson the next morning. Did he realize that he was easing himself into dating someone? As I entered the café, I saw him sitting on the porch. He motioned for me to come his way when he caught my eye. "What's this?" I asked when I saw coffee and a bagel waiting for me.

"I wanted it to be my treat," he said with a grin. "Cinnamon bagel and a mocha latte, right? You'd ordered that once before."

I chuckled and nodded.

"I can get you something else if you like," he offered.

"This is great," I said, sitting down. "I keep thinking about trying some of their other choices but rarely do."

"I like their house blend myself," he said, taking a sip.

"Thanks for doing this. Do you have a busy day planned?"

"I'm meeting with some inspectors this afternoon, and this morning I have two interviews set up, so I guess that's a pretty busy day."

"I'd say so!" I agreed. Just then, I noticed a man approaching our table.

"Excuse me, Claire. I just want to say good morning to you," Austen said, giving me a smile that looked as if it had been well rehearsed.

I was speechless. "Good morning," I mumbled.

"Dr. Austen Page," Austen said confidently as he extended his hand to Grayson, shaking his hand. "I'm sorry to interrupt," he continued. "I'm a friend of Claire's. I'm just visiting from Missouri."

"I see. Well, I hope you're enjoying Door County," Grayson said politely, his eyebrows slightly raised.

I could see from the look on Grayson's face that he was beginning to put the pieces together. I swallowed hard and tried to sound sure of myself. "Listen. I'm here to visit with Grayson, so—" I made eye contact with Austen and didn't finish my sentence, hoping he'd excuse himself.

"No, I understand," Austen responded, matching my even gaze. "We'll catch up later. I'll give you a call. It was nice to meet you, Grayson."

Grayson only nodded, glancing to Austen and then to me. At that, Austen made his way to the door.

"Is that the Austen I've heard about?" Grayson asked.

I nodded, embarrassed. "He showed up at my door without any warning," I explained, rolling my eyes. "We had quite a heated conversation, and I told him to leave. Of course, he didn't want to believe that I really wanted him to back off and insisted that we talk over dinner. I declined again. I'm so, so sorry that he barged in here. He's so sure of himself that he probably thinks I'm just playing hard to get."

Grayson listened intently and then said thoughtfully, "He obviously misses you very much and wants you back. I can't blame him. I'm not sure that I understand or approve of his methods, however. It strikes me as a bit heavy-handed."

"I have no desire to return to him. Seeing him act like this makes me surer than ever."

"Are you worried about him stalking you while he's here?" Grayson asked with a slight frown.

"I wasn't until now! How rude of him."

"I'm not offended. He probably thought interrupting us would have a different outcome. You handled it quite well."

I smiled weakly but didn't feel like I'd handled it well. On the outside, I wanted to appear strong, but on the inside, Austen's sudden appearance in my life had left me feeling off-balance.

"I guess you need to prepare yourself for a phone call or his next visit," Grayson warned.

"I will, so beware," I said, trying to sound brave as I forced a smile.

Grayson chuckled.

"On another and better topic, thanks for inviting me to the banquet."

"My pleasure. It'll be fun for both of us. Hopefully, we'll raise a lot of money."

"Well, we both need to get back to work," I said with a sigh. "Thanks again for the coffee and bagel."

"Claire, I know you're a grown, independent woman, but if you run into any problems with Austen, please give me a call," Grayson said kindly.

"I will. My greatest hope is that he'll go home."

Grayson helped me with my coat, and we walked out of the café together. When we said goodbye, our eyes met, and we held one another's gaze for just a moment—a wonderful moment. I didn't care if Austen was watching or not.

Chapter 8

It had been a bittersweet start to the day. Austen had managed to spoil what should've been a nice visit with Grayson. If Austen tries to call me today, I won't answer, I reminded myself. If he knocks at the door, I won't let him in.

On the way home, I picked up the mail. My phone was ringing in my purse. When I glanced at the screen, I could see that it was Harry. I was close to home, so I waited to call him back. Once inside, I tossed my coat on the couch and dialed him up. "Harry, how's it going?"

"I'm good. I'm sorry I didn't get to see you at the funeral luncheon."

"It was a lovely service, and you did a fine job. How's Rachael?"

"Better. She's going to stay with her sister for a few days. I think it'll be good for her. I'll keep an eye on the place and feed the animals."

"It's a good idea for her to get away for a bit. You're so sweet to help out."

"Charlie would expect it, and he would've done the same for me," Harry said, sounding choked up. "It looks like an early spring," he said, changing the subject. "Their place could get out of hand pretty easily."

"Is there anything I can do?"

"You can keep me company," he teased.

"Harry, you know what I mean. What about the barn quilts?"

"Rachael wants the business to stay closed for now. She mentioned that she has some orders to finish up, and that may be good for her when she returns. I think folks will be patient, considering the circumstances."

"The quilt will be ready anytime for the chamber's auction. Grayson Wills arranged it all. I hope we raise a lot of money."

"Speaking of Mr. Wills, you seem to fancy him these days from what I hear. Is that true?"

I paused to think about my response. I didn't want to hurt Harry's feelings. "Well, in a way. He reached out to me as a new chamber member, which I really appreciated. I find him to be very modest, smart, and a good father who's raising a teenager as a single parent."

"Yes, and a good businessman, just like his father. Just make sure he treats you right."

"We aren't that close, but I'll keep my eyes open, okay?"

He chuckled.

I hung up feeling good that Rachael was being taken care of. For now, I'd have more time to paint since I wouldn't be needed to help her at the barn. With the fundraising quilt on my mind, I decided to call Greta to find out if she'd finished quilting it. She was quick to answer the call and even quicker to get down to business.

"I thought I might hear from you any day now. Yes, it's quilted, and I'm getting the binding on as we speak," Greta said in her typical straightforward manner.

"Oh, that's great! We have the okay from the chamber to auction it off, so I'm excited about the prospect of raising a lot of money."

"I'll bring it to club so everyone can see it."

"Wonderful! I can't thank you enough for quilting it. It'll mean a lot to Rachael."

"I wish her well. I know it'll be hard. I'll see you at club then," Greta said before she hung up.

Greta was a hard one to figure out. She was always on guard and careful not to show any emotion. She was too possessive with the quilt club, but she got by with it year after year. So many things in that club truly perplexed me, but I couldn't think about that now. I needed to get started on my work.

I'd just settled into painting when Ericka called.

"I have the day off so I'm doing some planning. I also had to meet the delivery men over at Cher's condo. It's too bad that her move was delayed again."

"I know. She's so eager to get back here. I read that her new place is also a resort of some kind."

"Yes, it has some nice features. Living there, she'll meet permanent residents as well as tourists. I want to throw a little welcome-home party for her when she gets here."

"Well, I'll be glad to help. Do you think her quilt friends from the club will come if you invite them?"

"I'd hope so!" Ericka said.

"Rachael went to stay with her sister for a while, but if she's back by the time you plan it, I'll be sure to tell her about the party. I just want Cher back here. It's time!"

"Absolutely!" Ericka agreed.

Chapter 9

The next day, I was determined to attend the Moravian church service. I looked forward to attending the Episcopal church near my house once it opened again. That little chapel only holds services in the summer months because the building has no heating system. The morning was sunny, but very cold and windy. Tiny snowflakes were about to remind me that spring had not yet arrived.

I got to the church just as the service began. There was a vacant seat in the rear of the church in one of the two-seater pews. The woman next to me responded with a smile as I whispered good morning. As the service progressed, she didn't stand when others did, so I assumed that she had some physical limitations. When the collection plate was passed, she dropped in a one-hundred-dollar bill. It was another opportunity to begin a short conversation, but she didn't respond. That led me to think that she might have some hearing loss.

The pastor delivered an inspiring message. She talked about new beginnings. She said that God wants us to reach out to those in need and that we should reexamine our own intentions in life. I felt like I could easily relate to the sermon topic. When the service ended, my pew partner stood. I asked if I could do anything to help and she looked at me strangely.

"Thank you," she said softly. "I just take my time."

When I got into my car, I watched her being helped into a large black Cadillac. I wondered whether she had family or friends to watch over her.

Since I was in Ephraim, I decided to have lunch at Chef's Hat. I'd heard very good things about it. The side of the café overlooked the bay and offered outside seating in the summer. It was pretty cute inside, and the special of the day was shrimp tacos with rice, which sounded good. The diners at the table next to me were enjoying cherry cobbler, so I wanted to leave room for that or take some home with me. Everyone who worked there was so friendly, and I thanked them for being open. So many businesses closed for the winter months in this area.

Close to the restaurant was another popular tourist spot that was closed for the season. In warmer months, Wilson's Restaurant and Ice Cream Parlor, with its red-and-white awnings and geranium-filled flower boxes, was quite famous for its ice cream and hamburgers. It was located on the bay as well, so customers could get their treats and sit on the benches in the park across the street and enjoy their food. When Wilson's opened in late spring, I planned to do that! The Eagle Harbor Inn, where Austen was staying, was nearby as well. Hopefully, he was on his way home so I wouldn't run into him! I enjoyed my lunch immensely but ordered the cobbler in a to-go box. As I drove home, the sun was making the snowflakes disappear.

I was glad to be home. I made a fire and considered taking a nap. I got comfortable on the couch and picked up the Quilted Snow quilt. I decided that I could put a few more stitches in it. My phone rang, so I glanced to see who was calling. Thank goodness I did! It was Austen. Was he still here? I waited until it went to voicemail and then listened to his message, which said, "Did you enjoy Chef's Hat? I had dinner there last night, and it was quite good. Enjoy the rest of the day. You know where to find me."

I hung up with the realization that Austen was stalking me! Who should I tell? Did he know that I went to church? I felt that I had to be careful who I let know about this. I didn't want to call Grayson, even though he'd offered to help. Grayson shouldn't feel responsible for any part of my past life.

I decided to stay put on the couch and continue quilting by the fire until I felt sleepy. I wasn't about to go onto the porch to paint in case Austen might be watching. He'd likely booked the inn for a week or so, thinking I'd change my mind. Mom would be worried sick if she knew this! Cher would understand, but she had so much on her mind right now with moving. What should I do?

Chapter 10

At eleven that night, I decided to go to bed. Puff was waiting for me. I fell into a deep sleep until three in the morning, when tree branches hitting my window woke me up. I sat up in fear, listening carefully to make sure that was the noise I was hearing. The wind had picked up and it sounded like a storm was brewing. Once awake, I worried about Austen still being in town, since he might do things to scare or intimidate me. Sleep didn't come, so I checked my phone and found a text from Austen.

[Austen]
I remember your fear of storms. Let me hold you in my arms until it passes. Love, Austen

I couldn't believe it! Such behavior was out of character for him. He was trying to prey on my weaknesses. He doesn't even know who I am anymore! I wanted to call Cher and talk to her, but it was the middle of the night. Feeling that I needed some assurance, I took my chances that she'd answer and called her anyway. After several rings, she finally answered. I hardly gave her time to greet me before I said, "Cher, I'm sorry to be calling at this hour, but I just had to talk to you."

"Good heavens! It's three in the morning! Are you okay?"

"Yes and no," I said as I proceeded to tell her that Austen was still in town and was harassing me. I could tell that my news was upsetting to her as well.

"Good heavens, Claire! Have you ever seen this side of him before?"

"Not like this."

"Did he ever harm you physically?"

"No, but verbally. With Austen, it was all about controlling the least little thing. I found most of it funny at times, so I'd pick my battles as far as arguing with him. It just feels odd knowing that he's nearby. I don't know what to do."

"Well, you can threaten him by saying you'll call the police! I'm sure an upstanding physician wouldn't want that kind of publicity."

"I don't know what he'll do with a hurt ego. I've never challenged him before. You don't think he'd do anything to hurt Grayson, do you?"

"Grayson? Don't worry about Grayson. If you told him about Austen, Grayson is certainly mature enough to know how to handle it. It's just so weird after all this time that he wants you back. Why now?"

"Good question. I don't like the creepy feeling that he gives me. I sure don't like the thought of being watched!"

"Stay calm, cool, and strong. I know you can handle this, Claire Bear. I happen to remember when the mean girls in high school tried to get to you when they wanted you to drop out of the class president election."

I chuckled. "Cher, what in the world made you think of that?"

"I saw my friend hold her head up and not be intimidated in the least. You need to get that mindset again! You made the right decision by moving to Door County, and no one is going to talk you into going back to the life you had before."

"Okay, my friend, whatever you say. You'll be here next week, right?"

"Yes, for sure. I'm so ready, ready, ready!"

"I'll tell the members of the quilt club when we meet. Greta is bringing the quilt to show them. We'll all praise and thank Greta for her effort so she'll be happy."

"If the topic of membership comes up, please don't insist that I become a member again," Cher requested.

"Well, if it does, I think the group will want us both. If not, I'll resign and tell them to welcome you back."

"That whole situation makes me uncomfortable. I think it's either both of us or neither of us, if you really want to know how I feel. If you stood up to the mean girls, surely this little club shouldn't intimidate you."

"Okay, I get it. I'm sorry I woke you up, but what are friends for, right?" I laughed weakly.

She chuckled.

"Good night, Cher Bear," I said, feeling grateful for my best friend.

"Good night, Claire Bear."

Chapter 11

In recent months, there had been a knot in my stomach on the day of quilt club. As I ate breakfast, I tried to imagine what might happen at the meeting today. I checked my phone. Thankfully, there were no more messages from Austen. I walked out onto the porch, where I saw that the storm had taken down numerous tree limbs that now needed to be picked up.

As I left for the meeting, I was surprised to see three-inch jonquils coming up in the yard. Hopefully, there would be more surprises ahead. I thought of Grayson possibly being at the Blue Horse this morning. That would sure be more fun than what I was about to encounter.

Nearly everyone was in the meeting room when I arrived. I got a cup of coffee and decided to sit next to Frances.

"How are you, Frances?" I asked cheerfully. "It was so nice of you to come to Charlie's funeral."

"There are times when we have to unite and show support," she said simply.

"You're so right. I know that it meant a lot to Rachael."

"Ladies, ladies," Greta called out, banging her gavel. She carefully looked at her notes and then at us. "I have an invitation from the Red Cross for us to donate blood when they're here at the library next month," she began. "I also wanted you to know that I sent the library a thank-you note for letting us use the meeting room to sew the quilt for Rachael."

"Good," Ginger interrupted.

"Speaking of the quilt, I finished the binding and brought it with me today," Greta said as she pulled it out of the bag.

We waited with anticipation, and Ava jumped out of her chair to help Greta hold up the quilt. It was stunning, and everyone cheered and broke into applause. "You did a marvelous job," I praised. "You really got it done quickly!"

"Claire, would you mind explaining to the group the plans that have been made to auction this off at the chamber of commerce's dinner?" Greta requested.

"Sure!" I said as I stood. I explained how I'd requested Grayson's advice about how to best raise money for Charlie and Rachael. "He suggested the chamber's dinner auction rather than running around town trying to sell raffle tickets," I explained. "He got approval. The chamber keeps a small percentage, and the rest of the money goes to the worthy cause. I think it'll be quite successful."

"I agree with that," Marta chimed in. "It was so nice of Grayson to do that."

"What's also nice about this is that Rachael and Charlie have been chamber members, so I know many will want to help Rachael now that Charlie has passed," I added.

"How's she doing?" Olivia asked.

"She's away at her sister's house right now, which is good for her," I replied.

"Will you take the quilt and get it to the proper person?" Greta asked.

"I'd be glad to, and thanks to everyone again for helping with this great cause," I said. "The quilt is beautiful!"

"Thank you for making this happen," Ginger said. "I hope it goes to a good home."

"I was glad to do it, and it was good for our club," I said. "So many people don't know what we do or what we're all about." When Greta gave me a stern look, I knew I'd said too much.

"This group has never looked for publicity, Claire," Greta said stiffly.

"I didn't mean it that way," I said quickly. "I'm proud to be a part of this group, but I just think there's more that we could do." The room went silent.

"I hear that Cher will be back with us soon!" Marta finally said, breaking the silence. "I hope we see her back here."

"I'm not sure about that, but her moving plans are in place," I stated.

"Frances, would you like to start the show-and-tell?" Greta interrupted, clearly wanting to move things along.

Chapter 12

Frances showed a small quilt she'd made from funeral ribbons. Many of them were from her family's funerals. She gave a brief history of how the ribbons have changed through the years. Leave it to Frances to bring us back to the dead instead of to the living.

"I think I may have this framed," she mentioned. "What do you all think?"

"Oh, you should," Ginger said in agreement.

"But where would you hang such a piece?" Ava asked. "You wouldn't want to remember their funerals, would you?"

Frances smiled. "I'd like nothing more!" she stated proudly. "I think it's a piece of art."

"Well, Frances, we count on you to be unique," Greta commented. "Is that everyone today? Please pick up the latest newsletter from the library. I'll try to have a program for us next month, so if you have any ideas, let me or Marta know. I've asked Marta to lead the meeting next month because I'll be out of town."

"Before we adjourn, if anyone would like to get a ticket to go to the chamber's dinner, let me know," I offered: "You may want to bid on this quilt!"

"Thank you, Claire," Greta said without smiling. "Do I have a motion to adjourn?"

Ginger made the motion and Olivia seconded it. As soon as I could, I left with the quilt under my arm. I didn't want to have a conversation with Greta.

As I drove toward home, I saw Carl going into his gallery, so I decided to stop.

"Claire, how's that painting coming along?" Carl asked eagerly.

"Pretty well! I'll have it to you soon, as well as another Quilted Snow quilt," I assured him. Then I added, "Carl, I was thinking. What if I did a different quilt for each season? I was thinking about making one called Quilted Blooms for spring. Then I could do one called Quilted Sun for summer and then Quilted Leaves for fall. Someone might choose to buy them all."

"Claire Stewart, you're a genius. Count me in. I want one of each!"

"Seriously?"

"You bet! It's a great idea. I suggest making them all the same size for display purposes."

"Good idea. I just want to cover the whole town with quilts! There just isn't the appreciation for quilts here like I thought there might be."

"In other words, you think there should be a quilt in every window?" he teased.

"You're teasing, but I'd like to elevate the awareness of quilts as art. I see art in jillions of other mediums, but not in quilts."

"Well, I'm doing what I can. If you have any other suggestions, let me know."

"I will, Carl, and thanks so much for encouraging me to proceed with my ideas."

"You're good for me as well. You're bringing fresh eyes to the art community, and as art dealers, we should all be open to that."

I left the gallery feeling very inspired. When I got home, I looked at my painting and couldn't wait to get started on it again. As I munched on a tuna sandwich, I made mental notes of the tweaks it needed. I really appreciated Carl's support of my ideas. What else could I think of?

Chapter 13

The lighting was perfect as I mixed various shades of red to get the rich colors of the lighthouse. Out of the corner of my eye, I saw a car pull into the driveway and then turn around. Was Austen checking up on me? Seconds later, I saw him. He was back and got out of the car this time. He must have seen me on the porch. When he got up to the door, he stared at me from the outside.

"May I please come in?"

The tone of his voice belied the politeness of his words. Without saying a word, I stood and walked to the door. When I opened it, he breezed past me as if he were an invited guest.

"Busy painting, I see," he said, looking at my easel.

"I hope you're coming by to say goodbye," I replied.

"I did. I'm needed at the hospital."

"Well, have a safe trip home," I said without emotion.

"Did you think about what I asked you to do?"

"I didn't need to, Austen. I told you that I've moved on, and you need to do the same."

Unfazed by my response, Austen launched into what felt and sounded like a sales pitch.

"You see, Claire, I just don't believe you. I know you have a lot of pride. I can provide you with so much more than what you have here," he said, using a full-arm gesture to make his point.

"I'm very happy here," I replied, shrugging. "You need to go where you're needed." The expression on his face was a mix of anger and disappointment.

"Do you need money?" he asked.

"Austen, you can't be serious! I'm fine, so please leave."

"May I kiss you goodbye?"

"No. A kind word between us will do. You wish me luck, and I'll wish the same for you."

He nodded and turned to leave. I didn't want to give him the satisfaction of me watching him leave, so I went into the living room. I was relieved when I heard his car drive away. I sat down feeling relieved but noticed that I was shaking. Why did this have to happen? I was proud of myself for not giving in an inch. I was truly insulted by his offer of money. My phone ringing from the kitchen brought me back to reality. It was Harry. As I picked up the phone, I hoped that he wasn't calling to deliver any bad news.

"Hi, hon," he greeted me.

"Harry, how are you and Rachael?"

"She's been calling me every day to make sure I haven't forgotten to check on things at the farm. She said her nights are terrible."

"I can imagine."

"How are you doing?"

"I've been staying busy with a commissioned painting, which I hope to finish soon."

"That's good," he said. "Say, have you told Rachael anything about the quilt?"

"No, but I will. When do you think she'll return?"

"She didn't say, but she's worried about finishing up three barn quilts that were ordered. I offered to do the cutting for her. I'd watched Charlie a few times."

"That's so kind of you, and I'm sure she needs the income."

"I know. I need to have a serious conversation with her about the finances when she returns."

"Do you think she can keep the farm?"

"It's too soon to tell."

"Maybe we can put our heads together when she gets back regarding some promotional events. Maybe the Bayside could give her more hours, too."

"Good idea. You take care now, sweetie," he said, ending the call.

I hated to call Rachael at her sister's house, so I decided to text a couple of lines telling her I was thinking about her. I looked at my watch and thought of Austen once again. With any luck, he was on his way home by now. I made a roaring fire and put a frozen pizza in the oven. I then poured a glass of wine and walked out to glance at the painting. It was disappointing that I'd not made more progress, but I covered it up for the day. Grayson came to mind, and it felt good to entertain some pleasant thoughts. Now that Austen was on his way home, I was glad I hadn't told Grayson about Austen stalking me. I longed to hear Grayson's voice, but I didn't want to come across as too needy. My better judgment told me to move on to other activities for the evening. After all, Grayson was a busy man and father with many other things on his mind.

Chapter 14

The next day, the sun was shining, and I felt focused enough to get back to painting. I checked my phone, and there was a text from Rachael saying she'd be home in a couple of days so she could get back to work. I responded by offering my help.

I glanced at the lovely red-and-white quilt all tucked in a bag just waiting for a new owner. I decided to make a few notes about it for the auctioneer. Most men don't know much about quilts, but I knew that anyone bidding on it would want to know the size, the pattern name, and who made it. My phone rang with Ericka's name showing.

"Hey, Claire! Did Cher tell you that the movers are coming in a couple of days?"

"Well, it changes every time I talk to her. That's great."

"So that means I could host a little party for her on Friday night. I thought we could go with an Italian theme. She loves my cannoli, and I hope that you can bring a little something."

"Of course! I'll bring lasagna. Is it supposed to be a surprise?"

"No, I went ahead and told her because I wanted to be sure she'd come! By the way, feel free to invite anyone you want."

"I was thinking about telling Rachael if she's back. She may not feel up to it, though."

"Invite her anyway. I'm inviting the rest of the quilt club, but I doubt they'll come. Cher would love to see everyone again. Feel free to invite Grayson."

"Your condo isn't very big. Are you sure you want to invite so many people?"

"The more the merrier!"

"I wish I knew what to give her," I said.

"Well, I've been keeping an elephant ear plant for her since she left. I'm giving that back to her as a welcome-home gift!" Ericka laughed.

I chuckled. "Does that mean I can give Puff back as my gift?"

"Oh, you'd be in trouble there! She mentioned to me that Puff is completely attached to you now."

"Great," I lamented. "Okay. Thanks for the invitation," I said as I hung up. It was hard to imagine Cher living in the same town as me after all these years. I knew that my mother would miss Cher terribly. After her mother's passing, Cher had kept a careful eye on my mother. I also knew that Mom would be happy for Cher and me. I still hadn't said anything to Mom about Austen. It would worry her if I did. I hoped Cher hadn't ended up telling her.

Having no communication from Austen was comforting. I began to paint again. It was a good feeling knowing that this commissioned piece could be finished very soon. To my surprise, Grayson called around five.

"I can't contain my curiosity any longer. Did Austen go back to Missouri?" he asked.

His interest in my situation was flattering and made me smile to myself. "Yes, I'm pretty sure he did. Thanks for asking. I didn't want to bother you by calling about him."

"What do you mean?"

"He continued to stalk me the whole time he was here. I continued to refuse to meet with him. Finally, he came by to say goodbye. He said the hospital needed him."

"How do you feel about it?"

"Relieved." There was silence for a bit.

"It sounds like you could use a drink," Grayson suggested.

"Or a good friend," I teased.

"Is that an invitation?"

"I don't know how to answer that."

"I'll be there shortly," he said quickly before hanging up.

What had just happened? I looked terrible from painting most of the day, so I quickly freshened up and put on a different top with my jeans. It was only ten minutes later when I heard Grayson's knock at the door.

Chapter 15

"Hey, Grayson, come on in," I offered, unable to hide my delight at seeing him again.

"I brought a nice merlot that I happened to have on hand," he said as he entered.

"You didn't have to do that, but thank you. I'll get some glasses. Maybe you can put another log on the fire."

"Your wood supply is getting a little low. Do you have more?" he asked as he tended the fire.

"Yes, I have plenty out back."

"I love a real fire, but I finally got gas logs," he said.

I brought the glasses and he kept looking at me, perhaps expecting me to start a conversation about Austen. We just made small talk instead, and I told him that Rachael would be coming home soon. "I'll tell her about the quilt as soon as she returns. I hope she takes it in the right spirit."

"Explain to her that it's a big help to the chamber as well. I think she'll be fine with it."

"I hope she's doing better. The funeral was so sad, Grayson. I thought that Rachael was going to faint when she walked in and had to follow the casket down the aisle."

Grayson shook his head. "It sounds like you've had your share of stress yourself, Claire. Are you okay? I hope you don't think I'm trying to interfere with your relationship with Austen."

"I know."

"I guess I was a little worried that he'd try to change the relationship between us. I have to admit, when he interrupted us as we were meeting for coffee, I wondered what else he might be capable of."

"Sometimes you have to take a step back to be able to evaluate a person. When you're too close, you think everything's normal when it's not," I shared.

He nodded. "So true."

"I had no idea of the amount of daily stress I was under until I left town. I felt so much better physically as well as mentally after I moved here."

"So, you haven't heard from him?" Grayson inquired.

"No, thank goodness. I'm so relieved."

"You're a pretty strong woman, Claire Stewart."

"Don't give me too much credit. I called Cher right away because she knows him pretty well. She was really surprised that he had swallowed his pride and made the trip in the first place. She was pleased that I didn't give in."

"When does Cher arrive?"

"In a couple of days. Ericka is having a party for her on Friday night at the condo. She said I could invite someone." I smiled at him.

"If you're looking at me, I promised to take Kelly and her friends ice skating," he replied.

"How fun!" I said, trying to hide my disappointment. "I plan to say something to Rachael if she returns in time. I told

Ericka that I might bring Puff as a welcome-home present for Cher, but she advised me against it," I said wistfully.

He chuckled. "I think she likes it right here," he said as he stroked Puff's fur while she sat at his feet.

"Perhaps Kelly would like to have Puff," I offered.

His look was one of surprise. "Oh no you don't, Claire! I don't know why you'd still want to get rid of her."

"I know. Actually, we're doing fine. She seems to really like you, though," I said, laughing.

"You think so?" Grayson asked, laughing also.

"Grayson, you've told me a little about your work, but if you don't do much boating anymore, what do you do for fun?" I asked, hoping to learn more about him.

"I golf with clients every now and then, but most of my leisure time is decided by Kelly and her friends. However, lately I've been distracted by a pretty woman who just moved to town."

I smiled. "Do you read at night?"

"Occasionally, but to be honest, I get a kick out of watching old movies. You know, like some of the old classics."

"Really? Do you collect some of them?"

"A few. My favorite is *Casablanca* with Humphrey Bogart and Ingrid Bergman."

I smiled.

"It's great acting, and I love the famous line, 'Here's looking at you, kid.' How about you?"

"I love old movies, too. There's a channel that shows them all the time. I turn it on occasionally at night if I can't sleep."

"What's one of your favorites?"

"If you're asking me which one makes me cry the most, I have to say it's *An Affair to Remember.*"

"Yes, I know it."

"From the moment the movie begins, I feel caught up in it. Maybe it's the music. The scene that tears me apart is when he realizes that she's the woman in the wheelchair who bought his painting in the gallery. The look on his face is priceless. Then when he embraces her and they kiss, she's tearful and says, 'If you can paint, I can walk.'" Grayson seemed to know exactly what I was talking about. "It's funny how you remember certain lines that touch you," I remarked. "That's the way the older movies are. They don't have all the fancy special effects the way movies do now. It was all about the script and the characters."

"Exactly. I don't care much for comedy, but I do enjoy a good war movie every now and then," he said.

"More to drink?" I offered.

Grayson looked at his watch. "I had no idea that it was this late! I should go home, or your neighbors will gossip."

I chuckled. "Well, my neighbors have all gone to Florida, so we have nothing to worry about, but that daughter of yours doesn't miss much."

He nodded in agreement.

Chapter 16

Grayson stood and pulled me up with him. As we faced one another, our gazes met. He drew me close for a long, slow kiss that made me long for more of his brand of affection. "I'm glad I came by to see you," he said softly in my ear.

"Me too," I whispered.

"Did I make you feel better?" he asked with a sheepish grin.

"Much, much better," I replied, giving him a kiss on his neck.

"I could get into a lot of trouble if I stay much longer," he said while backing away from me. "I look forward to our upcoming date."

"Does tonight count as a date?" I inquired, smiling.

"It was better than a date," he said as he kissed my forehead and turned to leave.

"Thanks for the wine. We finished that whole bottle, by the way."

"I have more where that came from. Good night, Claire."

"Good night, Grayson."

I continued to stand at the door. I wanted to run out and give him one more kiss but didn't. Instead, I turned around and put the fire out for the evening after I watched him drive away. I kept thinking about how Grayson seemed so much more mature than Austen. Maybe it came from being a dad. Most men just think about one thing when they're with a woman. Grayson had a completely different approach. I wondered what drew him and his wife together when they'd first met. Could anyone come close to offering him what they'd had? Could that someone be me?

I smiled to myself as I carried our empty glasses to the kitchen. I was pleased that he'd made the choice to come over. I kept thinking about the things we'd talked about. I'd have to see the movie *Casablanca* again in light of the things he'd shared about it. Hearing his take on the movie was interesting. He was a sensitive man. What else would I discover about the man who wore the red scarf? It was two in the morning when I crawled under the covers, and Puff didn't move an inch. I had Cher's arrival to look forward to tomorrow. Life was good at this very moment. Thank you, God!

The next thing I knew, I was caught up in a dream. Austen was dragging me back to Missouri with a horrific expression on his face. I was protesting and crying, using every bit of strength I had as I tried to escape. Suddenly, I was wide awake and sitting up. Puff looked bewildered and probably wondered if it was time to get up. I looked at the clock, and it was only five.

Afraid I'd have another bad dream, I decided to get up. A long shower might be nice, and if I felt sleepy enough, I'd just go back to bed then. Most mornings, I tried to start my day by saying, "This is the day the Lord hath made; let us rejoice and be glad in it." I stepped into the shower and let the water wash over me. I stayed in there for quite a while before stepping out and toweling off. As I was drying my hair, I heard the phone ring. It was Cher. I hoped that nothing was wrong.

"I'm finally on the road, Claire Bear!" she announced, sounding elated.

"Great! You really got an early start! Are you excited?"

"Very much so! The van is ahead of me, but I'll still arrive before they do."

"Do you need me for anything?"

"I'm good. George and Ericka will meet me. I'll just see you at the party, but thanks!"

"I can't wait. I'm bringing lasagna. How about that?"

"Wow! That's awesome, Claire. Have you heard anything from Austen?"

"No, so I think he really did leave."

"Very good. Did you ever tell your mom?"

"No, I didn't want to worry her. Also, she knows that I'm really done with him."

"Okay, I need to stop for gas, so I'll see you later."

"Safe travels," I said as I hung up. I realized how much I was looking forward to seeing her at the party!

Chapter 17

As I began making lasagna, I watched the rain pour down outside. I really hoped that it wouldn't freeze on the roads. Even though Ericka's condo was close by, I was a big chicken when it came to driving on icy roads. I still couldn't think of a gift for Cher, but I knew there would be many opportunities to buy something for her once she knew what she needed.

As the afternoon wore on, I began to think about what to wear to the party. I supposed even jeans would work for tonight, but tomorrow night would be another story. I needed something special, so tomorrow, I planned to go to the Hide Side Boutique, where I knew they had great clothes. I'd popped in there once or twice before and was quite impressed by their selection of clothes that couldn't be found in a department store. I wanted a conservative look that still had a "wow" effect. Would that be possible? Not wanting to feel rushed, I got dressed early. Ericka called.

"I don't think I have enough wine glasses. Would you mind bringing about six of them?"

"Sure. My lasagna smells really good right now."

"Oh, I'll bet. I'm getting really nervous. I think I may have invited too many people."

"It'll be fine. Most folks won't stay long. I'll come early so I can help," I promised.

"Great! Just don't forget the glasses," Ericka reminded me.

When I hung up, I was glad that I wasn't the one hosting the party. As I gathered the glasses and put them carefully into a box, I wondered how Ericka would handle having to share her once-best-friend with me. I thought it might require some adjustment from both of us.

I did leave early, and the weather was just plain nasty. The lasagna I'd made was from my mother's recipe, and the aroma filled my car. Wine glasses clinked together as I drove. When I arrived, George and a few neighbors were already there. As I came inside, I could see that George had placed himself in the small entry area and had set up a small space where drinks could be served.

"Claire, good to see you again," George said, leaning down to kiss my cheek. "What would you like to drink?"

"Whatever you're pouring right now will do just fine. How have you been?"

"Very busy at work!"

"Are you staying in touch with Rob?" I asked.

"I am. He really got himself in a big mess, but I can't turn my back on him."

"I understand."

"Cher should be here anytime. I'm sure you're pleased to have her here," he said.

"You have no idea."

"I'm glad you're happy at the cabin," he said as he poured drinks for others who had arrived.

I walked into the kitchen and immediately got busy arranging the food. To my surprise, Brenda came. We had started to engage in conversation when a rousing noise came from the front room. Evidently Cher had arrived, as evidenced by the cheers of excitement. I slipped back in there to celebrate with the others. Cher was getting hugs and kisses from everyone as she made her way through the room. When she saw me, we embraced as if we hadn't seen each other in years. She was blinking back tears, so I knew that the party was something she appreciated.

"You're really here, Cher Bear!" I cheered.

"I'm sorry I'm later than I'd planned. I thought the movers would never get done."

"You have the rest of your life to unpack," I joked. "At least that's what they told me on moving day."

"The food smells amazing!" she remarked as she moved on to greet other guests.

Ginger and Ava were the only quilters from the club who came to the party. Why wasn't everyone from the club here? Ava, who seemed especially flirtatious tonight, appeared to enjoy every moment of the evening. I'd been a bit wary of her since the time I'd seen her remove a tip her friend had placed on their table that'd been meant for the waitress. It didn't take long for Ava to center in on an older neighbor of Ericka's. The bearded man seemed to enjoy her company very much.

Chapter 18

The small space was closing in on me since so many people had arrived. I finished my plate of yummy delights and decided to leave. No one would even notice. I found Ericka and gave her a hug goodbye. When I made my way to the door, Ava was sitting on the lap of the elderly man. It'd be interesting to hear what becomes of Ava and her new friend. Would he get his pockets picked, or would they end up in a relationship?

Cher followed me to the door.

"Oh, Claire, I'm so sorry that we haven't had time to visit tonight," she said, exhaustion showing on her face. "Your lasagna was delicious. Thanks for bringing it!"

"Ericka gave you quite the party tonight," I said, smiling. "Do you feel happy about being back?"

"Yes, of course!" she said, beaming.

"Look at all the gifts you got tonight!" I exclaimed. "Honestly, I didn't know what to get you, so drop me a hint when you think of something that you need."

"Did you notice all the wine that people gave me?" she asked, giggling. "I have nowhere to put it all, so I'll need you to help me drink it."

"I don't know about that!" I said with a laugh. "Did you get to talk to Ginger and Ava?"

She nodded. "Yes, and I think Ava has fallen for Ericka's neighbor."

I nodded in agreement. "It's hard not to notice."

"But that's what parties are for, right?" Cher joked.

I smiled but realized that I'd rather catch up with Cher without all of the background music and conversation. "I'm heading out if you don't mind," I stated.

"Not at all," she said, giving me a hug. "I'm tired too, but I think I'm stuck here for the rest of the party. You should've brought Grayson with you."

"I asked, but he had plans with his daughter," I explained.

"I'm so happy that the two of you hit it off," Cher shared.

"We'll see what happens. Enjoy the rest of your evening." I hugged Cher and exited, leaving the lasagna dish and wine glasses behind. I'd get them another time.

The drive home was icy but uneventful. I walked into my quiet cabin and drank in the peaceful atmosphere. It felt like a home should feel. Puff had already gone to bed, as if she knew I'd turn up eventually. Before I crawled under the covers, I checked my phone. I jumped when I saw a text from Austen.

[Austen]
You'll regret many things, Ms. Stewart.

I could only suppose that this was meant to be a threat for turning him away. Honestly, Austen always had to have the last word! He was probably hoping for a response, but I certainly wasn't going to give him one. I needed to keep this message. I'd deleted all of his other messages when I'd left

Missouri, but this one felt more threatening than any I'd ever received from him.

Later, in bed, I was kept awake by the anxiety I'd felt since reading the message. His feelings for me were strange and unhealthy. Austen had never been violent toward me, but he had been very controlling. When we'd lived together, I'd managed to convince myself that most successful men were that way. I did eventually fall asleep, but not for long. He popped right back into my head! I tried to wipe thoughts of Austen out by thinking of my upcoming date with Grayson. I knew that I'd share all of this with Cher, but not now because she was probably still at the party. I decided that I didn't want my mother to know anything about Austen's attempts to contact me. Exhausted, I tried to convince myself to just stay still and relax. With some luck, I knew that I'd fall asleep.

Chapter 19

It was almost noon the next day when Rachael called.

"Claire, I'm home!"

"I'm so glad. I've been thinking of you each and every day."

"Thanks. I just had to get these barn quilts finished that I'd promised to customers."

"If I can help in any way, just let me know."

"I will, but Harry did some cutting for me. That was a big help."

"I'm so pleased that he's there for you. By the way, Cher is back now."

"That's good news. I can't wait to see her."

"Rachael, I've been wanting to share something with you, but things kept getting in the way."

"Like what?"

"Even before Charlie passed, I knew that things were rough for you financially. I tried to think of a way to make things better. In Missouri, it's not uncommon to raffle or auction off a quilt to raise money for a worthy cause."

"A quilt? A raffle to help me?" Rachael asked. "You'd mentioned something like that when your mother was visiting, right?"

"Yes, but let me tell you how I managed to get a quilt made," I continued. "I got the quilt club members to make blocks for a red-and-white chain quilt. We met at the library to work on it, and then lo and behold, Greta offered to machine quilt it!"

"Greta? The club did it?"

"I know it's a first, but they think the world of you and wanted to help."

"How kind of them!"

"What happened from there is pretty exciting. At Grayson's suggestion, it'll be raffled off tonight at the chamber of commerce's Honors Dinner, rather than having members running around selling raffle tickets. Isn't that great? I think it'll bring a good amount."

"I don't know what to say. I haven't even seen it, and I don't know whether to be embarrassed or just grateful."

"I can drive out and show it to you or email you a photo."

"Oh, please don't go to the trouble of coming out here, plus I'll be working. Just email it to me. I don't know what Charlie would say about this."

"He'd be kind and laugh it off. I'm going to the dinner with Grayson tonight, so I'll let you know what happens."

"You're going to the dinner with Grayson?"

"Yes, things are moving along nicely."

"That's wonderful. He's a good man. Charlie got to know him pretty well when we had a sailboat."

"We'll see what happens, but he's good company. Keep your fingers crossed for a good outcome."

"I still can't believe you got the club to do a project like that!"

"I'll be out to see you soon and will bring lunch, okay?"

"You're something, Claire Stewart."

When I hung up, I was pleased that she had taken the news so well. It must feel weird to have to swallow your pride and accept help. I got busy and took a photo, sending it to Rachael before it slipped my mind.

The hours were ticking by, so I rushed out to get a new outfit for the dinner. It was nearly three by now. I was able to park right in front of the Hide Side Boutique.

When I entered the shop, I wasn't quite sure what I was looking for, but I knew I'd know it when I saw it. I declined the assistance of both salesclerks initially. I browsed the entire shop and then spotted a colorful rack of clothing near the front that I decided to examine more closely. The sign indicated that the items were all hand painted.

The dresses and jackets all seemed to be from the same designer. I was totally blown away by their style and unique splashes of color. I examined each one but kept going back to a sheer black jacket with splashes of pink, aqua, and purple. There were black crepe pants on the rack that matched the black in the jacket perfectly. I'd learned from experience that there are various shades of black. The clerk was quick to tell me that the designer's name was Goldie and that she was the artist as well. The pieces were stunning, and I liked the idea of supporting an artist. I looked at the rack of painted articles of clothing and wondered if I could do something similar with my painting skills.

The clerk sensed that she had a live one and followed me to the dressing room. As soon as I tried the two pieces on, I fell in love with them. The outfit was pricey, but I didn't care. I hoped it wasn't too dressy, but I knew this event was one of the nicer occasions in the business community, so

I decided to buy both items. When I got to the counter, I added earrings in the perfect shade of teal to go with my ensemble. It'd been a long time since I'd felt excited about fashion or about going to a dressy event. I hated to say it, but I knew Austen would love this look. I immediately tried to dismiss that random thought from my mind. I got in my car and decided that I needed to find out more about Goldie!

Chapter 20

I nervously took my time dressing for the big night out. Grayson was always on time, so I needed to be ready. I was right. I saw him get out of his car and noticed right away that he had a tux on underneath his overcoat. "Hello, handsome!" I greeted him.

"Well, look at you, gorgeous!"

"Do you like my new outfit?"

"Absolutely! There's a lot to like there," he said with a wink.

"Thank you!"

"We'd better be going since we're bringing the quilt. It needs to be set up for viewing."

"Okay. I told Rachael today what's going on and she's incredibly grateful."

"I'm anxious to see the quilt myself!" Grayson declared.

Grayson helped me with my coat and off we went to Alexander's. I was pleasantly surprised as I entered the spacious, attractive restaurant. The decor had an upscale black-and-white theme. The tables had black tablecloths with white napkins, and the beautiful crystal centerpieces showcased a variety of white flowers. I handed the quilt to the greeter, who promised that he'd take care of getting it properly displayed.

Grayson seemed to know everyone! I did see a few faces from a New Year's Eve party that I'd attended with him. I recognized some chamber members who served on some of the same committees that I served on, so I acknowledged them with a smile or a friendly hello. One of them was kind enough to ask how my art business was going. His wife then complimented me on my outfit and asked me if it was a Goldie design. I chatted with her about how I'd been unfamiliar with the line until today.

As Grayson and I viewed the items up for auction, I overheard a woman say how she loved the quilt and wanted her husband to bid on it. Grayson stopped when we got to the red-and-white quilt.

"This is striking! You pieced some of it, right?"

I nodded, feeling pleased with the way the quilt had turned out. That was all that was said, for it was hard to keep a conversation going with Grayson because of all the interruptions. Grayson was always gracious to everyone and took time to talk with the many people who seemed to have something to say to him. Eventually he was able to ask me if there were any other items that the two of us should bid on.

"The dinner for ten from Chives is tempting," I replied.

"Yes, it is. Let's see what it goes for."

We sat down, ready to enjoy a wonderful dinner. The salad was almost too pretty to eat. The main course was a small fillet and a piece of salmon with dill sauce. I enjoyed every bite. Awards were then presented for best leadership, best volunteer, and best small business. The awards were followed by the president's message while dessert was served. I wasn't disappointed when I received a chocolate melting cake with whipped cream and raspberry sauce. I was so obviously pleased with the food that Grayson began to tease me about it. After dessert, the auction started, and it looked as if the quilt would be the second item to be offered for sale.

"I think I need that quilt," Grayson said just loud enough for me to hear.

I smiled.

"Are you going to bid on it, Claire?" he asked.

"I'll have to if no one else does."

At that, the item from a spa in Sturgeon Bay was sold, and the quilt was presented.

Chapter 21

The auctioneer was quite good. He did an excellent job of letting the crowd know the details of the quilt using the information that I'd provided earlier. He started the bidding at one hundred dollars. The woman I'd heard expressing interest in the quilt put in a bid for two hundred dollars. A chamber officer raised the bid by fifty dollars. I was beginning to worry because I knew the quilt was worth more than that. Suddenly, from beside me, Grayson shouted out a bid of one thousand dollars! Everyone gasped in surprise and applauded. That was followed by a two-thousand-dollar bid from John, a friend of Grayson's in the back of the room. The crowd emitted whoops of excitement. When the noise settled, Grayson called out a bid of three thousand dollars! I looked at him in disbelief. His bid was quickly followed by the original woman bidder, who added five hundred dollars more to Grayson's offer! I was thrilled and thought the bidding was done because there was a break in the action, but then Grayson called out a bid for five thousand dollars, which stunned both the crowd and the auctioneer.

"Five thousand dollars going once, going twice," the auctioneer announced. "Sold to number one hundred fifty-five!"

I looked at Grayson in shock as the crowd clapped and shouted. Those at our table immediately congratulated him as I watched in disbelief. Rachael would never believe this, nor would the quilt club! When the noise died down, I leaned over and kissed him on the cheek. I hoped he knew how grateful I felt toward him.

The auction continued but we listened in silence, knowing we had achieved what we intended. Afterward, as the crowd began to thin out, Grayson and I sat at the table by ourselves and relaxed for a few moments. We chatted comfortably until it was time for him to pay for the quilt. I gathered from our conversation that Grayson had planned all along to pay up to five thousand dollars for the quilt. As we left, Grayson was still getting accolades on his purchase. The quilt was folded neatly, placed in a bag, and handed to Grayson. From there, we drove directly to my place and sat in silence in his vehicle.

"I don't know what to say, Grayson. This has been a wonderful evening. Rachael won't believe what just happened. It's just so good to know that you own the quilt."

"I had to step up the bidding, or we'd still be there increasing the bidding fifty dollars at a time. When I make up my mind that I want something, I focus on it until I get it or until I feel good about not getting it," he declared.

I chuckled. "Is that so?" I teased.

"Yes, so I guess I'm giving you fair warning," he teased back.

"Giving me a warning?"

"When I first saw you at the Blue Horse, I somehow knew you were different. I knew you were someone I wanted to get to know."

"You sure didn't show it!" I protested, smiling.

He laughed. "I also warned you about me being pretty green when it comes to flirting and dating."

"You're doing just fine. Your approach has been most appealing. I like it. Most men are so direct now, and I find that disgusting. I was out with some friends last year when a man came up to me and said, 'I'd like to get to know you as quickly as possible so we can get it on, if you know what I mean.' I was appalled and told him not to bother. How direct was that? I can play that game, too."

Grayson burst into laughter. Then silence settled between us and he said softly, "You know, I haven't been parking with a girl in a car in a long time." He turned to face me.

"Oh, I guess we are parking, aren't we?" I said, turning to face him.

"Well, I haven't been asked to go inside, so I guess the next move is up to me," Grayson flirted.

"As in a kiss? We used to call that making out."

Grayson nodded and smiled at me. "A kiss would be awesome," he said as he pulled me close to him and gave me a gentle kiss.

"Would you like to come in?" I offered.

"I really would, believe me, but I'm going to graciously decline. I know there's probably someone waiting up for me."

"Oh, I see," I replied. "It was a perfect evening, and I can't thank you enough for what you did regarding that quilt."

"Don't forget, the chamber benefited from that purchase as well. After their cut, I'll add what's needed to make sure Rachael gets a check for the full five thousand dollars."

"Oh, Grayson!"

"It's a win-win for everyone."

At that, Grayson walked me to the door with his arm around me, and another warm kiss followed.

Chapter 22

After a contented night's sleep, I was anxious to start my day. I waited until nine to call Rachael and give her a report on the auction.

She answered right away. "How was it?" she asked immediately.

"It was wonderful! I wish you could've been there. I'll send you some pictures that I took."

"Did they like the quilt?"

"They liked it very much! It was displayed beautifully, and it sold for a great price."

"Seriously? How high did it go?"

"Are you sitting down?"

"I am."

"It sold for five thousand dollars."

"No way! You're kidding me, right?"

"I am not! They started the bidding at one hundred dollars, and the bidding took off rather quickly."

"I'm speechless."

"People got caught up in the bidding. It was so exciting! Also, the chamber gets a small percentage of the selling price, so they were a motivated group."

"Do you know who got it?"

"I sure do!"

"Who?"

"Grayson Wills."

There was silence before Rachael finally asked, "Really? Did you make him do it?"

I laughed heartily. "No! I was as shocked as you are. He did love the quilt, and I thought he might bid on it."

"Well, I know he can afford it. Was he trying to impress you?"

I chuckled once again. "No, not really. At least I don't think so. I think that once his friend started bidding on it, it became a contest. He reminded me how much he thought of Charlie, too."

"I'll never be able to thank him enough."

"Well, he's pretty happy to be the new owner of the quilt. He made it clear that it was going on his bed, not Kelly's."

"So, the two of you had a good time?"

"Of course. He's such a gentleman. It's interesting to watch him when we're out in public. He has so many friends and lots of people know him through his business. He's so kind to everyone. It's interesting to see how he relates well to so many different types of people."

"Claire, it sounds like you've truly fallen for him."

"I'm afraid I have, but if it doesn't go any further, that's okay too."

"I don't think you should let him get away. Have you heard from Cher?"

"Not recently. I know she's overwhelmed with unpacking and getting utilities hooked up. Listen—the quilt club meeting is coming up, and I think it'd be a nice touch for you to be there to thank them."

"For sure! Is Cher coming?"

"I hope so. I know she's busy getting settled, but I hope that she'll make the time to come."

"They need to make sure that you're both welcome there."

"I agree. What are you planning to do today?"

"I'm in the mood to paint, so I'm getting some things done. Harry is coming soon to do some things outside. There's a lot to do before spring arrives."

"I'm so glad to hear that you're feeling like painting, Rachael."

"Do you have any idea how much paperwork there is when someone dies?" she asked, suddenly sounding perplexed.

"No, I don't," I admitted. "My dad's lawyer was also a dear friend and took care of much of that for Mom. I feel for you, but Harry will help you. If he can't, then I'd be willing to come out and try."

Before we hung up, I was going to offer to come out, but it sounded like she needed to be doing what she was doing. In fact, we both needed to be working on our painting projects, so I said goodbye and donned my painting smock. It felt good to make some progress on my project.

At noon, while I was eating a tuna sandwich, Mom called. She was curious about the chamber event, so I told her the details and about the handsome price the quilt brought.

"Claire, you should be so proud of yourself for having the idea to make a quilt and use it to make money for Rachael."

"Thanks, but I just wish I could get the club to do more of that sort of thing. There's so much need out there."

"One step at a time, honey. You're new to the club, and you don't want to give the impression that you want to take over everything."

"Good advice, Mom. What do you hear from Michael? I hate to admit that I'm not very far along in his book."

"I know it's a bit dry, but I'm so proud of him. I think he's doing well with getting some distributors to pick it up. You should give him a call."

"And talk about what, you?" I chuckled.

"Claire, you asked about him!"

"Okay, moving on then!" I laughed. "How's Mr. Vogel?"

"I guess he's doing fine. I'll see him on Tuesday at the senior center. Tell Cher I'm missing her calls to check in on me. I hope she's doing okay."

"I'll do that. I think she's glad to be back here. I love you!"

"I love you too, sweetie."

Chapter 23

I wanted to make a chicken divan casserole for dinner, so I picked up the phone to see if Cher wanted to join me. "Do you remember when I made chicken divan casserole for dinner the first time?" I asked Cher. I stifled a giggle.

"Yes, and when I saw the broccoli, I had a fit."

"But you ended up liking it, remember?"

"I did! Are you cooking?"

"I am. Are you free for dinner?"

"Oh, that sounds good. Ericka mentioned that she might like to get together tonight, but she hasn't called back."

"Then we have a date. I think the world of Ericka, but I don't think everything I ask you to do has to include her. I'm not good at sharing my best friend." While I was more serious about this comment than I wanted to let on, I made sure that I spoke in a lighthearted manner. It was a bit of a relief to me when she laughed.

"You're so right. I'll be there. I need a good meal."

"If you'd like to invite her it's fine, but I'm looking forward to having dinner to catch up."

"Oh, I can't wait. What should I bring?"

"Pick up some garlic bread. I'll make a salad."

After we hung up, I had to chuckle about our history as cooks. Our mothers were wonderful cooks, but we were truly lacking in culinary skills!

I went back to painting until four. I then cleared a place on the porch where I set a small table with a white tablecloth. I put a large candle in the center and then set two place settings of china and crystal. It'd be my first formal stab at entertaining since I'd moved here. I'd just finished setting the table when I saw the mailman approaching. That was unusual because I always picked up my mail at the post office. I opened the door to greet him.

"Are you Claire Stewart?"

I nodded.

"Sign this, please."

Naturally, I did as he instructed. His job complete, he turned and left. This was a curious occurrence. When I glanced at the envelope, my heart sank. It was from Austen. I went into the kitchen and sat at the table. Upon opening the letter, I could see that it stated my full name and that of my business. It was a notice to advise me that the following items had been taken from Austen's address. It first listed six pieces of fine jewelry that Austen had given me through the years. I knew each item was worth a thousand dollars or more. He then listed a laptop he'd bought for me when he'd purchased one for himself in order to get a better deal. He listed the china. Next, he'd calculated what the fair market in rent would have been for use of the studio in his house for five years. The total was absurd! At the bottom was the total due to him.

What in the world had gotten into him? He'd never mentioned me owing him for anything! He was known as a generous man. There were many times when I'd offered to pay for things, and he'd refused. I also knew there had never been any written agreement associated with our relationship. Did he really think this would scare me into coming back to him? The last paragraph informed me that if I didn't comply with payment and such goods, legal action would be taken.

I felt sick to my stomach. I threw the notice aside and told myself to put it out of my mind for now. I'd deal with him later and in a professional manner. I covered my painting and went upstairs to shower for dinner. As the water pounded on my face, it was mixed with tears. How could he be so hurtful? What was he trying to prove? As I got dressed, I decided that I'd ask Cher for a referral to a good lawyer. It'd be money I hated to spend, but Austen also knew that could be another way to hurt me. Taking a deep breath, I resolved that this experience wouldn't consume my visit with Cher tonight. This had every chance of being a fun evening, and Austen and his antics would not spoil it for us!

I came downstairs to put the casserole in the oven. As I whipped up the salad, I caught myself hitting the knife on the cutting board especially hard as I chopped the vegetables. Anger seethed within me. Austen knew me well enough to know that the letter he'd sent would make me absolutely crazy with anger. As Puff paced back and forth, she rubbed her fur against my ankles. It was if she knew something was up. Maybe she was just feeding off my nervousness. I picked her up and gave her a hug of reassurance. Her warmth was surprisingly reassuring to me. I went to the porch and gently placed Puff in her chair. I needed to calm down and concentrate on the opportunity to catch up with my best friend. I smiled at the thought of Cher being back in Door County. Would Puff be happy to see her?

Chapter 24

Cher was right on time, carrying a bottle of wine under her arm and a loaf of bread in her hands.

"You didn't have to bring all this," I said, giving her a hug as she entered.

"Do you know how many bottles of wine I received at that party?" she asked with a laugh.

"It looked like a lot," I agreed.

"Twelve bottles to be exact, and I don't know what to do with all of them!"

"That's it!" I exclaimed. "I'll get you a wine rack for a housewarming gift!"

"Hey, I'll take you up on that offer!" she agreed. Cher glanced around the porch as if to reacquaint herself with her current surroundings. "Claire, this table out here is so cozy. Why didn't I ever think of that? I only sat out here in the summer to get a cool breeze."

"Well, it's warm enough, and I have candles lit, so they provide a little more light."

"You're so creative. By the way, it smells heavenly in here."

"Did Ericka call you back?" I asked.

"No, and that surprised me a bit," Cher replied.

"I'm glad this worked out. Let's get something to drink."

Cher followed me into the kitchen. I saw her glance at the legal papers Austen had sent, but she didn't say anything. "Go ahead and take a look at them," I said, pointing to the papers. "They came by registered mail from Austen today."

Cher picked up the papers and her mouth widened in disbelief. "This is absurd, Claire! He's really lost it. He's so much smarter than this. Does he really think this will work to get you back?"

"It's almost laughable, but I think my response has to be on legal paper. Do you know a good lawyer in Door County?"

"I've never had to use one, but Ericka will know someone. Man, I'm sure glad you left that horrible human being!"

"Well, it's not going to spoil my little dinner party to welcome you home. Did you say hi to Puff? She should be in her chair."

"No, I haven't seen her," Cher said, looking around.

"She's been acting odd all day. She kept circling my ankles."

Cher laughed. "She wants your attention," she explained, as if that were something I should already know.

We took our drinks to the porch while the bread warmed up. We had lots of ground to cover as we discussed her party and the chamber's dinner. Within a short amount of time, the aroma of bread filled the house, so we went to the kitchen to get our food.

"Oh, this is such a treat, Claire. I love a beautifully set table, don't you?"

I nodded in agreement, looking wistfully at the china. "I guess I'm glad that Austen requested these dishes back. Maybe it's because I split the set in half." I shrugged.

"I thought that was most generous of me, don't you?" We laughed and returned our attention to the dinner in front of us.

"Claire Bear, this is delicious, and I'm not minding the broccoli one bit!" she said with a giggle.

"Very funny," I replied. "Cher, when was the last time that you went out on a date?"

She looked at me in surprise. "I have to think," she said, pausing to consider the question. "Linda fixed me up with a cousin of hers last fall. I don't know why she thought we'd be a match. He had three kids and was a real jokester, if you know what I mean. Now that I'm here, I may check out the Internet to see if there's someone in the area who'd be interesting to meet."

"Like a dating app?"

"Don't be so shocked. Just because you got lucky with Grayson doesn't mean it's that easy."

"Well, there's always George," I offered.

She gave me a funny look. "Yes, he's always looking."

"He hit on me when I first moved here," I confided.

"That doesn't surprise me. I can't quite figure him out."

"I think we should go to the Bayside when Rachael goes back to work. You never know who might be in town or who will give us a look," I said conspiratorially.

Cher giggled, and we then began telling old stories on ourselves. At one point, we were doubled over in laughter. After a while, our hilarity died down and Cher looked over at my nearby easel with its cloth draped over it. "Hey, I'm curious, Claire. Can I take a peek at the painting you're working on?"

"I guess. I hope I can take your criticism. Remember that I'm working from the client's photograph and have never been to the actual location."

"Oh, please!" she exclaimed, rolling her eyes.

"Okay, but look at this photograph first," I insisted. "I still have a couple of improvements to make."

As she looked at the picture, I uncovered the painting. Cher diverted her attention from the photograph to the painting itself.

"Claire Bear, it's beautiful! The sky is amazing. That's hard to do, but you captured the lighthouse so well. The contrast is breathtaking. Work like this takes a lot of time, and I hope you're charging enough."

"I'll leave that up to Carl. He knows the market here. The more he makes, the more I make. You should see him about selling some of your work."

"Too soon, I'm afraid. I don't have all of my clothes unpacked nor is my studio set up. I should be doing some of that as I speak," she lamented.

"I love this porch," I said as I looked outdoors.

"I loved it, too. It's surrounded by nature and is so inspiring."

"Well, here comes Puff!" I announced as I saw her sneak into the room.

"Where are the balls of yarn I gave her?" Cher asked, looking about.

"I had to finally get rid of them. Everything was getting tangled up—including her."

"Oh, no!" Cher laughed.

"What she likes more than anything is an empty shoebox that she can climb in and out of."

"Well, it sounds like the two you have it all figured out," Cher said, petting Puff as the cat rubbed affectionately against her legs.

Chapter 25

We cleared the table and I offered to make a fire. We both were yawning at that point, so Cher urged me not to bother. "It's only eleven, but I think I'm ready to head home to bed," she said as she yawned.

"I understand. I hope I can sleep after getting that letter from Austen," I complained.

"Forget about him. A good lawyer will put him in his place." Cher gathered her purse and keys as she said, "Remember years ago when we wouldn't even go out until eleven at night?"

We laughed, knowing that times had certainly changed. We hugged as we said our goodbyes. After she left, I picked Puff up from where she was waiting expectantly at my feet, and we went up to bed. Surprisingly, I fell into a deep sleep until the next morning.

Puff was ready for breakfast, so the two of us went downstairs to get our day started. There sat Austen's papers on the kitchen table. I needed a lawyer—and soon. I picked up my phone to call Ericka before she left for work.

"Well, good morning," she answered cheerfully.

"Ericka, I need your help again," I began.

"What now? Why me?" she asked with a chuckle.

"Because you're so smart, and because you know your way around," I answered. I then began my story about Austen visiting me in Door County. I told her that when I'd kept refusing his offers for me to return to Missouri, he went home angry. I then shared the letter I'd received. When I read the details of his demands, Ericka broke into laughter.

"You told me that this man is a doctor, right? He must certainly have more intelligence than to pull a stunt like that!"

"I thought he did. It's a ploy to harass me, so I need a lawyer to respond to him. I just don't know who to call."

"Well, George and I use the Steven Maxwell firm in Sturgeon Bay. They have different attorneys who specialize in various things. They've been around a long time."

"No one closer?"

"I can't help you there, but you could always ask Grayson."

"I'd rather not. This is personal, and I don't want to involve him in this mess."

"Well, give them a call. I talked to Cher a little bit ago, and it sounds like both of you had a great time last night. I called to apologize to her for not calling her back. Time got away from me."

"It was so fun catching up, but we're getting old, Ericka. Our wine consumption had us done by eleven!" I laughed.

"Well, it sounds like you shouldn't worry about this letter, but now he's going to make you pay for a lawyer."

"Yes, I'm sure that's his plan. Thanks for giving me some direction." We chatted for a few more minutes and then hung up.

I ate some toast and called the law firm. The receptionist asked a lot of questions and assured me she'd refer me to the appropriate attorney. It was obvious that I wouldn't be talking to Mr. Maxwell. She said I should hear from someone shortly.

Relieved at having that done, I dressed for the day and got back to my painting. If I stayed focused, I felt sure I could finish it today. I was interrupted by a phone call and was surprised to see that it was Olivia.

"Well, what's on your mind today, Ms. Olivia?"

"I've been thinking about our next quilt club meeting."

"Well, it's not for a while yet," I reminded her.

"I know, but Marta is going to be in charge. It's an opportunity for us to present some innovative ideas since Greta won't be there."

"I'm listening. What do you have in mind?"

"I think we could get the club to commit to another project. After all, look at the success of the quilt we just made."

Olivia's comment let me know that word had quickly gotten around about the selling price of the quilt. "I think you're right, Olivia. I'll be thinking, and so should you. Marta will listen."

"I knew you'd agree. I hope Rachael will come, and we could use some support from Cher if she's coming back."

"I'm on it, Olivia. Thanks for calling," I replied. While things were challenging right now in my personal life, I felt rather triumphant knowing that Olivia had latched onto the vision of the quilt club being able to make an impact in the community. Maybe Rachael would return, and I hoped that Cher would as well. I began to feel the strength that numbers could bring.

Chapter 26

I continued painting as my mind wandered to what Olivia and I had discussed. It'd be so great if every member chimed in with ideas. I needed to talk to Cher and then make sure that Rachael would attend the next meeting. However, my more immediate problem was sitting on my kitchen table. I still hadn't heard back from the law firm. Feeling stressed about the whole situation, I impatiently called them again.

"Yes, Ms. Stewart, I apologize," said the receptionist. "Matt Fairmore, your assigned attorney, just returned from vacation, so he just got your message. If you can hold, I can connect you with him."

When Mr. Fairmore answered the phone, I introduced myself. I felt silly explaining the ridiculous threat from an unhappy boyfriend. At any rate, he seemed to grasp my concerns and agreed that they needed to be addressed. We scheduled an appointment for the next day with the understanding that I'd bring the papers and set up an account with the firm. I was eager to get the whole situation resolved as soon as possible.

As we hung up, I already felt some sense of relief. I texted Ericka, thanked her for the referral, and informed her that I had an appointment. Cher also deserved a phone call since we'd discussed the situation over dinner the night before.

"What are you up to?" I asked when she answered.

"Everything! I finally got my TV and Internet going this morning. Now I'm rearranging things to see where to set up a studio."

"That's a lot. You don't have to do everything in one day."

"I'm finding that out. I'm quickly wearing myself out!" she agreed. "So, what are you doing today?"

"Thanks to Ericka, I have an appointment tomorrow to see an attorney in Sturgeon Bay. If you want to go with me, we could stop at the Barndoor Quilt Shop and Novel Bay Booksellers, not to mention getting some lunch, of course."

"Stop!" Cher pleaded. "Please don't tempt me like that! I refuse to have any fun until I'm more settled here. Plus, Claire, you don't know how long your appointment may last. I'll take a rain check. There are some good little restaurants in that area. I used to go to a book club at that bookstore years ago." Cher stopped talking for a moment and then said in a serious tone, "I sure hope the lawyer can help you."

"I just hope he's not too expensive. It makes me furious that Austen is putting me through this."

"I'm sure. By the way, your mom sent the sweetest welcome-to-your-new-home card today. Who does that anymore?"

"My mom. That's so her. She'd make Michael and me write thank-you notes all the time."

"She's so sweet. I miss talking with her because she was so close to my mom."

"I know you do. Your mom would be pleased that you're getting settled in here. It took a lot of courage for her to accept your coming back to take care of her."

"I kept telling her it was temporary. It made her happy when she knew you were holding my cabin for me."

"Yes, about that. We know how that's worked out, don't we?" We both chuckled. "It's so good to have you back!"

"Ditto!"

We hung up, and the rest of my evening was spent in front of the fire thinking about tomorrow's appointment and what I'd say at the quilt club meeting. From our conversation earlier in the day, I knew that Cher had too many other things on her mind to be thinking about the club right now.

Chapter 27

Mr. Fairmore's office was about four blocks down the street from the quilt shop and bookstore. The building was tall, and it appeared that the Maxwell firm occupied the first and second floors. I entered an upscale reception area where the walls were adorned with the credentials of the attorneys along with fine framed artwork. The receptionist gave me a form to fill out while I waited.

After a short wait, a handsome young man greeted me politely and requested that I follow him to his office. We started off with small talk before I began telling him all about Austen. He seemed to be intrigued that my best friend and I had basically switched living locations. He was easy to talk to and seemed to be a good listener.

After he'd heard my description of the events and had looked over the papers, he began, "What I've read in his demands is nothing new. His intent is quite obvious. He's not interested in a monetary settlement. He wants to harass you into feeling regretful. Sometimes a lawyer's simple letterhead response is effective—and sometimes it's not. It depends on how determined he is and how much money he's willing to spend. At some point, you can sue him for harassment if you feel it's necessary. The fact that he stalked you while he was here in Fish Creek for a week is a bit concerning."

"This just isn't like the man I knew. He was always controlling, but not scary like this."

"That's what concerns me. He has so much to lose by doing something stupid. To be clear, Ms. Stewart, you're not liable for any of the things he's demanding. You didn't have any contract, so just go about your normal life."

I thanked him for his time and felt I did the right thing by turning the matter over to him. I felt a lot lighter after talking to him. Despite the cold air, the sun felt good, so I decided to walk down the street toward the quilt shop and bookstore. I passed Lola's Bakery and Restaurant and decided that I definitely needed some lunch. It was a cute place located in a historic building, which I loved. I quickly ate an egg salad sandwich and chose a few delightful-looking pastries to take home with me. I felt better and wanted to pinch myself to make certain that I felt happy again.

Novel Bay Booksellers was a small, charming bookstore. It didn't take me long to notice that the owners called everyone by name as they entered. I particularly loved their section of Door County books and discovered that some were by local authors. I saw a woman looking at the book *Where the Crawdads Sing* and told her how much I enjoyed it. She thanked me and bought the book. Sometimes I felt I'd missed my calling by not going into sales. The children's section was adorable, and I wished I had some little people to buy for. I sat for a moment in a most intriguing wingback chair upholstered in a wild, attractive print. I got comfortable and read a bit of a book called *Fish Creek Echoes*. I thought it would be interesting for me to read as a new resident of the Fish Creek community, so I purchased it.

I left there and walked a block or so to where the Barndoor Quilt Shop was located. I walked down narrow, crowded aisles, which seemed typical of most quilt stores. The colors and fabrics were fascinating. I knew I'd be shopping here again soon. I asked for the owner, Carol, but they said she wasn't there. I wanted to thank her for giving our club a discount on the raffle quilt fabric.

Hanging near the front of the store was a lap-size medallion quilt of Door County. The shape of the peninsula was appliquéd in the center, and it was surrounded by blocks that represented significant things in the county, like cherries and lighthouses. It was red and white on one side and multicolored on the other. I could only imagine how the tourists would go for it.

"Is this quilt for sale?" I asked the young clerk.

"No, it's not, but we do have a pattern for it," she replied.

I told her that I'd take the pattern and then continued to look around. I loved all the cherry fabric they had in stock. This must have been where Cher had purchased some to make the kitchen curtains and tablecloth in the cabin. They had an abundance of samples, and I appreciated that so much. As I was checking out, I asked the clerk if they'd ever done a quilt show. The young woman looked as if she'd never been asked that question before.

I continued, "You know, in Sisters, Oregon, they have a wonderful outdoor show where they hang quilts on the buildings all up and down the street." Again, I got a look like I was from another planet.

"No, I don't think so," she said, looking uncomfortable.

I thanked her for her help, told her how much I'd enjoyed being in the shop, and made my exit. Outside, I realized that the afternoon was getting away from me. I knew that Olivia lived close by, and I should have visited her, but my instincts told me to get on home with my new book, pattern, and yummy treats from the bakery.

Chapter 28

Just after ten the next morning, I realized that I'd just put the last dab of paint on my painting! I stood back and admired my own work, which wasn't like me. I called Carl to see if he'd be at the shop.

"I'm not open, but I need to be there around noon if you can meet me then," he volunteered.

"Great! The painting is done, and I'm so anxious for you to see it. Please let me know what your client says."

"Great! I will."

I took a photo of the painting on my phone before I went upstairs to get cleaned up. I had another Quilted Snow quilt to give him as well. I was curious as to what I'd be paid.

Out of the corner of my eye, I saw Tom coming into my yard from the neighbors' house. Tom sometimes helped me with odd jobs around the cabin. "Hey, Tom! Come on in!"

"Oh, that's not necessary. I was just wondering if you wanted me to do a spring cleanup out here like I do for the Bittners."

"I'm sure I do, but is it time?"

"It is for some things. I clean out any flower beds that are experiencing early spring growth. Plus, there's always a lot of branches and old leaves that have settled in from the winter winds. I remember seeing your jonquils bloom. They make a pretty statement each spring."

"So, there does seem to be some work to be done now?" I confirmed.

"Mrs. Bittner has a lot more work over there. She loves a lot of flowers and likes everything manicured. Do you have enough wood in the house? You have a lot out here."

"I think I'm fine. Look—just do what you need to do, and let me know what I owe you."

"Just keep in mind that even in our spring season, it's chilly and folks are still making fires," he advised.

"Very well then. Bring me an armload."

By the time I got done dealing with Tom, I had to fix my face and be on my way to see Carl. When I arrived, Carl had the door wide open, ready for me to walk in. He must've seen me coming.

"Claire, I think I'm going to open up the shop earlier this year," he said with his hands on his hips. "If I'm going to be here working like I am, I may as well welcome some paying customers!"

"I agree! I see folks walking up and down the sidewalks in all kinds of weather."

"Let's see what you have here," he said, taking the wrapped painting from my arms. He carefully removed the wrapping and propped it up on a nearby empty display easel. Carl stood back and remained silent for a bit as he studied my work.

"I hope you like it," I interjected, suddenly feeling nervous about what he might say.

"I think you nailed it, Ms. Stewart."

I breathed in a sigh of relief. "Thank goodness. I'm pleased as well."

"I think our client will be very pleased. By the way, if he's not, I'll keep it and still pay you. I don't want anything going out of here that someone isn't happy with. This particular customer travels a lot, so I don't know how soon it will be before he sees this."

"I have another Quilted Snow for you as well," I said, placing it carefully on the counter.

"Very good. I'm tempted to send that one to my mother, but then I wouldn't have one for the shop. This has a better chance of selling during cool weather. When do you suppose your spring piece will be ready?"

"Oh, Carl, I haven't even started on it yet. All of my extra time has been spent on this painting, but I'll get started on it soon."

Carl got out his checkbook and quickly wrote me a check like he'd already had a price in mind. When he handed it to me, I couldn't believe how generous the amount was, not that I'd had a price in mind. "Thank you so, so much, Carl! I feel like I'm a working person in Door County now."

He laughed and said, "By the way, I heard your quilt at the Honors Dinner bought a pretty penny!"

"Yes, we were very pleased. The proceeds will be so helpful to Rachael right now."

"I donated a piece of pottery, but it didn't even bring the retail price, I'm sorry to say."

"That's too bad. It's a risk. We got lucky with the quilt."

"By the way, the space next door is supposed to be available by early summer. I'm trying to decide whether to take it or not. Do you think if I added more textiles like art quilts that it would pay for itself?"

I lit up, delighted that he was seeking my opinion. "If you're asking me, I wouldn't hesitate for a moment. You'd need some wall space and adequate hangers, but there's no one selling textiles like that. You now know the money some of them bring."

"Isn't there a quilt shop in Sturgeon Bay?"

"Yes, but she doesn't sell quilts. She only sells quilting supplies," I explained.

"I know there's a quilt shop in Jacksonport that sells Amish quilts, but I don't see that as the same kind of market. I hear that Amish quilts are very popular."

"Carl, I know some quilters here in the county who would love to sell their work somewhere. My friend Cher does similar work as mine. She just moved back to the area, and I know she'll be looking for a place to sell her things."

"Well, I have a little time to think about it. You just keep doing what you're doing!"

"Gladly! Thanks so much. I'll be waiting to hear how your client likes the painting."

Chapter 29

As soon as I got home, I called Cher to tell her about Carl's possible plan to open a shop for quilted art. My timing was poor. She was having trouble with her washing machine overflowing, so she said we'd have to talk later.

With Carl's encouragement and the prospect of making more money, I didn't waste any time making sketches for what I might want the Quilted Blooms quilt to look like. In Door County, cherry blossoms are so prominent that it'd only make sense to incorporate that flower in some way. The next decision would be whether to make it white like Quilted Snow or a solid color to reflect spring. I tried to picture what all four seasons might look like if they were displayed together. I quickly decided that complementary colors would work best. While I was contemplating what those colors might be, my phone rang. It was Cher.

"Is everything better now?" I asked.

She heaved a big sigh. "I hope this isn't a sign of more troubles ahead. I'm getting a whole new washing machine. I don't want to think about it anymore."

I gave her a quick update on Carl's plans, and I could tell that it was good news for her.

"I have so many ideas, and it just seems like now I have too many excuses to get started on anything," Cher complained.

"I understand. I felt the same way. Once you get settled, things will become clearer."

"Thanks, Claire," Cher replied. "By the way, I have a little gossip for you from home."

"What's going on?" I asked, not sure I wanted to hear what she had to say.

"Well, keep in mind what a small town we grew up in. It appears that Austen has told people that you left town because you created so much debt for him."

"Good heavens! Who did you hear that from?"

"Carole's daughter works at the hospital and heard it there. Of course, Carole and Linda both know better, and they defended you."

"It doesn't surprise me. He has to come up with some excuse as to why I left town so abruptly. I just hope Mom doesn't get wind of such rumors. It would really hurt her."

"That hospital is full of gossip. Don't let it bother you. It may not hurt to inform your lawyer that Austen is trying to ruin your reputation. By the way, did you like your lawyer?"

"Yes, very much. He seems to be resourceful and savvy regarding these kinds of situations. He assured me that I have nothing to worry about."

"Man, Claire, all I can say is that you must have really hurt his ego."

"That's what's so crazy! He's a successful, good-looking professional who can get nearly any woman he wants. Why can't he move on?"

"I hear you, Claire Bear. It's just gossip. Maybe I shouldn't have said anything."

"What are friends for? Well, so much for having a nice day!" I said with mock sarcasm.

Cher chuckled, and as soon as we hung up, I was ready to busy myself with getting something ready for dinner. I put a cheese enchilada in the oven and surprised myself as I angrily slammed the oven door shut. Was that little bit of gossip getting to me?

I made a fire and poked the logs until I had an impressive blaze going. I sat back and gave myself a pep talk. I couldn't do anything about how Austen was behaving, so I needed to let it go. He saw that I'm happy here in Door County, so he likely stewed all the way home about how to pay me back for my rejection. Those I care about know me better than that and shouldn't be swayed by idle gossip. I pulled dinner out of the oven and tried to think instead of my career possibilities with Carl. I had a plan now about how to proceed with my seasonal quilts.

My mind was exhausted, so I decided to turn in at nine and watch a movie from bed.

Chapter 30

I got up early enough to attend the chamber of commerce's breakfast meeting. I arrived at Husby's Food & Spirits in Sister Bay, where I hoped to run into Grayson. I filled my plate from the appetizing buffet and found a seat next to Allen, Ginger's husband. He introduced me to the owners of the Boathouse on the Bay, which is in Sister Bay. Everyone was chatty until the meeting began. Reports were given by various committee chairpersons and then announcements of upcoming events began. There was the Door County Half Marathon, the Blossom Run, and then the big St. Patrick's Day parade in Sturgeon Bay, which the chamber was going to participate in. Allen explained that the parade is a really big deal. He said it's like the official opening of spring and the beginning of the tourist season. Door County had more events listed on the handout given to us, but the only artsy thing listed was the Ellison Bay Spring Art Crawl. Too bad there wasn't anything quilt related on the lineup. Perhaps such a thing existed, but it wasn't mentioned in the chamber activities.

I asked the woman across from me if she liked quilts. She manages the On Deck Clothing Company in Sister Bay.

She politely nodded as I talked about how an outdoor quilt show would be fabulous along Highway 42.

"Claire, you should talk to Ginger about an idea like that," Allen encouraged. "She said as soon as the weather breaks, she plans to display some of our quilts outside in front of the shop to get people's attention."

"She has a great idea there," I agreed. "I'll talk to her. I think our club should be involved in something like that."

The chairman of the Honors Dinner then gave his report. He offered an additional remark about the generosity of Grayson Wills, who ran up the price on the quilt that was auctioned off. Everyone applauded, but there was no Grayson in sight.

I left the meeting feeling glad I went, but disappointed that I didn't get to see Grayson. I was close to the Piggly Wiggly, also known as the Pig, so I stopped in and stocked up on some groceries. After that, I ran by the post office to get my mail. It reminded me of our upcoming quilt meeting since we met at the post office building. When I arrived home, I saw Tom cleaning up the yard. He came to the car and offered to help carry in my groceries.

"I see that you've never used your outdoor firepit, but you have plenty of wood if you decide to make a fire in it, Ms. Stewart," Tom suggested.

"I'll remember that. It might be fun to have an outdoor fire sometime," I agreed. "Thanks so much for helping me again. You can just put the bill under the door when you leave."

"Sure!" he replied.

I went inside and had started putting the groceries away when I got a call from Cher. "How are you doing?" I asked.

"Fine. Did you have your phone shut off?"

"Well, I went to the chamber meeting in Sister Bay this morning. I put it on silent and guess I forgot to switch it back so I could hear the ringer. I hope you'll join the chamber when you get settled."

"I may, but I never really got too much out of it when I visited a few times."

"I thought since I was new, I'd give it a try for a year or so. I sat with Allen, Ginger's husband. Grayson wasn't there. In fact, it's been a while since I've heard from him."

"I'm sure you'll hear from him soon. I'm calling to hear what your lawyer told you. I got distracted by my washing machine fiasco."

"Why don't you come over tonight and we'll talk about it. I want to know more about the party, too. I bought fresh vegetables at the Pig on the way home. I can make us a big salad."

"You're treating me too well, but it sounds wonderful. I can bring wine. Goodness knows I still have plenty!"

"Okay, how about around six?"

"Sounds good."

I got busy with my chores and decided to make some quick brownies that I used to make on a regular basis. Austen would act like a little boy when I made them. Having these last-minute plans with Cher was exactly what I was looking forward to now that she'd moved back. We'd loved eating on the porch the other night, so I wanted to plan the same thing for tonight.

Chapter 31

I had everything prepared by six, and the aroma of the brownies consumed the house. I decided to change clothes. Minutes later, I heard Cher's knock. "Come on in!" I exclaimed.

"Here's some wine! Oh, what smells so good?"

"Warm brownies!"

"Oh, Claire Bear, you warm my heart, that's what you do! I love dining on the porch. I'll bet you and Grayson haven't done this, have you?"

"You're right. This will be our table," I joked. "Thanks for the wine. If you'll fill the glasses on the table, I'll tend to our bread."

"Okay. Did you do some cleaning up outside? It looks really nice."

"Yes, Tom has been doing some things for me. He's the one who put up my Christmas lights."

"That's nice to know. I suppose the Bittners will be back in the spring. One year, it was June before they came back." Cher joined me in the kitchen as I added a few finishing touches to our salad. "Did Ericka return your casserole dish and wine glasses, by the way?" Cher inquired.

"No, but that's okay," I replied. "That was quite a party!"

"I'll have you know that I wasn't the last to leave. George and some guys stayed pretty late, even after Ericka went to sleep."

"What happened with Ava, I wonder?"

"What do you think? Ericka said that she and the man she met there are a pretty good match."

The bread was ready, so we moved to the porch to enjoy our meal. Puff watched us from her chair and was likely confused watching her two mamas in front of her. I gave Cher a more detailed report on my lawyer's visit and she seemed relieved when I assured her that Austen had no legal claim. I added that I could even sue him for harassment.

"Claire, you wouldn't, would you?"

"It's hard to say. I can't believe he's doing what he's doing, considering his reputation."

"Let him talk all he wants. Anyone who knows you knows better."

"Thanks."

She smiled and changed the topic. "So, Claire Bear, what's your spring design going to be?"

"I think I'm going with cherry blossoms."

"You can't go wrong there," she said, taking another bite. "This is delicious!"

"Save room for brownies," I advised. "Cher, you know that quilt club is coming up, and you have to decide soon whether you're coming back."

Cher paused in thought and then said decisively, "Only if they take us both."

"Well, Marta is running the next meeting, so you have a little time to decide. I plan to bring up some things for discussion since Greta won't be there."

"Oh boy. I smell trouble. Like what, for instance?" Cher asked.

"Well, I plan to suggest we be a part of some kind of quilt show for the public to promote quilts as an art form."

"You've got to be kidding. You do know the quilt guild in Green Bay has one every other year."

"But that's not in Door County. We're the art capital of Wisconsin, don't you agree?"

"I suppose. The guild in Sister Bay had a show once in Anderson House that was just quilts from their members."

"Anderson House?"

"Yes, it's owned by the historical society. You should check it out sometime since you like history. The guild in Sister Bay has some exceptionally talented quilters."

"I'd love to go to one of their meetings. I met their secretary, and she said that I'd be welcome."

"Well, I wish you luck about even having such a conversation at quilt club."

"Naturally, I'll warn Marta. She may have already found a program by now."

"Look. You know I'll support whatever you come up with. I think the others will too, but just so you know, you'll be opening a can of worms."

"Carl from the gallery has really been encouraging me, but I can't do any of my ideas on my own."

"Events have to start with an idea and a vision. You can start small and see what happens."

"Good advice. Now, are you ready for some brownies? Do you want ice cream?"

"No ice cream for me. Just the hard stuff, please," Cher replied with a laugh.

Chapter 32

We took our chocolate in by the fire and continued our conversation. It was fun catching up on people we both grew up with. We talked comfortably together; however, Cher always got sheepish when I wanted to talk about her love life. I tried to introduce the subject once again.

"I don't have time for a man right now," she responded. "It'd just be another thing to worry about."

"That doesn't sound like you. When did this new attitude start?"

"Over time, I just realized that my life is full and has meaning without a man. My short marriage was a good lesson on that topic."

"You can't judge every man the same way, Cher. Don't you ever want adult male conversations every now and then?"

"Perhaps, but I know lots of intelligent women," she said teasingly, trying to get me to move to another topic.

"What if Grayson had someone to fix you up with?"

"Good luck with that, especially with someone from around here. I'm not worried, and you shouldn't be either. I want to get my work going again. I'm thinking of trying miniature pieces. What do you think?"

"As in quilts or paintings?"

"Whichever! I like working with smaller things. I did a piece for Carole, and I surprised myself at how much I enjoyed it," Cher revealed.

"I was thinking of a line of miniature paintings of quilts," I said.

"Great idea. I wonder how Rachael is doing with her barn quilt orders. Her commitment to make a real quilt block to match each barn quilt is time consuming."

"I'm sure it's a good selling point," I said. "It certainly sets her business apart from similar ventures. I sure hope Harry can help her figure out things financially. She has to be able to keep that farm."

"I didn't realize it was that serious. No wonder you were pushing that quilt for the auction."

"I think she'll need me when tourist season comes, so I'll probably go back to help her. I'm willing to do it for nothing, but she probably won't have it."

"You really liked it, didn't you?"

"Yes, especially during the Christmas tree season. Smelling that pine every day was divine."

"I know how you are about Christmas!" Cher teased. "Well, I'm fading, Christmas girl, so I'm heading home. You want some help cleaning up?"

"Not at all. You're my guest. How about a couple of brownies for tomorrow?"

"Sure!"

"Would you like to go to the Bayside Tavern on Saturday night when Rachael starts back to work? You might meet someone tall and handsome! We should ask Ericka too, so she doesn't think I'm trying to steal you away from her."

Cher burst into laughter. "Okay. It does sound like fun."

We hugged goodbye and then I sent Cher and some of the brownies home. I did as little as possible to clean up and headed upstairs to bed. I had to scoop Puff up from her nap in front of the fire. I dressed for bed and then remembered to check my phone before crawling between the covers. My heart stopped as I saw another text from Austen.

[Austen]
You're in serious trouble.

That was it. What in the world did he mean by that? Did he really think I was going to respond to his letter by sending him a check? Was he trying to tell me that I'm in serious danger? What was wrong with him? I sat back in bed and tried to think about my next move. I knew I had to add this text to my record when I talked to Mr. Fairmore again. I think Austen was hoping to catch me at a weak moment, thinking that I'd respond to him. This was harassment!

I rolled over and tried to think of my relaxing evening with Cher. I was glad the two of us were sticking together on our future with the quilt group. I had to remind myself to contact Marta.

After I finally fell asleep, my frustrations turned into a nightmare. There was Austen with a determined look crashing into my quilt meeting. He was telling the members what a terrible person I am. The members responded with, "I told you so." No matter how hard I tried, I couldn't convince them that he was the bad guy and that he was lying through his teeth. I woke up in a cold sweat.

It was four in the morning by then, so I got up and got a glass of water. I needed a distraction to go back to sleep, so

I turned on the TV. I turned to the old movie channel and thought of Grayson. Perhaps he was watching at the same time. This movie had Jane Wyman and Gregory Peck in a long love scene in a convertible. Now I could relax and get some shut-eye.

Chapter 33

The next morning, I was awakened by something fuzzy brushing across my face. I quickly realized that I'd slept later than usual, and Puff was letting me know it. Around ten, I called Rachael to see if she wanted some company for lunch. I wanted reassurance that she'd be at our next quilt meeting, so I wanted to talk to her about it over lunch. Thankfully, she agreed. I told her that I'd provide the food, so I called the Bayside Tavern and asked them if they knew her favorite sandwich. The guy who answered called out to someone named Bea. When he got her response, he confirmed that it was their French dip, which was basically a roast beef sandwich with cheese. It sounded good, so I ordered three of them in case Harry was there. I still had some brownies left from dinner, so I wrapped those up as well.

I picked up the food and headed out to Rachael's. I always enjoyed the drive, as it gave me time to think. I thought of Grayson, whom I hadn't heard from in some time. It also caused me to think of what Rachael might be going through right now and how I might help her. As I drove, I was happy about seeing teeny tiny signs of spring here and there. Rachael had said to come to the barn, where she was working. When I arrived, I could see evidence that Harry had been working on things outside, but his Hummer wasn't in sight.

"Claire, how nice to see you," Rachael said, giving me a hug.

"Wait until you see what I brought us for lunch," I said as I held up the large bag.

Peeking inside, she said, "Oh, it can't be what I think it is! I'd know that smell anywhere. Did you go to the Bayside to get this?"

I nodded and smiled, pleased that I'd surprised her with something she liked.

"I don't believe it! Thank you so much. Let's go into the lunchroom."

"I brought a sandwich for Harry in case he was here."

"No way! He was here earlier, but he's not getting this wonderful treat."

"You're a real meanie!" I teased. "Will you go back to the Bayside on Saturday night?"

"They sure want me to, but I haven't decided."

"Well, if I can entice you, I'm going there. I'm planning to come with some friends. I know Cher is really anxious to see you."

"Really?"

"I think you should go back to the Bayside. It'll be good for you to be with your friends."

"Okay, I suppose I will. I've gone back and forth about it so much," she admitted. Then she smiled and said, "But for now, let's eat!"

It was so good to see a smile on Rachael's face again. She took a big bite and began to chew slowly, savoring the flavors. In between bites, she couldn't say enough about how much help Harry had been to her.

"He brought his granddaughters over yesterday, and they love to come here. They fed the animals and came back so excited."

"You're so fortunate to have him, Rachel," I said. "I don't want to be nosy, but is he helping you with your finances? I know he has some concerns."

Her expression changed to one of pensiveness, and she finally nodded. "It's uncomfortable, but we're addressing some things. The quilt money took care of some of the medical expenses."

"Good. The club members were so pleased to help. We were all shocked at the amount it brought. I hope you'll be at the next meeting so you can thank them personally."

"I'll try to be there. I did send a thank-you note. I knew Greta would be looking for that immediately."

I snickered because I knew she was right. "I have another reason that I'd like you to be there," I said, hesitating.

"Now what?" Rachael asked, looking unsure.

"I want to discuss some new ideas for the club at this upcoming meeting. With Marta running it instead of Greta, I think we could make some changes."

"I'm more concerned that you and Cher get to remain in the club."

"Well, that will also come up," I assured her.

Chapter 34

"Rachael, I never saw the group so energized as when we were making the quilt. They were cheerful, talkative, and had a sense of purpose."

"Oh, Claire, that makes me feel so good."

"I hope to make more of that happen."

"You and Cher will both be there, right?" Rachael asked.

"It sounds like she will, which is another reason for you to be there."

After we ate, we went into the workroom, where Rachael showed me the barn quilts she was working on. "Claire, what's amazing is that even with closing for a while, I continue to get plenty of orders, which surprises me."

"I think having that quilt auctioned off reminded folks about your business. They all want to see you survive."

"I also sent a thank-you note to Grayson, just so you know."

"That was nice."

"Are things still good with the two of you?"

"I think so, but I don't hear from him very frequently. He's a busy man, and I have to keep reminding myself of that."

"That's right," Rachael agreed, nodding.

"Well, I need to be getting home. I sure hope we'll see you at quilt club! By the way, did you see Nettie and Fred at the funeral?"

She smiled. "I did. I was so touched. They sent flowers as well."

I gave her a hug and teasingly told her to get back to work. I left with a full stomach and warm feelings of friendship. On the way home, I decided to stop at Nelson Shopping Center to pick up some garden and flower seeds. I loved going to the large hardware store that had absolutely everything one could imagine. When I'd first arrived here, they'd had all the things I'd needed to get settled in the cabin.

When I walked in, there was a seed rack at the very front of the store. It was a great reminder that spring is on its way! I picked out seed packs of lettuce, spinach, and a few herbs. If I didn't have enough flowerpots in the shed, I could do like Mom always did and plant them between other things in the yard.

I was there for quite a while. I loved the gift area and even found a nice wine rack for Cher. She hadn't had time to pick one out yet, and I knew she would love this one. I found an oversized bow and a card to accompany it. When I checked out, I had them add several bags of potting soil. The store was crowded, and my cart had a few other impulse purchases, including a new pair of garden gloves in bright colors. The clerk told me that actual plants would start arriving soon, and he urged me to come back. I left there and went straight to Cher's apartment. She wasn't home, so I left the wine rack at her door. It would be a fun surprise for her when she returned.

When I got home, I began to unload everything. I carried most of my purchases to the backyard. I opened the shed to see what supplies I had to work with. There was a selection of clay pots, and I wondered how many owners of the cabin had used these clay pots through the years. The backyard was always shaded by the cliff to the rear of the property, so I'd have to keep that in mind as I placed the pots in the yard. No one could see my backyard, but I envisioned some color popping out between the rocks here and there. It took a little time and effort to get everything potted. When I got back inside, I washed up and fixed some tea. I started a fire so I could warm up quicker. I could feel the temperature dropping again. My cell rang, and it was Mom.

"Oh, I was thinking of you," I said right away.

"What brought that on?"

"I bought some seeds and potting soil at the hardware store. How about that?"

"You did?"

"Yes, with all the pots in the shed, it gave me thoughts about growing herbs and maybe some lettuce and spinach."

"Well, I'll be. I'm just going to buy two tomato plants to keep me supplied this year. I like going to the farmer's market at the park to get what little I need."

"Good idea. How are you and Mr. Vogel doing?"

"Odd you should ask. He was here for supper last night. I made a pot of chili and some corn bread, and he arrived with a big appetite. It's nice to cook for someone occasionally."

"Yes, I said the same thing when I made dinner for Cher and me."

"Bill asked about you."

Now Mr. Vogel had turned into Bill. I found that curious but didn't say anything. "That was nice of him," I replied.

"When he was at the bank, he heard that you have been struggling with a serious health problem, which was part of the reason that you moved away."

"Oh, good heavens! How crazy is that?" I asked, frowning.

"That's what I said. I told him I'd never seen you happier. I think he felt like he shouldn't have mentioned it to me."

"Nothing like small-town gossip!"

"Well, he frequently shares this and that with me about things he hears in the coffee room at the bank where he pops in every now and then."

Chapter 35

"I'm lunchroom gossip now? The only person who would spread lies like that about me is Austen."

"What? Now, that's nonsense."

"I may as well tell you that he's told folks I left town because I created a big debt for him."

"I just can't believe he'd do that," Mom protested.

"He's very bitter. He banks at Mr. Vogel's bank, so he probably dropped some remarks to one of the tellers."

"Claire, it's not that serious. Forget that I said anything," she urged. "How's Cher doing? I also keep wondering about Rachael and how she's adjusting."

I worked hard to settle myself down so we could talk about something else. "Cher is nearly settled, and Ericka hosted a really nice party for her. I went to see Rachael this morning. We raised five thousand dollars for her by auctioning off the quilt, so that will help her for now."

"Gracious me! Five thousand dollars? You never told me."

"Guess who bought it," I urged.

"Someone you know? Oh Lord, I hope you didn't pay that much!"

"Grayson outbid everyone."

"Well, I'll be! He's a keeper, honey. Are you listening?"

"Yes, Mom. He really did love the quilt and intends to use it for himself."

"I don't think we'd ever get over a thousand dollars for a quilt around here."

"I know. It was a wonderful outcome for the quilt project," I said. "Mom, how's Michael?"

"He said book sales have been steady. He asked me whether you have read the book."

I was taken aback at the question and hesitated to give an honest answer. After giving it some thought, I admitted, "Not completely. It's pretty dry, but parts of it are really good. I can tell that he put a lot of research into it."

"He sure did, and I'm very proud of him. He hopes to come by next weekend."

"Good. Tell him hello for me."

"Claire, he's your brother. I wish you two would communicate more often. You should call him yourself."

"I know," I replied. "I will. I need to run now. Take care. I miss you!"

"Love you, sweetie."

When I hung up, I returned to the subject of what appeared to be Austen's latest gossip about me. He was determined to smear my name. What an even dirtier act to spread something that he was certain would get back to my mother! I poked at the fire, trying to calm the feelings I had inside. I dialed Cher but her voicemail came on, so I had to leave a message. I reported, "Now the latest gossip is that I may be terminally ill here in Door County, according to some gossip at the bank which got back to Mom. He's up to no good again," I said before hanging up.

Still frustrated, I picked up a needle and started stitching the center of the Quilted Blooms quilt. Once started, I kept going and going, only stopping to rethread my needle. Since this was the first one, I couldn't wait to see the finished product. After a while, my phone rang. To my surprise, it was Grayson.

"What's up, Ms. Stewart?"

"I'm happy to report that I'm getting a lot of quilting done as I listen to some music."

"No old movies playing?"

"No, not this time. How about you?"

"Things are going very well. Everyone at the office is working on a large project, but I wanted to stop and give you a quick call. How's everything with you?"

"Pretty good. I went to see Rachael and had a nice visit with her. Then I went to Nelson's to get some things. I bought some seeds and got them planted today."

"That's great!"

"I was pretty pleased about how the day was going until I talked to my mother and she told me the latest gossip." I went on to tell him the story about me being seriously ill and that Mr. Vogel had shared it with my mother. "Austen seems determined to try to mar my reputation in my own hometown!"

"Well, he sure doesn't seem to care about his own reputation. That's too bad. Time will likely take care of it."

"Well, there's a little more," I said slowly. "I got another text from Austen informing me that I'm in real trouble."

"That sure sounds childish. I'm sorry that you're going through this."

"I did consult with an attorney, so I'll give him a call," I said, still feeling frustrated.

Chapter 36

Grayson said kindly, "I wish I could advise you, Claire. All I can do is give you a kiss and wish it all away like I do with Kelly."

I smiled at his tenderness. "That's sweet, but it's not your problem. Actually, I don't feel very comfortable sharing the situation with you."

"Aren't we good friends? You already gave me enough information to assure me that you made a good choice by leaving him. Since we're close, I feel I can only encourage you to take the professional advice that you're getting."

I sighed and decided to change the subject. "On a much happier topic, how's Kelly?"

"She's the reason I'm calling. Sometimes we leave messages for each other on the refrigerator. Today, she left me a reminder that I'm to invite you here for a spaghetti dinner."

"That's nice!"

"How about tomorrow?"

"I'm sorry, but I promised to bring some folks to the Bayside to welcome Rachael back to work this Saturday."

"That sounds like fun," he replied. "How about Sunday?"

"Sure. What can I bring?"

"I've been put in charge of the salad, so I think we're good," he replied with a laugh. "Kelly wants to be fully in charge of the spaghetti!"

"I make killer brownies. Let me bring dessert."

"Kelly would love that."

"Tell her that I make them with extra chocolate chips."

"Man, I could go for some of those right now," Grayson said.

"Great. I'll see you on Sunday." I hung up feeling fortunate to have a friend like Grayson. Making brownies for them would be a joy. Soon after hanging up from talking with Grayson, I made a call to Mr. Fairmore. I had to wait quite a while until he came to the phone.

"How are you doing, Ms. Stewart?"

"I'm feeling like a little child tattling on a big bully who is determined to harass me," I complained with a weak laugh.

He chuckled. "That's what I'm here for. I told you to keep me informed."

"Have you heard from him since you sent him the letter?" I asked, curious to know if there had been any progress.

"No, and that's a good thing for you."

"He sent another text, and this one sounds threatening."

"It sounds as if the pressure may be eating at him." At that, Mr. Fairmore listened closely as I told him about the texts and rumors it seemed that Austen was spreading in my small hometown.

"Let's give this a little more time. Do you feel physically threatened in any way?"

"No, I never have, but this is a mental game that disturbs me. I think he definitely wants me to feel threatened."

"I know it's difficult and frightening at times, but he's looking for a response from you. If you can send a message that he's looking foolish, that may be all it takes. The two of you never had any kind of written agreement, so try not to worry about anything."

"But now he's trying to ruin my reputation!" I protested.

"I've made a note of that, but it would take witnesses and interviews to follow through, so just sit tight. People who truly know you won't believe his nonsense."

When we hung up, I felt better. Austen's actions were on the record now. Perhaps the lawyer's letter did make him think twice and maybe that would curtail his anger. As I was turning the phone conversation over in my mind, my phone rang. It was Ericka.

"I just wanted you to know that I told Cher to count me in on going to the Bayside tomorrow night."

"Good! I think Rachael will be happy to see everyone."

Ericka's tone turned serious as she warned, "I have a strange question to ask you, Claire."

Chapter 37

"What is it?" I inquired. I honestly couldn't imagine what could be on her mind.

"Well, I had a couple of things missing after the party."

"No!" I responded.

"I didn't say anything to anyone right away in case I'd just misplaced them."

"What's missing, Ericka?"

"I'd rather not say right now, but Cher said that Ava from your quilt club has been known to have sticky fingers. That brings me to my question. Do you know if that's true?"

"Surely she wouldn't!" I replied. "She was very occupied with your neighbor, so I don't know how or when she could've taken anything. Maybe you should ask him."

"I thought about it, but it seems as though he really likes her, so I didn't want to offend him."

"It may be a risk you have to take," I said. Then I remembered the day when I'd run into Ava and her friend at the coffee shop. I said, "I witnessed her in action one day at a café when she came back later to pick up a tip her friend had left on the table. She doesn't know that I saw her, but it was strange behavior."

"How bold! What's her deal anyway? Does she need the money?"

"I don't know her very well. She really stands out in the quilt club in more ways than one. Everyone in the club is conservative except her. She also has a rather flamboyant personality, and then there's the cleavage ..." I said, my words trailing off.

Ericka snickered. "She's a little too old to be dressing and acting like she does."

"Your neighbor doesn't think so," I reminded Ericka. "However, she's quite a good singer. I'm told that when she was younger, she entertained the armed forces. You were lucky she didn't break out in song at your party."

"Oh, but she did! She was in the group that was the last to leave. They were singing all sorts of songs, and now that you tell me this, I recall that she was leading the pack. I went to bed. George was still there with them, so I felt that they wouldn't miss me."

"Ericka, I'm sorry to hear about the missing items. Perhaps the mystery will be solved shortly. Keep me posted, okay?"

"I will. I'll see you at the Bayside tomorrow night."

"It'll be fun!" I hung up with heaviness in my heart for Ericka and Ava. I wondered what in the world Ericka was missing. I freshened up and made a grocery list to take to the Pig. I also needed to stop by the post office to get the mail in case there had been a response from Austen. After speaking with the attorney today, I knew that I needed to stay on top of that situation. As I left the cabin and walked to the car, I waved to Tom, who was doing some more work over at the Bittners' house.

"Hey there, Ms. Stewart. The Bittners are coming back earlier this year, so I thought I'd better get things cleaned up."

"Well, that's good news!"

"I saw you messing around with some pots. I guess you're planting something."

"I planted a few seeds, so we'll see what happens."

"Are you thinking of a garden?" he asked.

"No. It's just too shady back there to grow many vegetables. I'm hoping to grow some herbs and maybe a little lettuce. I'm more of a flower gardener."

"If you need some help, just let me know."

"I will. Thanks!" I got on my way and began to think about the return of the Bittners. It would seem strange to have people so close by after the long winter.

The Pig was crowded. It didn't appear that they had any competition in the whole county! It didn't take long to fill my cart. I grabbed a few herbs that I saw for sale at the checkout counter.

When I got in my car, I decided to make a quick stop at the bookstore in the same shopping area. The Peninsula Bookman also had a location in Fish Creek. They have a wonderful collection of used books and a nice representation of books by local authors. I picked up the latest *Peninsula Pulse* newspaper, which I usually got at the library. When I arrived, the owner was assisting another customer, so I just gave the shop a quick look and found a book about Washington Island. I'd wanted to learn more about it, so I decided to purchase the book. Because of my vertigo, I may never get on the ferry to go there in person. Paging through the book, I realized that just looking at all of the winter photos made me chilly! Closing the book, I got the owner's attention and headed to the checkout.

When I got back in the car, the interior smelled delightful. I'd purchased a roasted chicken, mashed potatoes, and green beans from the deli at the Pig. I was looking forward to eating some comfort food for a change.

Chapter 38

The next day, I was looking forward to spending some time with the girls and seeing Rachael again at the Bayside Tavern. The weather was looking a bit more like spring, which gave me much to look forward to.

After breakfast, I opened the windows to the porch and sat there for a while just working on my quilt. Puff remained in her chair and seemed to love the fresh breeze as well. As I glanced out of the window every now and then, I noticed that traffic on Cottage Row was picking up. Could it be the return of the snowbirds? I spent the bulk of the day working on my quilt. I was pleased with the way it was coming along.

At five, I closed the windows. The temperature was dropping, reminding me that winter was still with us. I went upstairs to get ready for my big night out. The hamburgers at the Bayside were also something to look forward to as a dinner option. I dressed in warm and casual clothes since I planned to walk over there.

When I arrived, the first thing I saw was Rachael situated behind the counter pouring a draft beer. She gave me a quick smile and pointed to one of the high-top tables where Ericka and Cher were sitting.

"Hey, Claire!" Cher greeted me as she lifted her glass. "We got a head start on you!"

"I'll do my best to catch up," I teased as I took a seat.

"Good to see you all!" Rachael said, joining us. "What will it be, Claire?"

I ordered a drink and was pleased that Rachael had returned to work. I felt certain that the social atmosphere would be enormously good for her.

"Brenda is supposed to join us," Ericka informed me.

"Great!" I replied. "I really like her. I feel bad not reaching out to her more. She's invited me to so many things since I met her."

"Her daughter is such a sweetheart," Ericka mentioned.

Rachael arrived with my drink and pulled up a stool to join us. "I got here at about four today, so Ron said I should take a long break and join you."

"That was nice of him," I said. "I was hoping that would happen."

"I can't thank you enough for helping me through everything," Rachael said, making eye contact with each one of us as she made her statement.

"You're doing great," I bragged. "Charlie would be proud of you."

She smiled and then turned to address Cher. "Okay, Cher, are you coming back to quilt club or not?"

Cher remained unfazed by Rachael's directness and answered, "Only if they keep my buddy Claire Bear!"

"It's the perfect time to just blend in, with Greta not being there," Rachael advised with a laugh. "I can't believe how Greta takes that roll call every month!"

Each of us giggled, and Ericka raised her eyebrows in surprise. "I hate to say it, but that club of yours is like a high school sorority," Ericka teased. "It's a good thing I'm not a quilter!"

Everyone laughed.

"Everyone needs to be there if we're going to discuss any new ideas," I warned.

"What exactly do you plan to propose, Claire?" Rachael asked, looking directly at me.

"Well, when I visited with Carl at the gallery, I told him that a bigger emphasis should be put on quilts in the county. In other words, the area could offer something that the general public could view to demonstrate how quilts are art. That could mean something outdoors as people walk or drive by."

"Outdoors?" Ericka questioned.

"It's certainly been done before!" I assured them. "Quilters need to get their quilts out of the box!"

"You have a short window of nice weather here in Door County," Ericka reminded me.

"I know," I agreed. "There are many reasons to oppose my suggestion, like the weather, liability, and, of course, resources."

"For sure!" Cher agreed. Then she told the others, "I have to warn you that when you tell Claire Bear she can't do something, she'll find some way to prove you wrong!"

"Thanks, Cher," I chuckled. "I'm so glad you haven't forgotten."

"Hey, I also didn't want you to think I'd forgotten to thank you for the wine rack. It was perfect," Cher said.

"Back to the club. You can't be serious about wanting them to do something like that," Rachael said with a doubtful look on her face.

Chapter 39

"I think there should be some discussion about participating in shows of some kind," I explained. "It'd be interesting to know what the others think. Every event needs a driver. I know they'll be looking at me."

"You should and could be the driver," Cher said confidently.

"Perhaps, but I know that it also takes a village to make it successful," I added.

"Oh, for sure," Ericka agreed. "Around here, you'd better have the approval of the village."

"Do you really need the club to pull off a successful quilt event?" Cher inquired.

"Absolutely! I'd want their approval," I replied. "The club doesn't even have a name, so my approach would be to get the members' support individually."

"I think Claire is serious!" Cher teased, winking at me.

"Of course, having Cher Bear as my cochair would have to be part of the deal," I proposed, returning her wink.

"What?" Surprised, Cher leaned back in her chair.

"Oh boy! I'd love to be a little mouse at your next club meeting!" Ericka joked.

"We'll see how it goes," I said with a sigh. "It'll be interesting to see how far Marta lets us go as compared to Greta."

"Interesting thought," Rachael said. "I'll definitely be there. I sure hope the others will as well."

"I know that Olivia will be there," I mentioned. "She's just waiting for something like this to happen."

"She'd be a great one to have on the show committee," Cher suggested.

"It's been so fun to just sit and chat with you guys," Rachael said. "Do you want to order some food now?"

"We will, but you just enjoy the time they're giving you on this break," I advised.

"Okay, I will," Rachael said, shrugging her shoulders. Then she got an impish smile on her face and said, "Now, let's hear some romantic gossip." She rubbed her hands together and leaned forward as if preparing to hear some rather juicy conversation. Everyone laughed.

"Nothing from me," Ericka began. She sat back in her chair as if to indicate that other participants should take over from there.

"The only one with any romance going on is Claire," Cher offered, smiling at me.

"I'm smitten," I admitted. "However, I don't want any gossip, and at this point, there are no commitments or promises." I hoped that this simple admission would satisfy their curiosity.

"Well, there sure was some romance going on at my party between Ava and your neighbor, Ericka," Cher reported.

Silence followed until a surprised Rachael asked, "Really? Ava?"

"He's my neighbor in a nearby condo," Ericka explained. "He's got a comfortable life, but I think he's very lonely. He did indeed go gaga over Ava."

Rachael looked perplexed. "I thought she was married, but I guess not."

"Since we're among friends," Ericka said, "I have a concern about Ava."

"What's that?" Rachael asked innocently.

I was afraid that I knew what was coming, so I stared into my drink, trying not to make eye contact with the others.

Ericka continued, "I had some things missing after the party I gave for Cher. I'm told that your friend Ava may have sticky fingers, so I thought of her."

Rachael gasped. "You really don't think she'd be that brazen, do you?"

Ericka shrugged her shoulders.

"You really don't know for sure," Cher said in Ava's defense. "She was invited because she's in the quilt club with me."

"Is she the only suspect?" Rachael asked.

"Pretty much," Ericka said flatly.

"What's missing?" Rachael asked with interest.

There was a long silence before Ericka said sadly, "My rings." She then went on to explain, "I had a lot of food that came in that evening, and I was busy in the kitchen arranging things. At one point, I removed my rings and put them on the windowsill."

"My goodness!" Rachael exclaimed. "How many rings are missing?"

"Two," Ericka revealed. "One was a diamond ring I purchased for myself when I turned thirty."

Chapter 40

"How awful!" Cher said with a gasp. "Did you call the police?"

Ericka shook her head. "The whole idea of anyone stealing at my party is crazy," Ericka shared. "Nearly everyone that was there are friends that I know pretty well."

"It was probably too tempting for someone when they just saw them sitting there," I suggested. "Do you know who might have gone into the kitchen?"

"You've got to be kidding, Claire," Ericka said, exasperated by my question. "You were there! Everyone was in that kitchen at some time or another that night."

"It was packed alright," Cher agreed.

I remained silent, hoping to not upset Ericka any further. When I glanced at the door, I spied Brenda entering the restaurant. "Oh, here comes Brenda," I pointed out.

"Please don't say anything about the rings," Ericka requested as Brenda approached our table.

"Good to see you, Brenda," Rachael said. "I'm actually on duty tonight. What would you like?"

Brenda responded to Rachael with a big smile. "I'm glad you're back at work, Rachael. I think of you so often."

"Thanks, Brenda," Rachael responded. "Hey, if you guys want to order food, you'd better do it before the kitchen closes."

"Oh, then we'd better decide what we want!" I said as I looked at my watch. Surprisingly, it was already after ten.

"I'm starved," Cher declared. "I always get the same thing, so the Bayside burger it is!"

"I'll take the same thing but with sweet potato fries," I announced.

"I think you can repeat that order all around," Brenda said, looking to Ericka for approval.

Rachael retreated into the kitchen to put our orders in and then returned to her seat at the table.

"I'm so sorry that I couldn't get here sooner," Brenda apologized.

"Well, you missed all sorts of juicy stuff," I teased. "It's your turn to tell us what's going on with you."

"Not much," she reported. "I did finish a quilt for my daughter since I had less hours at work, but now the tourist season is slowly picking up so my hours should increase."

"I'll bet you get to meet such interesting people at the restaurant," Cher guessed.

"I do!" she agreed, nodding. "It's where Ericka introduced me to Claire."

"I'll bet it's just wonderful to stay in one of their lovely rooms on the premises," I said with a sigh.

"The rooms are charming and are decorated very tastefully," Brenda explained. "Claire, we haven't talked lately, but is Grayson still in your life?"

"Yes, we have a relationship of sorts," I said, blushing.

"More than she wants to let on, you might say," Cher laughed.

"That's great," Brenda responded. "He's such a fine man."

"What about you, Brenda?" Ericka asked. "Are you seeing anyone?"

She smiled. "No, I wish," she answered. "I meet a lot of nice men, but they gaze right through me most of the time as I wait on them."

"Well, some make better friends than lovers, so you might want to consider that," Ericka joked. "I have a male friend at work that I love spending time with, but we don't have a drop of romance in our relationship."

"Claire and I have discussed whether Grayson has any friends that he could fix me up with," Cher revealed.

"I've met some of his friends, but they seem to be taken," I explained. "I think Grayson's social life is mostly with his daughter."

"Have you met her?" Brenda asked.

"Only briefly, but tomorrow night, Kelly has invited me to a spaghetti dinner at their house," I shared.

They gasped in delight and surprise.

"Score!" Ericka exclaimed. "It sounds like you're in the club!"

I laughed.

"Are you nervous?" asked Cher.

"Not really," I shook my head. "It made me feel better when Grayson told me that Kelly was encouraging him to date."

"You're lucky there!" Brenda said. "Father and daughter relationships are pretty close in most situations."

I nodded in agreement. Just then, our food arrived, and everyone took the opportunity to concentrate on satisfying their appetites. Rachael returned to work, but I was grateful that the management had allowed her to spend some time with us on her first night back.

Chapter 41

Before we departed, Cher asked if I'd heard anything from my lawyer or Austen.

"No, it's been a while since Austen's last text," I reported. "I can only hope that the legal intervention has helped."

"I just can't wrap my head around why he'd risk his reputation over a woman who left him," Ericka said, shaking her head. Then she looked at Cher and me and quipped, "Men are so stupid, don't you think?"

We laughed at her silliness, but Cher pointed out, "Just look at the politicians who risk their careers over a pretty girl!"

"Austen has a huge ego," I explained. "He is admired by many, and who doesn't love a man who loves children and babies? He was humiliated when he was caught off guard by my move."

"Yes, dumb, like I said," Ericka reiterated, laughing at her own attempt at humor.

"Unfortunately, he has taken it a step further and is attempting to ruin my reputation," I replied.

"You left town. How can he do that?" Brenda inquired.

"Well, it's a small town, so it doesn't take much. He's trying to start rumors. He first said that I left him with a lot of debt. Now he's saying that I'm seriously ill. My mother still lives in that town, and I continue to have friends there. It's shameful."

"What a creep!" Ericka exclaimed.

"I agree," Cher echoed. "Just so you know, I'm going to pick up the rest of our tab tonight. You all have been so helpful and sweet since I returned."

"No way, Cher Bear," I insisted. "I told Rachael to split it up for us. There's nothing worse than a bunch of ladies trying to figure out what they owe on their food bill!"

They laughed in agreement.

"This has been great," Brenda said. "Thanks so much for including me. This place is bigger than I thought, just judging from the outside."

"I thought that at first, too," I agreed. "When I came here for the first time, Rachael introduced me to a couple of regulars, like Nettie and Fred, who are sitting at the bar tonight. They told me it was like their living room. They thought so much of Rachael that they came to Charlie's funeral."

"That's so sweet," Brenda said. "I'm sure that my daughter and her friends come here. She'll be surprised when I tell her where I've been tonight."

I smiled and nodded. When Rachael brought us the bill, we chose to leave her a generous tip. We hugged each other goodbye. It'd been such a fun evening.

When I got home, Puff wasn't around to greet me. Once upstairs, I could see that she was sound asleep near my pillow. That was taking too much liberty, so I picked her up and moved her to her regular spot. Her sleepy purr let me know that she didn't appreciate it. After I got under the covers, I decided to check my phone. Another text from Austen immediately made my stomach ache.

[Austen]
Two can play your silly game.

I rolled my eyes in exasperation. He must have gotten my lawyer's letter and was gearing up for a counterattack. Why did he have to say anything at all? Didn't he know that this was harassment? Was he getting any legal advice at all?

I turned out the light and resituated my pillow. I wasn't going to let Austen ruin a wonderful night spent with my friends. I had to smile at some of the funny stories and responses we'd shared over dinner. It made me happy that Rachael could participate. Friends had real value. It was something Mom always told me. She and Hilda had had what Cher and I have now. Before I drifted off to sleep, my mind wandered to the subject of how much I was looking forward to going to Grayson's house for dinner.

The next morning, I felt rested and began making Kelly and Grayson some brownies. I looked at my phone on the kitchen table. I was hesitant to check for further texts but thought that perhaps I should. Seeing none, I decided to call Mom and chat with her as I drank my coffee. I knew she was up doing the very same thing at her kitchen table. That was confirmed when she answered the phone so quickly.

"Oh, sweetie! How nice to hear from you! What's going on?"

"Well, I'm excited about going to Grayson's house for dinner tonight. Kelly is fixing spaghetti, and I'm taking brownies for dessert. It'll be nice to see the two of them together since they have such a close relationship."

"That's wonderful! They'll love your brownies. Call me tomorrow and tell me all about it."

"I'm a tad nervous," I admitted. I don't know which is worse—meeting someone's parents or their children!"

Chapter 42

We chatted a little while longer and I made a point to not mention Austen. After we hung up, I went about mixing the brownies. The phone rang and I was surprised to see that it was Marta. "Good morning, Marta," I greeted her.

"Hi, Claire. Am I catching you at a good time? Do you have a few minutes to talk?"

"Absolutely! I just finished putting some brownies in the oven."

"That sounds good," she responded. "Say, I'm calling about our next quilt club meeting."

"Yes?"

"I'm trying to make a plan for it, and I heard through the grapevine that you have a suggestion for a program."

I paused, knowing I had to choose my words carefully. "I guess I wouldn't exactly call it a program, but I wanted to express some ideas for the club and hoped others would do the same." I paused again and decided I should get some information from her. "Did you have a program in mind?"

"I'm kicking around some ideas for a demonstration," she informed me. "I guess I'm a bit hesitant to discuss ideas without Greta being there."

I drew in a deep breath and decided that it was time to speak my mind more specifically. It was risky, but there was no getting around it now. "That's why I'm suggesting this meeting for such a discussion. Members should be able to talk freely. As you probably know, they're intimidated by Greta."

"I understand what you're saying, but I hate to make it look like a rebellion of sorts. Maybe we could accomplish both somehow. We could start with a short demo and then discuss your ideas under new business."

"I like that idea, Marta. I'm glad that you understand."

"You certainly have brought a new perspective to the group."

"I'm taking that as a compliment," I said, laughing. "I also want to alert you that Cher and I will both be in attendance at the meeting."

"I thought as much. It'll be great to see her again. I think the less we mention it, the better. I certainly have no objection to the two of you remaining in the group."

"Thanks, Marta. That means a lot. I think everyone else feels the same," I replied.

"Not everyone," she said tentatively.

"I know," I admitted. "Perhaps time will help. I'm so glad you called, Marta."

"See you soon!" she said as she hung up.

A sense of relief came over me, knowing that Marta was on board with my plan. I had to wonder who had alerted her as to what I was planning, but I'm glad they did. I took the brownies out of the oven, and it was hard to resist cutting into the warm goodies, although I managed to leave them alone. I was glad that Grayson was picking me up to go to his house, so we'd have a little time alone.

I chose something that was casual but a little dressy to wear for dinner. I got ready in plenty of time and waited on the porch while doing some quilting. I loved watching the design take shape. It was like drawing with thread. I jumped when Grayson knocked at the door. "Come in! Come in!" I said.

Grayson came inside and asked, "Are you ready for a good dinner?"

"Yes! I hope you like brownies. They always smell so good as they're baking."

"They do indeed! The brownies will be a hit with Kelly."

I retrieved the dish of brownies from the kitchen and we prepared to leave.

"I'll carry those for you," Grayson offered.

I put on my coat and off we went. I was nervously hoping that only the very best things would happen this evening. I wasn't exactly sure where Grayson lived, so I asked him where he lived relative to his office in Ephraim.

"Our family has mostly lived around the Sister Bay area. Marina Park was the big attraction, of course. It's sort of what our family has been about."

As we got to the center of Sister Bay, we turned right off Highway 42 and onto a road I'd never traveled. "Where does Kelly go to school?"

"Now she's in Gibraltar High. Many times, I drop her off in the morning, which is what takes me to the Blue Horse so often. That happens to be the place where I met a very fascinating woman."

I laughed but returned my attention to our route. It was getting darker as we turned off the main road onto a more residential street. We pulled into a circle drive that showcased a very traditional brick house.

"This is lovely!"

He smiled.

We entered through the front door and it opened into a sizable entryway. Grayson then called up the stairway to tell Kelly that we had arrived. I looked around and was surprised to see so many beautiful antiques.

Chapter 43

"Hi, Claire!" Kelly's voice came from upstairs. "I hope you're hungry."

"I am," I responded. "My mouth has been watering all day just thinking about red sauce and spaghetti."

She chuckled as she came down the stairs. "Dad, you can show her anywhere around the house except my room," she instructed, sounding older than her years. "I'm going to finish some last-minute things in the kitchen."

"Can I do anything to help?" I asked as Grayson took my coat.

"No, I'm good, but thanks anyway," she said, making her way to the kitchen.

"She gave me strict instructions that you are to be our guest tonight," Grayson informed me.

"How sweet," I replied with a smile.

We began a limited tour as Grayson walked me around their lovely home. When we got to the large sunporch at the back of the house, I saw a snapshot of their lifestyle. "Grayson, this is lovely out here," I commented. "This is so you!"

He smiled. "We spend a lot of time out here and occasionally have dinner guests here in the summer. My family's history of sailing is depicted in many of these photographs." He pointed to a wall that housed a number of framed pictures. "We inherited this house after my wife's father died. We tried to make it our own by adding this sunporch overlooking the pond in the back. We were pleased with it and Kelly loves it here, so this has remained our home."

"It feels so warm and welcoming. You have a nice collection of art pieces out here."

He grinned. "I don't have something from the most famous artist in Door County," he teased. "However, I happen to have a gorgeous red-and-white quilt on my bed that she helped make."

I smiled, appreciating his warmth.

"Okay, you guys," we heard Kelly call from the kitchen. "Dinner is served in the kitchenette."

I looked to Grayson to take the lead. We walked by the spacious dining room and into the kitchen, where a nice casual table was set near a central breakfast bar.

"Claire, I didn't think a spaghetti dinner would be appropriate in the formal dining room, so I decided to serve it here in the kitchen, which is cozier," Kelly explained.

"I love it," I responded. "It has the feel and aroma of Italy!"

Kelly laughed.

"I said the same thing when I saw her use the red checkered tablecloth that we use for picnics," Grayson added.

"Dad, you light the candles while I turn down the lighting just a bit," she instructed.

"I'd be happy to," Grayson agreed.

When we were seated with our salad plates in front of us, Grayson took my hand and said a Catholic grace, followed by the sign of the cross. "We're delighted to have you as our guest, Ms. Stewart, so let me make a toast," Grayson said, lifting his glass.

I blushed with embarrassment. "I'd like to make a toast to the hostess with the mostest," I announced. "Thanks for inviting me."

We clinked our glasses, and the chatter began; conversation wasn't hard to maintain around Kelly. The garlic bread was perfect. Grayson and Kelly admitted that they were quite fond of garlic in most of their cooking. The spaghetti was served in a charming soup tureen with silver tongs. Grayson did the honors by filling our plates, and Kelly passed the Parmesan cheese in a crystal shaker.

"Kelly, this sauce is heavenly," I praised, wiping my mouth.

"It's homemade," Kelly modestly reported. "My mom would make this sauce on special occasions, or if someone requested it. It takes a long time to make."

"Well, I'm honored," I assured her. "Was this a request from your dad?"

"I did request it when she said she'd like to make spaghetti," Grayson admitted. "I wished I could have been home today to smell it. That's the best part."

"I've never made a red sauce from scratch, so this is really a treat," I said. "I can certainly tell the difference."

Chapter 44

Our lively conversation went all over the place. It was fun and interesting to hear Kelly engage in adult conversation. I asked her about her plans after graduation from high school.

"Dad's already looking at colleges," she said in a teasing way. "I'm leaning toward Marquette now, but who knows how I'll feel later. I love art and can draw well, but acting is also something I enjoy. I love to act in any play I can try out for."

"That's wonderful!" I replied. "Acting is such an art."

Kelly smiled.

"Kelly will succeed at whatever she puts her mind to," Grayson added, looking directly at Kelly.

"I want to see your artwork sometime, Claire," Kelly stated, taking me by surprise.

"Oh, sure! That would be great," I responded. I shared with Kelly that I'd just finished a painting from a customer's photograph. She was very intrigued by the idea. Grayson just sat back in his chair and listened to us as we chatted.

"Hey, I'm anxious to taste those brownies," Grayson eventually interrupted.

"Yes, yes," Kelly said, jumping into action. "Who wants coffee and who wants ice cream?"

"Count me in on both!" Grayson answered quickly.

"I'll have just a tiny serving of ice cream with my brownie," I stated.

Needless to say, the brownies were a big hit. As soon as we finished, Kelly insisted on taking charge of clearing the dishes.

"Thanks for all you've done to make this wonderful dinner, Kelly," I said sincerely. "Just let me know when you'd like to come over and see my artwork."

"You know, Claire is quite a quilter," Grayson bragged. "She helped make that neat red-and-white quilt on my bed."

"Yes, it's pretty cool, but Dad let me know right away that it was for his bed," Kelly said with a laugh. "My grandma quilted, didn't she?"

"She did!" Grayson replied, nodding. "We've stopped using some of her older quilts because we want to preserve them."

"I'm sure those quilts were made to be used and enjoyed," I urged. "If you just use common sense, they'll last a long time. By the way, keep the rest of the brownies for the two of you."

"That sounds good to me!" Kelly said, going into the kitchen.

"Let's go onto the porch for a little, or are you ready to head home?" Grayson asked politely.

"Actually, I'd like to see the night view from your porch," I suggested. "I see lights shining out there."

"Well, then, let me get our drinks and you make yourself comfortable."

The view was romantic and the glimmer from the moon with the lighting was gorgeous.

"It's a bit chilly, but let's step out on the patio to get the full effect," Grayson suggested. "When the flowers are in bloom, it's a sight to behold."

"I'll bet it is," I agreed.

"So many folks told us we should've put a pool back here, but we were always too attached to what nature had to offer."

"That's a great way to think about it," I said. "Anyone can build a pool, but not everyone has a moonlit pond."

"My neighbor keeps it stocked with fish because his extended family likes to fish when they visit."

"I feel very special that you're sharing all of this with me," I said, blushing.

"That's because you're special, or I wouldn't have asked you to come here," he said softly as he put his arm around my waist.

"I think we have to give Kelly credit for this visit," I teased.

"You're right," he agreed.

It was calming to take in the beauty of Grayson's backyard. Except for the occasional splash of a fish, it was blissfully quiet. Finally, I said, "It's been a wonderful evening, but I think I should go home. I don't want to overstay my welcome."

Chapter 45

We went back inside, and Grayson got my coat. I put it on as he went upstairs to tell Kelly that we were leaving. "Please tell her thank you once again," I told him as he ascended the steps.

"I will."

I glanced around the spacious living room while I waited for him to return. There was a lot to take in as I again noted that Grayson was surprisingly fond of antiques. I wondered whether they had been passed down from family members or whether he was a collector who looked for specific items to add to his decor. After a short time, Grayson came back downstairs.

"She was in her pajamas with her headphones on, but I did give her the message and a kiss on the cheek. She waved me on and said to tell you goodbye."

I smiled as we headed out to Grayson's vehicle. On the way home, we weren't as chatty as we had been on the trip to his house earlier in the evening. I was preoccupied with how he might have felt tonight having me over for dinner with his daughter. I was aware of the delicate balance between fathers and daughters, especially in this case when his wife had been taken from him so unexpectedly. When we got to my place, I felt like I wanted to get my concerns out in the open. After he turned the ignition off, I turned to him and said, "Grayson, did it feel odd to bring another woman into your house for dinner? I can certainly understand how strange that must have been for you."

"To be honest, you're the first woman I've invited to our house. I may not have gotten that far had it not been for Kelly encouraging me to have you over for dinner. I guess I was more concerned about how it'd feel to her."

"I would be too! You both have so many memories in that house."

"Good and bad, I'm afraid. I hope you'll be patient with me. I don't really know what I'm doing half the time with my personal life. I think it's why I'm so comfortable with you."

"How so?"

"There's no pressure. You're so easy to be with. I'll bet I'm a complete amateur compared to the men you've had in your life."

"Oh, Grayson," I said with a laugh. "Look at what a disappointment my last relationship was! You're totally different. There's no playbook on relationships. I'm glad you're taking this slowly, however, because I feel like it's good for both of us at this point."

"I'll walk you to the door. I've lost count on which number this date is."

We laughed. "I think that's a good sign, don't you?" I asked as we approached my doorstep. Grayson nodded and, with a smile, took me into his arms and gave me a wonderful kiss and hug. I loved the way he caressed my back as he held me. It was with reluctance that we separated, and I entered the cabin. I came inside feeling surrounded by a wonderful aura of warmth. My relationship with Grayson was of a different sort. I felt confident that whatever might happen in the future, I'd still feel good about knowing him.

The cabin was incredibly quiet. I went up to the bedroom and found Puff once again precariously near my pillow. I knew that she missed me. However, she wasn't getting by with that, so I moved her back to her place at the bottom of the bed. I undressed and quietly slid under the covers with a smile on my face.

The next day after breakfast, I sat at the kitchen table with my coffee and made some notes about what I wanted to say at the quilt meeting. Knowing I was going to have some support made my thoughts come a little easier. I was hoping the other members also had some ideas to discuss. My phone rang and interrupted my thoughts. It was Rachael. "Good morning!" I greeted her.

"Are you up and at 'em, like you always ask me?"

I chuckled. "I am. What can I do for you?"

"Well," she said with a pause, "since you were here when the woman came from The Clearing a while back, I wanted to tell you that she's following up on her request to have me lecture on quilt patterns!"

"I do remember her. That's great! I'll sign up for your class!"

"You will?"

"Absolutely! I'll bet other quilt club members would also if they knew about it."

"But I've never lectured about anything before. I feel a little nervous saying yes, even though it's a wonderful opportunity."

"So what? You know your subject matter, and that's what matters."

"She wants a commitment of several days, and I do get paid for it, so that's a really good thing right now."

"It sounds perfect. I hope you told her that you'd do it!"

"Not yet. I'll call her tomorrow."

"I think you have your answer. Do you have any printed material on the barn quilt business? If it shows a quilt pattern that you're mentioning in your lecture, it'd be cool for them to see it painted on a barn. It's also good advertising."

"Claire, you're a genius. I'll make a point to dig up some things we've used through the years. It's been a while since we've done a brochure."

"Glad I could help."

"You all really helped me a lot by coming by on Saturday night. I'd forgotten what it was like to be out with the girls, so to speak."

"I think everyone enjoyed it."

Chapter 46

I could almost hear my mother whispering in my ear, urging me to write Kelly a thank-you note for the lovely dinner in hopes that Kelly might do the same for others in the future. I sat down at lunchtime and got that little deed accomplished.

By two in the afternoon, the sun had come out and the temperature was a little warmer. It'd be a good day to venture out to the shed. I wanted to finish planting some seeds. I also needed to decide which flowerpots to use this year. I knew Nelson's would be stocking a beautiful array of flowers soon. I was pleased to see that the lettuce seeds I'd put in the pots were starting to sprout, unlike the spinach I'd planted at the same time. Again, I thought of Mom. She'd get such a kick out of me attempting to be domestic! I chose two matching pots to put on either side of my front steps. Hopefully, I could find some bright flowers that would detract from the dullness of the cabin exterior. Next door, Mrs. Bittner always planted a lot of geraniums, if I remembered correctly.

I walked over to my large, round firepit that Tom kept promoting. He'd stacked a nice pile of wood nearby in case

I wanted to make an early spring fire. That sounded like a fun thing to do with Grayson. I loved the vintage lawn chairs that Cher had left behind. It made the setting so inviting. When I went back inside, my phone was ringing. To my surprise, I saw that it was Michael. Because he rarely called, I immediately wondered if Mom had experienced some difficulty.

"Michael, is everything okay?"

"Yes, all is well. How about you, sis?"

"I'm sorry, but I always worry that something has happened to Mom when you call."

"I talked to her last night. She's perfectly fine. No worries there," he assured me.

"Good, good."

"I wanted to share with you that Jack Page, Austen's brother, came into town last weekend. You remember him, don't you?"

"Oh, sure," I said. Then, for some reason, I mentioned the most notable thing that had struck me the last time I'd seen him. "He was losing his hair, if I remember correctly."

"His head is completely shaved now. He looks good," Michael assured me, laughing at my weak contribution to the conversation so far.

"So, you had a great visit?"

"Yes, which is why I decided to give you a call." He paused. "Now don't take this the wrong way, but are you okay? I mean—you aren't struggling financially, are you? Go ahead and tell me if it's none of my business, but I'm just asking. If you need any help, I hope you know that you can reach out, and I'll be happy to help you."

I had to stop and think about why he'd ask such a thing. The call from Michael had taken me aback, and now I had to figure out where this conversation was headed. I decided to just be direct and cut to the chase. "Why are you asking?" I swallowed hard as he began to respond.

"Well, we never really talked much before you left town. I just assumed you had Dad's dream money to fall back on," he began.

"I still do, and I'm fine," I cut in. "Is this by chance coming from a rumor that Austen is spreading about me? He's told people that I left town because I put him in debt."

Michael paused. "Sort of. When Jack asked about you, I sensed that he was fishing around about why you left so suddenly."

"Oh, I can't believe he'd bring that up to you!" I was frustrated to have to attempt to explain myself, but I'd never really talked to Michael about my reasons for leaving Austen. I decided that now might be the time to clear a few things up. "Austen recently came to Door County to try to get me to come back. I refused, and it made him angry. He's been spreading rumors ever since, and he's even trying to force me to pay back rent for the time that we lived together. He claims that he needs to be reimbursed for the use of studio space there. We never had any kind of written agreement to support such a requirement on my part."

"Are you serious? So, you're okay, right?"

"Yes, I'm okay—with the exception of Austen's continuing harassment," I assured him. To let him know how well I was doing, I added, "As a matter of fact, I just got my first check from a commissioned piece I did for someone, which felt pretty nice."

"That's good to hear. Are you getting any legal advice about Austen's behavior? That's pretty cruel! Honestly, Claire, I had no idea that you've been going through this with Austen."

"Yes, I went to see a lawyer, and if it continues, I'll sue him for harassment."

"I'm so sorry, Claire. I can't believe he'd risk his reputation over this nonsense."

"He has a huge ego, Michael," I explained. "I caused it to burst, and this is what's happened."

"If I can do anything to help, let me know. I'll make sure that Jack is set straight. He obviously only hears Austen's version. Does Mom know about this?"

"Not really, and I'd appreciate it if you didn't tell her."

"Okay. I almost asked her about it, so I'm glad I didn't," Michael replied.

"I guess we should communicate more often. How's the book promotion coming along?"

"Decent. I can't complain. Now tell me the truth—did you read it?"

I chuckled. "Yes, but not to its completion. I will soon. I've been pretty busy."

"I'll bet it's a bit boring for you," he teased.

"It is a bit, but your research is impressive!"

"I'm actually starting another one."

"That's great! I'm proud of you, and Dad would be, too!"

Chapter 47

"Let's not go that far. I'm not really sure what Dad's measure of success was."

"I think we disappointed him with our arts and humanities mindsets."

"It's probably why he felt guilty and left us our dream money," Michael said with a laugh.

"Perhaps. If I end up buying this cabin from Cher, I may have to use it."

"Claire, are you pretty happy with the way things are now?"

"I am. I started seeing a guy who works in a family-owned boat repair business here in the county."

"Is that a promising relationship?"

"We'll see. His wife died in a boating accident several years ago, and he's raising a teenage daughter, so it's not perfect."

"I see. Let me warn you that when you're dating someone who's been widowed, they have a tendency to put that missing spouse on a pedestal, regardless of what they were really like. Just keep that in mind because you may never be able to fill those shoes."

"My, you sound like you've been there," I replied, hoping that he might share some more about the subject from a personal perspective.

"Okay. I'm not saying any more," he said, not taking the bait.

I chuckled and decided to let it drop. Instead, I asked, "Say, what do you make of Mom and Mr. Vogel?"

"I think it's a hoot! I'm grateful for it, aren't you?"

"I am. I think she's finally starting to call him Bill," I said with a giggle, feeling grateful for this time to connect with Michael.

"I think it's still Mr. Vogel when I talk to her. She had a great time at your place over the Christmas holiday, by the way."

"It was the best surprise ever, and you kept it a secret from me!" I responded, remembering how frustrated I'd been on one of our earlier phone conversations when I thought that he'd gone on a skiing trip and neglected Mom at Christmas. All the while, he knew of Mom's plans to surprise me by coming to Door County to visit me. I then said, "Cher is living back here now, and I know Mom misses her."

"I just may have to check out Door County for myself," Michael mentioned.

"I love it, and you'd love it as well."

"Well, I'm glad to hear that you're okay," Michael said, indicating that he was ready to end the call.

"Try to finish that book," I advised him.

"Okay, I promise. Maybe you'll be able to finish the second one!" he joked.

I laughed and then said, "Thanks so much for calling, Michael. I love you!"

"I love you too, sis," he said without hesitation.

After we hung up, I marveled at what had just happened. I felt connected to Michael as we talked. It was a refreshing feeling, and I longed to have it occur more often. Michael and I haven't been close, and I guess I've wanted a better relationship with him more than I've been able to admit. Anger then took over my thoughts as I pictured Austen spreading rumors about me. He'd used Mr. Vogel to get a negative message about me to my mother, and now Austen's brother had been used as a conduit to affect Michael. I can only imagine how alarmed Michael felt when he heard that I was in a financial bind and that he had to hear it from someone outside of the family! It wasn't true, but Michael didn't know that. Perhaps this recent event would have a good outcome since Michael had had the good sense to reach out and call me himself. Now he knows the truth, and it served to strengthen the relationship between us.

Since the day was mild with reasonable temperatures, I decided to go to the post office to mail my thank-you note. After that, I could stop in at the Blue Horse for some much-needed coffee. There would only be a slim chance of seeing Grayson there, but that was okay.

I didn't run into anyone I knew at the post office, so I mailed the letter and went to get some coffee. I walked into a packed café. The only person I recognized was John. He was two people ahead of me in line and was someone I'd met through Grayson. When he picked up his order, he turned around and saw me.

"Claire, good morning!"

"Hi, John!" I responded.

"Would you care to join me?"

His offer caught me by surprise, but I replied, "Sure, for a bit. Why not?" I got my simple order and followed him to a seat.

"Do you come here often? I know that Grayson does," he asked when we sat down.

"No, not as much as Grayson," I answered, laughing. "It's actually where we met."

"Really?"

I nodded.

"He's really busy right now, from what I hear," John commented. "The boating season is about to begin, so everyone wants repairs or inspections."

"I can imagine."

"Are things still going okay with you guys?" he asked, stirring cream into his coffee.

"I think so," I said. "Kelly fixed us dinner the other night."

"Well, you scored there!" John replied, leaving me to wonder what that meant.

"Kelly is so smart and talented," I remarked.

"She sure is," he agreed. Then he continued by saying, "I'm glad that you and Grayson are hitting it off. You're the first woman to really enter his world since Marsha's accident. Are you aware of that?"

"I'm not that sure about his recent past," I said, shaking my head. "My concern is being compared to her."

Chapter 48

"Marsha was a peach, and the way she died couldn't have been more dramatic."

"He's told me very little about it, but that's okay. I understand that it's something very personal."

"You're good for him," John went on. "I don't know if he'll ever want to marry again, but you never know."

"He doesn't get that pressure from me," I assured him. "It's not in my plan, either."

"Grayson said you left town because of a bad relationship," John shared. "I'm sorry to hear that."

"It's a long story," I said, shaking my head.

"We all have a story, Claire," John said empathetically. "Tell me more about your work."

"I create a mixed bag of quilting and painting," I explained, smiling.

"Speaking of quilting, that Grayson sure did outbid me on that quilt at the auction," he said with mock sarcasm.

I chuckled. "He did indeed!" I replied. "I was in shock. He's using it on his bed."

"I won't ask how you know that," John teased.

"That's what he told me anyway," I added by way of explanation.

John laughed as I blushed. "I'll have to tell Grayson about your remark."

"Stop!" I teased back. "I appreciated you running up the price on the quilt. I can't tell you how much Rachael appreciates the money that was raised."

"It was a fun evening."

"Hey, I didn't intend to stay this long," I said, looking at my watch. "I'd better be on my way. It was good to visit with you, John."

"I enjoyed it, Claire," John agreed. "Tell Grayson hello for me. I'm not sure when I'll see him again."

"You and me both," I joked. I found it a pleasure to visit briefly with John since I felt that I'd learned just a bit more about Grayson during the conversation. We said goodbye, and I walked out of the café.

I decided to make another quick stop at Nelson's before going home, to see if any flowers had arrived. To my surprise, they had some sitting outside in the parking lot. They were colorful pansies, which I knew did well in cooler weather. I pulled up by the door and got out to see which ones would work in the two flowerpots I'd decided to put at the front door. I liked the bright yellow ones the best. I also decided that a touch of red was always good with yellow, so I put a tray of those aside as well. When I got inside, I saw hanging ferns. I thought of my front porch. I could hang those right away. When I got to the checkout counter, I saw more herbs, which intrigued me. I bought two kinds of basil, which I especially liked to use on pizza. I returned home with a smile on my face.

It was late afternoon, but I was determined to plant the pansies in pots today. It was a great look when I placed a pot on either side of the front steps. I put the ferns inside on the porch until I could find hooks to hang them. With my leftover plants, I easily found little nooks in the yard and planted them. I put some around the base of a small tree, which looked very cute. I was a total mess, but I didn't stop until I had everything done and had the pots and tools put away in the shed. I went inside to shower and heard my phone. I remembered that I had left it by the bathroom sink. I ran to answer it.

"Claire, it's Carl."

"Hey, Carl. What's up?"

"I just wanted to tell you that your anonymous client was very, very pleased with the painting you completed."

"Oh, that's good to hear."

"I wouldn't be surprised if he commissioned you again."

"Well, I can't thank you enough for the opportunity to paint it. With this kind of encouragement, I don't know what to do first, paint or quilt!"

"Both, my dear," Carl encouraged.

I hung up feeling grateful for having made a client so happy. Art is so personal, and you never know what people are really expecting. I knew that I needed to be more disciplined with my work—instead of going to cafés and buying pansies!

Chapter 49

That evening, I took a closer look at the mail. I was pleased to see that the Church of the Atonement was going to be open on Easter Sunday. My intention was to attend a church close by on a regular basis. Now I could plan my Easter accordingly. I hated the thought of being away from Mom on Easter. I had such great memories of growing up—getting new Easter outfits and enjoying a special family dinner. Perhaps Mom would make plans with Mr. Vogel since they went to the same church. What I'd do was another question. What did Grayson and Kelly do? I knew that I needed to plan something to look forward to, just to make it more festive.

I read recently in the newspaper that there were egg hunts scheduled in Jacksonport, Sister Bay, and Baileys Harbor. Every holiday season in Door County revealed new activities and festivals. Because I hadn't lived here long, I was finding new ways to celebrate occasions. I couldn't wait until the cherry and apple trees started to bloom! I was daydreaming when I got a call from Brenda.

"Hey there! What's up?" I asked.

"I hope I'm not keeping you from something," Brenda began.

"Not a thing."

"Well, I wondered if you've ever been to a fish boil."

"No, I haven't, but I've seen pictures and heard folks talk about them. It's so funny that you'd call and ask about that. I've just been thinking about how I've enjoyed doing new things since I've moved here."

"Well, the White Gull Inn is working on the season's schedule of fish boils, so how would you like to join me at an upcoming one since I don't have to work it?"

"Sure! When are you thinking?"

"The first one is tomorrow night if the weather holds. We can also wait for the next one, but I may have to work."

"Tomorrow night works for me," I replied.

"That's great! I'll turn our names in. It's my treat."

"Brenda, that's not necessary."

"I want to. Just show up there at five on their patio and bring a big appetite."

"I'm getting hungry already!"

"Good! See you then!"

It was so thoughtful of Brenda to think of me. She was always the one to reach out to me, which I felt guilty about. She seemed to want to be my friend. I loved to have something to look forward to! At the end of the day, I fell into a restful sleep just thinking about what it'd be like to attend my first fish boil!

The next morning was clear and bright, so I decided to go to the Blue Horse for coffee. As I got dressed, I paid extra attention to how I looked just in case I ran into Grayson. As I drove there, I wondered if I'd be arriving at the same time that Grayson might be there, but that notion changed when I saw him coming out of the café. I quickly parked the car and called, "Grayson, wait up!"

"Hey! Good morning, Ms. Stewart!"

"I was hoping to run into you."

"Well, you certainly did!" he chuckled. "I'm sorry that you're catching me on the run."

"No problem. I had to do some errands, so good coffee was calling my name."

"I like the way you think! Is everything else okay?"

"Yes! I'm going to my first fish boil tonight at the White Gull Inn."

"Well, it's about time, I suppose," he joked.

"Brenda is treating me since she doesn't have to work."

"How nice. Let me know what you think. It's more of an entertaining experience for tourists."

"That pretty much still includes me. Please, I don't want to keep you."

"Tell Brenda hello and have some fun!" Grayson advised as he continued making his way down the street.

"I will," I said, but I wasn't sure that he'd even heard me since he was already on his way. He didn't even suggest getting together anytime soon, which was disappointing. Honestly, the whole interaction stung a bit after we'd just recently shared a wonderful dinner at his home. Had I misread our relationship altogether? I made my way to the Blue Horse and got in line to get coffee. When it was my turn, I always received a happy greeting from the staff. The girl waiting on me remembered to put a smiley face in my cappuccino. I was tempted to stay for a bit but decided to move on to the post office. When I got inside, I walked past the meeting room for our quilt club. I knew that very shortly, there would be a significant meeting taking place there. The club might never be the same after it!

Chapter 50

Five o'clock came quickly and I had little to show for my day except a little quilting. It appeared that the weather was holding steady for the fish boil even though it'd be chilly. I dressed in ample layers of clothing, not knowing how long we'd be outdoors. I left ten minutes early for my walk to the restaurant. From all the cars I saw everywhere, they were destined to have a great turnout. Brenda greeted me right away and told me she had a table reserved for us.

A big fire was blazing, and the event hadn't even started yet. Brenda quickly introduced me to boil master Tom Christianson. He assured me that I was in for a real treat, since it was my first time to attend a fish boil. Brenda explained that fish boils had been a Scandinavian tradition for over a hundred years, but the White Gull Inn started having them in 1961. The excitement in the crowd was building. Tom got our attention and began to explain the process.

First, he showed a giant basket of new potatoes that he was about to pour into the boiling water. After he dumped them in, he joked about adding a dash of salt. It turned out that his dash of salt amounted to a large portion of salt, causing everyone to laugh. He then doused the fire with splashes of kerosene, which resulted in huge flames. He explained that the kerosene would burn the fat off the top. Next, we saw a big batch of Michigan whitefish being dumped into the boiling water. Tom then assured us that it'd need another pinch of salt, so with encouragement from the crowd, he poured another generous dose in!

It was quite a show, and my appetite grew as time passed. The grand finale was another application of kerosene, which caused another impressive burst of flames. At last, he removed the potatoes and fish. The crowd knew what was about to happen, so they rose from their seats and moved inside the restaurant to be served.

"Brenda, this was really something to see!" I said, excited.

"I hope you'll find it tasty," she commented. "If you don't like fish, they have baked chicken."

"No, I want the whole experience," I assured her.

"I saved the table for two by the fire that you like so much," she said.

"You're too much, Brenda," I replied.

We settled in at our table and waited until the waitress brought us our plates of fish, potatoes, and a serving of coleslaw. Bread and butter were already on the table. It'd be wonderful to be served like this every evening! Like so many things I experienced, I wished that Mom could enjoy coming here for a fish boil. She loves fish and would really get a kick out of watching the boil master prepare the huge meal.

The dining area was noisy, but Brenda and I did our best to carry on a conversation. When we finished our plates, the waitress brought out a slice of the inn's famous cherry pie, complete with a scoop of ice cream on top. I was stuffed, but I wasn't going to miss out on that great dessert.

"Hi, Brenda," a man said as he approached our table.

"Hi, Pete," Brenda answered, appearing quite surprised to see him. "I didn't know that you were here."

"I came with a couple of guys from work who hadn't been to a fish boil before," he explained. "Aren't you going to introduce me to your good-looking friend?"

"Oh ... sorry," Brenda stammered. "This is Claire Stewart. She's fairly new to Door County."

"Well, welcome!" he said, shaking my hand. "Can I buy you ladies a drink?"

"Thanks, but I'll just finish my coffee," I responded.

"Not me!" Brenda lit up with excitement. "I'll have another chardonnay!"

"Coming up!" Pete announced as he motioned for our waitress to come by.

I was surprised at Brenda's interest in a man who seemingly came in from out of the blue. The way her voice and expression changed when he entered the picture, I figured that there was more between the two of them than was meeting the eye. The problem was that Pete's eyes were clearly on me and not on her!

"How long have you and Brenda known each other?" I asked, wanting him to focus on Brenda.

"I guess I've been coming in here for quite a while," Pete answered casually.

"Ever since I've been working here," Brenda answered, filling in the details.

"This is where I met Brenda as well," I mentioned. "She's the friendliest person here and has quite a following."

"I'll bet she does," he responded politely. "Claire, have you seen much of the county, or were you a tourist before you moved here?"

"I never really visited as a tourist. I had a friend who lived here. Through her, I learned a lot about Door County."

"Well, I'll let you two ladies get back to your conversation," Pete finally said. "Nice to have met you, Claire."

"Nice to meet you as well," I replied.

"Thanks for the drink, Pete," Brenda said in a flirtatious manner.

Chapter 51

When Pete was out of hearing range, I looked at Brenda and smiled. She smiled back like she knew what I was thinking. "Well, well, well! Is this man a special someone in your life?" I teased.

"No, Claire. It isn't like that," she responded, blushing.

"Not like what?" I chuckled. "It's obvious that you're attracted to him. Have the two of you gone out?"

"No, he's just someone I know from the restaurant."

"It appears that you know him very well," I guessed. "Is he single?"

She nodded. "That's about all I know about him. He's just always so friendly and is a big tipper."

"So why haven't the two of you gotten together?"

"He just flirts with me because he knows I'm also single," she explained. "Frankly, I think he came over to say hello because of you."

"Not true!" I protested. "He was being polite to one of your friends. Brenda, you know that we live in a modern age now where you can be the one to ask him out."

"Are you serious?"

"I know that we're both old school, but I think he may surprise you if you ask him. Maybe think of an event or have some kind of excuse to ask him, rather than just saying something out of the blue."

"I think we'd better change the subject before you really get me into trouble," she said, laughing.

We chatted for a while and then I decided to go home while there were still lots of cars around. I thanked Brenda for a wonderful experience and headed for the door. The air had cooled, and I pulled my jacket closer to my body. I was about to turn onto my street when I heard someone shout to me.

"Claire, Claire! Hold up!" a man's voice called out.

I couldn't believe my eyes. It was Pete. He'd pulled over and was getting out of his vehicle. My heart sank. "Hey, Pete. What is it?"

"Are you walking home?" he asked, walking toward me.

I nodded and stopped walking.

"I can take you," he said decisively.

"No, I'm fine," I assured him.

"Since you're new to the area and all, I'd be happy to show you around if you're available."

"Pete, that's very nice, but I'm seeing someone."

"I see. I should have known that you'd already have someone. Here's my card. I work in Baileys Harbor. Maybe we can just have a drink sometime."

"Sorry, Pete, but I have to decline. Thanks again."

"Just take my card," he insisted.

"Very well," I said, hoping he'd be on his way. I worried that he'd follow me, but he got back in his car and drove away. There was no way that I'd want him to know where I lived. I hoped that Brenda hadn't seen our exchange.

I was glad to get inside the cabin. I kept thinking of poor Brenda who had a crush on that guy. I sure didn't want to lose my friendship with her over someone like him! My gut told me that he was a womanizer and wouldn't recognize a nice girl like Brenda. She was so shy. I shouldn't have even taken his card. I hoped that I'd discouraged him.

Puff was happy to follow me up to bed. I had enjoyed the fish boil, but the evening had been tainted by my encounter with Pete. In bed, I tried to focus on the upcoming quilt club meeting to take my mind off him. It worked, and I fell into a deep sleep.

I was awakened the next morning by a call from Cher. It was only eight, so hearing from her at this hour alarmed me a bit. "What's going on? Aren't you typically still asleep at this hour?"

She giggled and then explained. "Oh, I had to get up early to let the cable guy in. I still can't get a good Internet connection here."

"It's pretty spotty around the whole county from what I understand," I replied.

"What are your plans today?"

"I'm quilting and thinking about starting a new painting since I got a good review on the last one."

"Any plans with Grayson?"

"No. I ran into him coming out of the Blue Horse, and he didn't say one word about getting together."

"Nothing to worry about, I'm sure. Well, we have the club meeting to think about. I stopped by Ginger's shop yesterday, and she said something that gave me some concerns about the meeting."

"Really? Like what?"

"She thinks that Greta has gotten word that the two of us are coming back to the group without her blessing."

"I can see that. Does she know anything about me bringing up some ideas for discussion?"

"I'm not sure. I think we need to be prepared for nearly anything. I'm sure that Greta has given Marta some instructions."

"Well, we'll see how it goes, Cher Bear."

Cher followed up my admonition with a deep sigh.

Chapter 52

"Let's not worry about it and see what happens," I urged. "We may get ignored just so Greta can bring it up at the next meeting."

"Oh boy!" Cher said sarcastically.

"I just hope everyone comes. Marta seems to be open-minded, but we'll see if Greta gets to her."

"Should I pick you up?" Cher offered.

"Yes, that would be a good idea. The two of us coming together will make a stronger statement. By the way, has Ericka said anything else about her missing rings?"

"No, but she's convinced that Ava has something to do with it."

"Do you know if she's approached her about it?"

"No, I haven't heard another word about it."

"Okay. I'll say a prayer that things will work out for us and Ava."

"Sounds good!"

Before I returned to quilting, I went outdoors to see if anything needed to be watered. It was great just to be outdoors, despite how chilly it was. I could see signs of spring, and it looked like the yard would need to be mowed soon. I walked around the cabin looking for things that should be done in advance of the coming season. Perhaps I should ask Cher if there was any maintenance that she hadn't gotten to when she lived here. I received a text, so I stopped in my tracks to see who it was from. It was Rachael.

[Rachael]
I have a date set for my quilt class at The Clearing! It's next Monday morning at ten. Please be there!

I replied,

[Claire]
Absolutely! Don't forget to come to quilt club.

[Rachael]
I'm planning on it!

I put the date in my phone right away after I hung up. I wanted to know more about The Clearing in general, and this class would provide a good excuse to check it out in person. I went back inside and had a bite to eat, despite wanting to crash and take a nap. After I felt refreshed, I went to my plain white canvas, which was set up and staring back at me. I remembered Carl saying that smaller artworks were preferred by tourists. There were places like the White Gull Inn that were popular and had been painted hundreds of times. I'll bet no one had ever painted it with quilts hanging from the beautiful balcony. Perhaps I could think of a different angle. I then decided to scroll through the photos on my phone to see if any other buildings struck me. I stopped when I got to the Thorp House Inn and Cottages. I loved the stately white house with the expansive front porch. I could easily picture quilts hanging from the four panels that comprise the porch. Perhaps painting quilts on buildings was my calling. It could be appealing to those who had stayed at the inn. No one else was doing it, so why not? Why not just quilt the whole town?

By dusk, I was mentally worn out. I went to the couch and picked up my small quilt. I was tempted to make a fire but wasn't sure I needed it. I put a chicken pot pie in the oven. I began to think about quilt club. If things didn't go well, I'd spend large amounts of time mulling it over. After I finished eating, I went upstairs to watch an old movie. The phone rang, and it was Grayson.

"Claire? It's Grayson. Am I calling too late?"

"Of course not. I just had a late dinner and decided to watch a movie. It's nice to hear your voice."

"I just came home to an empty house for a change. Kelly is spending the night with a friend."

"Oh, those are such fun years."

"Well, I actually prefer that she have her friends here, so I know what she's doing."

His seriousness made me chuckle. "You're such a sweet daddy. I'm sure that Kelly uses good judgment."

"Oh, you think so? I could tell you a story or two!" he claimed.

"I think you're doing a fantastic job with her."

"Well, there's no handbook, that's for sure," he said, laughing.

"So, did you have anything special on your mind?"

"Yes, I'd say so."

"Well, let's hear it."

He laughed again and then paused before he said, "I've acquired quite a habit of thinking of you when I'm not engaged with something else."

"That's not so strange, because the same thing happens to me."

We laughed and then continued to talk for another thirty minutes about this and that. He was finally the one to say that we needed to get some sleep. I was hoping that he'd suggest a date to get together again, but he didn't. Instead, it was a sweet good night.

Chapter 53

I was wide awake at six on the morning of quilt club. I almost convinced myself that I was ill. The thought of today's meeting was making me both nervous and nauseous. I prayed that God would keep me calm and guide me as to what to say. There had been so many times when I'd asked God to put His arms around me and keep me from feeling alone. So far, He'd never let me down. Feeling a bit more confident, I got up and showered. I reminded myself that Cher Bear, my partner in crime, was going to be by my side.

After Puff joined me downstairs for breakfast, I made myself some toast and checked my phone. Unfortunately, Austen's behavior always made me check my text messages first. Thankfully, nothing showed up. I thought about taking a show-and-tell item with me, but taking Quilted Blooms was premature, and if there was a negative outcome concerning my ideas, I might not want to be a part of the rest of the meeting. My makeup was applied, and I was finally ready to go. I kept looking at my notes to make myself feel more confident. Cher arrived fifteen minutes early, so when she drove up, I went out to meet her.

"You're not too anxious, are you?" she kidded.

"Not a bit. There isn't anything the two of us can't accomplish, remember?"

She giggled but then asked, "Have you heard from anyone?"

"No. Have you?"

She shook her head. "I hope there's coffee. I could use another cup. It'll be so strange seeing everyone again."

"I'll bet!"

When we got out of the car, Frances and Olivia had arrived and were getting out of their car. They were so happy to see Cher. They each gave her a hug and flooded her with questions. When we walked into the meeting room, there was Marta. She looked as nervous as I felt. She took a moment to give Cher a special welcome, which was nice. Ginger was the next to arrive. After she got her coffee, she came near me. Leaning down, she whispered a quiet "Good luck" in my ear. Lee arrived next and did a double take when she saw Cher. More laughter and chatter erupted. Where were Ava and Rachael? I left the meeting room to look outside. I was relieved to see Rachael coming my way.

"I'm sorry that I'm late," Rachael apologized, clearly out of breath.

"No matter. Have you seen Ava anywhere?"

"No, but she's often late. Is everyone else here?"

"Yes, and Marta is looking nervous."

"I don't blame her."

When we entered the meeting room, everyone stopped their chatter to welcome Rachael. Some members hadn't seen her since Charlie's funeral. I could tell that the welcome meant a lot to her.

"Well, it's time that we get started," Marta announced. Her voice was shaky from nerves, but she pressed on. "Cher and Rachael, we've certainly missed you."

"Thanks, Marta," Rachael responded. "If I may have a minute before we start the meeting, I'd like to express my gratitude for the wonderful quilt you made for the fundraiser." She began to wipe away tears that had sprung to her eyes. "You have no idea how touched I've been by your kindness. Thanks also to those of you who took time to come to the funeral. It was quite comforting to see so many friends. Charlie would have been pleased. My world has been so different without him." At that, Rachael swallowed hard and tried to manage a smile.

"You're welcome, Rachael," Marta said, fighting back her own tears. "We've known you for a long time, and if there's anything we can do, just let us know."

Others followed with comments of their own, all with the intent to comfort and encourage Rachael. It was a special moment that the club needed. I doubted if Greta would have allowed such interaction if she'd been leading the meeting.

"Cher, we've learned that you've settled in Egg Harbor," Marta stated, moving on to the next item of business. "We want to express our condolences on the passing of your mother."

"Thank you," Cher responded simply.

"Are you still quilting?" Marta asked, genuinely interested in Cher's response.

"I am!" Cher quickly replied. "I've been distracted by the move, but Claire is helping me stay on track now that I've come back."

"Very good," Marta said, nodding. "As you know, I'm filling in for Greta today since she's out of town. She'll be back at our next meeting."

There was silence until it was broken by Ava, who entered the room. "Sorry I'm late," she said nervously. "I had to wait for a repairman this morning. Good to see you, Cher and Rachael."

The three of them exchanged smiles and then everyone returned their attention to Marta.

Chapter 54

"Greta left it up to me to decide the program today, so I'd like to start with a short demo you all had requested at my farm meeting. I showed you one of my Flower Garden quilts that day and told you how much I enjoyed making hexie patterns. I do them by hand. I can't imagine doing them any other way. I brought a few quilts to show you where I used hexie accents. I have a small kit for each of you to try as you piece them together. Let's take ten or fifteen minutes to see if you can do it. Then I'm going to turn the meeting over to Claire, who wants to discuss some ideas with the group."

I was pleasantly surprised by her comment. So far, so good. I opened the tiny bag of hexies. Cher and I then exchanged glances. I knew that Cher detested hexies. We'd both just have to pretend to enjoy the process. Ginger was the first to get her pieces together. The others seemed to stall and required Marta's expertise to get them to an end point.

"Very good, Ginger," Marta praised.

"Thanks," she blushed. "I love handwork and do it in the shop when I'm not busy. It's mindless, and before you know it, you have something to show for it."

"Claire, I now will turn the floor over to you," Marta announced as the members returned their hexie attempts to their plastic baggies.

"Marta, thank you for giving me an opportunity to have an open discussion with all of you about the potential we have as a very well-known quilt club," I began as the room went silent. "I can't tell you how proud I was when all of you cheerfully agreed to make a quilt for Rachael. I saw energy and heard more chatter than I'd ever seen or heard here before. The community felt our outreach and supported us. Everyone in this whole county knows about our prestigious quilt club, but no one could ever tell me what you did, including my best friend Cher. Don't get me wrong—I was delighted and honored that you accepted my membership, but as a new person, I was anxious to be a part of something and make you proud that you accepted me."

Marta was squirming.

"So, ever since our success with Rachael's quilt, I've been thinking of creative ways that we could be a better part of the community."

"Claire, keep in mind that we're a small group," Marta interrupted.

"I certainly realize that," I countered. "It truly takes a village to do anything for causes and events. When I first arrived in Door County, it was so obvious that art quilters like me are barely recognized. Despite some small shows, and one lovely quilt shop, quilters are not acknowledged like the other artists. Quilters love to share their work."

"I agree with you there," Ava chimed in.

"My point here today is to bring ideas up for discussion. I'd like to hear from the rest of you about ideas that you may have regarding elevating quilts in general around the county." There was a pause.

"I know what you're saying, Claire," Cher agreed. "We're both from the Midwest, where quilters rule, you might say. It's not unusual for a town to have several quilt guilds and three or four quilt shops, if you can believe it. I know that not many of us here sell our work, but the exposure would help all of us. Quilts are art! I have a friend who is a quilt appraiser, and she talks about the value of trends all the time. Quilts are selling for big dollars. Look what Rachael's quilt brought at an auction!"

"Do you think our short tourism season has something to do with it?" Olivia asked.

"Perhaps it decreases quilt sales, but it shouldn't be a problem for quilt shops," I explained. "People quilt all year long, and from what I hear, Carol's shop does a great year-round business."

"There sure are a lot of women working on quilts at the Hygge in Egg Harbor," Lee added. "I love seeing what they're doing. I take my hand appliqué when I go there. Claire, do you have some ideas in mind? I'd like to hear them, regardless of what the club may decide to do."

"Yes, Claire, feel free to discuss them," Marta encouraged. "You've offered a fresh perspective to this group ever since you joined."

"She has!" Ginger agreed enthusiastically. "We may have limited time and resources, but I think it's interesting to entertain some new ideas."

Chapter 55

"I have to be careful because I had a teacher once tell me that if you suggest something, you'd better be prepared to take it on," I said, smiling.

Everyone chuckled.

"I agree with that," Marta said. "Ladies, keep in mind that we're just discussing ideas today. Without Greta here, we couldn't possibly decide on anything."

"Even if everyone agrees on something?" Cher asked.

Marta sighed. "We have rules that have kept this group together for decades," Marta reminded us. "Please continue, Claire. I didn't mean to sidetrack you."

"Quilters are artists, just like painters, potters, and sculptors," I began. "Our quilts are colorful and unique, and range from traditional to modern in design, so they suit almost everyone's tastes."

"That's for sure!" Frances responded. "Different strokes for different folks."

"Exactly, Frances," I said, nodding. "The problem is that most of our quilts are never seen. They're given away, kept in closets, or stuck on shelves in some shop, hoping someone will unfold them and perhaps buy them."

"Yes, like in my shop," Ginger agreed. "Seldom do they ever unfold them."

"Well, my out-of-the-box idea is to get quits out there," I began. "I mean out in the air where everyone can see and enjoy them, like they do at the plein air art shows."

"Outdoors?" Marta questioned.

"There are other places that have done it," I stated. "It's breathtaking to see. Can you just envision driving up and down Main Street or on Highway 42 and seeing colorful quilts hanging from balconies, clotheslines, and banisters? It can be a real drive-by quilt show for folks who have difficulty walking and those just arriving in our community. Who wouldn't smile at such a unique and colorful display?"

"How in the world would you ever get anyone to agree to hang their quilts outdoors?" Marta asked, concerned. "The sun is their worst enemy."

"With the limited time of eight hours, a quilt will survive, plus it wouldn't be directly in the sun for the entire eight hours," I explained. "Think of the use they might get in your home. Some people still hang their quilts out to dry after they're washed, so they get exposed to the sun then. Years back, they always had an airing of the quilts after every season."

"Easier said than done," Rachael pointed out. "Where on earth would you even get enough quilts to have a good display? I only have five or six, and I don't know if I'd take the risk."

"Then you should choose not to," I answered. "I don't have all of the answers, but maybe some of you do. I'm bringing this up to discuss. I talked to Carl from Art of Door County, and he thinks it's a marvelous idea. He's even thinking about expanding his gallery to display quilts."

"Well, after word getting out that someone was willing to pay five thousand dollars for a quilt, I'm sure that got his attention," Lee pointed out.

Everyone chuckled in agreement.

"I'm not fooling myself by thinking that this group would put together an event like this on its own, but if someone wanted to have an outdoor quilt show, would you consider helping in some way, or do you think the whole idea is crazy?" I asked.

"I'd help!" Olivia answered quickly.

"I would!" Ava said as she raised her hand in support.

"There's nothing about this that I don't like," Frances remarked.

"I'd be proud to be a part of such a display," Lee agreed.

"If Claire organized the event, it'd definitely be successful," Rachael added. "She has amazing ideas and is a hard worker. Take it from me."

"It'd be great for promoting the sale of quilts," Ginger said.

"You're quite a visionary, Claire," Marta stated. "It sounds like you received some valuable feedback today. You could certainly put that idea out there and see what happens."

"That's the spirit, Marta," I responded. "Everyone should be pulling their quilts out of storage to air them out!"

"Are there other ideas from anyone else?" Marta asked, trying to settle the group down from the excitement.

"I'm an active follower of The Clearing," Lee announced. "I want to take a moment to promote a lecture Rachael is doing for them on quilt patterns and how they got their names. It's coming up next week, and I for one can't wait to hear it."

"Congratulations, Rachael," Marta said, looking at her. "I'll try to be there."

"Thank you, Lee and Marta. I'm pretty nervous about it all," Rachael said, blushing.

Chapter 56

"Maybe it's because I'm an antique myself, but I'd love it if this club would do more regarding antique quilts," Frances remarked. "I'm at an age where I'm not making many quilts, but I cherish the history of quilts from the past."

"I agree!" Ginger echoed. Then she took a deep breath and said, "I know this is a sore subject, but I'd like to discuss why this club hasn't allowed more members."

Silence filled the room. Marta wore a panic-stricken expression and then blurted out, "If there are no other topics that you want to discuss, then let's move on to show-and-tell."

Ginger shook her head in frustration. "Oh, my word!" She looked at Marta for a moment and then made the decision to drop the subject. "I'll start since we're not going to discuss my concerns," she said sharply. "I brought kitchen quilts. They're small, which makes them easy to work up. Some of you probably call them potholders. They sell well in my shop, and I do most of them by hand." She passed them around for us to see. Ginger seemed to calm down as we studied her work and offered compliments on her skills.

Next, Ava brought out a small, solid black quilt that she'd embellished with white pearl buttons. Ava loved buttons and often wore button jewelry. As she showed her quilt, Cher and I looked at her hands to see if she happened to be wearing any new rings.

Marta showed a couple of table runners that she'd made for Easter gifts. I never knew how she produced so much quilting living on that farm of hers.

"I have a small quilt to show that features a block called Diamond in the Square," Olivia announced. "I love working with solid colors like the Amish use, and I guess it's what I like about the Gee's Bend quilts as well."

"I really love that," Rachael murmured. "I've done this pattern many times as a barn quilt."

"Your quilting really shows up well," I added.

"Thanks," Olivia smiled. "Losing my stitching in printed fabric is not very rewarding."

"Ladies, I think everyone has a lot to process from the meeting today," Marta concluded. "Thanks for making this meeting easier than I thought it'd be."

"You did great, Marta," I assured her. "Greta would have approved." My last comment was debatable, and Cher gave me a questioning look. "Maybe she'll never know," I quipped, just loud enough for Cher to hear.

"Well done, Ms. Stewart," Rachael said as we departed. "I think we're all safe—until Greta finds out!" Her comment produced a shower of giggles from the three of us.

"Who can do lunch?" Cher asked. "I'm starved."

"Me!" I answered quickly. "How about you, Rachael?"

She paused. "I guess so," she said, hesitating. "It feels weird. I usually had to rush home to relieve Charlie."

"He'd want you to come," I said softly.

"Okay then, where are we going?" Rachael agreed.

"I have a gift certificate to The Cookery," Cher called out. "I'll treat. It was one of many that I got from my party."

"Great!" I replied.

We decided to walk since the restaurant was nearby. Now that the stressful meeting was over, we all began talking at the same time. It was interesting to watch Rachael become a single person again. She was finding her independence, which was a new leg of the journey for her. After we got seated, Cher asked if I'd heard from Brenda lately. I told her about Brenda asking me to the fish boil.

"I've tried to call her, and she isn't returning my calls," Cher complained. "I'm beginning to wonder if she's alright."

"I can't quite figure her out," I admitted. "I know she's very shy."

"Claire, what's the next step regarding the quilt show?" Rachael asked, just as our food arrived.

"I don't know, other than I feel I'd have some support from the quilt club members after what I heard today," I revealed. "I think I'm going to talk to Carl again before I do anything else. He'll have good insight as to how the business community might respond."

"Maybe I'll go with you," Cher remarked. "I have a quilt that I'd like to consign."

"Good idea!" I agreed. "Oh, I love this whitefish chowder, don't you? I can't decide which restaurant makes it best."

"I wish I could make it," Rachael said as she took another bite. "Charlie and Harry love it, too."

Chapter 57

"How's Harry?" I asked, casually ignoring that she'd mentioned Charlie in a way that indicated she'd momentarily forgotten about his death.

She smiled, never catching her mistake. "He's been a rock for me," she said, blushing. "Today, he's painting that back room in the barn for me. He said I spend too much time in there for it to look so gloomy."

We laughed, and I suspected that there was some serious bonding going on between those two. "Why don't you bring him back a cherry pie from here?" I suggested. "I've bought them here before and they're delicious."

"What a great idea!" she responded.

We finished lunch and Rachael gleefully purchased a pie for Harry. My mind was filled with more ideas for the quilt show. When I pulled into my driveway, I saw all sorts of activity next door. It was the Bittners returning from Florida. They looked busy, so I didn't approach them. I was glad to know that they had returned. It gave me a better sense of security, I supposed.

I was tempted to take a nap but fixed a glass of iced tea instead. I had to digest what had taken place at quilt club today. I sensed a great deal of support, which I hoped would not go away when Greta found out. I just knew she'd have made a big deal out of both Cher and me remaining members of the club. I leaned back in my one comfy chair and asked myself whether I was truly serious about taking on such a project. An outdoor quilt show would be a lot of work! Having Cher by my side was encouraging. Now I just had to jump through the hoops required by the county board. I dozed off but then heard a knock at the door, so I jumped up to see who was there.

"Hi, Cotsy! Welcome home!" I exclaimed.

"It's good to be back," she said. "I just wanted to let you know that we're here. I hope you're well, and I noticed your new plantings right away. I love pansies, and I saw some pots in your backyard."

"Tom has been a tremendous help to me. He has been so good about cleaning up things outside, just as he's done for you."

"We couldn't do without him."

"Did you enjoy Florida?" I inquired.

"It was cooler this year than ever before. I can't believe it's Easter already. Do you have plans?"

"None that I've confirmed. I do plan to attend the Church of the Atonement on the corner now that they'll be open."

"Oh, it's lovely. I like taking guests there. Well, I'd better go. There's lots to catch up on. It appears as though you're adjusting nicely to the community."

"Yes, I am. By the way, did you know that Charlie McCarthy passed away?"

"Yes, I heard. I didn't know him well. I loved seeing his Christmas trees. That's where you helped out, right?"

"Yes. I really enjoyed it. It's been a shock for Rachael, his wife."

"I'm sure! Well, off to the tasks at hand. Nice talking with you again."

I went back inside and saw that I'd missed a call from Mom. When I called her back, there was no answer, so I left a message. As I prepared a salad for dinner, I thought about Carl and how I should keep him in the loop regarding the quilt show. Cher should also be included, so I gave her a call.

"Claire, you just caught me. I was about to leave to have dinner with some friends here at the condo."

"How nice! Say, I'm going to try to see Carl tomorrow morning. Do you still want to join me?"

"Yes! What time?"

"I'll have to check and see what time he opens up."

"I have a better idea. Why not have coffee at the Blue Horse first? I haven't been there in a while."

"That works for me!"

"Okay. I'll pick you up for coffee at nine thirty."

"Have fun tonight!"

When I hung up, I was a bit envious of Cher meeting up with friends for dinner. It was just like her to make friends quickly with her new neighbors.

Chapter 58

The next morning, Cher picked me up to take me to the Blue Horse. She brought a wall quilt with her. There were fewer customers at the café, so we got our order in no time and sat on the porch. We each chose a raspberry scone and brewed hazelnut coffee.

"This is what I was looking forward to when I knew you were coming back to Door County," I said as we sat down.

"It's nice, isn't it?" she said with a smile. "Claire, don't look now, but your lover just walked in the door."

"Lover?" I responded, turning around. He didn't see us sitting there, so I let him order before attempting to make my presence known.

"I can't wait to see the two of you together," Cher whispered.

"Oh, stop! He's just a good friend," I insisted. Sure enough, Grayson headed our way because he always sat in the same place on the porch if it was open. It was just seconds before he saw us.

"Hey, Claire!" he said, holding his tray containing a bagel and coffee.

"Good morning. Please come and meet Cher. She's my best friend," I explained as he gave Cher a friendly smile.

"That would be me," Cher said, extending her hand and giving his hand a warm shake. "Would you like to join us?"

"Thanks, but it's a brief stop for me this morning, and I know how you ladies like to coffee chat," he joked.

"We're having a quick coffee ourselves before we meet with Carl at his gallery," I explained.

"Very good! I'd like to stay longer, but another time perhaps," he said graciously.

"Absolutely. I'd like that," Cher confirmed.

"Later, Claire," Grayson said as he gave me a wink and went on his way.

"Man, oh man, Claire Bear! You sure know how to pick 'em!" Cher said in a low voice. "He's adorable!"

"I don't know if he's adorable, but he's easy on the eyes, as we used to say," I chuckled.

"The next time you're with him, tell him that your poor Cher Bear is all alone here in Door County."

I laughed. "I will. Just don't get any ideas about stealing him!" I jokingly warned.

"That's a terrible thing to say to your best friend," Cher teased.

"Speaking of friends, I had a strange experience with Brenda this week when I went with her to the fish boil," I shared.

"How so?" Cher inquired.

I explained to her about Brenda's infatuation with a man who comes to the White Gull Inn on a regular basis. I told Cher how he came over to say hello and focused on me instead of her. Cher nearly fell over when I told her that he approached me after I'd left the restaurant and offered to show me around Door County.

"Oh, how awful!" Cher responded. "Did she find out?"

"I hope not! He must know that Brenda is crazy about him. It was extremely uncomfortable, and by the way, he wasn't my type at all!"

"Well, she knows that you're involved with Grayson, so that should take care of it."

"I hope so, but it was in such poor taste. I'd love for Brenda to find someone nice. That guy couldn't be the one for her," I confirmed. "Look at the time," I said, looking at my watch. "We need to go."

That we did. Carl's shop wasn't far from the Blue Horse, so we were there in minutes. Carl was putting a painting in the window when we arrived. "Hey, Carl," I called out. "Meet my friend, Cher Clapton. She used to live here in Fish Creek, in the cabin where I live now. I think I mentioned that she's an art quilter like me."

"Nice to meet you, Cher," he said as he stopped working. "Come on in and take a look around."

"I'm very familiar with your shop," Cher assured him. "Claire is quite pleased to be doing business here, so I thought I'd show you a piece that I'd like to sell."

"Why sure!" he said as he took the quilt from Cher. He held it up and looked at it closely. "I like your bright colors and the peninsula sky. Do you machine quilt all of your quilts?"

"Sometimes I do both, like Claire does," she explained. "I recently got a new machine before moving back here."

"Your retail request is very reasonable. Did Claire explain our consignment percentage?"

"She did," Cher said, nodding. "She also told me that you may be adding art quilts of all sizes."

"I'm currently negotiating the rent increase for the extra space with the building owners. It's an added expense because I'll need to add some fixtures and get another person to assist me."

Chapter 59

"I think we have the sources to get you plenty of inventory," I suggested.

"Don't misunderstand me. I don't want just any quilts," Carl explained. "I don't think I'd be interested in bed-sized quilts, for instance. Also, I'd like the designs to connect to Door County if possible. I have a regular clientele that checks for that sort of art."

"That shouldn't be a problem," I assured him. "Carl, I also wanted to discuss the possibility of doing an outdoor quilt show here on Main Street."

"I knew you were intrigued by that idea," he said, smiling.

"Well, I got some valuable feedback from my quilt club, but they would not be the ones doing it."

"The club doesn't even have a name, so I'm not sure they should organize a whole show," Cher joked.

"In other words, the two of you and whoever else joins the parade would have to make it happen," Carl surmised.

"Exactly," I replied. "Listen—I know that villages have rules and regulations about outdoor things like this, so do you know what hoops I'd have to jump through?"

He paused. "You'll need a permit," he began. "It's called an event permit, but I don't know the details involved. I'd call the clerk's office and they'll tell you when, where, and how. You don't want to sell anything, right? They may not be keen on someone coming in from the outside to take away sales from the local businesses."

"No, it's not about sales," I assured him. "That's where you come in. Any interested party that wants to buy a quilt would have to see you. If you had your addition up and running by then, it'd be wonderful!"

"Oh, Ms. Stewart, you're something!" he said, laughing. "I have a lot to consider before then."

"Well, if you're looking for a good salesperson to run that end of the store, I'm available," Cher volunteered.

"Seriously, Cher?" I responded, surprised.

"Yes, I'd love it!" Cher said, clearly excited about the possibility. "I've had some retail experience in my day, plus I'm an artist and could perform demonstrations when I'm not busy."

Carl suddenly seemed deep in thought. "Well, leave me your contact information, and if this develops, I'll give you a call."

"Oh, that would be a win-win," I said, feeling extremely excited about the project. Cher filled out her consignment sheet and the two of us left the gallery wanting to do our happy dance.

"Claire, he liked my quilt, and now I even have a job possibility!"

"Don't get too confident about the job, Cher," I warned. "Do you really need the money?"

"Yes, I do!" she assured me. "The inheritance I received from Mom's estate gives me some security, but I need an income, just like you."

"Yes, I know what you're talking about," I said with a sigh.

"Thanks so much for taking me with you. Since I now owe you, I'll be happy to be your partner in the quilt show!"

"You will? Seriously?"

Cher nodded in agreement. We hugged each other right there on the sidewalk! Our day was going very well. When I got home, I waved to Cotsy, who was busily working outdoors. I took off my jacket and went up to the office. I needed a notebook to start planning the quilt show. I wasn't worried about finding enough quilts, but the permit had me concerned. I decided that first thing in the morning, I'd call the clerk's office. This event would need some seed money for advertising unless I could find a few sponsors. I found a blank notebook and immediately assigned titles to the committees needed for such an event. Then I made a list of people who might be advantageous to have involved. As I wrote and wrote about all that needed to be done, I began to feel overwhelmed. I decided to put it away until I knew more about getting a permit.

I went downstairs to eat a late dinner, and my phone rang while I was preparing a salad. It was Rachael. Before I discovered the reason for her call, I gave her a quick rundown about what was happening with my quilt show ideas.

"Girl, I can tell you're on a mission, but you'd better slow down until you know the rules."

"I know. I'm sorry to carry on so. How are you?"

"I'm fine," she said, hesitating. "Sunday is Easter, and I wondered if you have any plans."

"It is, isn't it? I know I want to go to the Episcopal church, which is right here. What are you doing?"

Chapter 60

"Well, Harry is insisting on cooking everything for a big meal that day at his place. He has his son and grandchildren, so he then thought of inviting you."

"That's so nice of him! Let me think about it."

"Well, as you can imagine, it's a big deal because of his granddaughters. He does a big egg hunt with them every year before the meal."

"That sounds like Harry. I'm glad you're going."

"I can tell that I'm getting a no from you. I'm surprised that Grayson hasn't asked you to do something."

"It's a family day, Rachael, and I'm certainly not part of his family."

"You will be one day, I'll bet. If you change your mind about joining us, just give me a call. I've got to work on Saturday night, which is always busy at the Bayside."

"Thanks for asking me, and please thank Harry for thinking of me."

"I will."

I hung up thinking about Harry and Rachael becoming more like a couple. I wondered if there was more than just a friendship developing. They certainly didn't need me in the picture on that holiday. After finishing my salad, I called Cher.

"Long time no talk," she joked.

"Are you busy?" I asked.

"Busy planning another quilt to take to Carl. Why?"

"I'm calling about Easter. I want to go to the cute little Episcopal church nearby and wondered if you had any plans."

"No, why? Easter isn't a big deal for me."

"Well, then, come with me and we can go to brunch afterward. Maybe Ericka could join us."

"I heard Ericka say that she and George are going to some relative's house."

"Well, what do you say?" I persisted.

"I guess so. No call from Grayson?"

"No, and I don't expect one. I just turned down an invitation from Rachael and Harry. I just didn't feel comfortable doing that."

"Okay, I'll come to the rescue. I'm curious about that church. Go figure—the whole time I lived in the cabin, I never attended their services."

"Well, it's time! The service starts at ten, so just knock on my door when you get here."

I went to bed feeling better about my Easter plans. It was only nine, so I turned on the classic movie channel, which always put me to sleep. I was reminded of Grayson, and sure enough, he called.

"Hey, you!" I answered cheerfully.

"Are you in the middle of something?"

"Yes, actually. I'm about to watch *Pride and Prejudice*. It's the one made in 1940 with Greer Garson and Lawrence Olivier."

"Wow! I didn't know there was one made that early. Are you a Jane Austen fan?"

"Not necessarily a fan, but I do love this movie. What a writer Jane was! I have a complete set of her books."

"So, do you think I have any characteristics of Mr. Darcy?"

I chuckled. "Let me think about that. I'll bet I could think of one or two. Do you think I'm at all like Elizabeth?"

He paused. "I think there may be a bit of her independence that I've noticed in you."

"Really? Just remember that it's her independence that's so attractive to Mr. Darcy," I said, giggling.

"I suppose you're right," he admitted. "I don't want to keep you, but I wanted to talk with you before the Easter weekend. Kelly and I will continue the tradition of spending Easter Sunday with Marsha's sister. They have a nice house on the lake, and they invite a lot of relatives each year."

"It sounds lovely!"

"Kelly has some cousins that she enjoys seeing, so we don't want to miss it. What are you doing?"

"Cher and I are going to attend the little church nearby and then go out for brunch."

"That sounds nice. I wondered if you were going to Missouri."

"I think that my brother will be with my mother, so I hope he doesn't disappoint her, which he sometimes does," I revealed.

"I hope you have a good Sunday. I've been curious about that church as well."

"You were sweet to call."

"Maybe we can go to that church together sometime."

"I'd like that very much. Tell Kelly hello for me."

"I will. Thanks!"

We hung up, and all I had to be happy about was that he had called. I guess it was good that he was still so attached to Marsha's family. It'd be very difficult for anyone to take that woman's place! As I was told recently, the deceased spouse is always put on a pedestal, whether they deserved it or not. At any rate, I was pleased that he hadn't forgotten about me.

As I drifted into a light sleep, I envisioned how Mr. Darcy would make peace with the independent Elizabeth Bennet. Their relationship was quite thorny until they finally found love with one another. It was something to remember.

Chapter 61

Good Friday always seemed more noteworthy than Easter Sunday to me. The Good Friday services that our family attended through the years described Christ's death in ways that often brought tears to my eyes. It was a time of true reflection. Then on Easter Sunday, my family created many memories by attending church, gathering with extended family, and capturing those memories in photographs year after year. Just as I was reflecting on those earlier years in my life, Mom called.

"Hi, Claire," Mom said, sounding out of breath. "I just wanted to tell you that Mr. Vogel is in the hospital. They think he's had a light stroke."

"Mom, I'm so sorry to hear that. Is he okay?"

"He's getting a lot of feeling back that was affected. I'll know more after I see him today."

"Was he alone when it happened?"

"No, thank goodness. He was having coffee with an old friend from the bank."

"It sounds like he got treated quickly, which is the key. Please give him my best."

"I will. He was so worried about me seeing him afterward. It was very scary, as you can imagine."

"For you as well, I'm sure. Mom, have you heard from Michael?"

"Yes, he's supposed to come tomorrow. He insists that we go to brunch instead of having me cook."

"That's a great idea. I'm supposed to have brunch with Cher after we attend that little church near here."

"Oh, how nice! You'll have to tell me all about it. I sure miss Hilda at a time like this."

"I know you do. This is Cher's first Easter without her mom, so I'm glad that we can spend it together. I'll also send Mr. Vogel a get-well card."

"Oh, he doesn't want a fuss."

"I want to, Mom. He's a wonderful man, and you think a lot of him."

"Yes, I have to admit that I do."

"I'll call you on Easter morning. You and Michael have a good day together."

"The same to you, honey."

I hung up wishing I could give my mother a hug right now. It was obvious that her feelings for Mr. Vogel were increasing. Her having him for a friend made me feel less guilty about leaving her.

I decided to attend Good Friday services at the Moravian church in Ephraim. The church was dark and quiet, and the atmosphere was subdued. No one was overly friendly like the first day I attended. The visuals and the sermon were wonderful, and the traditional message brought tears to my eyes. When the service ended, everyone filed out in silence.

As I drove home, I thought about my life and where I'm headed. When I arrived home, I didn't turn on the television or even listen to any music. I got a drink and picked up the quilting that sat next to me. I spent the remainder of the day in silence, quilting a bit more and eating a simple dinner.

The next morning, I made a mental note of the domestic duties around the house that I was very good at ignoring. Cher would be coming over tomorrow, so I wanted to make the place look clean and presentable. It perked me up a bit to know that we were going to spend some time together.

Ericka called in the afternoon to report that Rob's trial was coming up and that George was thinking of attending. It was so sad that Rob, George's friend, had turned out to be a disappointment to so many. His robberies in Door County had essentially ruined his life. I wondered how many years he'd spend behind bars.

"I'm happy that you and Cher will be together tomorrow," Ericka mentioned.

"Yes, especially with her mother gone."

"Cher has also been keeping me informed about the potential outdoor quilt show that you want to have."

"Good. We'll see where it goes after we figure out how to get the proper permits. It may entail actually meeting with a board of some sort. We're just in the beginning planning stages right now."

"If there's anything I can do, let me know."

"Thanks. That's very kind of you. You've been so helpful with many things already. I'm hoping that we can pull this off."

"Think of it as a start, and build on your dream."

"That, my friend, is excellent advice!"

Chapter 62

Easter Sunday was bright and sunny. It was cooler weather for Easter here in Door County, which I wasn't used to, but I actually put on a dress for the occasion, something I hadn't done in quite some time! I smiled, remembering my childhood days when we wore spring coats. Some of us wore new hats, and my mother made sure she had white gloves. We'd visit My Lee Hat Shop on the town square to pick out a new hat. I remembered sitting in front of a round vintage dresser mirror as the owner brought hats for Mom and me to try on. We always walked out of the store with new hats in fashionable round hatboxes. Times had certainly changed!

Cher arrived on time. Because of the nice weather, we decided that she should leave her car in the driveway while we walked to church.

"Don't we look fancy?" Cher teased when she saw what I was wearing. "I did the best I could. I know I'm wearing white slacks a bit too early in the season, but they went with my top."

"You look great! Happy Easter!" I greeted her as she returned my smile. "I'm sure you're thinking of your mom today. I know my mom is. By the way, she called last night to tell me that Mr. Vogel had a stroke."

"I'm sorry. Is he okay?"

I nodded. "I think so. He's making some improvements already."

"You're right. Mom was on my mind this morning. I still remember the egg hunts and Easter outfits."

We laughed together about our shared memories from childhoods spent in the same town, the same schools, and in close-knit families. It was hard to forget chilly Easter mornings with short little dresses and thin spring coats! We chatted all the way to the charming chapel.

A pastor greeted us at the tiny entrance. It was a good thing that we were early! Even then, we had to sit in the back row. The maximum capacity couldn't have been more than thirty people. We were in awe of everything in the compact space. It was informal, and the members seemed to know one another well. They were clearly happy to be reunited once again after the winter months.

The service began, and it had been a long time since I'd heard Cher sing, so it brought back many memories of the two of us singing along with popular songs on the radio. The sermon was simple. It was given by a traveling pastor from Green Bay. Her joy in telling of Jesus's resurrection was inspirational. After the sermon, a woman sang an a cappella solo. Her rendition of "He Is Risen" was beautiful.

As we exited the church, we found ourselves shaking hands with nearly everyone there. I was so glad that Cher and I had been able to share the service together. Cher then told me that she'd made reservations at Alexander's, so we walked back to get the car.

"Well, Claire Bear, we've shared another new experience together," Cher said with a big grin.

"It was special. Here we are, living in a new community and creating new memories for ourselves."

Alexander's had attracted a huge crowd, so the reservations saved Cher and me a long wait. I saw many familiar faces, including Ginger and Allen. The menu offered four specials to choose from, and they each made my mouth water. I chose turkey and dressing, and Cher chose the traditional Easter ham. Just as we were served strawberry shortcake for dessert, I brought up the quilt show. "We need to pick a time for the show so that when I go for a permit, I have something to tell them," I began.

"How much time do you need to put this event together?" Cher asked.

"From your experience living here, what time frame do I need in order to have a nice crowd attend?"

"I don't think you could possibly do it before the end of July," she said thoughtfully. "The Fourth of July has its own activities."

"If I targeted the end of July, it'd be tight. I could really use your help visiting some of the businesses that might offer sponsorship support."

"I can help with that. Making a personal connection would also be valuable because there hasn't been anything like it before; therefore, business owners may be cautious about having the responsibility of the quilt as it's being shown, too."

"I know. I think I'll have to get signatures from the building owners. I was also thinking that if it rains the day of the event, we could just put it off until the next day."

"I doubt that we'll have rain that time of year," Cher said as she took her last bite of strawberries.

Chapter 63

"What if I picked July 30?" I suggested. "It's a Saturday."

"You're asking me?"

I nodded.

"I guess, but where are you going to get all of those elves?"

I smiled. "They'll be available because it's not Christmas, and I prefer to call them volunteers."

We laughed.

"I can tell that you've already thought of everything. I know you too well. How do I get dragged into all these crazy ideas?"

"Look who's doing the dragging! You dragged me to Door County, remember? Let's start there. It's all your fault!"

We laughed so hard that we had folks staring at us. It felt so good to be in Cher's company, laughing together like always. Before we left, we walked over to Ginger's table to say hello.

"Ginger tells me that your idea of an outdoor quilt show just might happen," Allen said, sounding interested.

"With a little bit of your help, Allen," I teased. "I've got just the job for you, so don't let me down." The expression on his face led me to believe that I could indeed count on him.

"Whatever my boss tells me," he said, looking at Ginger.

"You're probably right. What she says goes!" I agreed as we laughed. Cher and I then made our way out of the restaurant. I noticed that Cher was smiling to herself about something. "What?" I questioned.

Still smiling, Cher replied, "You sure have a way of getting people to do things. This show will put your talents to good use."

"Our talents," I corrected. "We're going to do this together!"

It was two in the afternoon when we got back to the cabin. I was sleepy from the big meal.

"I'm so glad we did this, Claire," Cher commented.

"Me, too! This could be our new tradition on Easter Sunday!"

"It certainly could be. It was good to sit in church and reflect on things a bit. Life can change on a dime. This has been a vastly different year for me," Cher said quietly. Then she perked up as she said, "Oh, I forgot to tell you that Carole and Linda are definitely planning a trip to visit us this summer."

"Great! Have them come during the quilt show so they can help."

"Ha! Well, on second thought, I could suggest it. I think they'd like that."

"We'll get all of those details worked out. See you, Cher Bear!"

"You too, Claire Bear. Love you!"

When I got inside the cabin, I didn't waste any time finding my notebook to write down July 30 as the quilt show date. I added a place to list the volunteers that I'd gain along the way, putting Allen first on the list. I took a nap and spent the rest of the day enjoying the peace that Easter brings.

The next morning, I called the clerk's office as soon as I thought it might be open. When I explained my reason for calling, I could tell from the tone of the worker's voice that she thought I was crazy; however, she did tell me that I had to petition the board.

"The earliest opening we have on the agenda is in two weeks. You need to go to the Gibraltar boardroom that's located in the same building as the library. They meet at seven, so don't be late," she advised.

"Thank you. Please add another name besides mine. Cher Clapton will come with me."

"I'll send you a reminder, Ms. Stewart," she said before hanging up.

The first step had been taken. Now, I'd need to walk Main Street and begin getting a feel for who might allow me to hang a quilt on their building. Feeling like I'd already made some good progress, I called Cher. "The board meets in two weeks. That means we have two weeks to get feedback from businesses to see if they're willing to participate. Are you able to start in the morning?"

"We can't start then. Remember? Tomorrow is Rachael's lecture at The Clearing."

"Oh, I forgot. Well, we could have lunch after the lecture and perhaps catch a couple of shops."

"Here we go! What have I gotten myself into?" Cher moaned good-naturedly.

Chapter 64

The next morning, it was difficult to get out of bed. Most of the night, I'd been awake mentally reviewing the businesses on Main Street and wondering what they'd think of my idea. I dressed up more than usual, knowing that I'd attend the lecture and then begin to solicit businesses to gauge their interest in the quilt show. I quickly fed Puff and downed a bowl of cereal. I was busy watering plants when Cher arrived to pick me up.

"I'm anxious to see this place," I commented.

"It's really something! If there's time afterward, I'll drive you around the property," Cher offered.

"Not today, Cher Bear. Our time is ticking away, and we need to approach some shop owners."

"All you're hoping to get is a verbal commitment since we don't have any form for them to sign, right?"

"You're right, but it's a first step. If there isn't any interest at all, we may have to scratch the whole idea. If there's some interest, we'll just need to swing back to them and get their signature later on."

"Whatever you say, boss!" Cher said, making me laugh.

"The first place we'll stop is Carl's. He can give us some suggestions," I strategized. "Right now, though, let's get to The Clearing!" At that, we were on our way, continuing to chatter about the quilt show the entire time.

"Okay, here we go!" Cher announced when we arrived. "This is their main headquarters. We check in here and can also visit the gift shop. Some classes are held in this building as well."

"It sure is nestled in the woods."

"That's the whole idea of the experience. When we check in, they'll tell us where the lecture is being held."

As soon as we entered, a woman greeted us. We told her our reason for coming, and she took our money. She then explained that the lecture was off the main hall. My attention drifted to the gift shop, which was truly tempting.

We followed others who were there for the lecture and entered a large room with an expansive A-frame ceiling. One end of the room featured a gigantic arrow-shaped window that provided a view of the magnificent scenery outside. The windows on the side let in a lot of natural light. On the right side of the room was a group of women waiting for the lecture to begin. Some were at tables, and some sat in chairs arranged in curved rows facing the speaker. There appeared to be about thirty women in attendance, so I considered that to be a good turnout for the event, based on the size of the room.

"Here are two seats together," Cher pointed out.

We sat down, and I noticed that Rachael was surrounded by early arrivals who were eager to establish what the new expert might know. We were offered tea or coffee, which was a nice touch. A representative from The Clearing staff thanked us for coming and then introduced Rachael by giving a glowing description of her barn quilt business. Everyone applauded as Rachael blushed. I could tell that she was extremely nervous. For all that my friend had been through these last few months, I admired her bravery at doing something so out of her comfort zone. I said a quiet prayer for her.

"I can't believe you came to hear me today," she began. "I'm flattered and eager to tell you about the many quilt patterns I use to make barn quilts. Most customers come to me with a pattern in mind. Sometimes, it reflects a particular interest of theirs or a particular location. I just finished one for a couple from Iowa who lives on a sunflower farm. They wanted a colorful sunflower and it turned out to be beautiful." She then paused to look at her notes. "Like everyone who gets into quilting, it doesn't take long to realize how many quilt patterns and variations there are. We also quickly decide which ones are our favorites. I'm going to show you some patterns that have many names, depending on the area, family, or maker. Here's one called The Hole in the Barn Door, or Shoo Fly, or Churn Dash—take your pick!" Rachael's candor caused us to laugh while she showed us the pattern.

Rachael was becoming more relaxed as she warmed up to her new environment. She was able to keep some humor going by sharing the story of the Turkey Track pattern. She explained that in the Old West, it used to be called Wandering Foot because men would wander off and leave the women to search for work. Some of the men were never heard from again. This appeared to be new information for the crowd gathered, and they again chuckled. Rachael continued with her presentation, providing handouts with quilt patterns and their histories. She also included an advertisement for her barn quilt business in the materials.

Drawing the lecture to a close, she gave the crowd an opportunity to ask questions. Someone wanted to know how she started her business. Another was curious about whether she painted on any other surfaces. By this time, she was enjoying herself, and I could tell that she'd leave this lecture eager to think about other lecture topics she could develop.

Chapter 65

After a staff member thanked her for a marvelous program, Rachael was swamped with attendees who wanted to speak with her or ask questions. Cher and I didn't want to take up her time, so we headed straight to the gift shop. Many of the beautiful items were made by local artists. Time was ticking, so fifteen minutes later, I purchased a stone necklace with matching earrings, some hand-painted greeting cards, and a tiny print that looked just like Puff. Cher took the opportunity to tease me about how Puff was growing on me while she bought a journal and some greeting cards.

As we left Ellison Bay, we decided to have lunch at Wickman House. Cher said it had a wonderful wedge salad, which sounded perfect. She also suggested that the best drink to enjoy with it was a Bloody Mary. Both sounded wonderful.

"I'm so proud of Rachael for doing the lecture," I said as I sat down. "She's really thrown herself into her work since Charlie died. Of course, having Harry there to take care of the maintenance has really helped."

"I'm proud of her as well," Cher agreed.

"I do worry that she hasn't taken time to grieve, but that's her business," I remarked as our drinks were served.

"Would you look at this Bloody Mary, Claire? It has every vegetable known to man attached to it!"

We laughed as we examined the drink more closely. It was indeed an extravagant version of the classic drink! "I guess we really didn't need the wedge salad, did we?" I joked.

"The Bayside has a good wedge salad as well," Cher said, taking her first sip.

"Changing the subject, I don't remember you mentioning anyone that you dated while you lived here. Is that correct?"

"Nobody worth mentioning," she responded. "Every now and then, George or Ericka would try to fix me up, but nothing materialized. I'm counting on Grayson's sphere of influence," she said, laughing.

"I don't know if I'd count on that," I warned. "I'm not so sure that I can even count on him. He hasn't asked me out lately, but at least he called to see what I was doing on Easter Sunday. He didn't call, however, to include me in any of his plans."

We enjoyed our lunch, and I was particularly happy to have Cher's company. As for the restaurant, I decided that it was one I'd enjoy again sometime in the future. I looked at my watch and told Cher that we needed to be on our way to Carl's gallery. We paid our bill and drove to Carl's. When we walked in the gallery, Carl was busy with a customer, so we busied ourselves by looking around the gallery until he was free.

"Back so soon?" Carl asked, approaching us.

"Well, I just wanted to stay in touch, so you'd think of me," Cher said, smiling at Carl.

"Actually, the reason we're here is to ask which businesses to approach about displaying a quilt and maybe which ones to avoid," I explained.

"Think positively!" Cher chided kindly.

"I think you can count on almost everyone in this strip when you tell them that I'm on board with it. I'd start at the end with Pelletier's," Carl advised.

"Well, then, Claire, I could start on the other side of the street," Cher suggested.

"If you need to get permission from the actual building owners, that could really take some time. Some of them don't even live around here," Carl added.

"I just want an initial reaction and at best a verbal commitment," I explained. "We can always touch base with them later to get signatures. Do you have some paper to take notes, Cher?"

She nodded.

"Do you know how you're going to hang the quilts?" Carl asked, curious.

"I do, but each place will have their own special circumstances," I explained.

"Good luck going door to door, ladies!" Carl said as we left him.

"That's it!" I exclaimed, stopping in my tracks and turning to face Cher.

"That's what?" Cher asked.

"Door-to-door quilts! Get it?" I questioned, feeling excitement bubble up within me. "It will be a door-to-door quilt show!"

"Pretty clever!" Cher agreed as we went on our way. "Leave it to Claire Bear to ace it."

We laughed as we began our door-to-door experience.

Chapter 66

Cher and I each went our own way and decided we'd text each other if needed. I was excited that my first stop would be Pelletier's Restaurant & Fish Boil. They had a couple of unique places to hang quilts. Hanging two quilts on a building would be awesome! The manager of the restaurant was very pleasant when I explained why I'd dropped by. She didn't foresee any problem with the idea of hanging quilts there for the event. I continued moving from one business to the next, and for the most part, all the reactions were relatively positive. Sometimes there wasn't much of a reaction at all, but that wasn't very often. I kept taking notes so I could share them with Cher.

From a visual standpoint, it made sense to hang the last quilt on my side of Main Street at Gibraltar Grill. From there, Highway 42 continued to the Top of the Hill Shops. Maybe they would want to participate next year, but for this first year, I wanted the show to be limited to a concentrated area.

Cher sent me a text saying she was tired and needed something to eat and drink. After all the walking and speaking with people, I agreed with her wholeheartedly. I texted back that we should meet at Carl's and then head back to my house. Hopefully, Cher had also gotten good responses. At any rate, I was eager to hear about her experiences. By the time we met at Carl's, it was past five and Carl had gone home for the day. Ready to compare notes, we headed to my place for some conversation and a frozen pizza.

When we arrived at the cabin, I had to laugh at the bits and pieces of paper that Cher dumped on the table in the kitchen. She'd furiously taken notes, but they were in quite a messy heap! There was no doubt that we were both exhausted and eager to relax.

"Okay, did anyone yell at you or tell you it was the worst idea ever? Let's start there," I asked to get us started.

"No, but I got lots of looks—like the one from a teenager at some clothing place who looked at me like I was from outer space."

I laughed as I preheated the oven and prepared some drinks. "I know, right? I'm not sure how many took me seriously, but it was our first attempt at least."

"So, you did well?" Cher asked.

"Pretty much," I said as I slid the pizza into the oven. "Two shops pointed out that they didn't want their windows blocked so customers couldn't see their merchandise. I get that. It's not a big deal, because that's something we can work around."

"I believe the most positive remarks came from On Deck Clothing Company," Cher noted. "I think I talked directly to that store's manager. I'll check my notes in a minute."

"I'll get my notebook. We need to create a page for each store so we can make notes about their circumstances and who is in charge, so we don't get a different answer each time."

"Good idea! Let me get my notes organized," Cher said, skeptically eyeing her collection of papers.

The pizza was ready, so I refilled our glasses, and we took time to eat as we talked. As was typical when we got together, we got off the subject every now and then.

"Do you think Carl is serious about letting me work for him?" Cher inquired.

"I do, but first things first. First, he has to get the space secured. I think having your commitment will help him make his decisions."

"I sure would love the opportunity. I could quilt in my spare time when I wasn't busy."

"Yes, but remember, when you work for someone, it may require emptying the trash, ordering stock, or politely talking to the same tourist over and over again, not to mention watching for shoplifters!"

"I suppose you're right. My free time may not be actual free time. Is that what you mean?"

"I'm just saying that it won't be all fun. I can't imagine him paying you very much either. Most retailers make peanuts!"

"You're not going to talk me out of it," Cher declared, laughing. "Okay, let's start filling out these pages until we have a complete inventory of what we covered today. If I have to, I'll just sleep on that comfy couch over there."

"It's your couch, remember? You're most welcome to it," I teased.

She nodded and laughed as we got down to business. Two hours later, we almost fell asleep at the table. Cher insisted on going home. I didn't argue as I lugged myself upstairs to bed. It had been a very full day. My dreams took me from The Clearing to going in and out of the Main Street shops.

Chapter 67

The next day, I awoke feeling joyous about the quilt show. Knowing I'd need to designate an area to work on it, I set up the kitchen table as the office for the Door-to-Door Quilt Show. My phone rang, and I didn't recognize the number.

"Ms. Stewart, this is Margaret from the clerk's office. We just had an issue pulled from tomorrow's agenda. Is that too soon for you? Can you and the other person come on such short notice?" she asked.

"Oh, the sooner the better," I assured her.

"Okay. The meeting starts at seven tomorrow evening," she replied. "See you then," she said before hanging up. I called Cher immediately to tell her about the meeting.

"This is all happening so fast!" she responded.

"You're available, aren't you?"

"I guess," Cher said, "but you'd better be the one doing all the talking!"

I chuckled. "I have plenty of notes, so don't worry. I think they'll be pleased about the responses from the businesses."

"Well, it's still all talk, so I'm not sure it'll mean much."

"We'll get those signatures when it's time. I just worry that they may bring up something we're not aware of."

"Don't be too disappointed if we don't get to do this, Claire Bear."

"That's not going to happen. Listen—don't be late. I'd rather get there early to get the lay of the land."

"I know. I know."

Filled with excitement, I went back to the kitchen table to review my notes. I wanted to size up how much manpower would be needed. Since I wasn't backed by an organization, I was going to have to recruit individuals who could take responsibility for the action items I'd listed. When I looked at the column titled "Sources for Quilts," I decided to go ahead and call Kathy Luther from Joe Jo's Pizza and Gelato to see how many quilts she could help me find. She held an office in her quilt guild, so I knew she had access to quite a few quilters. I only had the restaurant number for her, so I used that. When I asked for her, they asked me to hold. It seemed that I'd caught her just as she was going out the door. "Remember me? Claire Stewart?" I asked quickly when she answered, sensing that she might be in a hurry. "I'm the quilter from Missouri. We met at a chamber event you hosted at the restaurant some months ago."

"Oh, sure! What can I do for you?"

I briefly told her that I wanted to have an outdoor quilt show in Fish Creek and that I was in the process of getting an event permit to do it.

"An outdoor show?" she questioned.

"Yes, I know it's risky business, but it's just for one day," I explained.

"I've heard of places doing that," she remarked thoughtfully.

"I know you can't speak for everyone, but do you think some of your members would allow their quilts to be shown?"

She paused. "I don't know. We've done displays before, but never outdoors. What if it rains or if someone steals a quilt?"

"Those are good questions, and I plan to have answers, but we're just in the beginning stages of planning right now. I'll only be able to control so much, but can you just imagine what a stunning visual art show it'd be?"

"Yes, I can. I can tell you this, Claire. We have what we call 'second-tier quilts' in the collection that my husband and I own. They're nice, but not our best of show, if you know what I mean. I know we can give you ten or so of those."

"You can?"

"Sure! They're in storage and need to be aired out anyway. I know you'll put precautions in place to protect them."

"Oh, Kathy, that's such good news! I'm sure that others will follow suit if you act as an example."

"We have some risk in the restaurant as well with the ones we have hanging, so we'll work out something."

"Thanks so much. I'll keep you posted. If you get a response from your members after you ask them, please let me know."

I hung up feeling like I'd found a pot of gold! The more quilts I could get from one person, the better. I listed her ten quilts as a commitment. Once we knew the buildings we could use, we could assign sizes needed and specific accessories they needed for hanging. If I asked Carole and Linda to bring quilts, they would have other sources as well that they could ask. They could spread the word to their quilt guilds. I sure couldn't count on the one that I belonged to—not yet anyway! I then thought of my mother's full cedar chest. She could send her quilts with Carole and Linda! Buoyed by the response from Kathy and counting on help from the people I knew who made quilts, I convinced myself that getting quilts wouldn't be a problem. The problem at hand was to convince six board members to do something in their community that they'd never done before!

Chapter 68

I almost convinced myself to take a nap, which I seldom do, but I was beginning to feel overwhelmed just thinking about the show. I jumped when the phone rang. It was Rachael. "Well, what a pleasant surprise! What's up?"

"I just need to talk to someone," she said quietly.

"Oh, Rachael, what's wrong?"

"I miss Charlie so much." She began to sob into the phone.

"Of course you do," I soothed. "You haven't taken much time to grieve, and I can see that you've thrown yourself into your work."

"Maybe so, but I get so confused."

"Confused?"

"Please be honest with me, Claire. You probably know me better than almost anyone right now."

"I promise to be honest with you, but what are you confused about?" I asked.

"You know how grateful I've been to have Harry's help since Charlie died. Charlie would really appreciate all that Harry has done for me. I didn't have a clue about all the things that have to be done around this place."

"Harry loved Charlie and wants to be helpful."

"That's the problem. The two of us miss Charlie so much that a lot of the time, we end up crying on each other's shoulders. I don't know what I'd do without him."

"I understand."

"He even comes around at mealtimes so he can cook for me. He knows I have so much work to do with the barn quilts," she explained.

"That's great!"

"Is that normal?" she asked. "When one of us gets down, we hug each other, and honestly, it's been so comforting."

"That's what friends are for. What's so confusing about that?"

She paused. "I shouldn't even say anything about it, but it really kept me awake last night. I just need to talk to someone who can help me get a grip."

"What's really bothering you?" I asked softly.

She paused again before she implored, "Please, please, keep this to yourself."

"You know I will," I assured her.

"Harry was here last night grilling steaks for dinner, and we had some wine. We cooked out on that little patio behind the barn where Charlie and I would grill once in a while."

"That's nice."

"It really was. We talked a lot about old times. Sometimes we laughed, but sometimes I'd break down in tears. Harry is always good for one of his bear hugs."

"I'm sure he is."

"The next thing you know, we're embracing—and we kissed! It felt like it was the most natural thing to do, like Charlie and I did all the time. Neither one of us was thinking, plus we'd had a couple of glasses of wine, so our defenses were down. We kissed several times, Claire."

I paused, wondering what I should say. Then I offered, "Rachael, it was a natural thing you were both used to doing with your spouses. Perhaps it wasn't romantic. It sounds like you were comforting each other."

"That's what I keep telling myself. We were both embarrassed and taken aback by it. The worst of it is that I kissed him first! I hope Harry doesn't get the wrong idea. I'd never want to do anything to hurt him."

"Now just hold on. It's going to be okay. You both felt awkward, and that's a good sign."

"I'm so embarrassed. That was two days ago, and I haven't heard a word from Harry since! That's not typical."

"Well, perhaps he's taking a time-out. He's not going any-where. Frankly, I think the two of you will laugh about it one day. You're good friends. Things will sort themselves out."

"Thanks so much for saying that. I hope you're right. I need him so much."

"And he needs you, too. Try not to worry about him. I'd call him if you haven't heard from him in a couple of days. He'd be very relieved to know that he didn't hurt you. Just call and ask him a question about the farm."

"Okay, I will. Thanks so much for understanding."

When I hung up, I sat down at the kitchen table to process what she'd told me. It was shocking and yet not. They were two people who were hurting, and they comforted each other. Harry had been divorced for some time, but Rachael was a new widow. Harry could easily be falling in love with her. I just hoped their innocent connection wouldn't destroy their friendship. They really needed each other.

Chapter 69

The next morning, I was up at the crack of dawn going over my notes for that night's meeting. I was pleasantly interrupted by a text from Grayson.

[Grayson]
Are you free for a drink at the Bayside around five? I'm dropping Kelly off at band practice.

[Claire]
Sorry, I have a meeting with the board regarding my idea about an outdoor quilt show. Rain check?

[Grayson]
Moving ahead I see! Good luck! Let me know how it goes.

Grayson's text cheered me up. It was good to know he hadn't forgotten about me, even though I might only be something to do while he waited on Kelly. Hopefully, I'd have good news to tell him. Then my phone rang. I was thinking that it might be Grayson again, but it was Olivia.

"I heard you're going to the board meeting tonight."

"Yes. How did you know?"

"I may live in Sturgeon Bay, but Door County is a small area. Word gets around."

"It must have been Cher."

"It was," Olivia confirmed with a laugh. "She's pretty nervous. Do you want me to go, too?"

"Oh, Olivia, you're so sweet to offer, but right now, I have just the two of us signed up to present. Thank you so much for offering, though." I then gave her an update on everything I planned to present to the board. I told her I'd already secured ten quilts to hang.

"Quilts are not your problem, girlfriend. I have good sources for quilts. You'll need some excellent publicity! As soon as you get your event permit, I'll talk to Carol at the quilt shop and have her get it on her social media."

"That would be great. I have you and Frances down for getting quilts from your area. I'm counting on our club members to participate, whether they realize it or not."

"I like your confidence, Claire." Olivia then offered, "I have a small collection of Gee's Bend quilts, and some I made as reproductions. They would make a fine display together."

"Indeed! I'm glad you mentioned that. I'd like to have some displays on the lawn of Noble House, and yours would be perfect there. My friend Brenda volunteers there now, so I'm sure we can get permission. Maybe their museum has quilts in their collection that they'd like to display. I'll mention it to her." I hung up feeling even more excited! I hoped I wasn't doing all this planning for nothing. I decided to call Cher around four to go over everything.

"I hear you're just a little bit nervous," I teased when she answered.

"You bet I am! From what I hear about this board, they're not eager to make many changes."

"Don't worry." I filled Cher in on my phone conversation with Olivia, and she was pleased as well. I reminded her to get there early. Once we hung up, I showered and dressed. I decided to wear a navy business suit with a white blouse. I wanted to appear businesslike instead of dressing like the flamboyant artist they might be expecting. I should've cautioned Cher to do the same. I went downstairs to try to eat a bite, but I was too nervous.

When I arrived at the library building, I was pleased to see that Cher was wearing a black suit with a polka dot blouse. We smiled at each other. "Is this the beginning of our business career?" I joked.

"Could be!"

"I have my notes, but feel free to jump in and make comments."

"I don't think I'll do that—unless I think you're in trouble!" she joked, laughing nervously.

Chapter 70

Down the hall in the library was the Gibraltar room. Before we entered, Cher lifted her pinky finger.

"Remember this?" she asked playfully.

"Let's see if it still works!" I returned, linking mine to hers.

A woman approached us and asked, "Are you ladies here for tonight's meeting?"

We nodded.

"Please have a seat out here until we call you." At that, she retreated, and it was just Cher and me again. The area was so small that I could see why they only heard one case at a time. Other folks sat nearby, but no one was talking. I was curious as to their reasons for being there, but they were likely as consumed with their thoughts as we were.

"Ms. Stewart and Ms. Clapton," the woman announced as she opened the door for us. We were ushered into a cozy room.

"Good evening," the chairman greeted us. "Please have a seat. We understand that you're here to obtain an event permit for an outdoor quilt show on Main Street in Fish Creek."

"Yes, that's correct," I responded.

"This is certainly a request we haven't gotten before, but we're willing to listen to your proposal."

"Thank you so much." To my dismay, my voice cracked. I was more nervous than I'd expected, but I forged on. "I appreciate being able to get on your agenda so soon because we'd like to have the event on July 30 of this year."

He nodded, indicating that I should continue my presentation. From that point on, I felt like I was in the twilight zone. Every board member was male and each of them regarded me with somber expressions. I forged ahead, explaining what we intended to accomplish by having the event. Cher appeared to be frozen in her seat. I could tell that she wasn't going to be much help, so I continued explaining the plan. I tried hard to speak slowly and mentally reminded myself to breathe. The board members continued to offer me nothing more than even gazes until they sensed I was about to wrap it up.

"Have you ever executed an outdoor quilt show before, Ms. Stewart?" one asked. Each board member was wearing a name badge, but I was unable to read his name.

"No," I answered.

"There is a great deal of liability involved. I don't know if you're aware of that," another man said. "Can you imagine the outcome if something happens to one of the quilts or if inclement weather affects the show? That could result in lawsuits not only for you, but for our county. When shop owners themselves put merchandise outdoors, they're responsible for whatever happens to that merchandise."

"I understand," I stated. "When I visited the shops about this idea, they were more concerned about anything blocking their own inventory, not whether it'd be stolen or rained on. As I told you, we'd have a list of the participating buildings and businesses and would get consent forms signed by the owners of the buildings."

"What hours did you mention?" the man at the end of the table asked.

"I hope to have them all hung by nine that morning and plan to have them down at four that evening before the shops close at five. It's my intention to have enough volunteers to make that happen in an expedited manner."

"I'm not sure this endeavor will be worth all that effort," one man said.

I glanced at Cher. She looked uncomfortable, and I could tell that she felt bad for me but didn't know how to improve the direction of the questioning. Then, surprising me, her expression changed, and she sprung to her feet. "If I may, gentlemen," Cher began, clearing her throat. "I can certainly understand your reservations. All innovative ideas are risky. Let's remember, however, that Door County is known for being a champion of art from its earliest existence. Visitors expect the finest and most unique art when they come here. My friend and I don't own a business. We won't make one penny on this endeavor. In fact, it'll cost us time and a fair amount of money if we don't get some sponsors. As Claire explained, we have many people just waiting for the board's approval. We see this as a successful first event—and one that will grow year by year! Can you just picture lines of cars driving slowly to see not only the quilts displayed in Fish Creek, but eventually those in many of the villages north and south of us? It presents an opportunity for the elderly and for those who can't walk to enjoy a show—and it's free!

Businesses will benefit because it'll bring foot traffic to the streets. There'll be tourists looking for food, purchasing fuel, and needing lodging. Wouldn't you like Fish Creek to be the first to offer such an opportunity? I guarantee that if my friend thinks this is a good idea, I know her well enough to know that she'll make it successful!"

Chapter 71

Cher's speech made me want to stand up and applaud! This was a side of Cher that I'd never seen before, and it left the board members speechless. There was a lengthy pause before anyone spoke.

"Thank you, Ms. Clapton," the chairman finally said. "Please step outside while we discuss the matter. We realize that time is of the essence for your planning, so we know we don't want to put off making a decision."

"Thank you," I replied. "As you can tell, we're quite excited about the idea. We appreciate your consideration and time."

The board members maintained their somber expressions as we left the room. As soon as the door closed behind us, I looked at Cher and gave her a hug. "You were wonderful, Cher Bear! Even if we're turned down, you're the best partner I'll ever have!"

"We're not going to get turned down," Cher said confidently. "We've got this!"

"Thank goodness we'll get an answer this evening," I said. It seemed like an eternity as we waited outside the door. I said a small prayer for strength and for a good outcome.

Finally, the chairman stepped out of the meeting room. He held a piece of paper in his hand.

"Good luck with your Door-to-Door Quilt Show," he said, showing the slightest hint of a grin.

"Thank you so much!" we said in unison. We left the building feeling exuberant. When we got to our cars, we broke into a happy dance.

"Let's head to the Bayside! I'm buying!" Cher declared.

"I'm in!" I replied. It had been a while since I'd felt such excitement about a project. After we got a table, we went over every detail, sometimes talking simultaneously. It was too bad that Rachael wasn't working tonight because she could've celebrated with us. After we got our drinks, I made a toast. "Here's to the Door-to-Door Quilt Show by Cher Bear and Claire Bear of Door County, Wisconsin!" We both burst into laughter. Out of the corner of my eye, I caught a glimpse of someone by the door. I couldn't believe who had just walked in. Grayson spotted us and headed our way.

"I'm not crashing this victory party, but I just wanted to extend my congratulations. I told the bartender to put your drinks on my tab."

"Thanks, Grayson!" Cher replied.

"How did you know?" I asked in disbelief.

"I have my sources," he teased. "You make a formidable team, and if I can do anything to help, just let me know."

"That's wonderful!" I responded. "Please have a drink with us."

"I wouldn't think of it," he said, shaking his head. "You'll have me hanging quilts and who knows what else if I stay. You two just enjoy yourselves."

"Thanks, Grayson," I replied, smiling. He kissed my cheek and off he went.

"Now that guy is a keeper—at least until the quilt show is over," Cher said with a laugh.

I chuckled and kicked her leg under the table. "Every now and then, he really surprises me. He called me earlier and asked me to have a drink with him, but I told him about our meeting and declined his invitation."

"Don't let him get away, my friend," Cher advised, shaking a finger at me and smiling.

"I can control some things and can't control others," I stated simply. "Anyway, let's have another toast to pulling this off," I suggested.

"Cheers to the Bears!" Cher exclaimed.

For the next hour, we talked mainly about the show, but eventually landed upon the subject of Ericka's missing rings. Cher said, "I don't think Ericka has been able to move past the missing ring situation. She mentioned to me last week that I should keep an eye out for the rings whenever I see Ava. How in the world can I do that? Ava's got more jewelry than anyone I know!"

"There were so many people at your party, Cher. I don't know if Ericka should focus solely on Ava."

"It's because she's heard us talk about her sticky fingers," Cher said with a sigh.

"I don't know how seriously to take that," I responded. "I want to give her a job at the quilt show that doesn't have her handling quilts, so I guess I don't fully trust her either. Perhaps she'd be good with public relations."

"That brings up security," Cher pointed out. "The bigger this becomes, the harder it'll be to keep an eye on things.

Some of the shop owners told me they don't want to be responsible for the quilt that's displayed at their store."

"I don't blame them," I agreed.

"Oh, my goodness, I didn't realize that it was this late!" Cher exclaimed, looking at her watch. "They're closing soon!"

At that, we agreed to leave and placed a nice tip on the table. We hugged as we said goodbye, feeling triumphant that we'd just gotten permission for the first ever Door-to-Door Quilt Show!

Chapter 72

After a few hours of sleep, I got up early and began thinking of jobs and who might fill the various roles. I was eager to get the show started! I hadn't been long at my task before Puff eagerly ran down the stairs, not wanting me to forget her breakfast. I fixed some coffee and sat down at the kitchen table. Opening my quilt show folder, I realized that I had to alert some people that the show was really going to take place now that we had the permit. The quilt club needed to know—that was certain. I also needed to call Carl and arrange to meet with him. He was my business contact for Main Street. Even though it was early, my phone rang. It was Mom, my biggest supporter. She couldn't have called at a better time. "Good morning!" I answered cheerfully.

"Well, you sound mighty alert this morning."

"I am! Did you know that last night was when Cher and I were going to see the county board about our show permit?"

"No, I didn't. How did it go?"

"We got it! I still can't believe it," I exclaimed.

"Congratulations!" she said enthusiastically.

"You should've been there to hear my Cher Bear. They were asking me lots of tough questions and sounding very critical when Cher stood up and went to bat for us. She gave a wonderful closing about how successful the event would be for the community and told them that if I was involved in the event, it'd be successful. I nearly fell over. She was fantastic!"

"She's always been your greatest cheerleader. I can recall many times when she came to your defense through the years."

"So now, I'm here at the kitchen table setting up the committees."

"You're on the ball, I'd say," Mom said. "I'm happy for you and know that you'll really enjoy planning such a big event." Then she asked, "How's Grayson?"

"He's fine. He heard about our good news last night, so he stopped in at the Bayside where Cher and I were having a drink to celebrate."

"That was nice of him. Perhaps he can be involved in some way as well."

"I hope so," I agreed. Then I remembered that she'd called me and that she must've had a reason. "Is everything okay there? How's Mr. Vogel?"

"Everything is going well here. Mr. Vogel is working hard to recover. He seems to be in good spirits," she replied. Then she went on to say, "The nicer weather is wonderful, but I just can't do all the yard work like I want to. Kenny from down the street still does the lawn, but my flower beds need so much attention."

"Pay him to help you. Have you heard from Michael?"

"As a matter of fact, he called last night. He mentioned having dinner with a girl named Ellen. I don't know if she's a girlfriend or not."

"Yes, I doubt it, knowing him."

"I saw Carole and Linda at the Hallmark store this week. They said something about visiting you this summer."

"I heard. Cher hopes to convince them to come during our quilt show so they can help."

"That sounds like a good idea. They sure miss Cher."

"I know. She misses them, too," I replied. "Hey, do you think you could loan us some of your quilts for the show? We'd take good care of them," I said.

"Absolutely! Do you want me to go ahead and send them to you now so you'll have them?"

"Let's wait and see what Carole and Linda do. Perhaps you could send your quilts with them. It would save you all that expensive postage."

"Great idea. Well, I'll let you go. You have a lot of work to do. Tell that handsome Grayson that I said hello when you see him again."

"I will," I said with a big smile. I hung up feeling a pang of homesickness. I regretted not being able to see my mother more often.

Then my phone rang again. It was Matt Fairmore, my attorney. "Mr. Fairmore, is something wrong?" I asked, immediately beginning to feel nervous.

"I just wanted to give you an update on the news I've received from Dr. Page. He has an attorney. I received a letter from his attorney encouraging you to settle the matter as soon as possible."

"So, it's another threat, right?"

"Yes, but I'm not surprised. A letter from his attorney sends the message that Dr. Page is serious about the matter."

"Do you know how to respond?"

"Yes, of course. I'll draw something up and send you a copy. Don't concern yourself."

"Thank you," I said as a heaviness fell over me, despite his words of confidence.

Chapter 73

I hung up, stood, and paced around the tiny cabin, trying to digest this latest news. How could I get Austen to leave me alone? I had to trust that my lawyer was telling the truth when he said he'd seen behavior like Austen's before. If calling Austen would calm him down, I'd do it, but Mr. Fairmore had advised me against it. He said it was probably just what Austen wanted and might cause him to think he could get me back. Keeping silent wasn't easy for me.

I began to think about my time with Austen. He always liked to think he had monetary control over me. Austen would sometimes say, "It's a good thing that I know people with money so they can buy your work." He didn't seem to think that my work was good enough for them to want to buy it on their own. When Carl immediately purchased a quilt from me, I regained some confidence that I'd lost. I'm sure Austen suspected that I came to Fish Creek broke. I never told him about my father providing dream money for Michael and me, and now I'm so glad I didn't. If I decide to buy the cabin from Cher, I'll need it. It's such a shame that Austen and I couldn't part as friends. I heard a knock at the door. When I looked out, it was Tom. He was wearing a big smile.

"What's up?" I asked.

"I'm going to mow the Bittners' lawn tomorrow for the first time since last year. Do you want me to start mowing yours as well?"

"Sure! Just go ahead and mow mine when you come to mow theirs."

"You're accumulating more branches from these big trees, so I'll get that cleaned up as well. Your flowers sure look nice."

"Thank you. I'm pleased with their progress. My herbs are doing well also," I replied.

"I keep putting branches in your firepit thinking you'll make a fire sometime soon."

"Thanks," I said. "Someday soon, perhaps." I had to chuckle at the thought of sitting outside at my big firepit all by myself. So far, I'd not done a good job at inviting anyone over to enjoy it with me. Tom was such a good helper. Perhaps he'd be willing to help out with the quilt show. The phone rang. I was relieved to see that it was Marta. I excused myself from Tom and took the call.

"Claire, this is Marta."

"Hey, good to hear from you," I said.

"I'm calling to congratulate you on getting the quilt show permit."

"Oh, how nice. How did you know?"

"Well, it's public record, but my friend Cornelia is the recording secretary for the board, so I heard it from her. She said the two of you gave quite a nice presentation, and she thought it was a great idea."

"Thank you, Marta. That's good to hear. I hope you know that Cher and I represented ourselves and not the club. If Greta gets wind of the permit, make sure she knows that."

"I will. Don't worry."

"We're starting to put committees together now. Can we count on you?" I asked, hopeful that she would help us.

"I'll think about it. Please don't take this personally, but I don't want any of my quilts hanging out in the sun all day."

"I understand, but there are other ways you can help. I need a person to collect the quilts as they come in. First, I have to find a place on Main Street where that can take place. The person collecting the quilts has a lot of responsibility and must be someone who understands how to handle quilts. You'd be great in that position."

"I think I may have a suggestion about where you can collect them, but I'll have to ask," Marta offered.

"Really? Where?"

"The Community Church is closed until they get a new preacher. If we could use their meeting hall, it'd be a perfect location."

"It would be! Would you mind asking? See? You've been helpful already!"

"I'll give the custodian a call and see what he has to say," she said.

"I'd really appreciate it. So, it's important that the person receiving the quilts is detail oriented. You have great organizational skills. Would you consider taking that position?"

Chapter 74

Marta paused and then said, "Oh, I don't know if I could do that."

"I don't know of anyone better! You of all people would make sure that everyone's quilts are handled properly."

"Well, if you really think so," she said, but I could hear the hesitation in her voice.

"It'd be a big relief to have that critical position filled, Marta," I urged.

Marta breathed a deep sigh and said, "I guess I'm just one of those folks who can't say no when I'm needed."

"Marta, thank you so much! Aren't you glad you called?" I heard her chuckling at my enthusiasm. I hung up from the conversation confident that God would work out all the details needed to make the show successful. Overjoyed to have that position filled, I picked up the phone to share the good news with Cher.

"Marta just called to tell me she got the news about our event permit. I think she wanted to remind me that it shouldn't be sponsored by our quilt club, but instead I talked her into being in charge of packing the quilts in receiving and pickup! She didn't want her quilts in the show, but she did agree to help us!"

"She's perfect for that job," Cher agreed.

"There's more. She's going to try to arrange for the Community Church to be our quilt headquarters since they're not having services this summer."

"It's a perfect location. That's awesome news. Way to go, Claire Bear!"

I felt like I was full of news to share, so I continued, "I talked to Mom this morning and she saw Carole and Linda recently at the Hallmark store. It sounds like they plan to come here for a visit, so would you try to convince them to come for the show? They were planning to stay with you, correct?"

"Yes, that shouldn't be a problem."

"We'll assign them duties if they agree to come," I said with a laugh.

"Yes, boss, I'll take care of it," Cher shot back as we laughed together. "Anything else?" Cher asked.

"Yes. Ask them how many quilts they can bring to display. Mom can then send her quilts with them," I suggested.

"Okay, I guess I'd better get on this," Cher agreed.

As we hung up, I began to realize that I had the potential to sound rather bossy during this planning process. I needed to be more mindful of how I was coming across to others as I put the project together. After all, they would be volunteers, and I needed to express my appreciation for their contributions. I also had to be careful that this event wouldn't come between Cher and me.

At the end of the day, I closed my quilt show folder, reminding myself that Rome wasn't built in a day. Tomorrow,

I planned to approach each quilt club member to see if they wanted to be involved. I poured myself a drink and went out on the porch, where I opened some of the windows to get the wonderful breeze. I sat in the dark with Puff, who was settled comfortably in her chair. We were now a pair, like it or not. The peacefulness made me think of Grayson. I wondered if he might be thinking of me. My phone showed that I'd just received a text from Cher, and that made me smile.

[Cher]
Carole and Linda are on board about coming for the quilt show. They will count their quilts and let us know how many they can contribute to the cause. I thought that since it'll be their first trip here, they could serve as monitors. We'll need some people walking up and down Main Street making sure that people are not touching the quilts. When I made that suggestion to them, Carole said that we need to print signs as a simple deterrent indicating that people shouldn't touch the quilts. Linda is excited about coming and has claimed the couch because she says she doesn't sleep well at night. I think they're both pretty excited about being involved. You may not see this until morning, but I just had to tell you right away.

I replied quickly.

[Claire]
Oh my gosh! That's great news! I love the idea of having them be monitors. I agree about the signage. Good job, Cher Bear!

It appeared that Cher had the quilt show bug now and that made me happy. If she got the job at Carl's gallery, it'd be icing on the cake.

Chapter 75

The next morning, I looked out the window just in time to see Ericka drive up. I was curious as to why she'd drop by, so I greeted her at the front door. "Good morning! What did I do to deserve an early morning visit?"

"Can I come in?" she asked.

"Of course! How about some coffee?"

"Sure, but I only have about fifteen minutes," she replied. "George called me late last night," she explained as she followed me into the kitchen. "He said that Rob has been sentenced to fifteen years at the Wisconsin State Corrections in Kewaunee."

"Goodness! That had to upset him. What a shame."

"Yes, he still blames himself for not helping Rob more with his problems," Ericka shared.

"Drug dependency does terrible things to people. They do things that they wouldn't ordinarily do," I said, trying to be consoling.

"George plans to visit him next week."

"Maybe he'll get out earlier with good behavior. Rob was a very kind person."

Ericka gave me a curious look. "You liked him, didn't you?" she asked.

"Yes, and he liked me, too. I trusted him. He could've stolen from me many times, but he didn't."

"You're right. I'm sure he's going through a huge adjustment right now."

"What about his family?" I asked.

"They aren't saying anything, but we get the sense that they somewhat blame George for what happened."

"Poor George!"

"Don't be surprised if he tries to talk to you about it," Ericka warned.

"I don't know how I can help, but I know that it's not his fault," I said.

"Oh, I talked to Cher," Ericka mentioned. "She's over the moon about how the meeting went. I hope you guys know what you're getting into."

"Did she also tell you that she may have a chance to work at Carl's gallery when he expands?"

"She did, but I doubt if that's going to happen anytime soon, do you?"

"It might, and she'll be ready. Carl has already been so much help with our show. It'll be a big plus for his business if he can get that expansion open before the show."

"Before I run, how are things going with Grayson?" Ericka inquired, heading toward the door.

"Slow, but steady," I replied, realizing that I didn't really know how to answer her question.

"That's great! Well, I've got to run," she said, heading out the door.

After she left, I went back to the kitchen still thinking about poor Rob. Thank goodness I didn't get any closer to him than I did! My phone rang, and it was Carl.

"Hello, Ms. Stewart. I hope you're quilting because I just sold another one of your little quilts."

"That's great news!" I exclaimed. "However, I have to admit that since we got the permit for the show, I've only been working on that."

"You got the permit?"

"Yes! How about that? I'm anxious to talk to you about it," I informed him.

"Congratulations! I'll help in any way I can," he offered.

"I need your advice on prospective sponsors," I replied. "That would give us the startup money we need."

"I'll consider being a sponsor if it's not too pricey."

"That would be great. I know this whole project is risky business, but with Cher's help, I think we can do it!"

"I'll let you know when I sign on the dotted line for the space next door. It's looking pretty good," Carl said.

"I hope so. It's all Cher talks about. I'll stop by soon, okay?"

"Sounds good," Carl said.

When we hung up, I wanted to get back to my quilting, but my business would have to come to a halt if I wanted to get the quilt show on the road. Time was running out. I wanted to make a good first impression with the show, or else it would never happen again. As I was fixing a glass of tea, I saw a call coming in from Rachael.

"How's it going?" she asked, sounding happy.

"Everything's good! How about you?"

"The same. I'm calling to ask you to dinner tomorrow night. I know it's the last minute, but Harry just bought a quarter of beef and he thinks we should use some for a barbecue. It's an all-day affair for him."

"Wow! That's a lot of meat! Does he freeze the rest?" I asked.

"Yes, or sometimes he gives a lot away. You know Harry. We thought it'd be nice if you'd bring Grayson. Harry has asked his son to come, and the girls will be there, too."

"Thanks! It sounds wonderful. I can't answer for Grayson, but I'll be there. What can I bring?"

"Harry is taking care of the meal, so why don't you bring dessert?" Rachael suggested. "See you around six then, okay?"

"Sounds good."

Chapter 76

I considered Rachael's request, but wasn't sure what to do about inviting Grayson. He was obviously busy since I hadn't heard from him. I'd have to give it a bit more thought before choosing to call him. I went to bed with a lot on my mind. My mind flip-flopped between thinking about the quilt show and picturing myself with Grayson at Rachael's farm. Sleep finally came, and I overslept the next morning. I awoke to Puff walking all over me to get my attention. Finally, I gave in and got out of bed.

It was a beautiful day. The temperatures were getting warmer and warmer each day. The tourist traffic was increasing as well. I convinced myself that a walk down by the marina would do me good. It was lovely down there. I didn't take advantage of its beauty often enough. I ate some toast and got dressed for the day. I took a few moments to water the flowers before taking a walk. Mrs. Bittner was out, but I didn't feel like going next door to visit.

I left the house, and it occurred to me that the sky was the prettiest blue I'd ever seen. I could smell spring and summer at the same time. As I approached the marina, there seemed to be more activity than usual. I walked to the dock and stood for a few moments watching the boats launch. The thought of a restful ride on the water made me feel envious of those vacationers at first, but then I remembered my vertigo and was grateful that a boat ride wasn't on the docket today.

"Well, look who's here!" a man's voice said from behind me.

It was Grayson. "Hi," I greeted him in surprise. "What are you doing here?"

"I should be asking you the same thing."

We chuckled. "I'm just out for a walk. It's so pretty here. I'm pretending that I'm one of those tourists seeing this for the first time and about to set sail."

He laughed. "I think I told you that I keep a boat here. A friend is going to take it out today, so I came to check on it."

"That's awfully nice of you. How are things going in general?"

"Good. Things are very busy this time of year."

"Well, being the busy man that you are, would you be too busy for dinner tonight?" I offered.

He paused. "Just supervising my daughter," he said lightly.

"Well, I know where there's going to be a very good barbecue this evening, and you and Kelly are invited to join me."

"You're cooking?" he teased.

"No, but Rachael called and invited me to come out and enjoy some of Harry's barbecue. He's quite a chef and will be cooking all day. She wanted me to ask you, but I know you've been really busy. It's a fairly small group that's coming."

"Man, that sounds good, and I'll bet Harry's a master at it."

"I had a taste of some of his cooking during a tailgate party at a Green Bay Packers game, and it was amazing."

"Well, I'll tell you what. I'll check with my boss and see what kind of reaction I get."

"She'll love the farm, the animals, and the company, of course."

"I'll bet she will! I'll let you know as soon as I can."

"That's great. I'd better get going. You both can meet me there if you want."

He gave me an incredulous look and then protested, "That's not how I treat a woman who has asked me out!"

I laughed. "I'm sorry that it's a last-minute invitation, but Rachael just called last night."

"Okay then. I'll call you as soon as I can."

I watched Grayson drive away. What were the chances of him being at the marina? I was proud of myself for inviting both Grayson and Kelly. Somehow, it just seemed right. As I walked back to the cabin, I had a skip in my walk. Seeing Grayson made me feel lighthearted. I saw some wild Queen Anne's lace along the wooded area and decided to pick some. The bouquet reminded me of home, where I looked forward to seeing them every year. I wish I could paint the detail of one of those flowers. Their intricate detail was truly art in nature. Wouldn't it be wonderful to capture that beauty in quilting?

When I arrived back at the cabin, I arranged the flowers in a cream pitcher and positioned it on my kitchen table. It brightened up the whole room. It was late afternoon when Grayson finally called.

"If it's not too late, we'd like to accept your invitation," Grayson confirmed.

"Wonderful! I'll give Rachael a heads-up. Did you have to twist Kelly's arm?"

"No, she just shrugged her shoulders and asked what time we needed to leave."

"Okay," I said, grateful that we could finally spend some time together. After I told him the time, I hung up. It wasn't long before I began to feel butterflies in my stomach. I knew I needed to distract myself, so I preheated the oven and got busy making some brownies.

Chapter 77

Grayson and Kelly were right on time when they pulled into the driveway. They were in a vehicle that I didn't recognize. Grayson came to the front door with a big smile on his face. I greeted him with a smile as well. Tonight, I was wearing jeans and a jean jacket. I had my hair pulled back and wore a yellow ball cap that matched my shirt. I picked up the brownies and we headed outside. He gave me a quick wink as I said hello to Kelly. "I hope you're both ready for barbecue," I said, smiling.

"It sounds really good!" Kelly responded, sounding happy to be included. "Dad can cook some, but I really have to watch him when he grills anything."

"Hey, I just like my barbecue rather crispy," he replied in defense of his grilling aptitude.

"I like your outfit," Kelly said.

"Thanks." I blushed as Grayson took notice of me with an admiring glance and a quick wink. Kelly kept up a constant chatter until we arrived at Rachael's. Rachael was pleased to see us and immediately made us feel welcome. When Kelly saw Harry's granddaughters running around, she quickly engaged herself with them.

"Claire, Grayson, this is my son. Kent is the father of those baby girls running around," Harry said.

"Pleased to meet you, Kent," I responded, shaking his hand. "I've already had the pleasure of meeting your darling little girls."

"Thanks," he said, appearing to be rather shy. "They're a handful, but they really love coming here."

"Harry gave them a ride in a wagon attached to the tractor last week," Rachael bragged. "They loved it!"

Watching Harry cook where Charlie typically grilled took me a bit aback. However, Harry was right at home in front of a grill, and my mouth began to water from the aroma. I helped Rachael with some of the side dishes and reminded her that I'd brought brownies for dessert.

"I thought I smelled those in the car," Kelly said, overhearing our conversation as she played with the little ones. "Dad, did you know?"

"Well, when I winked at Claire, she thought I was winking at her, but I was really approving of the brownies I smelled," Grayson joked.

"Thanks a lot!" I joked back.

"I can't wait to try them," Harry said as he rubbed his round tummy.

As the evening progressed, I realized that being with Rachael and Harry was like being with a married couple. They helped each other out in one moment and ordered each other around in the next. Eating outdoors was always a treat for me. Rachael had put red-and-white tablecloths out with ivy centerpieces. One table held all the food, and the other was where we sat to eat. All the picnic favorites were available, including corn on the cob and a baked bean casserole. Grayson and I were distracted by the conversations around us, but occasionally we'd make eye contact and smile. Kelly sat at the table with the little girls, and she seemed fine with that. Of course, the little ones loved her, and there was no shortage of shrieks and giggles from them. Everyone ate more than they intended. I hadn't had good ribs in a long time, and these fell off the bones. It reminded me of the barbecues in my hometown. Grayson teased me about my bib and messy hands. I was relieved that the brownies were a big hit. Everyone enjoyed vanilla ice cream with them. I promised Kelly that if there were any leftover brownies, they could go home with her.

Chapter 78

I refilled my glass of lemonade as everyone sat around enjoying the refreshing breeze. It was really my first outing of the season, so I was ready for the temperature drop later in the evening. Grayson sat down next to me and patted my hand. I was keenly aware that Kelly witnessed that simple gesture. I knew we had to be careful about showing affection when Kelly was around.

Harry was on top of everything. When he wasn't getting us more refreshments, he was cleaning up so Rachael wouldn't have to do anything.

"Rachael, I want you to know how much I enjoy the red-and-white quilt I purchased," Grayson shared.

"I'm so glad," she said with a big smile. "It was very generous of you to purchase the quilt."

"I'm going to steal it from him one day," Kelly teased.

"Kelly, I think I need to squeeze some time in and show you how to make one of your own," I suggested.

"Seriously?" she responded. "That would be so cool," she said, but then got distracted by a cat that had approached us. She watched the cat for a moment and then asked, "Rachael, what's your cat's name?"

"Oh, he or she doesn't have a name," she replied. "She or he just started hanging around here the last couple of days. It probably belongs to a neighbor, but I've been feeding it."

"I'll bet it's a he," Kelly guessed.

"That's what Harry thought," she said, nodding. "I love the white ring of fur around his neck."

"I've never seen a cat like that before," Kelly murmured. "He's really friendly."

"Yes, I'm surprised that no one has come to ask about it," Rachael said.

"Well, he needs a name," Kelly insisted as she watched the cat.

"You're free to name him, as far as I'm concerned," Rachael said.

"Well, Kelly, you could probably just give that cat a home," Harry interjected.

"I could? Dad, what do you think?"

"I'm not sure that's a good idea," Grayson responded with a serious expression on his face. "He may belong to someone who is trying hard to find him."

"I doubt it, since no one has even asked about him," Harry replied.

"Dad, could we?" Kelly begged.

Everyone looked at Grayson and waited for his response. "Let's give him another week to be found. If no one shows up for him, we'll give it a try."

Kelly's eyes lit up as she reached down for the animal. "Maybe I'll call him Spot," Kelly joked. "Claire told me about Puff and Spot being in the early reading books."

Everyone laughed together.

"I think that's a great name," Rachael said with a giggle. "Perhaps it was meant to be that he wandered over here."

Kelly picked up what she hoped would be her cat. Grayson just shook his head like he knew there would be heartache ahead. Kent remained rather silent the whole time as he diligently kept his eye on the girls. I couldn't help but wonder how he felt about Rachael getting closer and closer to Harry. After a few minutes, Grayson suggested that we be on our way. It was then that Rachael pulled me aside.

"Claire, I'm guessing that you'll be busy putting the quilt show together so it won't be convenient for you to work at the shop with me," she queried.

"I'm afraid you're right," I agreed. "I'll try to be available for the Christmas season, though."

"I'm happy to help with the quilt show, so just tell me what to do," she offered.

"I will," I said, giving her a hug. "Thanks for a wonderful evening. I'm not sure that Grayson will feel the same way since he got a cat in the bargain."

She laughed and then everyone said goodbye. Kelly was thrilled to take the leftover brownies. She gave the cat one last hug. Once we got on our way, Kelly couldn't stop talking about the cat and all she'd do if she got to keep him. There wasn't time for Grayson and me to have much of a conversation, but all in all, it was a good evening spent with friends. When we got to my place, I gave Grayson a kiss on the cheek and told them goodbye as I got out of the car. I could tell that Grayson would've liked a nice hug, but this wasn't the time or the place.

"Thanks for the brownies, Claire!" Kelly called.

"You're welcome," I responded. "I'll keep my fingers crossed about the cat."

Kelly flashed me a big smile at about the same time that I caught Grayson rolling his eyes at me.

Chapter 79

The next day I got out my quilt show folder and made up a form for each participating business to sign, giving permission for a quilt to be hung. I planned to make copies at the post office when I went to pick up my mail. As I looked over the list, I wondered who might consider being a sponsor. I had no idea what our advertising expenses would be. I also needed to find someone to head up that area.

About midway through the day, I decided to give Brenda a call. "How are you?" I asked when she answered. "I haven't heard from you since we went to the fish boil. Is everything okay?"

"Yes, I've just been busy," she said curtly.

"I'd like to get together and give you an update on our quilt show. A lot has happened," I shared.

"Well, I don't think I can right now. I'll get back to you."

"That's fine, but are you okay?" I asked, surprised by her lack of interest or energy.

"Claire, I'll talk to you later. I've got to run right now."

There was no goodbye. She just hung up! I was shocked by her abruptness. What was eating her? This wasn't the Brenda I knew. I wondered if Ericka knew anything about what might be going on with her, as she was the one who had introduced us at the White Gull Inn. Regardless, I would have to bypass her and talk with the management at Noble House about getting permission to use their lawn for the event. Thankfully, it only took one quick phone call to secure that area for the quilt exhibits. I was jotting those notes when my phone rang, and I was surprised to see a Missouri area code.

"Claire, it's Linda!" the caller announced.

"What a surprise! How are you?"

"I'm doing well. Carole and I are planning to come there in July. The timing should work out so we can be there for the show."

"That's so cool! Did Cher tell you she thought the two of you would make good monitors on that day?"

"Yes, I think we can handle that. It's also a good opportunity to see the quilts up close. We both have quilts for the show, and I hear that we're bringing some from your mother."

"That sounds wonderful. I really appreciate it. Do you have any idea how many quilts you might bring?"

"I'm guessing around ten or so. Is there anything else we can bring?"

"Just some jelly donuts from my favorite bakery," I joked.

She chuckled. "You've got it. We're so excited! I'll just warn you that Carole and I can get into a lot of trouble."

"Somehow, I seem to remember," I said, laughing.

We chatted for a while longer before hanging up. Hearing her voice and laugh made me think it was just yesterday when we were all in school together. Carole and Linda also had a flare for art. Linda was of Native American descent and owned a collection of beautiful turquoise jewelry. She loved trying to reproduce other pieces that reflected her heritage. We always referred to Carole as a foodie because cooking and baking were her thing. During our high school years, we loved hanging out at Carole's house in the country, where we'd enjoy some good home cooking. All her jobs revolved around food, so she finally wrote her own cookbook. She dubbed it *Carole's Cooking*. This trip to Door County would broaden their experience. I was certain that they would have a great time here. Then, I was surprised when my phone showed a call from Olivia.

"Hey, how's the quilt show coming?" she asked.

"Right now, the show is contained in a folder," I said, joking.

"Well, I have a lot of commitments from quilters who are willing to show their quilts. When do you need them?"

"I'll let you know. I have to hear from Cher regarding how many buildings we have. Marta was going to secure the Community Church for our headquarters since the congregation is not currently meeting in the building."

"Marta's helping?" she asked in disbelief.

"Yes, big time. She's agreed to head up quilt receiving and pickup, which is huge."

"Wait until Greta finds out," she warned.

"It'd be nice if Greta would join us, but I guess that's too much to wish for."

"That's for sure!" Olivia exclaimed.

"All of the other quilt club members seem excited about it," I said.

"Listen—just email me when you're ready. Do you have email addresses for the quilt club members? If not, I can send them to you."

"Thanks so much, Olivia. I'd appreciate that. You've been such a trooper, and I'm grateful for your help. Recently, I've gotten permission to use the Noble House lawn for special exhibits, so that's where we'll put your Gee's Bend quilts."

"You're on top of it, Claire. I'm excited!" she declared just before she ended the call.

Chapter 80

The next day, it was my mission to organize our first quilt show meeting. Marta had secured a key to the church and Olivia gave me a complete email list. Now I needed to make a list of others who might help, like Carole, Linda, Tom, Carl, and hopefully Grayson and Harry. It took time to make the email message sound official. I included the time, the place, and an agenda. I took a lunch break and watered my flowers before going back to actually send the email. I was surprised when I got immediate responses from Lee and Ginger. Olivia answered saying that she'd tell Frances because she wasn't good about checking her emails. Olivia also promised to give Frances a ride if she needed one. Surprisingly, Grayson responded quickly via text.

[Grayson]
I see that you're off and running! Sorry I can't attend your meeting, but plan on me to help. I'll encourage Kelly to do the same. See you soon!

[Claire]
I didn't think of Kelly. Good idea. I could use another $200 sponsor. Can you suggest anyone?

[Grayson]
Sails Again will be happy to.

I'd hesitated to ask outright if Sails Again would be a sponsor. After all, Grayson had already done so much by purchasing the quilt at the auction.

[Claire]
Thanks so much!

I went to the computer to make a form for sponsors. I continued with paperwork until evening, when Mom called. "Mom, it's good to hear from you," I said.

"I thought I'd call before I turn in. I'm pretty tired today."

"Are you okay? What did you do to make yourself so tired?"

"Not that much, really. I have days like this every once in a while."

"Have you been to see Dr. Carron lately?"

"No, I'm fine. How are you doing?"

"Well, I've had a very productive day working on the quilt show. I even got good news from Carole and Linda. They're planning to come to the show."

"That's great! Does Cher have room for them to stay with her?"

"She says she does. They'll have a wonderful time."

"Do you think they'll have room to bring my quilts?"

"Yes, they're planning to bring yours," I assured her. "Have you seen Mr. Vogel lately?"

"We saw each other at the senior center last week," she volunteered. "He seems to be doing what his doctor says, according to him, anyway."

"Tell him that I said hello. Mom, if you don't feel better soon, I wish you'd make an appointment with Dr. Carron."

"I will. I'm just getting old, you know," she said with a laugh.

We hung up, but I was bothered by the fact that she wasn't her usual chipper self. With Cher not there to look after Mom any longer, I was going to have to pay closer attention to her. For a moment, I wished that Michael and I had produced some grandchildren, but we hadn't. That made me feel sad for her as well. However much I loved to be around children, I was always happy to come home to some peace and quiet. I guessed that God just had a different plan for me.

I decided to call it a day and fixed something to drink. I was pleased with today's progress on the show, so I decided to email Cher and share the details with her. After all, she was my cochair. I went out to the porch and began writing an update. After I sent it, I took a shower to help me relax. I didn't want to wear my worry cap to bed and think about all the things that could go wrong like I sometimes do. I sighed as I thought about how a call from Grayson would complete my day. As I slid into bed, I received a text. I was hoping it was Grayson, but it was Cher.

[Cher]
Holy cow! Good news regarding our meeting. I didn't see Greta on the group email list, though.

[Claire]
Well, she didn't offer to help, and chances are that she's pretty disgruntled with us. The next quilt club meeting might be brutal!

[Cher]
Not to worry. The Bears can handle it!

I smiled and snuggled deeper into the covers.

Chapter 81

It was rainy on the day of the quilt show meeting. I hadn't heard back from everyone, but since it was such short notice, I wasn't worried. I sat on the porch to drink my coffee as I watched the rain and heard it hitting the rooftop. A phone call from Rachael startled me.

"I'm just calling to give you an RSVP. Harry and I will be at tonight's meeting."

"That's great. I really need help from both of you."

"Well, it gets better."

"How so?"

I talked it over with Harry, and we decided that McCarthy Barn Quilts needs to be a sponsor."

"Oh, Rachael, thank you! It really is a good way to promote your business."

"Yes, we sure wish we could sell our barn quilts there."

"Not this year, though. The board was concerned about taking business away from the shops involved. Frankly, if this goes over, I think there will be a way to have vendors in the future. Now I have three sponsors! I'm using the sponsor funds to promote the event. I've recently gotten Ginger to oversee advertising because she's so familiar with it, and Ava is helping her."

"That's a good job for Ava. Until we figure her out, she shouldn't be around the quilts," Rachael warned.

"I'm trying not to think of Ava that way. She's been a longtime quilt club member, and she just marches to her own drum."

"I still wonder if she's dating Ericka's neighbor."

"I don't know, and I don't care," I responded with a laugh, certain that I had more pressing issues on my mind.

"Well, I'll let you go. I got some new barn quilt orders yesterday. They're from some of the women who attended my lecture at The Clearing."

"That's great! You should think about doing more lectures there. I also think that quilt clubs and guilds would be interested in your program. Aren't you glad that you accepted their invitation?"

"My friends are always looking out for me," Rachael said, sounding thankful.

After I hung up, I realized that in a relatively brief period of time, Rachael had become a good friend. Cher was still my soulmate, but Rachael had welcomed me with open arms when I moved to Door County, and that meant a lot.

As I did some chores, I kept checking my computer to see if there were any more responses. Marta called to remind me that she'd be at the church early to open up. She had no idea how grateful I was for everything she'd already done to help with the event. I began to wonder if Greta knew about the meeting. At around four, I checked in with Cher by calling her. "It's not too late to back out," I teased.

Cher laughed. "Don't talk that way, Claire Bear. We're in this together!"

"Marta has been wonderful. She'll be there early."

"Should I bring tea or coffee?" Cher asked.

"I haven't seen the building, so I'll leave that up to Marta. The meeting shouldn't take very long. It's really just hearing reports from committee heads about what they've been assigned. They'll also need to give everyone an idea of how far along they are."

"I'm going out in a little bit to meet up with a few more businesses," Cher said.

"Great. Do you still have plenty of forms?"

"I'm good. I'm getting a little pushback from some places. I can't believe how many businesses have building owners who don't live around here."

"We'll have to work with what we have, so don't worry about it," I advised.

"Two places I've called on want the quilt to be shown inside the window, which is fine, I suppose," Cher remarked.

"Yes, that'll be fine. Thanks for all your hard work."

"Sure. Hey, I'd better get back to my job. See you tonight!" she said as she ended the call.

I smiled to myself as I got back to my quilt show folder, which was sitting on the kitchen table. Cher and I made a good team. Whether we failed or had success, it sure was nice to know that I had someone to experience it with.

Chapter 82

As I checked over the details of the meeting, I realized that tonight could really change my focus here in Door County. Was I really ready for what was about to happen? I hoped I hadn't bitten off more than I could chew! I picked up the newspaper and glanced through it absentmindedly. I thought that Ginger would have placed an advertisement for the show in there by now, but I didn't see one. I was startled when the phone rang, especially when I saw who was calling. It was Greta. "Good morning," I answered.

"Claire, I'm calling in regard to your quilt meeting tonight."

"Yes! By the way, you're very welcome to join in," I offered.

"The reason I'm calling is to make it very clear that our club is not the entity organizing or endorsing the event in any way. Therefore, I caution you not to give that impression at the meeting since we're so well known."

"Oh, I absolutely understand, Greta. I want you to know that after I described my vision for the show, each club member made their own decision as to whether they wanted to be a part of it. Cher and I are cochairing the event and we're happy to include anyone who wants to participate."

"Well, it was unfortunate that I had to miss that last meeting. It seems that many things were discussed. The only subject not addressed was the membership policy as it pertains to you and Cher," she commented.

"Well, we have a meeting coming up, so I'm sure it can be discussed then. Greta, please know that I'll make sure everyone knows who's sponsoring the show. I want you to be happy that we're promoting quilting right here in Fish Creek with this outdoor show. I'm excited because this has never been done before in this area."

"I think that hanging those quilts outdoors is disrespectful, and it's unfortunate that you used our meeting to corral your support," she declared.

"Oh, Greta, I'm so sorry you feel that way. I assure you that we'll take hanging the quilts very seriously."

"We'll take that up later. I just made this call to make everything clear."

"I understand," I said quietly.

"Very well, Claire. I wish you well," she said as she hung up.

My heart sank as I hung up the phone. How could anyone who loves quilts as much as Greta object to this show? I immediately gave Cher a call. "Can you talk?" I asked when she answered.

"I'm filling my gas tank right now but go ahead."

My voice shook as I described the phone call with Greta. Cher listened without interruption. She finally responded when I paused to catch my breath.

"You're not really surprised, are you?" she asked.

I sighed. "I don't feel good about this at all. Upsetting Greta is not good for the club."

"Don't worry about the club. They're on your side."

"The next quilt club meeting sure won't be pleasant! Of course, she had to remind me about our membership and that it wasn't brought up at the last meeting like it should've been," I complained.

"I think everyone is of the same mindset. It's both of us, or neither of us," Cher said matter-of-factly.

"It's so unfortunate. I hope she doesn't badmouth the show to everyone. She knows a lot of people, and they know she runs the club."

"I think she knows better than that," Cher replied. "How's the response for the meeting coming along?"

"Decent. Grayson is going to be a sponsor, which is very cool. I think that will give Ginger plenty of money to work with."

"That's great. The On Deck store here wanted to know if their other locations would be decked out with a quilt."

"Pun intended, right?" I teased. "Tell them not this year."

"Okay. I'll see you tonight then. Try not to worry, Claire," Cher urged.

I hung up feeling a little better. I appreciated Cher so much. I'd make every effort to get us through this show together without hurting our relationship.

Chapter 83

It was the first time I'd entered the Community Church. I peeked into the sanctuary and saw that it was charming and historic to say the least. Following the sound of voices, I found the meeting room, where I also smelled coffee. I saw Marta talking to Ginger and Allen, who had arrived early.

"Nice of you to make coffee, Marta," I said, smiling.

"Not to mention that she brought her famous peanut butter cookies," Ginger added.

"Oh, that's so thoughtful!" I exclaimed.

"Well, it's just a welcoming touch for our first meeting," Marta said, blushing.

"Thanks so much!" I said. "This meeting area is really nice, and we certainly have lots of room."

"Allen and I moved some tables around so we'd have a head table."

Just then Cher walked in, and her expression indicated that she was pleased with the setup. Within the next fifteen minutes, almost everyone who had committed to coming had arrived. I wanted to be punctual and not keep folks any longer than necessary, so I started on time.

"Everyone, welcome to the first meeting of the Door-to-Door Quilt Show!" Everyone smiled, and one or two people applauded. "Some of you may not know everyone, so let's go around and have each person introduce themselves." They all obliged, and some took longer than others. That done, I continued by saying, "Thank you again for volunteering to help with this art show, because that's basically what it is. It's a new venue for Fish Creek that I hope will grow throughout Door County. I've assigned committee responsibilities after speaking with some of you. I'd like the committee chairs to describe their jobs and the progress they've made thus far. The show must be up and ready by nine that morning and taken down exactly at four so businesses can close at five if they desire. The businesses have been approached by Cher and me already. Eventually, we'll need to get letters of permission signed in order for us to hang a quilt on their premises. We want to be very sensitive as to where they would like their quilt hung so it won't take away from their own displays. Only a couple of shops have requested that we display their quilt inside their shop windows. The designated area of the show is from this end of Main Street to Gibraltar Grill. Basically, it ends before going up the hill. We may have a gap or two, but that's okay. If there's a chance of rain, we'll postpone the event until the next day. If there should be a pop-up shower, we'll provide plastic drop cloths for emergency use. Marta is going to champion the care of the quilts. She'll accept them, label them, and bag them up so they can travel to the proper shop. At the end of the show, she'll be the one to examine each quilt and give it back to the proper owner. Hers is a particularly important job because these are not our quilts. We want them to stay as safe as possible. Cher will photograph the building where each quilt will be hung. That photo will be attached to the bag with the needed hanging equipment, such as clothespins, for example. We have a committee of volunteers who will hang the quilts. Lee is in charge of any special exhibits, and those will be on the Noble House lawn. So, let's get started." Just then, Ava walked in, so I asked her to introduce herself. When she did, she announced that she'd be helping Ginger with publicity.

"Ginger, do you want to begin?" I said, glancing at her. Addressing everyone, I said, "After everyone is done, we'll be happy to answer any questions."

Ginger stood up and presented her publicity schedule. Next, Olivia explained that it was her job to collect quilts for the display. Cher followed her and described the assorted sizes of quilts that would fit specific buildings. Marta simply said that she felt good about her duties because she was concerned about the safety and care of each quilt. Lee then stood and mentioned that she was securing some exhibits and that the guilds were also welcome to sell raffle tickets in the park. Allen announced that he'd need more volunteers to help hang the quilts. I then finished up by announcing the sponsors that we had secured so far but assured everyone that we could use more.

The meeting lasted over an hour, and any questions were mostly about safety concerns. That's when I explained that we had a group of volunteers to monitor each side of the street. I also mentioned that a sign would be attached to each quilt indicating that they weren't to be touched. Near the end of the meeting, Carl entered the room and I introduced him. I announced, "Carl has been very supportive of our idea and has agreed to help hang the quilts as well."

Chapter 84

"Thanks, Claire," he responded. "If anyone wants to sell their quilts in the show, I'll be happy to handle the sales."

"That's wonderful!" I responded. "It was very important to the board that we not take away any sales from local merchants."

"Claire, I also have an important announcement to make," Carl began. "After noticing a particular interest in art quilts from my customers, I'm developing a new addition that will be able to accommodate them in my shop. I hope to have it in decent shape by the time of the show."

"That's great news," I said. "We wish you well." I looked at Cher and she was already doing a happy dance.

"Thanks, Claire," Carl replied. "It was you who encouraged me to take a look at that market."

I felt myself beginning to blush. "Well, if there are no other questions, we'll adjourn," I announced. "Please feel free to stick around for refreshments. Thanks go to Marta for the special treats."

As everyone started to disperse, Cher immediately went over to Carl to congratulate him. His announcement was great news for her. After most of the attendees had left, I helped Marta put the cookies away. I thought this might be a good time to tell her about my phone call earlier in the afternoon. "I got a call from Greta today," I revealed.

"Oh? What did she have to say?" Marta asked.

"She was very concerned about tonight's meeting."

"I'm sure," she said, nodding.

"She reminded me not to present the show in any way that would make people think it was being sponsored by our quilt club."

"I see," Marta said quietly.

"She said they would take up the topic of my membership at the next meeting since we didn't take care of it at the last one. I think she's quite determined to remove the new member who has stirred the pot," I said, grinning weakly.

"I wouldn't worry about that, Claire."

"I'm not," I assured her. "However, perhaps it might be better for the group if I just dropped out."

"I don't think that should happen," she protested, shaking her head. Then she changed the subject and said, "I think the meeting went very well, don't you?"

"I think so. The good thing about this first show is that we have nothing to compare it to. This is the first, so we have no place to go but up!"

"That's the spirit!" Marta said, laughing. She then began packing up her things, getting them ready to take to her car.

"Claire," Cher said, coming over to where I was standing. "I actually start helping Carl on the addition next week!" she said with excitement.

"I think we should use this as an occasion to celebrate, don't you? Let's go somewhere," I suggested.

"I'm in! Should I ask Carl?"

"No, I think tonight should be a Claire Bear and Cher Bear celebration," I said.

"I think you're right. Bayside?"

"Bayside it is!"

We waited until everyone had left the church except Marta. I could tell that she took pride in playing her role in this show. She locked up and waved us on, telling us to have a good time.

When we got to the Bayside, it was full of people. We each ordered a beer and an appetizer of chicken wings, something Cher particularly loved.

"I never drank beer until I arrived here," I confessed.

"It used to be just wineries here in Door County, but then the breweries started moving in. They came into fashion with all of their different flavors. I love this raspberry lime, but it's not for everyone."

We raised our glasses and clinked them with joy. "To the Door-to-Door Quilt Show!" I toasted.

"Cheers to our success!" Cher followed.

After we had discussed the intricacies of the meeting that had just ended, our conversation turned to the quilt club and our current membership predicament. I said to Cher, "Marta says not to worry about the next meeting, but I am worried. I'll gladly bow out if necessary."

"If so, I'll quit," Cher said. "They can then continue doing their thing."

"Cher, I don't think you understand. I don't want to negatively affect the group in any way. I just want to make it stronger and more noteworthy. I'll always be grateful to them for accepting me under the circumstances. This show wouldn't be happening if I hadn't joined the group."

"I know. Hey, let's get off this subject and feast our eyes on the guy standing over at the register."

I turned in that direction and had to laugh. Because she didn't date much, it was easy to forget that Cher was a single person always ready to look at what was available.

Chapter 85

"Cher Bear, why don't you head in that direction and see if you can get him to buy us a drink? I'll bet you have the touch," I proposed.

"Seriously? Are you daring me?" she asked, frowning at me.

"I dare you."

She gave me a sassy look and got out of her chair. After taking a drink of her raspberry-lime concoction, she bravely walked over to the hunk she'd admired. After a few moments of shared conversation, he glanced in my direction, which made me think that she must've told him about my dare. In no time, she returned with two drinks in her hands and a triumphant smile on her face. Whatever she did certainly worked! As she approached our table, I saw him slip out of the bar.

"Well, that was a short and sweet relationship," I pointed out.

She burst into laughter. "His name is Leroy, and he was just in here to get a quick bite before picking up his kids from basketball practice."

"He's married then?"

"Those beautiful blue eyes and that perfectly trimmed mustache belong to someone else. That's always my luck," Cher said, shaking her head slowly and wearing an exaggerated pout.

"I'm sorry, but I can't see you going out with anyone named Leroy in the first place."

She giggled. "We got a free drink, didn't we? I think he was flattered that I noticed him. Not too many women would come up and do that."

"Trust me, Cher Bear, I think you're wrong. It's a different world than when we were in college."

We continued our conversation with our favorite topic being men. We decided that we couldn't live with them and couldn't live without them. As Cher and I finally parted ways, I told her that I was going to the chamber of commerce meeting in the morning and invited her to join me.

"Carl's a member. Maybe I'll see if I can use his gallery name when I attend. I'm not sure the membership fee is worth it for me right now," Cher said thoughtfully. "I don't think I'll make the meeting tomorrow."

"Well, it's one way that I can see Grayson," I admitted.

"Good luck. I may not see you until the quilt meeting. It may be the last one, you know."

I sighed at the thought. "Okay. Go home and get busy on quilts for the new gallery."

"Sounds good."

It had been a good day, and I had a lot to be thankful for. The meeting had gone well, and Cher officially had a job with Carl. When I slipped under the covers, I received a text alert from my phone sitting on the bedside table. It was from Austen.

[Austen]
Do you really want to keep on fighting? It's going to be very expensive. Call me on my private number.

What the heck did that mean? Was he drunk and thinking of me at this hour? The text reminded me of times when he'd haughtily educate me about things being costly when he was aware that I couldn't purchase expensive things like he could. I sighed. It was too late to call my lawyer. Austen couldn't possibly ever collect on his nonsensical requests. He had to know that from his lawyer. This text was probably him just trying another approach. Once again, Austen had a way of spoiling anything good for me, like tonight. I knew Cher would still be awake, so I called her.

"What?" Cher asked with surprise in her voice. "Did you forget to tell me something?"

"Austen just sent me a text," I informed her solemnly.

"Not again!"

I read the text to her word for word.

"What's the deal, Claire? He really doesn't think you're just going to pick up the phone and call him, does he?"

"He might. He's counting on me being afraid of debt, and he knows that I'm a sensitive sort."

"Wait a minute. Does he know about your father leaving you the dream money?"

"No, and I'm so glad that I never told him. Mom advised me against it, and I'm so glad that I listened to her."

"Honestly, does he seriously think that you're still in love with him? Never mind. I can answer that one."

"Thank you."

"Well, I knew you were infatuated with him, but you never talked about him like you did about what's his face," Cher said.

"Do you mean Bill?"

"Yes! What was his last name again?"

"Bill Harmon. Yes, I was young and very much in love. It's too bad that he treated me poorly. As you'll remember, he eventually broke up with me."

"With Austen, I think you were taken with the idea of dating a doctor."

"Okay, so just ignore the text?"

"Yes, and definitely report it to your lawyer."

"Okay. I guess we'd better get some sleep."

"Good idea. Good night, Claire Bear."

"Good night, Cher Bear." I turned over and fell into a restful sleep.

Chapter 86

The next morning, I awoke feeling truly rested. I was excited about the work I had to do on the quilt show. I thought about skipping the chamber meeting, but then I'd possibly miss seeing Grayson. After some thought, I decided that I wanted to go, so I took extra time doing my hair and makeup. The meeting was to be held at Sister Bay Bowl. I'd be seeing it for the first time.

When I arrived, I could see that the bowling alley was closed, but the restaurant was teeming with activity as chamber members arrived. As I glanced around the area, I saw Grayson getting coffee, so I headed his way.

"I was hoping you'd be here," he said, greeting me with a warm smile. "I thought of you last night. Did the meeting go well?"

"Very well," I assured him.

"I'm proud of you," he said simply, indicating that we should move to occupy two open seats nearby.

Thankfully, we had a chance to visit a bit before the meeting started. While I had a difficult time following some of the business that was put before the membership, when they asked if anyone had any announcements, I stood up.

"On July 30, Cher Clapton and I are having a free outdoor quilt show in Fish Creek. It's the first art show of its kind around here. Some of you have given us permission to hang quilts on your buildings, which we appreciate. It's from nine to four, so I hope you'll take time to drive down Main Street and enjoy it."

To my surprise, everyone applauded. "I hope I didn't say too much," I whispered to Grayson after I took my seat.

"You were great. People typically don't clap for an announcement."

"I guess you're right," I said, smiling.

The meeting ended and Grayson said he needed to be on his way, but he assured me that he'd give me a call. I always felt a bit sad when Grayson and I parted because there never seemed to be enough time to visit with him, but then people started coming up to me to ask questions about the show. It was gratifying to see that they were excited about the upcoming event.

The Piggly Wiggly was close by so I stopped to get some things. I loved that store and took advantage of anything they sold that was prepared and ready to go. Today, I chose a chicken, corn, and broccoli casserole. On my way back to Fish Creek, I surveyed the shops at the bottom of the hill. At the very end was a darling Irish retail store called O'Meara's Irish House. I knew that Cher had not approached them, so I pulled into their parking lot. It looked like a place where I could spend a lot of money if I got carried away.

A young woman wearing a tag that identified her as the manager approached me. I introduced myself and told her about our show. When I finished my explanation, I asked her what an Irish shop was doing in Scandinavian country. I then shared a bit about the Stewart family history.

Her response to the show was quite positive. She agreed to participate as long as we didn't cover her sign with a quilt. In fact, she said that she owned an Irish Chain quilt that would be appropriate. I loved the idea, and she even agreed to hang it so we wouldn't have to.

"That would be wonderful," I replied. "The quilt has to be up by nine and taken down exactly at four, just like the others."

"Sure," she agreed. "I'll put it on our website, too."

"Thank you so much. We'll be dropping off flyers for you to hand out," I assured her.

"Great! It was nice to meet you, Claire."

I was so happy that I'd taken the time to stop and visit with her. It might just be my opinion, but I think the business owners had been looking for something new to promote. I arrived home, put my groceries away, and then headed straight to my quilt show folder to add my updates.

Chapter 87

The arrival of June reminded me of hot Missouri summers. In Door County, flowers are abundant everywhere. Cherry trees can be found in various stages of spring growth. It was wonderful to see some of the trees loaded to the max with vibrant red cherries. Ericka told me that June was her favorite month, and I could see why.

June is my birthday month. On June 17 of my birth year, I arrived weighing seven pounds and eight ounces, with blue eyes and a determined spirit. My blonde hair is now streaked with gray, but my determined spirit hasn't faded. I'm looking forward to celebrating my birthday in Door County.

As I showered for the day, I tried to rehearse what I was going to say at today's quilt club meeting. I wanted to appear confident, but I also wanted to be respectful to Greta. I knew that Cher would be nervous as well. The whole ordeal made my stomach hurt a little. I decided to wear black capris and a black-and-white lightweight sweater. As I was getting dressed, Cher sent a text saying that she was running late, so that meant I definitely had to be there on time.

I parked in my usual spot and saw Ginger pull up next to me. There was no sign of Cher's car.

"Good morning!" Ginger greeted me. "That really was a good quilt show meeting. I don't know how you pulled so much together in such a short period of time."

"Thanks, but there's still so much to do. I really appreciate Allen's help as well."

"Oh, he's used to doing a lot of things like that with our business. I know some good quilters, and I plan to ask for quilts from them."

"Great!" I replied. Then I said, "Ginger, I'm worried about this meeting. Greta isn't happy with me."

Ginger gave me a look that told me she didn't understand. However, there was no time to explain since we'd arrived at the meeting space.

"Good morning!" Marta said as we entered the room.

"Good morning," I responded. "Ginger just complimented us on our quilt show meeting."

"That's nice!" Marta responded. "I thought it went very well."

There stood Greta with her arms folded in front of her. That wasn't a good sign.

"Good morning, Greta," I greeted her.

"Good morning, Claire and Ginger," she replied, sounding serious.

As everyone arrived, I noticed that the usual chatter was kept at bay. We each got coffee and sat in our familiar spots. Cher slipped in last and took a seat.

"It appears that everyone is here now, so let's get started," Greta said, ready to use her gavel. "I'd like to begin by thanking Marta for filling in for me last month."

Marta smiled and nodded.

"I hear that the demonstration on hexies was well received. After we take care of some unfinished business, I have a project that everyone might enjoy."

There was complete silence as everyone gave Greta their full attention.

Greta took a deep breath and continued, "As you may recall, our longtime tradition of having nine members needs to be discussed. That number was set a long time ago, so we'd have an uneven number of members for voting purposes. We're approached daily by quilters who'd like to join, but we've turned them away to honor our rules. We only accepted Claire Stewart's membership because Cher Clapton moved to Missouri. After some consideration, we accepted Claire at Cher's request until Cher was able to return. Cher has now returned, so as much as I'd like to make another exception, we need to keep our membership count to nine. We've certainly enjoyed having you, Claire. Is there anything you'd like to say?"

I could feel color and heat creeping up my neck and onto my cheeks. I swallowed hard, and as I stood, I saw Cher sitting in the back row with her mouth open.

"Before you respond, Claire," Olivia interrupted, "I'd like to make a motion that we continue to keep Claire as a member and increase our membership to ten."

"I second that," Ginger said quickly.

I took the opportunity to sit down while Greta looked stunned. "I see that there has been some politicking going on while I was gone," she said crisply. "Let's have the discussion then. Marta, you have your hand up. Go on."

Chapter 88

"Thank you," she said softly, looking at the floor. "I just want to say that after last month's meeting, there was some discussion about changes that the group wanted to make. Greta, I appreciate your respect for tradition. There's much to be said for that. When it pertains to the membership of Cher and Claire, we're all comfortable having both of them remain in the group. Claire has offered us a fresh perspective, and the two of them have good ideas for the quilting community in general. That's all I've got to say on the matter."

"I agree!" Frances said exuberantly. "I'm the oldest of the group, and until we did that quilt for Rachael, I didn't realize how stagnant our group had become. It's no reflection on you, Greta. You've been a good leader."

"There's just so much more we could do," Lee chimed in. "Sometimes, fresh eyes reveal what we don't want to see."

Cher and I were in a daze as we listened to the responses. I could feel my heart beating in my throat. We remained silent and watched Greta stiffen more and more with each comment.

"I think all of you have spoken your piece, and I'm obviously in the minority. As a result, I resign as your leader and as a member of this group. My time has come, and with my resignation, you'll still have the membership count as required."

"Greta, please," I said, standing up. "We won't allow you to do that. Cher and I will resign. We talked about this ahead of time. We meant no harm. You've been a member of this group for many years and have run it like a ship. We both appreciate the support that each of you have shared, but it's Cher and I who created this problem, not any one of you. The two of us have a big project ahead with the quilt show, so our time is best spent there."

"Claire's right," Cher agreed. "This group would not be the same without you, Greta. You've put your heart and soul into it, and we have no intention of causing problems."

Greta was shocked at our responses as she stood there in silence. With that, Cher and I quietly left the room, knowing we were doing the right thing. The other members appeared dumbstruck. As we exited, I'm certain that you could've heard an appliqué pin drop. When we got outside the building, we looked at each other and smiled.

"Why do I feel happy?" Cher asked with a smile.

"For the same reason I feel relieved that this is over. I'd feel terrible if Greta left that group. It's what she lives for."

"That's the truth," Cher agreed.

"I think we did the right thing. The others will respect us for that. We're the newest members, and what do we know?"

We giggled and shrugged. It was disappointing to leave the group, but the quilt show was calling us now, and there was much to accomplish in a short amount of time. Cher must've been thinking similar thoughts because she turned to me wearing a solemn expression.

"We have a lot of work to do," she said in a serious tone. "I hope the members who are helping with the show won't back out after this."

"It's not likely, but so be it if they do. I have to get the flyer ready and to the printer today."

"I have more visits to make," she said. Then she drew in a deep breath and said, "Boy, I'd love to be a fly on the wall in that room right now."

I nodded in agreement, still feeling tense from the exchange we'd experienced. At that, we went our separate ways. I knew that we'd run over the events of the morning again and again in our minds.

When I got back to the cabin, it was time for lunch. I felt a sense of relief as I tried to find something to eat after my stomach had been feeling tense all morning. I fixed a quick salad and added some tuna. Dutifully, I sat down at the kitchen table and worked to construct an idea for the flyer. I wanted it to show a quilt or quilts hanging from buildings so people would get the idea. After a while, I encountered no real success. I knew I needed help, so I called Carl to get his advice.

"Oh, sure," Carl responded when I told him what I needed. "Try the 2forU Design & Gallery. I've used them before. They're on Bluff Lane, off Highway 42."

"Great! Thanks, Carl."

Chapter 89

My chat with the gallery went very well. They said they'd come up with a few ideas and send them to me for approval. After I hung up, I also called the newspaper to get some advertising rates. I couldn't expect Ginger to do everything. The marketing portion of this project was a huge responsibility. I hoped that Ginger could contact quilt groups and visit with Carol at the Barndoor Quilt Shop in Sturgeon Bay. As I thought about Ginger, I heaved a big sigh. Ginger is Greta's niece, and I hope that Cher and I didn't create a rift in their family because of the quilt club situation. My thoughts were interrupted by a call from Rachael.

"I can't believe that you did what you did! How could you give in—just like that?"

"It's okay, Rachael. It really is. Cher and I no longer fit in, and you know it. Besides, we have our hands full with the quilt show."

"If you ask me, you should've let Greta leave when she offered," Rachael retorted.

"I appreciate your support, but it's for the best," I said, hoping to ease her distress. "What else is new?"

"Harry has a place over on Washington Island, as you know. You haven't been there, and I know you'd love the lavender fields. They're in bloom now, and I'd like you to go with us to visit the island. If you're going to live in Door County, you have to experience it."

"Oh, I'll bet it's beautiful! I really want to go, but getting on that ferry is scary to me. I'm afraid that my vertigo will kick in. Anything unstable and wavy like that can set it off and make me really sick."

"Oh, I didn't realize that. Can you take something before getting on the ferry like people do before they get on an airplane?" she suggested.

"I do take meclizine when I feel it coming on. It worked the last time I flew to Missouri, but it was a smooth flight, not a bumpy boat."

"Please just give it a try. If the wind and waves kick up, we won't go. You sure don't want to visit in the wintertime, though."

"When are you going?"

"Friday. That's the plan."

"Well, I have no plans, so let me think about it," I agreed, feeling thankful that they thought to invite me.

"We'll pick you up. You'll love it!"

"How's Harry?" I asked.

"The poor guy had to help me big time yesterday. I lost one of my baby goats. It was so sad."

"Oh, my goodness!" I exclaimed. "I'm so sorry to hear that. How many goats do you have now?"

"Six, and they all have names."

"I'm sure that you have each of them spoiled rotten," I said. "Well, I'll get back to you, okay?"

"Sure. Really think about it, Claire. I know you'd enjoy seeing the island."

When I hung up, I knew I couldn't say no to Rachael's invitation. Visiting the island was on my bucket list, and I knew it'd be more fun to go with friends.

By early evening, I was ready for a meal. I thought of the White Gull Inn. If I left right now, I'd still be able to catch Brenda's shift. I grabbed a light jacket and walked briskly to the restaurant. When I arrived, only a few people were dining since it was not yet the dinner hour. I saw Brenda from a distance. She was busy cleaning off a table, so I walked over to say hello. When she saw me, she gave me a weak smile and returned to her task. Confused, I asked, "I haven't seen you in a while. Are you okay?"

She nodded. "I'm here," she responded, sounding aloof. "Do you have a table?"

"No, I just got here. Where should I sit? Can we chat for a bit?" I asked.

"This is fine," she said, indicating that I should sit at the table she'd just wiped off. "I'll get you a menu."

"Thanks," I replied. I watched her return to the hostess station to get a menu. She wasn't acting like herself at all, and I didn't know why. Perhaps I shouldn't have come. When she brought the menu and a glass of water, she placed both in front of me and walked away, moving on to check on customers at a nearby table. I glanced at the menu and was pleased to see that the whitefish chowder was the daily special. While I waited for Brenda to return, I checked my phone.

"So, it's probably the whitefish chowder, correct?" she stated when she returned. "I'll bring it out shortly."

At that, she turned around and was gone! What was wrong with her?

Chapter 90

Five minutes later, she brought me the chowder, some bread, and a glass of iced tea. She then looked around. It was almost as if she thought someone could be watching her. I decided to break the silence. "Brenda, I've been anxious to talk to you about how the plans are coming along for the quilt show."

"I've heard all about it," she said curtly. "Congratulations."

Her tone was flat and bordering on sarcastic. "What's going on with you?" I asked as gently as I could.

"Not a thing!" she said, shaking her head.

"What's changed, Brenda? Did I do something to offend you?"

She rolled her eyes and asked sharply, "You really don't know, do you?"

"No, I don't," I assured her. "Please tell me."

"I heard about Pete offering you a ride home," she began. "I heard it directly from him, as a matter of fact."

"I hope he told you that I refused his offer," I said, hoping to clarify what must be a misunderstanding.

"In a roundabout way, of course," she admitted. "I know it's not your fault, but you must have encouraged him in some way."

"Brenda, you'd just introduced me to him! I saw the glimmer in your eyes. He's a friend of yours, so I wanted to be nice. Let me be clear: I have no interest in him whatsoever. I happen to be involved with Grayson Wills. You know that." I purposely kept my tone quiet and even, hoping to defuse the conflict. She looked away, and I saw her eyes fill with tears.

"I'm sorry," she said quietly. "Enough said. I need to get back to work."

When she didn't immediately walk away, I reached out and gently touched her hand. "I'm so sorry that he hurt you," I told her. "I don't know him at all, but in my opinion, you deserve someone better."

"I'll call you," she replied. "I appreciate that you came in."

"I'll be glad to have you call me. I consider you a great friend."

"Thanks, Claire," she said as she walked away. I studied what was left in my bowl and realized that I didn't have much of an appetite anymore. I did manage to finish and quickly went on my way. When I got home, I called Cher to tell her about my encounter with Brenda.

"Why do I feel as if you're back in high school?" she joked after I relayed my restaurant experience to her.

"Well, it's very real to her. She's so sensitive. I hope she does give me a call."

"I hope she does, too," Cher agreed. "Hey, I want to switch to a happier subject. You're going to have a birthday next week!"

"Don't remind me."

"How about a party of some kind?" Cher offered happily.

"No, and I really mean no. I hate drawing attention to myself."

"We've got to do something! We've missed a lot of birthdays while living apart."

"You're right," I agreed. "I'd really like it if just the two of us did something."

"Well, I'm not a cook, but I can treat you to dinner," she offered. "Now, if Grayson calls and wants to take you out, we can do it another time."

"I don't want him to know, so let's just meet up and have a birthday drink and a hamburger at the Bayside."

"Actually, that sounds great. Maybe I can talk you into one of those Bayside Coffees that they set on fire."

I chuckled. "They look so dangerous. I don't know about all of that!"

"Well, you know how we are when we get together," she reminded me.

I smiled, knowing that the birthday plan would mean we'd enjoy the evening, and it'd be filled with lots of laughter. "Rachael and Harry want to take me to Washington Island. I want to go, but I'm scared silly about having my vertigo act up."

"Oh, I think you can handle it. Just stare at one spot, and don't look out on the water. However, if it's crazy weather, tell them you'll wait for them in the tourist center there by the dock."

"That's a good idea. Okay, I'll plan to go. Harry supposedly has a little cottage on Schoolhouse Beach."

"Nice! I wonder what that's all about."

"I guess I'll find out."

By the time I hung up, Cher had, as usual, put me in a good mood. I'd not only made the decision about going to Washington Island, but I also had a date for my birthday!

Chapter 91

Harry and Rachael wanted to leave early so we could catch the first ferry over to Washington Island. As I waited for them to arrive, I decided to find out some information about the island. I read that it was the largest island of the county and that the ferry ride would last about thirty minutes. Surely I could endure a trip that short! The island is home to unique businesses, eateries, museums, festivals, and a theater. Cher had told me earlier that she loved the bookshop there called Fair Isle Books & Gifts. If the opportunity presented itself, I'd like to spend some time there. I'd already heard about the beautiful beaches, parks, and lavender farm.

Harry beeped his horn when they pulled up in his Hummer. I blew Puff a kiss, grabbed a jacket, and flew out the door so they didn't have to wait very long. Rachael revealed that the game plan was to get on the ferry at Gills Rock, which was the last village on Highway 42. I'd been there to turn around and had watched vehicles get on the ferry.

"Guys, if the water isn't calm, I might not get on the ferry," I cautioned.

"You're in good hands," Harry assured me. "We won't make you do anything you aren't comfortable with. My place is nothing fancy, but my son and I call it our man cave. We like to go there and fish when we can."

"He's had this property forever, Claire," Rachael bragged. "I'll bet it's worth a pretty penny today."

We arrived at the deck and Harry paid for us to drive onto the ferry. I could tell that Rachael was keeping a watchful eye on me. I surveyed the water and said, "Okay, I'm game. I don't want to spoil this for anyone, and it looks pretty calm out there."

As we began crossing, I stayed in the vehicle while Rachael and Harry got out to enjoy a better view. When I realized that there was no turning back, I almost panicked. I'd taken a pill, so I told myself to sit still and concentrate. I made sure to keep my eyes off the water. At first, Rachael kept checking on me, and I finally started to relax.

"We're here!" Rachael announced happily. "See? That wasn't so bad."

I took a deep breath as Harry slid back into the Hummer and prepared to drive us off the ferry.

"Good job, Ms. Stewart," Harry said, smiling. "My place is on Schoolhouse Beach, right off the main road. When we get there, I just need to check it out and make sure no one has been messing with anything. While I do that, you ladies can relax and have a cold beverage."

"That sounds good!" I said. I was prepared to enjoy the remainder of the day trip now that the ferry ride was over. I listened to the chatter between Rachael and Harry as they pointed out places of interest that we passed along the way. Harry was right. When we arrived at the cabin, it was like something from the movies. Harry walked around the cottage to check things out while we waited for him to unlock the door.

"This place is so hidden, it's a wonder it survives," Rachael murmured. "Harry will know if anyone's been around. Do you think Grayson would enjoy a little place like this?"

"No," I responded. "I've never heard him talk about going fishing. He told me that his wife had died, but did you know that she lost her life in a boating accident?"

"It's been such a long time," Rachael replied. "I know that it was very difficult. Has he ever shared any details? That must still be so hard for him."

"I'm surprised he even shared that piece of information. He said he rarely goes out. I'm sure with his business, he's reminded of that incident every day."

"You're probably right about that," Rachael agreed. "Oh, here's Harry."

"Come into my palace," Harry teased as he opened the door with one hand and waved a spiderweb out of his face with the other.

Once inside, I stood in one place and glanced around, taking in the makeshift decor while Cher got us sodas out of the refrigerator. Even though I knew Harry was well off, it sure didn't show in this primitive little cottage.

"I said it was nothing fancy, but I sure do have good memories in this place," Harry shared. "I've got a nice fishing boat outside, and sometimes, I just get in it and leave all the stress behind."

"That's great," I said, smiling. "I think the place suits you, Harry."

"Well, if we're going to tour the island and see the lavender field, we need to get going, Harry," Rachael said, glancing at her watch.

Harry sprang into action at Rachael's suggestion. We crawled into his vehicle and the adventure of Washington Island began!

Chapter 92

Harry continued to describe various places as we drove along. I was trying to picture them in the winter when the weather was brutal. I saw the bookstore and would have loved to stop, but Harry was in charge, which was fine with me. I was surprised at how much of the island was wooded and was impressed with the many walking and biking paths. When we arrived at the Fragrant Isle Lavender Farm & Shop, I thought I'd arrived in heaven. The fragrance was indescribable, and I couldn't wait to take photos of some of the twenty thousand plants they bragged about. It was a self-guided tour and Rachael suggested that we gather bunches of lavender to take home. She told me it was the largest lavender farm in the United States. I couldn't wait to visit the gift shop.

I must have posed a hundred different ways as Rachael took photographs. I also took some of Rachael and Harry. The way they stood next to one another made it clear that they'd made peace with being a couple. It did my heart good to see them so happy.

Just as I suspected, the gift shop was delightful. It offered a wide array of soaps, lotions, and edibles made from

ANN HAZELWOOD

lavender plants. We helped ourselves to some lavender tea. The visit was magical, and I was so glad that these friends had invited me to share the day with them.

Much too quickly, it was time to head back to the ferry. Rachael mentioned that next time, she'd like to take a Cherry Train tour, which told more about the island's history and stopped in several places like the historic Stavkirke church and Schoolhouse Beach. We approached the ferry again and the return trip was more enjoyable since I knew what to expect. It was six that evening when they dropped me off at the cabin. "Thank you so much for inviting me to go with you today," I gushed. "I enjoyed it so much."

"If you get really brave, I'll take you out on that fishing boat," Harry teased.

"No, thanks, Harry," I replied, laughing. "I'll leave that for you and your son to enjoy."

I hugged them and gathered my purchases. Being with Harry and Rachael all day was like being with a married couple. They teased each other playfully, and I could see the fondness they had for one another.

Puff was the first to examine the bags I dropped on the couch. She seemed to be attracted to the scent, so after I emptied one of the bags, I gave it to her to play with. I quickly put some things in my bathroom to remind me of the lavender fields.

I munched on raw veggies and dip for dinner. I could barely find room on the kitchen table to eat since it also served as my office for the quilt show. Between bites, I wondered what Grayson was doing. Why didn't he want to see me more often? Did he think I'd want a commitment if we spent more time together? I wondered how he might feel about a woman calling him. A telephone call from Mom jerked me out of my pity party.

"How did it go on the ferry ride to Washington Island? I've been thinking about you," she began.

"I did fine with my little pill. I can't say that I enjoyed the ferry, but at least I didn't get sick."

"Good. I mailed your birthday present today. It's not much, but I wanted you to keep an eye out for it since you have to go to the post office."

"Mom, that wasn't necessary. I wish Cher hadn't remembered, but after some discussion, we decided to meet up for a hamburger like we used to do."

"That's nice. I wish I could be there. I just talked to Michael and he said he remembered to send you a card. How about that?"

"It says a lot that he remembered! Did he have anything new to say?"

"Not really. He hates when I ask him if he's seeing anyone. He assures me that he has no female friends at the moment. I sure would have liked to have had some grandchildren."

"Mom, you know that both he and I are too old to have children now unless we marry someone with a ready-made family."

She chuckled. "I know. I know. I'd settle for that!"

Chapter 93

"How are the show plans coming along?" she asked.

"Very well. I'll check in on the committees tomorrow, and the flyers should be ready soon, so we're getting there. Did you decide which quilts I can have to show?"

"Yes, I did. I hope you approve. Will Carole and Linda have room for them?"

"I'm sure that Carole's SUV is quite adequate."

"How's Grayson?" she inquired, turning her focus to my dating life.

"I really can't say. It's been a while since I've seen him," I admitted.

"Just remember that he's a busy dad as well as a business owner," she advised.

"That's what I keep telling myself."

"Well, honey, I'll call you back on your birthday. Let me know when you get your gift."

When we hung up, I realized that I missed her very much. Maybe it was the talk about birthdays that made me homesick for her. At any rate, Cher and I would have a great time together at the Bayside on my birthday.

The next day, after Puff and I had our breakfast, I started making phone calls to get updates on the show. I made notes next to each response. I was really pleased with Ginger's report.

"Claire, I need those flyers. Everyone is asking for them. Allen just put it on our website. The newspaper said they'd write a feature story about it since it's a new event. They'll probably call you. I haven't heard back from any of the other newspapers yet. I told them that we may have a Door County quilt contest."

"Not this year, I'm afraid. This show is being put together very quickly. If we were having a contest, the quilters wouldn't have time to make anything. On the flyer, I just put that there would be special exhibits on the lawn of the Alexander Noble House." We spent a bit more time going over some details until I was assured that things were moving along in a positive direction. Then, Ginger changed the subject.

"Now, on to something else that's been on my mind," she began. "The quilt club members are in a dither about what to do about next month's club meeting. What happened at that meeting was appalling. There's talk of everyone boycotting the next meeting."

I was glad that we were on the phone so she couldn't see my horrified expression. "Oh, please don't do that," I pleaded. "Greta will just quit if that happens, and the club means the world to her. Besides, Cher and I have our hands full with this show. Perhaps time will help the situation."

"She'll just come back more powerful than ever since she succeeded in getting you out," Ginger responded.

"Well, maybe so. I just hope she doesn't talk any of the members out of helping us with the show. I worry about Marta being strong enough to handle her. Marta is a godsend to this show."

"You just keep moving forward, Claire. The show will be wonderful. Allen said he may have another guy who can help out."

"That's great. I think we'll have the hanging labor covered, but we can always use more help."

"Just keep me posted on the quilts you have committed," she requested.

"I don't have an exact number yet from Kathy Luther. She's double-checking with her guild."

"Thanks so much for all you're doing," Ginger said.

"It's a win-win for everyone involved. I'm certain of that," I replied.

"I hope so!"

The rest of the day, I remained focused on the show details. Cher texted me every now and then to report on where she'd been as she visited more businesses. Hopefully, the part of getting commitments from business owners would be finished soon. By eight that evening, I was mentally drained. My mind drifted to Grayson once again. Should I call him? The more I considered the idea, the more I convinced myself that he could take my mind off things, so quite out of the blue, I gave him a call.

"Grayson here," he answered brusquely. "Claire?"

"Yes, it's me," I said, now worried that I had interrupted him. "I'm winding down from a busy day and wondered how you were doing." When there was silence from him, I nervously filled it by saying, "I just thought I'd call and say hello."

"I'm feeling kind of the same way," he said slowly. "I'm sorry that I haven't called. I've been pretty frustrated with Kelly recently."

"Really? How so?" I inquired.

"She's been a different person lately and seems determined to make my life miserable," he confided.

"You mean she's acting like a teenager?" I replied, trying to lighten the conversation.

"I guess, if that's what it is." He went silent again.

"She's at an age where she's trying to be independent," I said softly and slowly.

"I think she's being disrespectful about nearly everything, and she doesn't want to talk about it. I've never seen her like this before!" he shot back.

"I'd guess she's learning to deal with hormones. They can cause her to do and say crazy things."

"That's what the women at work told me. She embarrassed me in the office this week, so she's been grounded. That doesn't even seem to bother her," he said, clearly exasperated.

"I'll bet she still has her phone, right?"

"Yes, I didn't have the heart to take that away. I guess I'm a failure."

"Grayson, you're a wonderful father. Daughters and fathers have a special relationship, so it has to be hard to discipline her. I know that it was hard for my dad."

"It's nice to know that you understand," he said. Then he added, "I just don't think that right now is a good time to see you until Kelly and I get this worked out."

Chapter 94

"Has she expressed an opinion about you seeing me?" I asked, curious to know how I had come across to Kelly.

"In a roundabout way, but I know she didn't mean it, like so many things that she blurts out lately," he confessed.

I drew in a sharp breath, surprised by his answer. "I see," I said, trying to keep the disappointment from my voice. "Whatever you think is best."

"I appreciate that. How long do these mood swings last?"

I chuckled. "I'm not sure. Everyone's different, so just be patient."

"I didn't mean to dump all of this gloom and doom on you."

"That's okay. What are friends for?" I asked.

"I'll give you a call. Thanks for understanding," he said.

"Absolutely! Good luck," I replied as I hung up. My heart was broken. I shouldn't have called. I wanted to be able to consider what Grayson was going through, but now my feelings were hurt. Was he always going to put Kelly first? Of course! That was a good wake-up call. I needed to keep my feelings at a bay where Grayson was concerned. I turned out the lights and noticed that Puff was already asleep. How lucky she was.

Not able to sleep, I reviewed all those intimate moments I'd shared with Grayson. Those led me to believe that he had real feelings for me. I kept imagining that at some point, we'd certainly share more wonderful moments as we grew closer. I wondered now if he'd ever had the same thoughts about me since he still loved his wife so much.

After I'd worn myself out thinking about it, I decided to back off completely from him. He might not even want to help with the show. I determined to stay away from the Blue Horse and possibly even from chamber meetings. I tossed and turned and prayed that God would help Grayson with Kelly. I also asked Him to help me use good judgment with Grayson in the future.

With little sleep, I got up early so I could stay busy and productive. While I was busy working, it suddenly dawned on me that it was my birthday! Happy birthday to me! No one even knew except Cher and my mom, so that was good. I was really looking forward to getting together with Cher tonight so I could tell her the latest. She always understood and gave me good advice. I received a text alert and knew that it was Mom.

[Michael]
**Happy birthday, sis! I hope that my card arrived.
From your favorite brother. With love, Michael**

I couldn't believe it! His text put a huge smile on my face. This wasn't like him. I texted back.

[Claire]
Thanks so much! Love you, too!

Well, this would have to do for making my day, I told myself. However, not long after, I received a call from Mom, who wished me a happy birthday. It was nice to chat with her again. After I hung up, Puff wanted my attention, so I stroked her back. It wasn't long before I received another text. To my surprise, it was from Austen.

[Austen]
Too bad you gave up those birthday memories we shared. I guess this makes you another year older.

I reread his text over and over and couldn't figure out his point. Was he trying to be funny? He knew that I was sensitive about getting older. That must be it. He always gave me generous birthday gifts, but I always felt that he used them as a means to impress our friends. Why did he contact me at all? I had no intention of responding.

The day seemed especially long and quiet. I saw Cotsy out working in her yard, but I wasn't in the mood to visit. I poured another cup of coffee and walked over to my easel. I thought about starting a painting, but I couldn't drum up any motivation. I also wasn't ready to open my quilt show folder and make phone calls. I needed something physical to keep me occupied, so I got out the vacuum and started cleaning. My mind went back to times when Austen was out of town. I'd think about crazy things and start cleaning. By late afternoon, I felt better. It was finally time to think about my big night out. As far as what to wear, it was definitely a jeans night, but which top should I choose?

I'd just finished putting on my makeup when the phone rang. It was Matt Fairmore, my lawyer. "Mr. Fairmore, what's going on?" I asked.

"I hope you're sitting down. I have some good news for you today," he replied.

I remained silent and waited for him to speak.

"Dr. Page has dropped all the charges against you."

"Seriously?" I asked.

"As I told you, no judge was likely to hear his case. He just wanted to harass you, so he really had no choice but to eventually drop it. By doing it like this, he still had control and got to do things his way."

"Yes, that's just like him! I actually got a strange text from him this morning because it's my birthday."

"Well, happy birthday! This is a nice birthday present, I guess."

Chapter 95

I hung up feeling tremendous relief. Even though I knew Austen had no case, he was always full of surprises. I took time to thank the Almighty for a good birthday present. Cher said she'd meet me at six, so when I walked into the Bayside, she was already there. She gave me a wave.

"Happy birthday, Claire Bear!" she greeted me. Standing up, she gave me a warm hug.

"Thank you! Why are you sitting back here in the corner where it's kind of dark?"

"Oh, we can move. Where do you want to sit?"

"Let's move over there, closer to the bar." Cher gathered her things, and we took the table that I'd indicated.

"How has your day been so far?"

"Interesting!"

She gave me a questioning look. After we ordered drinks, I told her about the text from Austen and the happy news I'd received from my attorney. Then I told her about the disappointing result I'd gotten when I called Grayson. I told her that calling him had been a big mistake.

"You should've called me first, like we used to do," Cher joked. "I could've stopped you! Never, never call a man on a whim. It's an old-school tip that still works today."

I nodded in agreement. "Well, I did it, and now I know why he's been keeping his distance. Why did I think he cared so much for me?"

"Oh, for heaven's sake! He didn't leave you for another woman! He just has his hands full right now," Cher countered.

I could always count on Cher to tell me the truth, whether it hurt or not. "You're right. Okay, let's place our order. I'm starved. I cleaned the whole cabin today trying to keep my mind off Austen and Grayson."

Cher laughed because she knew my tendency to clean when I felt stressed. Then she said, "Well, look who just walked in—Brenda and Ericka!"

I turned to look. They headed our way like they were on a mission.

"Happy birthday!" Ericka said, leaning down to give me a hug.

"Happy birthday!" Brenda exclaimed, giving me a friendly smile.

"How did you guys know?" I said, looking at Cher.

"Look! Rachael just walked in!" Cher announced with exaggerated surprise.

"Happy birthday, girlfriend," Rachael called as she, too, headed our way.

"Oh, my goodness," I said, feeling embarrassed. "I didn't want a party. This isn't fair, Cher Bear." I said the words in a lighthearted tone, but I was beginning to feel a little overwhelmed.

"Hey," Allen and Ginger called, coming our way. "We heard there was a party going on!"

"Oh, well, there does seem to be one gearing up!" I responded, giving Cher an uncertain look. "It's good to see you."

"I wasn't going to let my wife go out and have all the fun without me," Allen teased.

"I hope you don't mind being the only guy," I teased back.

"I don't think I am, because Carl just came in the door," Allen said, giving me a wink.

"Good heavens!" I said in disbelief.

"George said he'd try to stop by," Ericka added.

I was overwhelmed as I watched Allen and Carl rearrange our tables and chairs to accommodate everyone.

"Harry wanted to come too, Claire, but he had another commitment," Rachael informed me. "He said to tell the bartender that he'd buy a round of drinks on his house charge."

Carl then came up to hug me. He said he felt honored to be invited by Cher. I asked if he knew everyone, and he seemed to act as if he did.

"Hi, my name is Kevin," the server said. "If anyone wants to order, I'm ready, birthday girl. I understand that someone has ordered the Bayside burger followed by the Bayside Coffee."

"Cher, what did you do?" I asked in disbelief. I had an uneasy feeling that she had more surprises up her sleeve.

"Kevin, that order is correct," Cher verified. "Okay, Claire Bear, you'd better feast your eyes on who just walked in."

There was Grayson, looking more handsome than ever in jeans and a black leather jacket. He could tell that I was surprised to see him.

"Happy birthday, Claire!" he said as he gave me a kiss on the cheek.

"Grayson, I'm sorry if you felt you had to do this," I stuttered. I felt acutely uncomfortable now.

Grayson just laughed and turned to greet everyone else. It was obvious that the party had started. Cher moved out of her seat, which was next to me, and gave it to Grayson. I felt I was on another planet right now. Now my only worry was that Bayside Coffee!

Chapter 96

In no time, the laughter and chatter became louder and louder. George showed up and chose to kiss me on the lips, which came as one more surprise added to the evening. Thank goodness Grayson was looking the other way.

"Please don't tell me that you invited the quilt group, too," I nearly hissed at Cher, who seemed to take quite a bit of joy in my discomfort.

"No, no, I wasn't that organized," she teased. Then she said quietly so only the two of us could hear, "It was a last-minute thought. Just enjoy! Hey, I got Grayson here, so what more do you want? I told them no gifts, or you'd really be upset with me! I have a little something for you, but I'll give you that later."

"Cher Bear, you're something!" I said, shaking my head. Everyone then began teasing me about singing "Happy Birthday." I won my case and was able to stifle that idea. When the Bayside Coffee showed up, others were nice enough to share the potent drink.

Later, as some started to leave, Grayson offered to walk me to my car. I smiled and then began saying goodbye to the rest of the crew that I knew would stay there until quite late.

Grayson and I stepped outside, where the air was clear and where I could hear without him having to shout in my ear over the noise of the bar.

"Last night, it took all I had to keep from saying that I'd see you at the Bayside," Grayson admitted.

"I feel bad that Cher made you leave Kelly to make an appearance for me," I blurted out.

"She said to tell you happy birthday, by the way," he said gently.

"She did?"

He nodded. "She can be a devil at times, but she has a good heart. Cher was insistent on her no-gifts policy, so I don't have one for you. I'll make it up to you somehow."

"Your gift was showing up tonight. Please consider Kelly first. Hopefully, things will get better." From the glow of the streetlight, I could see that he was sad and tired. While I wanted to protect my own feelings, my heart went out to him. He just wanted to be the best dad to Kelly, and they had definitely hit a snag recently. Grayson turned to look at me.

"Well, I'm glad that I could share this party with you. I'll tell you good night then," he said as he pulled me close, giving me a light kiss on the lips.

"Do you want to come back to the cabin?" The words just tumbled out before I could think clearly.

He paused. "Claire, I get mixed signals from you, so let me just give you a big birthday hug and we'll stay in touch."

Ouch, that hurt! What exactly did he mean? Mixed signals? My thoughts began to spin, and I could feel my heart rate quicken. One thing I knew for certain was that I didn't want to have a serious discussion in the Bayside parking lot. "I hope so," I said quietly. "Good night." My beloved Grayson could be leaving for keeps tonight. How could he say that I was giving him mixed signals? He was the one sending mixed signals! I slipped into the driver's seat of my car and pulled away, afraid to look back.

When I got inside the cabin, I began to resent Cher's attempt to make my birthday special by asking others to join us. It wasn't what we had planned. However, when I thought more about it, I suppose it was fun—until Grayson walked me to the car! I crawled into bed and started going over every word that Grayson had said. At least he was nice enough to respond to Cher's invitation. I had to face the reality that I'd always be number two in Grayson's life if we remained a couple. Thankfully, I fell into a deep sleep, but the next thing I knew, my phone on the bedside table was ringing.

"You're still in bed?" Cher joked after I answered with a raspy morning voice. "It's ten o'clock! You never sleep this late!" Then she lowered her voice to a whisper and said, "Hey, if Grayson is still there, don't say a word. I'll hang up."

"I can't believe I slept this late!" I exclaimed. "No, Grayson isn't here, and it doesn't look as if he will be in the future."

"What in the world do you mean by that?"

"I'll explain more later, but our conversation didn't go all that well last night when he walked me to the car. It was an awkward goodbye. I think he just showed up to be nice," I explained. "Cher, that was such a fun evening, and I can't thank you enough for your kind gesture."

"Everyone had a wonderful time, including Grayson, by the way," Cher said. "I thought that it was sweet of him to walk you to the car."

"That's because he's a gentleman," I explained.

"Claire Bear, you're a little crazy about all of this. I'm so sorry things turned out that way."

"I'll be okay," I assured her. "I just need to concentrate on the show. Grayson wished me good luck with it, so it sounded like he wouldn't see me until then."

Chapter 97

"I still say you have this all wrong, but you're correct—we have a show meeting tonight, and we need to get prepared," Cher declared.

"With the show, our big concern is weather, but it's too soon to get a reliable forecast," I said.

"I have a quilt count from Linda. They're so excited."

"I hope they can stay long enough for me to visit with them," I said wistfully.

"They want a pretty good tour of the peninsula, so I don't think they'll rush home," Cher informed me.

"Did you remember that tomorrow is the quilt club's first meeting without us? Wouldn't you like to sit there as quiet as a mouse to witness it?" I asked.

"Oh, I think there will be plenty of little mice there to inform us," Cher replied, giggling.

"Okay, I've got to get going. I need to call Marta to make sure she'll open up the church early enough."

After my conversation with Cher, I brushed away any thoughts of Austen or Grayson. I fixed myself some hot tea and sat at the kitchen table to call Marta. I was happy when she picked up the phone.

"I was hoping to hear from you, Claire," she said quickly. "Tonight, I thought I'd show everyone the process I'll be using to log quilts in and out. They'll need to know what to do with the quilt bag."

"Good idea," I agreed. "I'll remind Cher to bring photos of each building so we can show an example."

"Claire, do you remember Billy, my grandson? He said he'd be happy to help if you need him."

"Yes, I do remember him. That's wonderful! Bring him with you to the meeting tonight. He can help distribute the flyers that I'm bringing."

"Everyone needs to take some tonight to get the word out," Marta said.

"Thanks so much for all your help, Marta," I said sincerely.

"No problem," she stated simply. "Well, the garden and canning are calling. Because of all that I have to do with the harvest, it'll be a relief when the quilt show is over!"

The next thing I did was to text Cher an update. She texted right back and asked if she could give me my birthday present after the meeting. We agreed to go out for pizza at Husby's after the meeting.

I had already accumulated a stack of bills related to the quilt show. Rachael had paid for her sponsorship. Hopefully Carl and a few others like Grayson would bring their checks tonight so I could get the bills paid. My mind began to wander. Maybe Grayson would change his mind about being a sponsor after last night's conversation. One thing was certain—I wasn't going to call him!

I took a break around two in the afternoon, still hoping that the flyers would arrive soon. I went outdoors to water the plants. There was something satisfying about watering plants. It was too bad that I wasn't doing more cooking because my herbs were healthy and beautiful. As I assessed my little place, I was reminded that I'd soon have to decide whether to buy the cabin. Cher was happy with her condo, so I knew she wouldn't want the cabin for herself any longer. I wasn't tempted to go elsewhere, but more space would be divine. However, I had to admit that I was getting spoiled living in the middle of Fish Creek. Tom, who had been working next door, spotted me. He made a waving motion to get my attention.

"I got your email about the meeting tonight, but I'm not able to be there," he informed me.

"That's okay," I replied.

"The day of the show might not work out either. There's a possibility that I have to go to my grandmother's place in Green Bay," he explained.

"Well, if you're not there, we'll have to make it happen without you," I teased. "Thanks for offering. I wish you could see the show, though."

"Cotsy said she's going to take a lot of photos. She thinks it's exciting."

"That's great. I think a lot of people will enjoy it."

Tom and I had returned to our tasks at hand when I got a special delivery. It was the flyers! I broke open the package, eager to see what I had ordered. There it was in print. It was really going to happen! "Door-to-Door Quilts" was written beautifully across the top of the page. I proofed it carefully and everything seemed to be in order. I was bursting with pride. I could only hope that my helpers would feel the same.

Chapter 98

The aroma of coffee and peanut butter cookies filled the meeting room as Cher and I arrived. "Marta, you're spoiling us," I teased as I gave her a hug. "It looks like we're going to have a good turnout."

"I think so," she agreed. "Lee called. She's running late but wants to be put on the agenda."

"Okay! I see that you brought Billy with you," I said as I gave him a smile. He seemed eager to help so I filled him in on some of the things he could do as a volunteer. It turned out that he was also the one who did most of the baking of the cookies for the meeting tonight. I could see how having a responsible young man at the quilt show could be a big asset.

I glanced around the room and then at the clock to see if it was time to start the meeting. Most of the people I expected to attend had filtered into the room and taken a seat. I tapped on my nearby glass to get everyone's attention. "Welcome, everyone!" I began. "It's good to see you again. Marta brought her grandson tonight because he's going to be helping us, so maybe we should introduce ourselves to him."

"Hi. I'm Kathy Luther. I'm the representative from a local quilt guild, and I'm pleased that we'll be showing some of the members' quilts in the show. We'll also be selling raffle tickets on the Noble House lawn."

"Thanks, Kathy," I responded. "Your group has been so helpful. Please thank them for us." The remainder of the group introduced themselves, and I then began the business portion of the meeting. "Before I call on the committee chairs, I want to let you know that Carl, the owner of Art of Door County, has agreed to be a sponsor. Carl, we're appreciative of your sponsorship because the bills are starting to come in."

"You're welcome," he replied.

"Marta, I'd like you to start tonight so you can explain the process that's in place when someone brings us a quilt to hang."

"I'd be happy to," she began. "When quilts are brought in for the show, the owner fills out a form that goes in our file. It states how many quilts are being dropped off and provides a description of each one. Cher then decides where it'll be hung. If it's going to be hung at the White Gull Inn, for example, a photo of the location is put with the quilt and attached to the bag, showing exactly where the quilt is to be hung. If it needs any additional hanging support, like clothespins, they will go in a little bag and will be attached to the quilt bag. When those who have volunteered to hang quilts come to get them that morning, they will know exactly where to go and will have a picture of where each quilt is to be hung. After the quilts are in place, the bags will come back to me until it's time to take them down. Volunteers can begin taking down quilts at four that evening, and all quilts will be brought back to me so I can check them off. At that point, the owners can take them home." She concluded with, "I'm responsible for these quilts every step of the way, so please follow the rules." She made an exaggerated nervous expression and several people giggled.

"Thanks, Marta," I said. "I don't think they could be in better hands. Ginger, how's the publicity going?"

"Well, we have beautiful flyers available now, so please take some to share with others to get the word out. Billy will make sure that everyone leaves here with some. We're expecting some interviews about the show, and we're encouraging all participating businesses to advertise on their own social media platforms. If you have any ideas or more information, please see me after the meeting."

"Thanks, Ginger," I said. "We have plenty of quilts to hang at this point. In fact, we have over a hundred! We can always use more, and I happen to know that more are coming our way." At that, everyone applauded and there was a sense of excitement in the room. I moved to the next item of business. "Carl, do we have plenty of volunteers who can help hang the quilts?"

"Yes, I think we're in good shape," he replied.

"Cher, do you want to say something about security?" I inquired.

"Yes, I'm happy for the opportunity to remind everyone how important security is," she stated. "We can't afford to have any incidents. I have some volunteers who will be responsible for watching people closely so they don't touch the quilts, even though there'll be a sign on each quilt. We could use a couple more monitors at this point." I paused and then said, "Lee, I see that you made it. Do you want to talk about the special exhibit area that's going to be on the Noble House lawn?"

"I'd be happy to," she said, standing up. "This year, we have just a few special exhibits because we got started on the show so late. The historical society will display some of their antique quilts, which will be a rare treat for us. We'll also have a nice display of Gee's Bend quilts from Olivia Williams. If you haven't heard of them, it'd be good for you to check them out. We also have a local quilt guild selling chances on their raffle quilt. Next year, we hope to have a contest for making a Door County quilt. I'll be there the entire day to watch everything, so let's hope for a pretty day."

"Great progress," I responded. "Did you notice how everyone is planning next year's show and we haven't had this one yet?" Everyone laughed and clapped.

Chapter 99

"Does anyone have any questions?" I asked.

"Yes," a male voice boomed from the back of the room. It was Grayson. "Who do I give my check to for a sponsorship?"

"That would be me, I guess," I said, blushing. "Would that be from Sails Again?"

He nodded. "It is, and I also brought a check from the Blue Horse. They asked me to bring theirs."

"Oh, that's wonderful news," I said as everyone applauded. "Let's remember to support these generous businesses. McCarthy Barn Quilts has also given a check, and we're so appreciative. If there are no more questions, we'll adjourn. Please feel free to stay and have some refreshments."

"Good meeting, Claire," Marta said, smiling.

"It's those homemade cookies, Marta," I teased.

"These cookies are mighty good," Grayson said as he approached our table. "Peanut butter cookies are my favorite."

"It's good to see you here, Grayson," I said. "Thanks for the sponsorship."

"My pleasure, plus I like making this woman smile," he said, winking at Marta as he motioned in my direction. She grinned. "How about I buy you a drink?" he said quietly, leaning toward me.

I opened my mouth to tell him I'd made plans with Cher when she joined us.

Cher was quick to chime in with, "Well, Grayson, if you don't mind being the third wheel, we are going to get a pizza at Husby's."

"That sounds great," Grayson said. "I haven't had any dinner."

I looked at them, wondering how the evening would turn out. I wanted to feel happy. After all, I'd be sharing dinner with two of my favorite people. "How did you manage a check from the Blue Horse?"

"I didn't have to twist their arm. We're both good customers," he responded. "They even mentioned that they're having a quilt hung on their place."

"I'm so grateful for their sponsorship. It means a lot," I replied. "Well, Cher and I will just meet you at Husby's if that's alright," I suggested.

"Sounds like a plan," he agreed.

"Good deal," Cher added as we left. "I have your gift in the car. So how about that, Claire? Grayson shows up and puts whipped cream on everything with two sponsorships!"

I didn't reply because I was simply speechless about it myself! When we got in the car, Cher handed me a pretty wrapped gift box. Once I had removed the paper, I took the lid off to reveal four hand-painted coasters of different Door County locations.

"Cher, did you paint these? I've never seen anything like them before."

"I did! I love working with a tiny brush. I'm pleased with them."

"Girl, these would sell in Carl's shop. I love them! You spent a lot of time on them. There's so much detail. Thank you so much!" I gave her a hug, and off to Husby's we went. Grayson was already there when we arrived and had secured a high-top table for us. After we sat down, Cher suggested that one of their sixteen-inch pizzas would be plenty for all of us. Grayson asked if we wanted a salad.

"Not for me," I stated.

Cher declined as well and announced, "I'm treating tonight since you got us those two sponsorships, Grayson."

"I can't let you do that," Grayson argued. "Besides, I owe the birthday girl something."

"Oh, your sponsorship was quite enough," I assured him.

"Your being here is a gift to Claire," Cher teased.

I kicked her under the table. "She's right," I said. "I'm glad that you could come."

At that, we put our order in and began to talk about the meeting we'd just attended. It had been filled with excitement for the upcoming event, which was gratifying to me. After a few minutes of chatter, Cher wondered aloud why we didn't see Rachael.

Chapter 100

"She's really busy with her barn quilts," I explained. "Since her lecture at The Clearing, she can hardly keep up."

"I think she's making more time for Harry," Grayson teased.

We chuckled. "What do you mean by that?" I asked with a smile.

"The looks exchanged between the two of them say it all. It may be untimely, but it's there."

"Do you agree, Claire?" Cher asked.

I paused before I spoke. "I wouldn't be surprised," I said slowly. "They both loved Charlie and have really leaned on each other through a really tough time. It'd be great if they could find love again."

Our pizza arrived and we continued to chatter, moving from one subject to the next. It was hard for me not to stare at Grayson. I still wondered about what he'd said in the parking lot of the Bayside. We finished eating and Cher made good on her promise to foot the bill.

"Cher, I'd like to take Claire home if you don't mind," Grayson asked, taking us by surprise.

"Have at it," Cher answered with a laugh. "On that note, I think I'd better get on home myself."

We said goodbye and Cher went on her way. When she was gone, Grayson looked at me with an inquisitive expression. "You don't mind, do you?" he asked with a wink.

"I'm flattered." We got on our way, and I began to feel my confidence returning regarding Grayson's feelings for me. When we arrived at the cabin, we sat in silence.

He pulled his key from the ignition, turned to me, and asked, "Aren't you going to do the polite thing and ask me in?"

Surprised, I answered, "Oh, of course. It's pretty late, so I figured that you had to be on your way."

Without another word, he drew me close and kissed me. Still holding me in his arms, he whispered, "I can't remember a time when I brought you home and didn't want to stay."

"Stay?" I asked as my voice caught in my throat.

"You're so loving, and your little cabin reflects your good taste. You've taken that space and made it feel like a home. Not everyone has that capability, and that's one of the things I love about you."

I swallowed hard and offered an awkward, "Well, thank you. Please come in." Once inside, I busied myself by pouring us something to drink while Grayson examined some of the photos on the mantel.

"It's been a while since you've mentioned Austen's name. Have things gotten any better?"

I nodded, smiling. "Yes, he finally dropped all the charges after he realized that he really didn't have a case."

"Well, perhaps he meant it as a strategy to get you back."

I paused. "That never even crossed my mind because it's not a possibility."

"I hope not because there's a lot at stake."

"Oh?" I asked, confused.

"I wouldn't like someone taking away someone I love."

I had to think for a moment about what he'd just said. "That's very sweet, and I'd feel the same way."

"I've wondered to myself if I'd ever find someone again after loving Marsha for so many years. I know she'd want me to keep on living, but I have to admit, I've made Kelly my priority. Things have just been simpler that way."

"Of course! I think what you're experiencing happens to many. They say that people who've been happily married and experienced the loss of a partner long to experience that feeling again. I don't say that to scare you, but it's human nature to want that feeling back again."

"My days are pretty busy and focused, so when I come home at night and know that Kelly is okay, I find myself thinking about you." He tenderly embraced me, making me feel wanted and loved. Something was different about him tonight. As we kissed and held one another, I felt closer to him than ever before. At the same time, I found myself holding back my desires because I wanted to be sensitive to his. As we wordlessly continued to move closer physically, we were close to being at the point of no return. "I want to stay here with you tonight," he said softly, breathlessly.

"I'd love that, but you can't," I said, trying to regain my composure.

"I can't?" he responded, looking surprised.

"No, you can't. We'll know when the time is right," I said simply. "I don't want you to have to explain where you were to your teenage daughter."

Chapter 101

He tilted his head slightly and smiled at me. "Claire Stewart, you have way too much control in this relationship. Do you realize that?" he accused with a devilish smile on his face.

I chuckled. "Well, one of us has to keep a level head! I miss feeling close to someone," I admitted. "You could very easily twist my arm and get your way."

He stood up and took my hand, drawing me into his arms. He then held me tighter than ever before. I wanted to stay there forever. "You're a cruel woman, Ms. Stewart," he teased. "I'll do whatever you say, beautiful." With that comment came another kiss and we said goodbye. I reluctantly watched him leave. I should've known from the very beginning that the handsome guy with the red scarf at the Blue Horse was going to get me in trouble. I'll never forget how he caught my eye that day when I first saw him.

Puff was already sound asleep in her favorite spot on my bed. I smiled. I didn't think that Puff would take too kindly to another person occupying her place. Once I was settled in bed myself, I replayed every word and touch that I'd received from Grayson tonight. What had caused his change of heart? There was certainly no mention of mixed messages this evening! Now, we were talking about love. It took every ounce of self-control for me to slow things down tonight. I had to remind myself that there are three parties in this relationship, and I didn't want to be the one to be eliminated.

The next morning as I was eating breakfast, my mind wandered to the quilt meeting that was now taking place without Cher and me. Would all the members come, or would some make their feelings known by staying away? Would Cher and I be missed? I sighed, feeling rather sad about the whole ordeal. I had to admit that I'd miss the group regardless of how odd it was. Greta was quite likeable when she wasn't playing the role of drill sergeant. I was sure it wouldn't be long before Cher or I would hear what happened this morning. I busied myself by filling the dishwasher, and my phone rang. It was Cher.

"Good morning! Did you forget to pick me up for the quilt meeting?" I joked.

"Funny, funny," she responded. "Can you talk?"

"Of course!"

"Are you alone?" she teased.

"Of course! I deserve a medal for it," I said with a laugh.

"Tell me more! Tell me more!"

"I think I can relax a bit regarding Grayson. He almost said the L-word last night."

"Praise the Lord! I saw it coming!"

"You did? I sure didn't. I really don't see him very much, and he's trying so hard to figure out where Marsha and Kelly fit into his relationship with me."

"I can imagine. You're going to have to be patient about that, my dear."

"I'm not really looking for marriage, and I don't want him to feel that's where this relationship has to go," I explained.

"You'll just have to be patient and see how everything develops," Cher replied.

"Good advice, Cher Bear."

"Don't forget, you're supposed to ask him if he has a friend for me!"

"I will. He certainly got to know you a bit better last night."

She chuckled.

"Hey, let me know if you hear from any of the quilt club members," I requested. "I'm curious about how things turned out."

"I will. Love you, Claire Bear."

"Love you too, Cher Bear."

By four, it seemed odd that we'd not heard from anyone, so I decided to give Rachael a call.

"Oh, girl, I didn't go. I'm sorry," Rachael answered when I inquired about the meeting. "I just have too much work to do. Besides, it won't be the same without you and Cher."

"That's so nice of you to say, Rachael. I'm just curious to know how Greta decided to handle our absence."

"Don't call Ginger because she didn't go either," Rachael advised. "She came out here to pick up some more small barn quilts to sell in her shop. They've sold very well for her."

"That's interesting. I wonder who did show up," I said. "I'm glad that you and Ginger have worked out an arrangement that benefits both of you."

"I sure wish I could set up a booth somewhere at the quilt show," Rachael lamented.

"Not this year. I have to make sure that we promote the businesses that allow quilts to be hung this year," I explained.

"Okay. I'll hold you to it for next year, though. Hey, I've got to go. Harry has to make a delivery for me, and he wants to tell me something."

"Okay. Please tell him that I said hi."

We hung up, and the thought of Harry and Rachael working together so nicely made me happy. I went back to the kitchen table to get my mind off the quilt club meeting. I also needed to give some more thought to this wonderful quilt show.

Chapter 102

Over a week went by before I heard from Grayson again. I was beginning to wonder if I'd imagined our last encounter. I was watering the flowers when I got a call from him.

"Hey!" he began. "What's my sweet woman doing today?"

I had to pause for a second. His enthusiasm was commendable, but why was it more than a week late? "I happen to be outdoors watering the plants."

"Well, I wonder if I could interest you in going to Sturgeon Bay. A while back, you said you'd like to see the red lighthouse you'd painted for a customer. Kelly has plans for the day, so how about it?"

It was a wonderful invitation and was something that I'd wanted to do in warmer weather. "I'd love to! What time?" I answered, feeling excited about this turn of events in my day.

"How about in the next hour?"

"Sure! I'll do my best to be ready." I hung up and quickly went inside to get ready for this unexpected trip. It appeared that I did cross Grayson's mind when Kelly wasn't occupying his time. For now, why not? Just as I finished getting changed, my phone rang. It was Marta.

"Yes, boss?" I teased.

"Claire, get serious for just a minute," she said, taking me aback.

"Oh! I'm sorry. Is everything okay?" She didn't answer right away.

"We had our quilt meeting. Have you heard anything about it?" she asked in a businesslike tone.

"No, I haven't heard anything. I thought of all of you and hope that all went well."

"We didn't have a quorum, so we couldn't have a meeting. I was the only one there."

"Really?"

"It was obvious that everyone is unhappy about you and Cher departing. I tried to explain other reasons to Greta, but she blames the two of you."

"No! We didn't want that to happen. We felt like we were the problem, and that it'd be better if we both left so the club could carry on."

"I tried to tell her that, but she's taking it personally," Marta explained.

"If you asked each member why they weren't there, they'd probably have a legitimate excuse. I know that Rachael was truly overwhelmed with work."

"Greta thanked me for my loyalty, but she feels that the group will probably disband."

"That's crazy! What can I do?"

"I think you've done all you can. In the end, I suspect that Greta will have a change of heart and come back next month as if the last meeting never happened," she predicted.

"I hope so. I'm so sorry that it's come to this," I said.

"So am I. It's been all her own doing, I'm afraid," Marta decided.

I saw Grayson drive up. "Don't worry, Marta. Thanks for calling to tell me," I said. After we hung up, I closed my eyes for a few moments to collect my thoughts. It certainly wasn't ever my intention to move to a new area and close down a quilt club!

Grayson greeted me with a sweet kiss on the cheek and off we went. As we drove, he said, "You look great, but you aren't smiling. Are you okay?"

I hated to start our trip with a downer, but the feelings I had turned out to be hard to shake. I told him about the phone call, and he listened very carefully.

"You know, Claire, there's still a lot I don't know about the opposite sex, so it's best that I don't comment. Giving you any advice about that would be crazy."

"Smart answer," I said, laughing at his candor. "Thank you for listening."

We arrived at the U.S. Coast Guard station in Sturgeon Bay in no time. I was expecting to be able to drive right up to the water to see the lighthouse, but we had to park in a lot and walk to the waterfront. We did, and there it was in all its glory. It was a bright lipstick-red structure encased by a vivid blue sky. I took a deep breath, wanting to take it all in. I thought of my painting and wondered if I'd captured its true beauty.

"Do you want to walk all the way out to get a closer look?"

"It's pretty far out, and that walkway looks a little narrow to me," I said, surveying the situation.

He chuckled. "That's true, and it's a bit windy. Let's just walk out a little closer. I nodded and took his hand. I stopped in my tracks when the first splash of cold water hit me. I also saw a passing boat, which caused me to turn around. The last thing I wanted was to set my vertigo off!

"Stop a minute. Let me get a photo," Grayson requested. He got the images he desired and then we turned around and began the trek back.

"It's amazing, Grayson. I'm so glad I got to see it in person," I confided. When we got back to the car, we realized that we were hungry. Grayson said he'd been craving Mexican food and suggested a popular restaurant called Old Mexico. It sounded great!

Chapter 103

The restaurant was fairly crowded when we arrived. We were happy to get seated right away. Grayson asked, "Should I offer to help Carl hang quilts?"

"Sure, if you're free," I replied, "but your sponsorship is more than enough."

"Let me just say that the two of you are amazing the way you're pulling this off."

I smiled, feeling happy to accept the compliment. "Thanks. It's a big undertaking, but it's something that will elevate fiber art of all kinds in the area. You'd mentioned that Kelly might want to volunteer. If she'd like to be a monitor and guard the quilts, I could really use her in that capacity."

"I'll ask her again just to make sure," Grayson agreed. He then proceeded to order a variety of the most requested items on the menu. The guacamole was delicious, and I honestly think I ate it on everything they brought to the table. I thoroughly enjoyed the food and the company.

On the ride back, Grayson held my hand as he drove. This was something new for us, and I wondered if being with me was comforting to him. It was a beautiful day, and I didn't want it to end. However, the daytime date did come to an end because we were both busy people, and our responsibilities called to us. Because of that, our goodbye was short and sweet.

That evening, I decided to turn in earlier than usual. However, just as I was about to head upstairs, I got a call from Olivia.

"I hope I'm not calling too late, but I wanted to tell you that I got great news from the Barndoor Quilt Shop today. They think they'll have at least twenty quilts from their employees and customers!"

"Oh, that's great! We can use them."

I'll get with Cher so she can start placing them. At the shop, Carol said there's a lot of excitement about the show. That's a great place to display those flyers."

"All good news, Olivia! Did you hear anything about the quilt meeting?"

She paused. "I didn't stay away on purpose, but I did have a terrible headache that morning. Frances said last month that we should boycott the next meeting, and frankly, I agreed. We needed to send a message."

"I feel bad. Neither Cher nor I wanted that to happen. Marta called and said that Greta feels like the club is done for."

"Well, I can't speak for the others, but it was a childish maneuver on her part last month. It didn't have to be that way."

"I agree."

"Cher is all excited about her friends arriving from Perryville," Olivia mentioned.

"Yes, Mom is sending her quilts with them."

"I can't wait to meet them."

"I can't thank you enough for all of your help," I told Olivia.

"My pleasure! I agree that we're all set without another meeting."

I hung up and crawled under the covers with a smile of contentment on my face.

Chapter 104

The next day when I arrived at the post office, I saw Ava leaving. I flagged her down to say hello. "Ava, how are you?" I quickly noticed that she looked quite sad.

"Okay, I guess. Did you hear?"

"About the club?" I asked.

"No. My husband left me," she said, tearing up.

"Ava, I'm so sorry," I said, trying not to let on that I didn't even know she was married.

"I'll be fine," she assured me. "How's the show coming?"

"Pretty well. I'm dropping off some flyers here."

"I have some in my car. I try to drop a few off wherever I go," she told me.

"Thanks, Ava. Cher and I are so grateful for everyone's help. I hope things work out better for you."

"Thanks," she replied. "As far as the club is concerned, I'm not sure I'm going back after what happened at the last meeting."

"Oh, Ava, you must. Cher and I would feel terrible if you didn't."

"We'll see. I'd better run. I'm glad I ran into you."

"Me too! Take care of yourself," I said. After I delivered the flyers, I checked my mail and picked up my birthday package from Mom. When I got back in my car, I called Cher to see if she could meet up for lunch.

"Oh, I'd better not," she replied. "I want to finish this painting for the gallery. I got a call from Carl, and he has officially rented the next space!"

"That's great news. Will he open in time for the show?"

"He's getting it painted now and asked if I could come in tomorrow to help him with some things."

"I know you're excited, but just be prepared for whatever he might ask you to do."

"I know, and the pay is pathetically low, but it'll be so cool to be in that environment," she said, clearly happy about the possibilities at the gallery.

"It will indeed," I agreed. "Don't get so involved there that you forget we have a show to put on," I warned.

"Don't I know it!" she laughed.

"Hey, I saw Ava at the post office. Did you know that her husband left her?"

"You know, I wondered if she had one," Cher said slowly, "but you sure couldn't tell by her flirtatious behavior."

"Maybe the guy at Ericka's apartment had something to do with it after all," I suggested. "She then told me that she might not go back to quilt club."

"We sure opened a can of worms, didn't we?" Cher moaned.

We hung up after covering some details about the show. I then headed to the Pig to deliver flyers and pick up some fresh vegetables and turkey. That grocery store always struck me as such a happy place as I watched neighbors visit with one another in the aisles. On the way back home, my phone rang. I glanced at it and didn't recognize the number.

"Claire, it's Kelly," a voice said shyly.

"Kelly, what a nice surprise," I replied.

"My dad said I could help at the quilt show. He mentioned that you need monitors. I'd just watch people, right?"

"That's right. You won't be the only one. You'll just stroll back and forth on your assigned block and discourage anyone who tries to touch the quilts."

"I can do that," she agreed. "Another thing. I want to bring Spot over to meet Puff sometime."

"Kelly, no one told me that you were able to keep Spot! That's great!" I exclaimed.

"Well, Dad isn't all that happy about it, and he complains about the smell," she informed me.

"Oh dear! Just keep changing that litter box! Your dad will get used to having an animal indoors. Please come over any time. I am curious to see what Puff will do."

"Where do I check in the morning of the show?" she asked.

"Do you know the Community Church on Main Street?"

"Sure!"

"Just show up there by nine and we'll have a badge for you so people will know it's your job to look out for the quilts."

"Oh—like the quilt police?"

I laughed. "Sort of, but with a big smile on your face."

She chuckled. "I'll be there."

Chapter 105

Carole and Linda arrived yesterday, so Cher said she'd spend today driving them through Door County. I told her that I'd like to take them to lunch tomorrow at the White Gull Inn and then show them the cabin. Today, I planned to meet Marta, Olivia, and Frances at the church to start assigning quilts to Cher's photos and then attaching the photos to the corresponding quilt bags. I'd gotten up early to make some brownies to take with me because everything quilters do involves food of some kind! On my way, I'd get my mail and check the newspaper to see if our article was in there. The day was warm, and I longed for an air conditioner. Now I knew why Cher spent so much time on the porch in the summertime. I could also see why she even slept there every now and then.

When I arrived at the post office, I first went to pick up a newspaper. "You have a big weekend coming up," a woman behind me said. "I can't wait to see all the quilts."

"Yes, thank you! I'm glad to see that there's no rain in the forecast."

"You can't go by that," she said, shaking her head for emphasis. "Around here, we can have a pop-up shower at any time. Are you prepared for that?"

"We are," I assured her, "if the shop owners do what they're supposed to do. We've tried to think of all the potential obstacles so everyone else can just relax and enjoy the show."

"Well, good luck to you," she said kindly. "That was a nice piece the newspaper ran about it."

"Thanks," I said. She went on her way as I scanned the newspaper and spotted the article. Since Ginger was doing most of the publicity, they used one of her quilts in the accompanying picture. As I read it for the second time, I was relieved to see that it was accurate. I was hopeful that the article would be one effective means of drawing people to the event. I picked up the mail and scurried on to the church, where I was the last to arrive. I shared the article with the others, and they huddled around to see it. As they gave the article their attention, I noticed a huge pile of quilts.

"Wow! There are a lot of quilts, Marta!" I exclaimed. "Tell us how we can help."

"Claire, I'll have you start the assembly line by looking at the photo of a building and attaching it to the corresponding quilt bag. Frances or Olivia can insert the drop cloth and any additional hanging supplies."

"Okay, good plan," I agreed.

"We want to keep all of the quilts for each block grouped together. That way, it'll be more organized when the volunteers hanging quilts come to pick them up."

I was impressed by Marta's organizational skills. She had thought through the process very carefully and knew exactly how she planned to execute her part of the event. That was particularly comforting to me since the safety and security of the loaned quilts was of utmost importance.

"This table is for the special exhibits," Olivia pointed out. The table was a mass of vibrant color and texture. I was excited to take a look at Olivia's Gee's Bend collection.

"Will the raffle quilt and the historical society's quilts show up that morning?" I asked, just to make sure.

"I sure hope so," Olivia responded with a nervous laugh.

"The work that each of you has put in has made this job so easy," I said. "Help yourselves to some brownies, even though I know they won't compare to Marta's cookies." At that, the work began. Our small team accomplished a lot, and it was all done with good attitudes and a fair amount of lighthearted teasing and laughter. We worked diligently until four that afternoon. When additional last-minute quilts were dropped off, Marta got right on it.

When I got home around five, I was exhausted, but in a good way. I poured myself a drink and headed to the porch to enjoy the warm breeze. It looked as if it could rain, which would cool things off. Just as I sat down, I got a call from Grayson. It couldn't have come at a better time.

"Claire, how did your day go with the quilts?"

"It was good and very productive," I bragged. "I'm sitting on the front porch with a glass of wine. Do you want to join me?"

"Oh, I'd love to, but I'm in Green Bay at a dinner meeting. I had a bit of time, so I thought I'd give you a ring."

"Nice! I've been thinking of you, too. By the way, I got a call from Kelly. Did you have to twist her arm to get her to help with the show?"

"Not at all!" he laughed. "She has an artistic bent, and I think she's intrigued by the idea of the show. I'm glad she reached out to you."

"I think it'll be a pleasant experience for her," I replied. "Hey, she shared the news about her getting to keep Spot. You never mentioned that."

He paused, and then I heard a big sigh on the other end of the line. "I'm afraid that I didn't have much choice. Honestly, I just couldn't say no to Rachael. However, I'm not used to having animals around, and this cat is pretty sneaky if you ask me."

I found myself stifling a giggle. He was so serious, and I didn't want to offend him. "You should've seen me when I realized I'd inherited Puff! I wasn't very happy about the indoor cat situation at first either. For Kelly's sake, try to be patient. Now, Puff and I are doing fine, but I'm still convinced that Cher was a much better mother than I am when it comes to little Puff."

"I see," he said, but I could tell that he was distracted and needed to end the call. "I'd better get in the dining room. Things are getting started in there. Enjoy your drink."

"Thanks for calling to check on me."

"Always, my sweet," he said as he hung up.

I smiled to myself. My sweet. I'd never heard him refer to me in that way before. I felt entirely and wonderfully smitten, and I thought he was too, but would it last? I relaxed for a while, enjoying my drink as I'd been advised, and then decided to go upstairs early and watch a television show in bed. I picked up Puff and took her upstairs with me. As I carried her, she relaxed in my arms, probably also thinking that an early bedtime was a good idea. As I undressed, she curled up on the quilt like a good cat. When I didn't crawl under the covers because of the warmth in the room, she glanced at me to determine whether the change in routine was acceptable to her. After a few minutes, she tucked her head alongside her front paws and closed her eyes.

Unfortunately for me, it was time to put on my "worry hat" for the day. Was I forgetting something regarding the show? Would we have a pop-up shower? Would the volunteers show up to do their jobs? Would any people come to the show? Were Cher, Carole, and Linda having a wonderful time without me tonight? Would Grayson continue to think about me through his dinner? My mind raced through so many questions and came up with so few answers. I was finally able to close my eyes and fall into a restful sleep.

Chapter 106

The next morning, I cleaned the cabin, keeping in mind that Carole and Linda would be seeing it for the first time. I went outside and watered the plants since the rain hadn't shown up. Everything looked pretty good, but it didn't compare to the beauty of the Bittners' yard. Their gardens were exquisite, full of blooms and fragrances.

I sent Cher a text telling her that I'd made reservations for noon under my name. The White Gull Inn was a place Carole and Linda had to experience if they wanted to get the flavor of Door County. I arrived a little early, hoping to see Brenda. When I didn't spot her, I asked another employee about her. They commented that she wasn't on the schedule for today. I then waited on the porch for the others to arrive. It was good to see some familiar faces from my hometown. There were lots of hugs and some friendly laughter before we went inside.

"Before I forget," Linda said, "I'm supposed to give you a big hug from your mom."

"Thanks," I said, smiling. "I know she's thinking about all of us being together right now. Our table is ready. Cher, did you tell them about this place?"

"Only about their fish boils and that we have a friend who works here."

"Oh, Claire, this place is so charming, and I can't believe you live so close," Carole exclaimed. "Cher pointed out the cabin. You're so lucky to be this close to the water, too."

"I know," I agreed, nodding. "Thanks to Cher Bear, I have that opportunity."

Everyone followed the hostess to the inn's best round table. It was surrounded by windows. I loved it because you could see the cottages beyond the patio. Everyone seemed to be talking at once about the tour of the peninsula yesterday.

"What was your favorite spot?" I asked Linda and Carole as we surveyed the menu.

"That incredible Christmas shop in the church!" Carole replied. "I could've stayed there all day."

"We can go back before you leave," Cher assured her.

"I loved Al Johnson's food, and I'm truly impressed with all the galleries I see everywhere," Linda added. "I'm thinking of talking with some of them about consigning my jewelry."

"Oh, I'm sure plenty of them would be interested," I assured her. "I'd try to do that before you leave. Perhaps we can give you some guidance about the best places to approach."

"I brought some copies of my cookbook," Carole mentioned. "I thought I could see if any of the shops here had some interest in them."

"Great idea," I agreed. "You've come to the right place!"

Carole and Linda had so many questions. I'd forgotten how much I missed their humor and the excitement they brought wherever they went. It was curious how quickly we reconnected even though we had been separated by so much time and distance. It created a warm and satisfying feeling within me—a feeling of home.

"What delicious whitefish chowder," Carole complimented. "I could eat this every day."

"This fish taco is delicious as well," Linda added. Changing the subject, she said, "I can't wait for the show. Thanks for letting us be a part of it."

"I'm glad that you could come," I assured them. "Your responsibilities as monitors are to observe the people and the quilts at the same time. By the way, Grayson's daughter, Kelly, is also going to be a monitor."

"Listen—just wait until you meet Grayson," Cher bragged. "He's candy for the eyes, and Claire has him hooked!"

"Not so!" I responded, blushing.

"So, do you think you'll marry him?" Linda asked, her eyes widening as her curiosity grew.

"No, no, and a final no," I said, shaking my head. "His wife died in a horrible accident, and no one will ever fill her shoes. Since then, he lives every moment for Kelly."

"She's lying," Cher claimed. "I can tell that he adores her. You both just need some time. I'm telling you girls, there will be a wedding someday. Austen will be so sorry that he didn't take her to the altar."

Cher's expressions were so convincing that all of us erupted in laughter. "Don't believe her," I advised Carole and Linda. "She's exaggerating."

After a full lunch topped off with the inn's famous cherry pie, we took a walk to Sunset Beach Park. The view of the bay was as stunning as ever. There was a sailboat going by in the distance, creating a perfect picturesque scene. We took a seat on the stone wall and shared more stories and laughs from the past. After a while, Linda summoned her courage and walked down the rocky steps to put her feet in the water. It was just like something we'd have done as children in Missouri. She took a first step in. I watched her carefully and then turned my gaze to Cher and Carole, who were keeping an eye on Linda as well. Here we were, four adults who had remained close friends for decades. Where had the time gone?

Chapter 107

"If I lived here, I'd come down here every day and meditate," Linda declared after she'd returned to her seat on the wall.

"I used to come here a lot," Cher said quietly. "When the tourist season was at its peak, I didn't walk here as much. I'd only see romantic couples and families posing for photos. After a while, I realized that it depressed me a little to see everyone else with someone while I remained alone."

"Oh, Cher, you never told me," I said gently.

"Like at anyone's home, we have good memories and bad ones," Carole added.

"I love this breeze," Linda said as she held out her arms. "The humidity in Missouri is the worst."

"There've been a few days like that here," I pointed out. "So, what do you have planned for tomorrow?"

"Washington Island," Linda eagerly responded.

"Oh, you'll love it!" I assured them. "I just went there for the first time myself."

"We'll spend most of the day there," Cher said. "Claire, maybe we can meet up with you later."

"Let's wait and see," I answered. Leaving the plans at that, I said, "I think it's time that you come on over to the cabin."

"Linda and I can walk, Cher," Carole suggested. "We'll meet you there."

"I'll walk with you," I replied. "I need the exercise." At that, Cher headed to her car and the remaining three of us set off for the cabin.

"It's good to see Cher back here and happy again," Carole mentioned. "She took the death of her mom really hard."

"I know," I said. "Thank goodness she had my mom and friends like the two of you." We settled into a few moments of silence.

After a short while, Linda said, "Tell us more about what we really do as monitors for the show."

"Sure," I agreed. "You'll have a name tag and gloves so folks will know that you're associated with the management of the show." They nodded.

"What if someone gets irate?" Linda asked.

"First, go to the shop owner," I suggested, "or you can also call me. You shouldn't have any problems." They repeated their nods. When we reached the cabin, Cher had already arrived and was admiring my herbs.

"Cher, tell them the history of the cabin," I requested before they came inside. I went on in, and it was a good reminder that Cher still owned the cabin and that I was just renting. Minutes later, they joined me inside.

"This is so cute," Linda exclaimed.

"You're making effective use of every little space, aren't you?" Carole observed.

"I had to," I said, smiling.

"She saw things and found places that I never noticed," Cher revealed. "I love what's she's done, and I hope she keeps it."

"I want to live here a little bit longer before I decide," I explained. "I do love it despite the lack of square footage."

"Hey, how about meeting up for a pizza at the Wild Tomato while Carole and Linda are still here?" Cher suggested to me. "They want to go there before they leave, so if not tomorrow, then another time."

"Sure," I agreed. "I love their pizza. Tomorrow, we'll do the final assignments of the quilts, so please bring them to the church before you go to the island."

"Sure, we can do that," Cher agreed. "Are you sure you don't need me?"

"I think we're good," I assured her. "Don't forget to take a lot of flyers to the island."

"Thanks for reminding me," Cher said.

It was after four in the afternoon by the time they left. I was exhausted from so much talking. At five, Grayson called.

"I know it's the last minute and that you have friends here from out of town, but would you be available for dinner? I understand if you're already committed."

"I think it's a great idea," I agreed, knowing that I'd have to perk up some before I'd be good company for dinner.

"I had a complicated problem at work that got resolved, so I want to reward myself," he confessed.

"What's Kelly doing?"

"She left with her aunt and won't be back until tomorrow. The timing is good."

"Well, I'll need to change into something else. Is it casual?"

"Casual it is," he stated.

"Okay, I'll see you soon."

Chapter 108

It didn't take long for Grayson to arrive, and I could tell that he was in a very good mood. As I was about to get into his SUV, he scooped me up and gave me an enthusiastic hug.

"Do I need to put on a blindfold?" I joked.

He laughed and replied, "No, I think you're good."

"Oh, I see you brought a cooler."

"Yes, it was necessary for our dinner."

"You cooked?"

He burst into laughter and shook his head. "Not exactly."

I was intrigued but decided against asking any more questions. I felt content to just go with the flow and enjoy Grayson's company. On our way north on Highway 42, we chatted about my Missouri friends. When we arrived in Sister Bay, we pulled into the parking lot of the Sister Bay Marina.

"Is this my first clue?" I asked, taking a careful look around. He smiled and nodded as he made his way out of the vehicle and into the area where the cooler was situated. "It's so beautiful here," I commented, taking in my surroundings. Seeing that Grayson was occupied by the items that he'd brought, I asked, "What can I carry?"

"Just take this bag, and I'll take the cooler. Follow me, sweetheart."

With only those simple directions, we walked along the pier where the water's edge was lined with beautiful boats that cost more than Cher's cabin. We then stopped at an exceptionally large boat that had been dubbed *Sally.*

"Claire, meet Sally," Grayson said, mimicking a formal introduction. "She's owned by our company, and we use her for company entertaining."

"Grayson, I didn't think that you boated anymore, and you know how frightened I get," I said, feeling my pulse quicken.

"We're not going anywhere. Make yourself at home," he urged.

Not feeling quite as enthusiastic as the hopeful expression he wore, I followed his lead, wanting to trust him. As we boarded, it was like entering a lovely cottage that offered every convenience.

"We'll set up shop here where we can see the sunset. From this spot, it'll be magnificent." Grayson began to arrange some of the items he'd brought while he described the vessel. "It sleeps up to six people, so it's perfect for a big family to take out on the water."

"It's so beautiful!" I said, feeling more comfortable as I realized that the waters were calm tonight. "These chairs look so comfy," I noted as I eagerly occupied one.

"I brought your favorite wine, so you just relax and let me do a few things. I even have a nice warm throw if you get chilly. I know that the temperatures will begin to drop soon."

While he worked to organize what he'd brought, I noticed all the detailing on this gorgeous boat. I watched him carefully set up a small table by my chair. Within minutes, he'd filled the tabletop with sushi, cheese curds, crackers, and sausages. Until I saw the spread before me, I hadn't paid any attention to my appetite. Now, I found myself extremely interested in his selection of foods for our dinner. Grayson finished off the presentation by placing a small lantern on the table, which provided a warm glow. I smiled, realizing that the fanciest restaurant couldn't compete with the setting he'd just constructed.

"Seriously, Grayson, where did all this come from—and why?"

He looked as if I'd insulted him, but he recovered quickly and innocently replied, "Have you heard of this place called Piggly Wiggly?" I burst into laughter. He continued by saying, "I like it here in this spot. I wanted to be with someone I could truly relax with, so I thought of you."

I got out of my chair and went over to him. "You're a sweetheart, Mr. Wills," I said, giving him a kiss on the cheek. "I feel comfortable being with you as well, and I'm honored to be your guest." He then pulled me close and gave me the real kiss I was hoping for.

"Look in that direction," he said, pointing to the sky, "and very soon, you'll see the sunset. It'll be a showstopper tonight." He smiled at me. "How's the wine?"

I smiled. "It's as sweet as you," I replied. "I've never had sushi, but it looks good."

"Surely you love Wisconsin curds," he teased as he put one in my mouth.

"There isn't much I haven't liked since I moved here," I shared. "This afternoon, as Cher was showing the cabin to our hometown friends, I realized that I need to decide soon about whether to purchase it or not."

"What are you unsure about?"

I paused before I answered. "I'm changing. It was perfect for my needs when I first arrived. It had nearly everything there for me, including a cat, which I've finally accepted." We smiled at my reference to Puff.

"What's changed?"

"Well, now that I have friends, I'd like to entertain. The cabin is very, very small. I do like having a well-lit place where I can paint, so that's a plus. Maybe I just need more time to figure things out."

"I think it suits you, but that's where you were living when I met you, so maybe that's why I think that. Remember the Bittners' Christmas party?" I nodded. "I saw you when you arrived, and you looked fabulous. I was hoping to walk you to your car until you said you lived next door. When you consistently turned down my offers to walk you home through the snow and ice, I was disappointed."

I remembered the evening well, and his offers to walk me home. At this moment on this fabulous boat, I gazed at him with my heart full of love. "Frankly, I'd have loved it, but I didn't get the sense that you were ready for any woman in your life just then."

"I'm sorry that it showed," he said, looking down. "I know that Marsha would want me to get on with my life, but when I feel brave, Kelly comes to mind. With you, I'm experiencing feelings that I didn't think I could have again. The whole thing has taken me a bit by surprise."

"I know. I feel the same way. I wasted so many years with the wrong man." I fixed my eyes on the horizon, realizing how different my life was now.

"Had you hoped to marry him?"

I chuckled. "I guess every little girl thinks she might marry a doctor one day, but my fantasy certainly eroded when I moved in with him. That was a big mistake."

Chapter 109

"That's when I should've given Austen an ultimatum," I said. "He had his cake and ate it too. As time went on, we lost the best part of what we saw in each other. Does that make sense?"

"Oh, yes, I totally get it, but now, you seem so well adjusted and happy."

"I am, and I'm glad that it shows," I said as I kissed his hand. We watched the sunset in almost complete silence as Grayson kept his arm wrapped around my shoulders. The wine, food, and romantic atmosphere were good medicine for us. It felt like a scene in the movies. After the sun disappeared, the air became chilly, so we moved inside the cabin, where pleasant music was playing.

"So, do they call this the *Love Boat* at work?" I couldn't resist asking.

He laughed. "Families mostly take advantage of using the boat. I tell them that the first tank of gas is on me. We have rules posted, too. Most of the employees have boats of their own, though."

"Isn't it convenient that no one had a romantic date scheduled for tonight besides the boss?" I teased.

He grinned. "We're doing way too much talking," he said, pulling me closer. "I'd like to hold you all night long if you'll let me."

I could feel the electricity surging between us. Within minutes, we were reclined next to each other on the couch. I could feel his heartbeat. His arms drew me close in an embrace that felt new and captivating. I drew in a sharp breath, and it took all of my internal strength to pull away from something that offered me so much pleasure. I was sure where this would lead if I didn't. I was breathless, hot, and enticed—all at once.

"Are you okay?" Grayson asked, surprised.

I remained silent and then sat up, furiously thinking about what to say. I finally mustered, "Grayson, you're incredible, and it's obvious that we have a romantic setting that's perfect, except ..." I paused, searching for the right words to say.

"Except what?"

"I don't want to ruin what we have together," I blurted out. He looked confused.

"You don't have to worry about that," he said finally. "I'm very attracted to you—the strength within you and your determination. I feel so good when I'm with you. Always."

Our eyes met as he spoke. I swallowed hard, trying to find my voice. "I know," I said softly. "Believe me, I know." I stood up, clearing my throat. "I'm going to get more wine." He smiled.

"Then you take the lead between us, and I'll follow. I'll be good with whatever makes you comfortable."

Within moments, the uncertainty between us had diminished, and I began to feel at ease again. We left the cabin in favor of some fresh air on the deck. There, we engaged in light conversation as we drew in deep breaths of air that had indeed gotten even cooler.

"I look forward to helping Carl hang the quilts," he said, starting us on a new subject.

"I can't tell you how much I appreciate you and Kelly helping out."

"Of course," he said simply, as if volunteering for a quilt show happened to be the most natural thing ever. It was after midnight before we left the marina. We held hands all the way home. I hadn't become accustomed to the feel of his skin next to mine yet. It stirred up a warm feeling within me that felt risky and wonderful all at once. When he pulled up in front of the cabin and turned the vehicle off, the gaze he offered warmed my heart. At the door, he wore a look of disappointment on his face. "It's getting harder and harder to leave you here, Ms. Stewart," he said softly.

"I'm sure that the remarkable boss of Sails Again can find the strength to carry on."

He laughed, pulled me to him in a firm embrace, and then gave me a long kiss that made me want to melt into him. We parted slowly. He paused and reached for my hand, pressing the back of it to his cheek for just a moment before releasing it. With that, he turned and walked to his vehicle.

I went inside, and as I got undressed, I questioned whether I'd done the right thing by cooling things down tonight. Perhaps I just wasn't ready for a physical commitment. I needed to be strong—to stand my ground—and yet convey to him the love that I feel. Would I be able to strike that balance? I went to sleep knowing that just hours before, I'd spent time with the man I was falling in love with.

I got up early, acutely aware that I had a full day ahead. Marta, Olivia, and I met to work on the show. I let Marta know that Cher, Carole, and Linda would come by to bring us the last of the quilts that needed to be assigned. We went over everything we still had to do.

"Be sure to take notes about what could make it better next year," I suggested, winking at them.

"Did you hear that, Marta?" Olivia teased. "She's already thinking of next year, too! She called it out at our last full committee meeting."

"She's right to begin thinking about it. I already have some ideas myself!" Marta admitted, laughing.

Chapter 110

Cher and the girls showed up, and it was obvious that they were all in a good mood. They entered carrying armloads of quilts that they deposited on a nearby table.

"Claire, are you sorry that you didn't meet up with us last night?" Linda asked with a twinkle in her eye.

"I'm sure I made the right decision," I said, smiling. "Grayson and I went to the Sister Bay Marina to watch the sunset."

"Of course you did," Cher teased.

"Oh, that sounds so romantic," Carole sighed.

"Yes, you made the right decision," Linda concluded, chuckling.

"Okay, we need to be on our way!" Cher advised. With Cher in the lead, the three exited the church, and we began the tedious chore of matching up quilts to the assigned buildings. I was pleased when I saw which quilts Mom had decided to send. I needed to remember to take pictures of them on the buildings. I knew that would please her very much.

We worked until five, when we decided that we were finally ready for tomorrow! Now we just had to hope for clear weather and that everyone helping with the show would show up. I had relaxed a little about the number of people who might come to enjoy the show. Even if folks had not seen our publicity, there were always enough tourists who might be pleasantly surprised to find themselves in the middle of an outdoor quilt show!

I was already looking forward to getting together afterward for a celebration. I'd have so many people to thank. Marta said we could still have the church if we needed it, so maybe we could meet there. I expected to have enough sponsorship money left over to fund a simple gathering for everyone who had helped in one way or another. I'd just arrived home when my phone rang. I thought it might be the girls reporting in, but it was Grayson.

"How did it go today?" he asked.

"Great. We're ready. Right now, I don't care if I ever see another quilt again!"

He chuckled. "I'd wait until the show is over to say that," he teasingly suggested. "Kelly and I will be on time. You'd better rest up. It'll all be over soon."

"I'm waiting to hear from the girls. They went to Washington Island today. I don't want to go to bed until I hear from them."

"Well, good luck tomorrow, sweetie. I'll see you soon!"

We hung up and I was touched that he'd called to ask about my day. It was now ten o'clock and I still hadn't heard from Cher, so I decided to call and check on them. Her phone rang and rang. I finally went to bed and didn't wake up until morning. Today was show day, and there hadn't been any word from my friends. I jumped out of bed, quickly got Puff fed, and made toast for myself. After I downed my simple breakfast, I checked my phone again, and there still wasn't even a text from Cher. Marta and I had agreed to be at the church by seven so we could meet the volunteers who would begin hanging quilts at eight. Cher, Carole, and Linda weren't needed until nine, but now I wondered what kind of shape they'd be in. Before I left for the church, I tried Cher one more time.

"I'm awake, Claire Bear. Not to worry," Cher said immediately.

"You'd better be. How are Carole and Linda?"

"They're just getting up, and it's very quiet. Don't worry, we'll be there."

"Are you all hungover?" I asked, anticipating that the answer would be affirmative.

"We had a good time. I'll tell you more about it later," Cher answered. "Is there a problem regarding the show?"

"No, everything's good," I replied, rolling my eyes at the situation.

"We're good too, boss. See you soon!" Cher quipped.

"Okay," I said, realizing too late that Cher had already hung up!

Chapter 111

When I walked into the church, I was met by the aroma of coffee brewing. A few steps later, a platter of donuts caught my eye. "Good morning, Marta! Donuts? Yum!" I exclaimed.

"Not just any donuts," Billy chimed in. "Grandma makes these from scratch!"

"You must have gotten up mighty early, Ms. Marta," I teased.

"I'm just like any other farmer's wife," Marta replied humbly.

"Billy, I'm glad that you'll be helping us today," I said as I watched him take another bite of his donut.

"Good morning, Carl," I said. "You're early. Is the new part of the gallery open today?"

"Not like I'd hoped, but we'll get there in the next week," he replied.

Carl and I went to fill our coffee cups as others trickled in. Everyone looked like they really needed that first cup of coffee! When Grayson and Kelly showed up, I felt relieved and grateful that they'd decided to support this event together.

"Hi, Claire. Are any of the other monitors here yet?" Kelly asked as she looked around.

"No, but they should be here any moment, so help yourself to a homemade donut."

"Today is the big day, isn't it?" Grayson asked, smiling.

"This is the day that the Lord hath made, so let us rejoice and be glad in it," I recited, smiling back at him.

"Nicely said," Grayson commented as he slipped his arm around me. "Show me my stack of quilts so I can get started. I think I know the drill."

"Good morning, Grayson," Harry said when he arrived. "I guess these ladies are ready for us. Give me a short, easy block, Ms. Stewart." He winked at Grayson and laughed a hearty laugh. Harry could certainly fill a room when he entered it.

"Of course," I said with a smile.

Everyone seemed to be present except Tom, but then I remembered him saying he'd probably have to go out of town. As folks enjoyed their coffee and donuts, there was a lot of joking around, and I was glad to see it. In no time, all the quilts were distributed. If Tom did show up, I'd send him to one of the larger blocks in town. Finally, Cher, Carole, and Linda arrived. They were smiling, but Carole was limping.

"What in the world is this all about?" I asked, giving her a mortified look. The three of them broke into laughter and could hardly regain their composure!

"It's just a sprain," she said between giggles. "It'll be fine."

"Well, that sounds like a story for later," I declared. "Help yourself to some donuts and coffee. I want you to meet Kelly, who is also going to be out with you."

"It's nice to meet you," Cher said graciously. "I know your dad. It's so nice of you to help us with the show."

"Me too," Linda said. Then she added, "None of us have been streetwalkers before today." The three of them were reduced to guffaws again! Kelly eyed them with widened eyes, not sure what to make of her new friends.

"Take breaks whenever you want, but don't take your eyes off people when they're around the quilts. Here are your tags. Be nice and friendly to everyone. The volunteers hanging the quilts have already pinned on the do-not-touch signs," I instructed.

"It's almost nine," Cher stated, suddenly sounding authoritative. "Here are our phone numbers if anyone needs to call us for any reason." At that, Carole, Linda, and Kelly filed out of the church, ready to carry out their responsibilities. I was glad to see Linda take Kelly under her wing as they were leaving. Then, it seemed as if no time had passed before those hanging the quilts began drifting back in with their empty quilt bags.

"Any problems?" Cher immediately asked them.

"None that we didn't solve," Allen answered. "You both need to go out and look across the street. It's an amazing, colorful art show."

At his urging, we stepped outside. My eyes filled with tears of joy. It was breathtaking. "It's just like I imagined," I said quietly.

"I've got chills going up my spine," Cher stated. "Look at the Blazing Star from here. You can see that from several blocks away!"

Marta stepped outside. Situating herself between the two of us, she put an arm around each of our waists. "Well done, ladies!" she said. Her voice was filled with emotion.

"We couldn't have done it without you, Marta," I said. "I'll be sure to send the church a donation for letting us use this place." Marta smiled and nodded her head, continuing to take in the colorful scene. Minutes passed as we stood there. To our surprise, some of the quilt club members stopped in to congratulate us.

Chapter 112

"You two need to walk down the street and look at all the quilts," Marta suggested. "You deserve to reap what you've sown. I'll stay here."

Cher and I looked at one another and agreed. "We do need to check on the monitors and see if they need any support. I'd also like to take some pictures that we can use to help us plan next year's show," I said.

"Hey, let's get through this year first!" Cher said, shaking her head.

Within minutes, we were walking down a street that had been transformed. Quilts of all colors and styles could be seen. As we got closer to some of the shops, we were able to hear the wonderful compliments coming from those who had decided to enjoy the show on foot. The first monitor we saw was Carole. She was sitting on a bench and situated where she could see an entire row of quilts. She was in a perfect spot to see a lot.

"I hope you don't mind that I'm sitting here," she explained. "I can see pretty much what's going on. I had to get off my foot."

"No, I'm glad that you found a bench," I said. "You probably do need to be off of your foot."

"I'm meeting folks from all over the place!" she claimed.

"That's fantastic!" Cher replied. "It'll be interesting to see how many have come from Missouri."

We kept walking north until we saw Linda and Kelly.

"Hi, Claire," Kelly greeted me. "I had to tell this kid not to touch the quilts. There were beads on the quilt and he kept touching them."

"Good job!" I responded. "Did he listen to you?"

"Yes, he jumped back like he didn't expect me to say anything," Kelly said with a little giggle. "His mom pulled him away after that."

"That's exactly the reason we need monitors," I confirmed. "These are not our quilts, so we have to protect them while they're in our procession."

"Ms. Stewart!" a man's voice called as he came toward me.

"Yes?" I answered, curious.

"You may not remember me from the county board," he began, "but I want to compliment you on this show. My wife has a quilt hanging on the window of the Fish Creek Market down the street. She's quite proud of it and insists on sticking around to hear what the people have to say about it."

"That's really a great idea," I replied. "Cher, let's encourage quiltmakers to do that very thing next year. Having them available to answer any questions during the show could be a good teaching tool."

"Or not," Cher joked.

"Thanks for sharing that with us. I deeply appreciate the board giving us permission to execute this event," I told him.

"Did you see the special exhibits at the park?" Cher asked him.

"Yes," he said, nodding. "It's a perfect setting. I'd never heard of Gee's Bend quilts before. They sure are colorful!"

"That's where we're headed now," Cher said as we moved along.

As we walked away from him, we marveled at our good fortune. We were delighted to have run into a board member who was enjoying the show. "It sure didn't hurt that his wife is a quilter," I stated.

"Claire, Claire!" a voice called out. It was Kathy Luther.

"Kathy!" I responded. "I was hoping to run into you."

"I just came from the park, and the quilt raffle tickets are really selling well."

"I'm so glad," I said, relieved. "We're headed that way now. Have you met Cher? She's my cochair."

"Not officially," she responded. "Thanks for doing this show."

"I'm glad that you like it," Cher replied modestly.

"We can help more next year if you need us," Kathy offered.

"That's good to hear," I replied, nodding. "You've helped us a lot by getting so many quilts from the guild members."

"Oh, my husband is so proud," Kathy bragged. "Cher, he's a quiltmaker as well and has two of his quilts hanging at the On Deck Clothing Company store down the street."

"Wonderful!" Cher responded. "It's nice to meet you."

We said our goodbyes and walked to the park. The color from a distance was stunning. There was a nice crowd, especially around the raffle quilt. Not too far from there was Olivia, who was standing by her Gee's Bend quilts. She was busy talking to people as they enjoyed looking at her collection.

"Olivia, this is such a grand addition to the show," I exclaimed. "They make an absolutely stunning exhibit."

"Thanks so much," she said proudly. "The labels tell which ones are reproductions and who made the others. I have a handout for those who want to know the story behind the Gee's Bend quilts."

"What a great idea," Cher agreed. "I can see that education needs to be a part of this show."

"You're right," I said, nodding. "Let's go buy a raffle ticket while we're here."

As we wrote out our names and contact information on small printed slips of paper, we teased each other about who would buy more and who might win the quilt. Closer to the Alexander Noble House was the unique display of antique quilts. As we got closer, we were amazed at how old some of them were.

Chapter 113

"Look at this incredible broderie perse appliqué on this pillar print," Cher exclaimed.

"I'm impressed that you know what that is," I joked. "Broderie perse is such an art. Look how close the stitches are. It's cool, but it's a bit too much for me. I like simple geometric designs like we used in the chain quilt we did for Rachael."

"Do you think that Grayson really liked the quilt that much?" Cher inquired.

"Yes, I think he actually uses it and enjoys it very much. I'm so glad we did that project."

"I think he likes it because you helped make it," Cher replied, smiling at me.

I returned her smile. "I need to get Kelly started on quilting while she's interested."

"Well, that's certainly a good way to score more points," Cher teased.

"Let's see how Carl is doing," I suggested, hoping to change the subject.

As we walked along, I noticed some things about the attendees. There was no question that most of them were women. For the event's first year, I was pleased with the overall turnout. When we arrived at Carl's shop, it was filled with customers! Carl was busy assisting customers and manning the cash register while another woman answered customer questions. The shop was buzzing with activity! I smiled and asked, "Is the show increasing business today?"

"Very much so," he said, nodding his head. "I sure wish I had that extra space ready and stocked with more merchandise, but at least they can see that I'm expanding."

"Do you need some more help today? I can stay if you need me," Cher offered.

"There shouldn't be much wrap-up from the show, so I shouldn't need you," I agreed.

"That won't be necessary because I have some extra help today. Oh, I meant to introduce you to my sister. Jan offered to help me out," Carl said. He motioned for the woman to come over and join us and then introduced us to one another.

"Nice to meet you," she responded. "I live in Green Bay, so I'm close by. Good job on the show. It's beautiful."

"I'll be back at the church to help with takedown," Carl said. "Jan can handle things here."

"Nice to meet you, Jan," I said as Cher and I departed.

"I want to see all the quilts up to the top of the hill. Gibraltar Grill and O'Meara's are the last displays up there," I said. We chatted and admired what we saw on the way to my cabin to get the car. Our time was running out to get back to the church.

As we drove north, we did see some gaps in the display that we wish weren't there, but all in all, we were pleased. The last two businesses did a magnificent job, and the Irish shop owner did indeed use her Irish Chain quilt. It was hung beautifully by her sign.

When we arrived back at the church, Grayson, Allen, and Harry were already there, ready to pick up their empty bags. They were eager and ready to take down the quilts, bringing our successful first show to a close.

"Good turnout, Ms. Stewart and Ms. Clapton," Grayson complimented, nodding his head at us as he mentioned our names.

"Thanks," I responded. "I think Kelly is enjoying herself. She certainly isn't shy."

Grayson chuckled. "I think she took her job seriously. I'm sure that I'll hear all about her experiences later on today."

"Thanks again for your help," Cher said to Grayson before she went over to assist Marta. Her words were a reminder to me that I needed to get busy and send out thank-you notes as soon as I could after the event. Everyone who had volunteered to help had really made the show a success. Cher and I couldn't have done it without our small army of dedicated helpers. I watched as a small crew gathered the empty bags and headed out to carefully take the quilts down. I went to check with Marta to see if she needed any help.

Even before the volunteers were back from removing the quilts, those who had donated quilts for the event were starting to gather at the church. Those who were local and those who had driven in to see the show themselves wanted to pick up their quilts. That certainly was more convenient for us as well. Marta, Cher, and I would be holding our breath until each and every quilt was returned safe and sound.

Allen and Harry were the first to return with quilts. I felt anxious just watching the process. Marta opened the bags and carefully inspected the quilts. When she was satisfied concerning their condition, they were passed on to Cher. Cher checked them off the list. The quilts then came to me to make sure they were put in the hands of the correct owners. Owners completed the process by signing a paper indicating that their quilt had been returned in good shape and that they had picked it up. During the process, people gave us compliments again and again. It was gratifying to hear their comments. Not all assessments of the show were positive, however. There were a couple of sour comments. One woman said she was unable to find where her quilt was displayed, and another woman said she saw someone touch her quilt and cautioned us to keep a closer eye on things in the future. So far, none of the complaints uncovered serious flaws in the execution of the event. I listened patiently to everyone regardless of their viewpoints and tried to make mental notes about how the show could be improved.

Chapter 114

Carole, Linda, and Kelly all returned around the same time to turn in their badges. Linda bragged about what a good job Kelly had done, and Kelly beamed with delight.

"It was fun except I couldn't eat and drink as much I wanted," Kelly voiced. I smiled at her and expressed my gratefulness. It was a long time for someone Kelly's age to be responsible for something as important as someone's expensive and often one-of-a-kind quilt. She had stayed on task and I was proud of her.

"Carole, how's your ankle?" I asked, concerned.

"I did fine since I sat down whenever I could," she responded. "Maybe the sprain turned out to be a good thing. It kept me from being tempted to sneak into the businesses and shop!"

"We'll do that tomorrow if your ankle will tolerate it," Cher suggested.

"I met a woman from St. Louis today, and she knew all about Perryville," Linda shared. "Everyone was really nice, but I'm really exhausted."

"I think we'll crash and order pizza tonight," Cher decided. Carole and Linda agreed. They looked at me for a response.

"I'll see," I said. "Grayson will be back soon to get Kelly, so I want to stay until he returns for her. He said he had a quick errand to run after he dropped off the quilts that he'd removed." At that, the three friends left for Cher's home. They knew that the best medicine for Carole was to get her foot propped up for the remainder of the day.

More time passed. All of the quilt owners who had come for their quilts had left. It was six in the evening by now and the only people left at the church were Marta, Billy, Kelly, and me. I could tell that Marta was exhausted and needed to go home.

"I'm relieved that it's all over," Marta admitted. "I had several concerns, but everything worked out."

"You weren't the only one who was worried," I said, patting her on the shoulder. "I knew that it was risky, and that we'd learn a lot from this first show."

"Your system worked," she pointed out. "I know that some got a little impatient while waiting for their quilts, but it had to be done correctly."

"By the way, have you noticed the new friendship budding between Billy and Kelly?" I asked, nodding in the direction of where the two were seated and talking furiously to each other. Marta nodded and smiled.

"Yes, I noticed. I think they know each other from school," Marta pointed out. "Kelly sure is a sweet girl."

"She is," I agreed. "I just can't get over how the two youngest volunteers stayed with their responsibilities all day long and carried them out just as well as any adult could." I paused for a moment and then said, "I honestly can't thank you enough for all you've done, Marta. I hope it doesn't hurt your relationship with Greta."

"Oh, she'll eventually come around," Marta said. "When something's not her idea, she has trouble embracing it."

"Hi, ladies," Grayson said as he came through the door. "Has anyone seen a cute little teenager hanging around?" We chuckled as Kelly heard Grayson's voice and gave him a smile.

"She's enjoying Billy's company," I told him.

"She doesn't know a stranger."

"Let's go, Billy," Marta called out. "Claire, let me leave the key with you so you can lock up. You can give it back to me later."

"Thanks again, Marta," I said, giving her a hug and clipping the key on my keyring. She and Billy gathered the donut platter and off they went. That left just the three of us.

"I'm starved, Dad," Kelly said, giving Grayson an imploring look.

"That likely makes three of us," Grayson responded.

"Wild Tomato?" Kelly suggested.

"Sure! How about you, Claire?" Grayson asked, regarding me with raised eyebrows and a questioning look.

"I'm game!" I answered. "Let me put some things in the car. I'll just meet you there." I noticed that Grayson looked somewhat disappointed at my suggestion. I wanted to make sure that the church was left in decent shape, so I straightened up a few things after they left to get us a table. In the silence, I clicked off the last light. In the dimness, I wondered if it had all been a dream. How did the simple thought of a door-to-door quilt show become a reality so quickly? I knew that Mom would be wondering how everything went, so after I got in my car and freshened up, I decided to give her a call.

"It all worked, Mom!" I shouted excitedly into the phone.

"I'm so glad. I almost called you, so thanks for taking the time to call."

"I'll send you some photos in the morning, so don't forget to check your email."

"I will. I'm so proud of you, honey."

"Are you feeling okay?" I asked. There was something in her voice that sounded different.

"Oh, I have my ups and downs. You know that," she said, brushing off my question.

"How's Mr. Vogel?"

"His daughter is in town visiting, so I haven't seen him."

"Well, that's nice for him. Tell him that I said hello. I'm about to meet up with Grayson and his daughter for pizza. I'm famished."

"I'll bet you are. Tell them all hello, and thanks so much for taking the time to call."

Chapter 115

I wondered what Mom meant by saying she had her "ups and downs" due to her age. I'd better check in with Michael soon to see if he knows anything. I didn't like her tone. She was usually much more upbeat. For now, I put my concerns aside and headed to the Wild Tomato.

Grayson and Kelly were lucky to find us an outdoor table. Kelly started to chatter about her day while Grayson listened and smiled at me from time to time. Since I was so tired, I mostly listened to what the two of them had to say. When the pizza was delivered to our table, Kelly helped herself to a slice and asked, "Claire, when can you teach me some quilting stuff?" Instead of digging into her meal, she paused and waited expectantly for my response.

"Anytime," I offered. "Now that the show is over, I'm looking forward to getting back into quilting again myself," I explained. That satisfied Kelly and she began to consume a fair amount of the pie. I only had one slice of pizza before I began to feel completely fatigued. When it was time to part ways, Grayson kissed me on the cheek and whispered that he'd call me later. I thanked them for including me, climbed into my car, and headed home.

When I arrived, I couldn't wait to stand under a hot shower. I headed there first thing and let the water rain down over me while I felt my muscles begin to relax. I stepped out onto a bathmat and began to dry off. When the phone rang, I'd already forgotten that Grayson had said he'd call later.

"I hope you weren't asleep," he said as I answered.

"No, I just got out of the shower," I explained.

"Are you feeling pretty good about everything? I didn't want to ask when Kelly was with us."

"I do feel pretty good, but frankly, I can't think too clearly right now."

"I certainly know more about quilts than I did before!" he said, laughing.

"Good!" I exclaimed. "Did you see the quilt at Noble Park that's similar to the one you bought at the chamber auction?"

"I didn't get to the park. I'm sorry."

That's okay. You did a fantastic job, Grayson. I appreciate all that you did to help out."

"I wish I could hold you right now," he said, cutting right to the chase.

Ever since the evening on the boat, there had been a heightening of attraction between us. I felt it, and I knew he felt it, too. I could see it in his eyes when he looked at me. When he brushed against me, I felt as if my senses were on overdrive. "I wish you could, too. You have a wonderful way of making me feel calmer."

"Well, let's try to plan something next weekend, okay?"

"Sounds great."

"I care for you, Claire, like I never thought possible," he said. Usually when he said such things, his voice was gentle and quiet. This time, his tone was different. It was like something was emerging from him. His former uncertainty was diminishing, and his ability to declare his love for me was developing before my very eyes.

"Oh, Grayson, I feel the same. Good night." I hung up wondering when I might hear the three magic words from him. I think I could actually say them to him. Something had moved us to a different place in our relationship.

Later, I fell into a deep sleep and dreamed about hundreds of quilts blowing in the wind. Suddenly, all of them blew away. I did everything I could to catch them, but despite all my efforts, they eluded me and were caught up in the sky. I woke myself up gasping for breath as I tried to rescue the lovely quilts that flew upward and out of my reach.

By then it was six in the morning, and I convinced myself to get up and tackle the lengthy list of chores that needed to be done. Puff reluctantly followed me downstairs. She didn't want to miss her sleep, but even more, she didn't want to miss breakfast. I glanced at the quilt show folder on the kitchen table. While things were fresh in my mind, I wanted to make some notes as I drank my first cup of coffee. At eight, Cher called, which surprised me.

"Good morning, Claire Bear," she greeted me. "Are you alone?"

I could hear Carole and Linda giggling in the background. "Quit asking me that!" I complained, laughing at her persistence. "You know better than that."

"Sorry. Hey, Carole and Linda want to go shopping today. They can go on their own, but if I'm not needed for anything, I'll join them. They saw some shops yesterday that they think might carry their items, so they want to check them out."

"Good for them for trying to drum up some additional commerce while they're here. Do you think that you could stop by for just a bit? I need your opinions on some things, like who to send thank-you notes to."

"Of course. The shops don't open until later anyway, so I can do that," she agreed.

"Great! See you soon." I made a list of questions to ask her when she arrived and then went outdoors to water my flowers. I saw Cotsy Bittner doing the same.

"I loved the show," she called from across the yard.

"Thanks," I called back. Cotsy's opinion mattered to me because she and her husband had good taste. I was happy to receive a positive endorsement from her.

As I returned inside, I glanced at my easel on the porch. Painting memorable scenes of Door County on a quilt was a clever idea and could also serve as an effective advertisement for future quilt shows. My mind began to review various businesses and locations that had flavored my impressions of Door County since I'd moved here. I stopped and shook my head as if to erase the subject at hand. Did my mind ever stop? I wished I could start working on those designs right now, but unfortunately, I had unfinished business to do. My ringing phone brought me back to the kitchen table. Without checking to see who was calling, I picked up the phone that I had left next to my quilt show folder.

Chapter 116

"Claire, it's Austen."

My first impulse was to hang up. However, I knew that he would call again, whether it was right away or weeks or months from now. I decided to get the conversation over with. "What is it?" I asked with no emotion in my voice.

"Well, that's not a very friendly greeting. I was hoping that you'd be nicer to me since I dropped the charges."

I paused, hoping that a few moments would help me gather my thoughts. I sighed and said evenly, "I don't think you had much choice, and you know it."

"I didn't call to debate the matter," he informed me.

"Then why are you calling?"

"I want to see you. I want to put all of this behind us and start over. Everything around me reminds me of you. I've been angry with you, Claire. I didn't want to admit my part in the demise of our relationship. I've just had so much anger. I've also had time to reflect. I've cooled down, and the more I think about things, the more I can see how wrong I was about so many things between us. I was wrong. I'm sorry, Claire. I never meant to hurt you. I love you, and I'm sorry for the things I did."

I couldn't believe my ears! "Do you honestly expect me to believe everything you've just said?"

"Maybe not now, but if we can spend some time together, I think you'll see that I'm completely sincere. I've changed and grown. I'm not the same person you left when you moved to Wisconsin. Please, Claire. I can be there tonight if you just give me the word. We can have a nice dinner together. I know a perfect place that we'll both enjoy. All I'm asking is for you to hear me out."

"Austen, I've told you that it's over," I reminded him.

"Claire, remember how we met?" he said, as if I'd not uttered a word of rebuttal. "I remember it like it was yesterday. We knew we were meant to be together. We were certain of it. I should've married you right away. I wish we'd gotten married then. Waiting was a mistake. It was my mistake."

"Austen, please listen to me," I pleaded as I took a deep breath. "I don't think it's a good idea to—"

"I'll listen to you tonight," he said, not wanting to hear the rest of my response. "I won't interrupt you then. You can hit me, yell at me—and I'll still want you in my arms again. You'll see. I love you."

I heard a click. He hung up! I immediately tried to call him back and the phone rang and rang. Then I received an automatic message informing me that his mailbox was full. I needed to stop him from making that trip! Feeling frantic, I called the main number at the hospital. They told me that Dr. Page was on vacation and that Dr. Webb was taking his calls. I wasn't sure what to do next. I glanced out the porch window and saw Cher coming up the driveway.

The sight of Cher on my doorstep was such a relief that tears sprung to my eyes as she walked in. She instinctively took my arm and looked at me for an explanation. I had spoken to her only a short time ago and had been fine. Now, I had tears streaming down my face and she could feel my body shaking as she kept a steadying grip on my arm. "Austen just called and insisted on coming here. He said he still loves me, and he wants us to start over."

"Oh, Claire Bear, what an idiot he is," she said, immediately taking my side like any good friend would. "You told him no, right?"

"I did, but he never, ever listens to me! What a nightmare it was the last time he was here!" I nearly shrieked. "That same horrible feeling has returned. His mailbox is full, and he has Dr. Webb taking his emergency calls while he's out on vacation."

"You absolutely can't see him," Cher said, keeping her voice even and firm. "He's such a controlling human being. Plus, he's counting on you to respond as you typically would, Claire. He's certain that you will accommodate him again."

"I know. I know."

"Call your lawyer and alert him. You could even call Grayson and let him know," she suggested.

"No, no," I said, feeling calmer. "Grayson can't be involved in this mess."

"Okay, let's get a drink of water or coffee and think about this," she said, walking me into the kitchen.

"Cher, everything was so great with the show, and then Grayson said such wonderful things to me last night. Now this!" I dissolved into more tears.

"Hey, Claire Bear," Cher said as we both took a seat at the table, "you're the strongest woman I know. You left him, remember? If he arrives, you don't have to see him. Call the police if you have to. I can be here too—but only if I have to," she concluded, ending her comments with a bit of humor.

I looked at Cher and grinned, feeling grateful for her companionship. I took a deep breath and a long swallow of coffee. I had to be the grown woman I am and stop this silly nonsense. "Okay, I'm good," I said, calming myself with deep, measured breaths.

"Now, let's get back to the reason I'm here," Cher said, knowing that the best thing for me right now was to concentrate on something else. "Who needs a thank-you note?"

"I have a list," I assured her, turning to that page in the folder. "Cher, would you agree to cochair again next year?"

"I'd be crazy not to," she chirped. "It was quite fun, and I sure got to know a lot of shop owners. Now that the business community saw all the traffic it created and how it put money in their pockets, they should be really excited about next year. It looks like the county board shouldn't present a problem either."

"Oh, Cher Bear, I love you!" I said, leaning over and giving her a hug.

"Let's just forget about Austen and put our heads together about what would make the show better next year," Cher said decisively.

We did just that as we munched on grapes, cheese, and crackers. Several hours later, Carole and Linda texted Cher to tell her they were heading to Wilson's in Ephraim for ice cream. We immediately closed the quilt show folder and decided to join them. I was especially in favor of meeting up with them since Cher had sacrificed the opportunity to shop with them earlier and had remained with me instead.

When we arrived at the locally famous icon, we saw them digging into huge ice cream sundaes. When we joined them underneath the red-and-white awning, they immediately began telling us about various shops that were interested in Carole's cookbooks and Linda's jewelry. It had been a productive morning for them! Once that topic was exhausted, I realized I had a question that had been puzzling me for two days. When I asked Carole again how she'd sprained her ankle, Linda and Cher looked at Carole and the three of them broke into gales of laughter once again!

Chapter 117

"Claire, I think that what happened on Washington Island needs to stay on Washington Island," Cher advised, sending me a look of warning and a smile. Carole and Linda nodded their heads energetically while looking at one another conspiratorially.

"You just had to be there," Carole explained, shaking her head and wiping tears of laughter from her eyes.

"I'm okay with that," I agreed, shrugging. "I'm just glad that you had a good time. I hope you've enjoyed the entire visit, even though we made you work a full day at the show. When do you have to be back?"

"I'd like to leave tomorrow because of some plans I've made back home," Carole replied. "Linda would like to see more of the Lake Michigan side, so maybe we'll take that route."

"I can't thank you enough for helping with the show," I said. "Your quilts were wonderful, and I really appreciate your bringing Mom's quilts with you. Let me know how she's doing when you see her, will you?"

"Why do you ask?" Cher wondered.

"I think something's going on," I shared. "She hasn't been herself lately. She said that Mr. Vogel's daughter has been in town, so Mom hadn't been seeing him."

"We'll spend a little time with her," Linda suggested.

I breathed a sigh of relief. "I'd honestly appreciate that so much," I assured them.

"Okay, I'm going to drop Claire off and meet you back at the condo," Cher said, standing. We shared a tearful goodbye and Carole and Linda promised to throw a party the next time I returned to Perryville. I was thankful that Austen's name hadn't come up.

"Seriously, I'm really scared about Austen just showing up at any time," I said as we were driving home. "I told him that we are over, but what if he hung up the phone and just jumped in his car? I wouldn't put it past him to try to surprise me like he did the last time."

"That settles it. I think I need to stay with you tonight."

"What about Carole and Linda?" I asked.

"They're fine. In fact, I think they're planning to go to the Bayside later, and I know I'm not up for that. I don't know where they get their energy! Even with ankle pain, Carole doesn't slow down."

"Are you sure you can stay?"

"Claire Bear, we can do anything together, remember?"

I managed a weak smile. "What will we say to him?"

"We'll tell him that we have plans, and we'll remind him that you told him not to come."

"Okay," I nodded, thankful that a plan had been launched.

I was relieved that Cher had decided to stay. She let Carole and Linda know about the change of plans. At dinnertime, I pulled out two pot pies I'd purchased at the Pig and put them in the oven. Cher made a simple salad with the Pig's fresh, ripe tomatoes. As we sipped wine and chatted, I almost forgot the reason she was there. Then I remembered. "You'd think he'd call and give me a heads-up that he's almost here if we're supposed to go to dinner," I said, feeling resentful that Austen had put me in an uncomfortable spot once again.

"Nothing that guy does or doesn't do surprises me anymore," Cher declared emphatically. Then she tried to divert my thinking away from Austen by saying, "This pot pie hit the spot, but I could use a refill of that great wine."

"You go ahead. Two glasses are my limit, plus I have to think straight in case he arrives."

"Would you like to watch a classic movie?" Cher suggested as she got comfortable on the couch. I picked out one of our favorites and pretended to be engaged in the familiar story, but my mind was on Austen, who could knock on my door at any minute.

At nearly midnight, the movie ended. Cher looked at me. "I think he's a no-show, Claire Bear," she said. Then Cher's phone rang, startling her. She nodded and responded to the other side of the conversation with a serious look on her face. I wondered if Carole and Linda had run into some trouble at the Bayside. Cher stayed on the phone, but her expression remained the same. She wasn't talking at all but was listening intently.

"What's happened?" I whispered, leaning closer to her. Rather than answer, Cher hung up the phone.

Chapter 118

"Cher, who was that?"

"It was Carole. Austen won't be coming," she said slowly.

"What do you mean? How would Carole know that? I don't understand," I replied.

"He's had a serious accident in Springfield, Illinois. He was on his way here."

My heart dropped to my feet. I stared at her, waiting for more information. "How in the world does Carole know that?"

"Carole's daughter is a nurse at the hospital where Austen works. They got word that he was in a really bad accident involving a tractor trailer."

I swallowed hard, not knowing how to respond.

"No one knows any details. The man driving the tractor trailer didn't make it. Carole said she'd keep us informed. She didn't mention the name of the hospital he's at in Springfield, but you can imagine their shock at Perry County Memorial. Do you know anyone in his office who would talk to you?"

"No, not anymore," I said, realizing that my hands were beginning to shake. "I think I'll call Mom. Maybe she's heard something." Suddenly, I realized that I was the cause of this tragic accident. Why couldn't I have stopped him from coming?

"I know what you're thinking," Cher said, looking grim. "It's not your fault."

"Maybe I was too hard on him and should have given him another chance."

"Claire, get a grip. That would be the worst reason to take him back! I'll stay with you tonight."

"No, please go on so you can be with Carole and Linda," I insisted. "I need to be alone and think this thing through."

"If you want," she said with hesitation. "I love you, Claire Bear, and I'll say a prayer for him. He'll probably be fine."

Surprisingly, I was glad to have Cher leave. I went upstairs with Puff following close behind. I stretched across the bed still wearing my clothes. Puff jumped on the bed and came to look directly in my face for a few moments. She finally nestled next to me, and I found her companionship comforting tonight.

I didn't wake up until the sun shone its first rays through the window. My first thought was Austen. Was he dead or alive? I got up, washed my face, removed yesterday's street clothes, and donned a fresh outfit, all while wondering what news today would bring.

As soon as Puff was fed, I called Mom. She was in a cheerful mood, which told me she hadn't heard about the accident. "I tried to tell him not to come, and he hung up. I couldn't reach him after that," I explained.

"Honey, I'm so sorry. Why don't I give Bill a call and see if he's heard?"

"No, please don't involve him," I requested.

"Okay. It sounds like Carole's daughter is going to be your best source," she maintained. We said goodbye and I really regretted upsetting her. It was a small town, so I figured she'd probably heard something. I poured more coffee and sat on the couch, staring straight ahead.

Chapter 119

Cher texted ten minutes later saying that a local news program had him listed in serious condition instead of critical. Cher said that was a good sign. After we hung up, I tried to think of anyone I knew in my hometown who could give me more information. I'd left town with rumors flying, so I was sure that no one would care to give me an update on Austen. I tried to get my mind on other things. After all, there was nothing I could do. At some point when he was well enough, I'd try to talk to him.

The days passed, and it was time for the quilt club to meet again. It'd be the second meeting without Cher and me. Would everyone show up or would they boycott like some did the last time? I picked up my quilt of cherry blossoms and continued sewing on the binding. It was mindless work, but it was something I could do to be productive. Interestingly, Puff didn't leave my sight. She knew that something was up. In the early afternoon, Cher drove up to the cabin. It led me to believe that she knew something.

"Good to see you working on something," she said with a big smile. "I went by Carl's, but he wasn't there. We need to get with him soon about his ideas concerning next year's show."

"You're right," I agreed. "Did you hear anything else about Austen?"

She shook her head. "I'm sure that he's in good hands, and I'll bet the local press is watching his progress. Have you called his cell again, just in case someone else picks up?"

"No, but I'll do it now," I agreed, wondering why I hadn't thought of that before. I got the same recording telling me about his full mailbox and ended the call.

I made Cher a glass of iced tea and we moved onto the porch, where it was quite pleasant. She changed the subject by saying that she'd read a good report about the quilt show in the local newspaper.

"I'll get a copy when I get my mail," I promised her. My phone rang, and it was Marta.

"Have you girls recovered from the show?" she asked cheerfully.

"Yes, we have. In fact, Cher is here with me now. She said there was a good review in the paper today."

"It was good news, and I have even more," she said.

"Oh, let me put you on speaker so Cher can hear you."

"Hi, Marta," Cher chimed in.

"Hi, Cher," Marta said. "Well, for starters, you're talking to the new president of the club. Greta stepped down and made a motion that I be the one to replace her. Can you believe that? I even got a compliment about how I helped to organize the quilt show!"

"Marta, congratulations!" I said quickly.

"Well deserved," Cher added.

"Did the show come up?" I asked, curious.

"Yes, which leads to my other good news."

"What?" I asked.

"Greta said that you and Cher accomplished a great feat for quilters in this county and that you were to be commended for it. As we sat there in shock, she suggested that we expand the membership of the group and ask the two of you to come back."

"Unbelievable," I responded. "Are you sure?"

"I'm sure! Will both of you return?"

We looked at each other and I could tell that we wanted to burst into laughter. We knew what the answer would be.

"Sure, I suppose so," I said as Cher nodded her assent.

"We value what both of you bring to the group, and everyone thought we could be of more help to you next year if you were actual members of the club," she explained.

"It's hard to believe in a way, but it's very good news," I responded.

"There's more!" Marta said with excitement. "We have a name!"

"A name for the group?" Cher asked, like she hadn't heard Marta correctly.

"What's the name, for heaven's sake?" I asked.

"We're now known as the Quilters of the Door!" Marta announced proudly.

"Oh, my! We love it, don't we?" I asked, looking at Cher.

"It's perfect. I still can't believe that all of you agreed to these changes."

We thanked her for calling and hung up. Cher and I looked at one another in disbelief. We knew that together we had demonstrated what quilters can do if they work together. We did our happy dance, regardless of the apprehension we still felt for Austen. We knew that once we were fully inducted back into the club, we could have an even better Door-to-Door Quilt Show next year. The Bears were back!

WHITE GULL INN'S
Door County Cherry-Stuffed French Toast

Yields 6 servings.

---

1 loaf unsliced egg bread

2 packages (8 oz. each) cream cheese, room temperature

2 cups tart Montmorency cherries*, drained and divided

3 eggs

½ cup milk

Cinnamon (as needed)

Powdered sugar (as needed)

Trim the ends from the loaf and cut the bread into six 1½"-thick slices. Make a cut three-quarters down the middle of each slice. (The bread will appear to be two separate slices but will be joined together at the bottom.) Set aside.

In a small bowl, mix together the cream cheese and 1 cup of the cherries. Spread approximately one-sixth of the mixture into the pocket of each slice of bread. Gently press the slices together, evenly distributing the filling.

In a separate bowl, beat the eggs and milk together. Dip the stuffed slices into the egg mixture and coat all sides. Place immediately on a lightly oiled, heated griddle and sprinkle with cinnamon. Cook over medium heat until golden brown, turning to cook the second side.

Remove the cooked slices from the griddle and place on a cutting board. Gently cut each piece in half diagonally, forming two triangles. Arrange pairs of triangles on individual plates. Sprinkle with powdered sugar and the remaining cherries. Serve with maple syrup and butter.

Thanks to The White Gull Inn in Fish Creek, Wisconsin, for serving such a delicious breakfast and for sharing this recipe with us.

* *For information on where frozen Montmorency cherries are sold near you, please contact Seaquist Orchards in Ellison Bay, Wisconsin, by emailing Robin Seaquist at robin@seaqistorchards.com.*

About the Author

Ann Hazelwood is a former shop owner and native of Saint Charles, Missouri. She's always adored quilting and is a certified quilt appraiser. She's the author of the wildly successful Colebridge Community series and considers writing one of her greatest passions. She has also published the Wine Country Quilt series and East Perry County series and is now writing the Door County Quilts series.

booksonthings.com

Cozy up with more quilting mysteries from Ann Hazelwood...

WINE COUNTRY QUILT SERIES

After quitting her boring editing job, aspiring writer Lily Rosenthal isn't sure what to do next. Her two biggest joys in life are collecting antique quilts and frequenting the area's beautiful wine country. The murder of a friend results in Lily acquiring the inventory of a local antique store. Murder, quilts, and vineyards serve as the inspiration as Lily embarks on a journey filled with laughs, loss, and red-and-white quilts.

THE DOOR COUNTY QUILT SERIES

Meet Claire Stewart, a new resident of Door County, Wisconsin. Claire is a watercolor quilt artist and joins a prestigious small quilting club when her best friend moves away. As she grows more comfortable after escaping a bad relationship, new ideas and surprises abound as friendships, quilting, and her love life all change for the better.